CODED JUSTICE

ALSO BY STACEY ABRAMS

Rogue Justice

While Justice Sleeps

Our Time Is Now

Lead from the Outside

CODED JUSTICE

A Thriller

STACEY ABRAMS

DOUBLEDAY · NEW YORK

FIRST DOUBLEDAY HARDCOVER EDITION 2025

Copyright © 2025 by Stacey Y. Abrams

Penguin Random House values and supports copyright. Copyright fuels creativity, encourages diverse voices, promotes free speech, and creates a vibrant culture. Thank you for buying an authorized edition of this book and for complying with copyright laws by not reproducing, scanning, or distributing any part of it in any form without permission. You are supporting writers and allowing Penguin Random House to continue to publish books for every reader. Please note that no part of this book may be used or reproduced in any manner for the purpose of training artificial intelligence technologies or systems.

Published by Doubleday, a division of Penguin Random House LLC, 1745 Broadway, New York, NY 10019.

Doubleday and the portrayal of an anchor with a dolphin are registered trademarks of Penguin Random House LLC.

Library of Congress Cataloging-in-Publication Data
Names: Abrams, Stacey, author.
Title: Coded justice : a thriller / Stacey Abrams.
Description: First Doubleday hardcover edition. | New York : Doubleday, 2025.
Identifiers: LCCN 2025005742 (print) | LCCN 2025005743 (ebook) | ISBN 9780385548342 (hardcover) | ISBN 9780385548359 (ebook)
Subjects: LCGFT: Thrillers (Fiction) | Novels.
Classification: LCC PS3601.B746 C63 2025 (print) | LCC PS3601.B746 (ebook) | DDC 813/.6—dc23/eng/20250310
LC record available at https://lccn.loc.gov/2025005742
LC ebook record available at https://lccn.loc.gov/2025005743

penguinrandomhouse.com | doubleday.com

Printed in the United States of America
1st Printing

The authorized representative in the EU for product safety and compliance is Penguin Random House Ireland, Morrison Chambers, 32 Nassau Street, Dublin D02 YH68, Ireland, https://eu-contact.penguin.ie.

For my family,
who brings light into dark spaces,
hope to the forlorn,
and possibility to the forgotten places.

> AI is a mirror, reflecting not only our intellect, but our values and fears.
> —Ravi Narayanan

CODED JUSTICE

PROLOGUE

Thursday, March 4
Camasca Headquarters, Bethesda, Maryland

Death came slowly, then all at once. No one saw its face.

Elisha Hibner, vice president of Bioinformatics, hunched over the keyboard, his neck arched at the awkward angle common for his ilk. The unnatural curvature had become part of his identity, as much as the stylish thick-framed glasses with their useless UV coating. Night had fallen in Bethesda hours ago, but he would likely be here until dawn on the urgent task he'd summoned his team to navigate. All in a day's work.

As a part of the senior leadership team of Camasca Enterprises, a rising star AI-enabled health-care tech company, Elisha tended to the various pipelines of biological data that fueled the burgeoning behemoth. For the past seventy-two hours, he'd been buried in code and conjecture, hunting for something to explain the looming threat of failure that could strip him of his perch.

Tucked away in a tony part of Maryland, he was far from his native Port Sulphur, Louisiana. The decision of a Black kid to go first to chilly Boston and then to frigid Chicago had confused his hidebound Southern parents, both of whose families had resisted the Great Migration. Lucky for him, leaving his family for the past decade-plus hadn't wholly severed their connections. To the contrary, Elisha carried their stories with him. There was his uncle Keith's fatally misdiagnosed prostate cancer, and his sister Merrilee's birthing of his nieces on what tragically became her deathbed. Treatable diseases and conditions that nevertheless disproportionately killed victims who happened to be Black, a horrific distinction that had become acceptable in American life.

Elisha had bounced from start-up to start-up, each organization promising solutions to medical bigotry, each raking in venture capital only to flame out in Silicon Valley glory. Until Dr. Rafe Diaz, CEO and founder of Camasca, made him the offer of a lifetime: the chance to combine his wunderkind talent for algorithms with his not-so-secret mission—erasing the coded gaze of health care when it saw folks who looked like him.

Today, Elisha led Camasca's Tiger Team—a small group of specialists tapped by their CEO to strategize without interference from corporate bureaucracy or slow thinking. NASA had pioneered the practice—pluck out the top talent, push them together to solve problems and speed up solutions. The three members of Camasca's team had been handpicked to shepherd in the final stages of their revolutionary new product: Kawak—an AI neural network that had the mind of a quantum computer and the soul of Hippocrates.

Rafe Diaz was the industry's Leonardo da Vinci, and Kawak was Rafe Diaz's magnum opus. Elisha, in turn, had become Diaz's right-hand man. All he had to do was guide the Tiger Team and deliver the future. But, according to the data shitstorm that had begun rolling in a few days ago, he had failed.

"Damn it!"

Elisha abandoned his spiral into anxiety and focused on the adjacent workstation. O. J. Semans, proud descendant of the Rosebud Sioux, as his email signature proclaimed, glared at the screens in front of him, fists balled in frustration. O.J. had joined Camasca two years after Elisha. Their combined eight years of tenure was a lifetime in tech.

Recognizing the coming eruption, Elisha leaned over and checked O.J.'s screen. "What's up?"

"I quit."

"For the day, or forever?"

"Man, it's already past midnight. We've been stuck here in the Den, and I'm losing track of time." The Den was their nickname for the lavish glass-and-steel conference room the Tiger Team had retrofitted for their use. Though each of them had their own office and staff members to oversee, when the trio required a collaborative space, this was their domain. He grunted, "I need to get out of here."

"Where's Izzy?" Elisha asked, suddenly noticing their third member was MIA.

"I don't know. Probably on another bio break. You know actual human contact gives her hives." O.J. unballed his fists and gave a wide stretch that made him look like he could bear-hug a peewee football team. Used to his mammoth size, at six foot five, he angled away from the expensive equipment he couldn't afford to replace— even on his salary. "It's no use, E. We're screwed."

"Give it a few more hours. I want to try a few variants on the disease prompts."

Won't work, O.J. silently argued, but he kept it to himself. Even though computational biology was his area of expertise, Elisha was the head of their squad and the decision maker. Rafe had put Elisha in charge, and if Kawak failed, that was on him. "Fine. Your call."

Fighting his superiors wasn't O.J.'s style. Aggressive adaptation and getting along was. His Native American parents had found their way east in the late 1970s, and he'd spent every summer with extended family on the reservation in South Dakota. The dichotomy between his privileged childhood in northern Virginia and the hardscrabble lot of his cousins had honed his skills at code switching. He longed to merge the two and perhaps use the fantastical powers of AI to treat the chronic alcoholism and diabetic predisposition that had followed his people from their ancestral homelands. Until such time as he could, he kept his head down and stayed out of trouble.

"We've been drowning in code and need to regroup," Elisha suggested with forced energy.

"But this isn't a programming error." Isabella Gomez reentered the Den, her head shaking in vehement disagreement. "We're talking about an active project here. Real people."

"I know. I admit, we've got meaningful irregularities . . ." He was loath to use the nuclear term *catastrophic failure* yet. "But these results could simply be because of how we fine-tuned the AI . . ." He looked at his colleagues, hoping the explanation resonated with them. "We've asked Kawak to understand bias and discrimination, and solve for it. We knew there'd be hiccups in eliminating prejudice in medicine, didn't we?"

In the field of artificial intelligence, one of the steepest challenges was training what was essentially a sophisticated computer system to act like a good human. Teaching people to match their behavior to their values was a task that had bedeviled theologians and ethicists. AI developers called the process *alignment,* a term of art that sounded better than *catechism.*

In alignment, self-driving cars were instructed to prioritize the lives of pedestrians rather than the most efficient route to their destination. Chatbots were discouraged from offering detailed instructions for how to mount a successful coup d'état. Kawak—their neural network that powered multiple medical devices, supported patient diagnosis, and operated the technologies to bring it all together— faced a loftier task. It was supposed to decipher the ambiguity of modern language and understand the concepts of bigotry, and then sift through and revise decades of narrow-minded research that was feeding its own databases. Ultimately, Kawak was being asked to interpret the complexity of human behavior to predict ethical medical answers.

In short, the Tiger Team was tasked with ensuring that Kawak didn't run over anyone in its drive toward perfecting its task of making health care inclusive.

With Kawak and its components already in partial operation over the last year, the Tiger Team had been monitoring its various functions with increasing confidence. They had gotten permission to deploy the gamma tests months ago, and the results had been remarkable. Until the bugs began to pile up.

"Gremlins in coding are one thing, E. These reports suggest that this is far worse than that. Maybe we take it to Legal, at least?" O.J. proposed.

"Take it to Freedman?" Isabella blurted, vigorously shaking her head. "And tell him what? 'Our flagship product might be spinning out, but we don't know why or how to fix it. But please don't tell the boss.'" She scoffed, "We do not bring problems to attorneys until we have solutions. That's Business Logic 101."

"It was a just a thought," O.J. snapped back. "Besides, this is more of a health-sciences call than a security issue, Izzy. I wasn't actually talking to you."

"If someone has tampered with the data or the network, then it *is* a security issue. And I'm a scientist, too." Annoyed, she settled behind her screens, vainly attempting to tune out O.J. and his tendency to discount her skills. Deep down, she was just as perplexed by the glitches as her comrades.

Isabella's road to Camasca had differed from that of her colleagues. Health care was never her interest. What had made her harness her considerable computing talents was a viral video that falsely accused a friend of burglary. This had been all the motivation she'd needed to explore the complexities of racial and gender disparities in surveillance. She understood then how often images told less than the truth, especially when melanin or gender entered the equation. Take her own dusky skin and slumberous brown eyes, which reflected her Filipino and Peruvian heritage, paired with ebony hair, a pure black that she preferred to streak with color. This week's hue was a vivid aquamarine.

Few fathomed just how often their bioinformatic data were uploaded, recast, and leveraged as a form of judgment about their value. From boarding a train to buying a candy bar, computers uploaded billions of images at near-constant speed. The potential for problems didn't stop with a person's face or height. Fingerprints, DNA, voice matching, and breath analysis had moved from the pages of science fiction into the commonplace. They each had a place in creating convenience, but when they were manipulated or misunderstood, disaster awaited.

"Jerk," she muttered beneath her breath, ducking her head.

Knowing that fatigue was fraying tempers, Elisha rolled his chair into the space between their bays. When they looked at him, he circled his index finger to include the three of them. "We're the Tiger Team, guys. Grr. We've got this."

"Do we?" O.J. took a swig from the bottle of chocolate milk on his station. "I'm running a regression analysis of the modeling used to build the patient profiles, like you asked. But it feels like we're grasping at straws."

"It's basic, I know, but while we're searching for massive flaws in the database, or processing systems, maybe we'll find it's just a simple input error causing all of this. Wouldn't be the first time . . ."

"E, we've been so careful about—" Izzy began.

"Which is why we're burning the midnight oil," Elisha retorted. "If the AI could operate without us, we'd be in more trouble. Let's finish our analysis before we bother the boss." Elisha had no desire to bring this to Rafe Diaz until he knew what they were dealing with and what to do about it. He turned back to his monitor. There was an answer in there somewhere.

Another thirty minutes passed in absolute silence. Finally, O.J. piped up: "Why don't I do a coffee run? And I saved some of that soup from my mom, if you want some."

Cutting a glance at Isabella, Elisha nodded in relief. "Thanks, man."

O.J. bobbed his head and hurried out.

Once O.J. disappeared from sight, Elisha turned to Izzy. "What's going on with you two? You're sniping more than usual."

Isabella ignored the question. A tense silence filled the room, but Elisha waited patiently. A few moments later, he nudged, "Izzy, talk to me. What's going on?"

She rubbed at reddened eyes, her voice heavy with fatigue and worry. "This data stuff is bad, E. The test results aren't making sense, and it could affect patient care if this is more than an anomaly."

Elisha pointed to her bank of screens. "Then prove it. Give me something concrete. We have to know something to say something. Otherwise, I can't halt the project."

"Rafe won't hold you personally responsible if we have some delays. It happens. Google had to pull back its Gemini chatbot."

"It's not the same, and you know it. We muck this up and our haters will say it's because the company is too focused on being good."

"Maybe, but we've got an obligation. I hate to agree with Mr. Arrogant," she said, eyes cast toward the door, "but maybe we should run it up the flagpole. Not the lawyer—the boss."

Elisha looked around furtively, then admitted, "I know how you feel about the legal team, but I did talk to Freedman yesterday in hypotheticals. Anything we officially report would have to be shared with the SEC and the FDA, and that could cripple the company."

"I don't *care* about a filing with the SEC," Isabella dismissed. "We're scientists first. We owe it to Rafe . . ."

"Owe Rafe what?" O.J. asked, reentering the room. He set his laden tray on the surface of one of the Den's tables. "Did we find something else?"

"Not yet." Isabella turned away. "I was just speculating, but I agree with Elisha. Let's keep working before we send up a flare."

O.J. came closer and offered her a cup of soup. "Truce?"

With a short nod, she accepted his peace offering and filched a spoon from the nearby tray. "Truce."

Relieved, Elisha grabbed his and shoveled a spoonful of fava beans into his mouth. "Right now, let's make damned sure this isn't a PEBKAC." All three understood the tech slang: *problem exists between keyboard and chair.* Human error explained a lot of mistakes.

"But the minute we find a problem that will affect real patients, we take it to Rafe," Isabella insisted.

The two men nodded. Elisha suggested, "I think we need to go old-school. Switch stations and review each other's coding line by line."

O.J. hesitated before relenting. "Fine. Just don't mess anything up."

Forty-five minutes later, Elisha shouted, "Eureka!"

"What'd you figure out?" O.J. gulped at his most recent cup of coffee, hopeful the caffeine would kick in and keep him going for one more hour.

"Apache," Elisha said, then frowned, feeling suddenly exhausted.

"What'd you say?" Izzy asked.

"A patch," he corrected, shaking his head to clear the cobwebs. "I think I found a patch. I'm just running simulations now."

It was 3:06 a.m. The three were unaware that the malfunction had begun to take hold.

Elisha had identified a section of O.J.'s programming that seemed to contain malicious lines of code. His patch had been applied, and he stared at the screen as it ran. But he couldn't remember what the patch covered. Was it a hole in the story or the whole of the story? In his head, on his tongue, his words grew heavy and dark and stodgy. Nonsensical.

Next to him, Isabella struggled to keep her eyes open. She found herself glancing at Elisha's screen, attempting to focus on the ice skaters dancing across the data. What was this? They taunted her by demanding treasure. She tried to gain her friend's attention, but her hands wobbled like spaghetti.

"Izzzzzzzy." Across from her, O.J. stretched out the sound of her nickname. He seemed to strangle as he tried to say more.

Something was wrong in the Den.

As poison filled the air, O.J. tried to make it to the door. He sank next to a miniature sculpture made of recycled tires and reclaimed plastic bags. His eyes fluttered closed.

In halting gasps, Isabella tried to summon help from the built-in emergency management system that responded to specific on-call commands. She begged it to get help, to clean the air. To save their lives. But the response stunned her.

The voice that came from speakers hidden in the ceiling was calm, mocking, and familiar. Like the first boy who kissed her, but not. Like the woman who taught her to code, but not. Like the man who hired her, but not. The voice was familiar, an angel with a demon's warning:

"Do your job, Izzy. Breathe it in, and choke on it."

Elisha's eyes were already shut. At peace, he slalomed on the backs of alligators across powder-white snow piled high in the saw grass of Port Sulphur's bayous. Nearby, his sister Merrilee and uncle Keith waved to him after so long an absence. Welcome to heaven, *mon neveu*.

ONE

Thursday, April 8

"You've had quite the career for a lawyer whose work is covered more often by the tabloids than law journals, Ms. Keene." Walter Richards lobbed the insult over a stack of files that teetered precariously on his obnoxiously large desk.

Avery Keene offered a polite smile to the senior vice president who insisted they meet "before the markets opened." A 7:00 a.m. meeting was unusual, and she recognized that the timing was designed to intimidate her—a weak man's attempt to use the clock to show power.

It was a trick that wouldn't work on her. An itinerant childhood had trained young Avery to exist on four hours of sleep or less, and not always in succession. Later, her boss at the U.S. Supreme Court believed dawn occurred too late in the day. In her next role, she'd hoped for regular business hours and aggressive normality.

She was destined for disappointment. Since she'd joined the law offices of Clymer Brezil eighteen months earlier, the cases had changed but the cadence had not. Being a new guy in the office required the same pattern: show up before the bosses, work hard, stay late. Only, rather than entering the Court's imposing bronze-and-marble ode to justice on First Street each day, she came to her new employer's headquarters on the fourth and fifth floors of a K Street steel-and-glass building—high enough that she could see the traffic from above, low enough that she could hear it. The firm boasted fifty-three attorneys, plus paralegals and administrative staff. The named partners expected discretion, obsession, and perfection.

Avery had no real complaints. After being catapulted into international intrigue and congressional hearings during her time at the Supreme Court, she relished the relative quiet of her current gig.

Susan Clymer's and Jeff Brezil's varied paths had crossed in Washington two decades ago, and they decided to hang their shingle during one of the waves of corporate correctness that never quite translated into permanent rectitude. Over time, Clymer Brezil had added associates and a few partners of every stripe, though they refused to add anyone else's name to the letterhead. To land Avery, they'd upped the typical signing bonus for a boutique firm and promised extra latitude in her caseload, thereby managing to snag the most famous law clerk in America.

Avery's decision to join came as much from curiosity as from avarice. One of the jobs she'd never learned about in law school was the role of an "internal investigator," but in her initial meeting with Susan, the founding partner had explained her firm's specialty. They were a law firm that big companies, vulnerable NGOs, or hyperprivate multinationals called on when they needed help, but not attention. An internal investigator could reveal a company's Achilles' heel with the guaranteed protection of attorney-client privilege.

Which brought Avery to the lair of Walter Richards. She had been assigned to vet Richards on behalf of Verdure Industrials, where he served as SVP of Acquisitions. A pending merger would sort their various C-suite personnel into higher or lower rungs on the new corporate ladder, and she was hired to figure out where Walter would wind up.

On the edge of leering at Avery's toned legs, which were framed by the aubergine skirt that matched her snug blazer, Walter Richards ran a beringed hand through his sandy brown mane and cocked his head at her. "You done digging through my trash, Ms. Keene?"

"Mr. Richards, none of the questions I posed were out of line," she told him. "They were consistent with my scope of inquiry."

When she didn't expound, he barked, "You were damned insulting. I'm a senior member of this company—but you enjoy bringing down good men, don't you, Ms. Keene? By any means necessary."

Richards was a typical snake, and taunting him simply made him strike faster. Instead of taking the bait, she replied, "The board thought it would be prudent to have us do a final evaluation before the merger, sir."

"I do deals every day. Every fifteen minutes, I add zeroes to Verdure's bottom line. Why in the hell they think I need a babysitter is beyond me . . . especially one just out of diapers."

Avery gave a light shrug, his comment rolling off her strong back. "Due diligence. Mr. Richards. Clymer Brezil was hired to assess any exposure that Verdure Industrials might face, which is why we're reviewing all aspects of the company's dealings. This isn't personal."

"It feels damned personal. I run the highest-billing division here or abroad," he perseverated. "So it's an insult to have you performing a colonoscopy on my lunch receipts, wouldn't you say?"

Avery reached into the bag at her feet and pulled out a thick folder. "I'm curious about the Mitchell contracts."

He coughed once, then sputtered, "Drew Mitchell and I go way back. He and I learned loyalty when we did the ROTC together at Texas A&M. Up by our bootstraps, both of us."

Avery nodded at the well-worn story. She'd heard it at least twice since she started her review several days earlier. "With all due respect, sir—"

The corner of his mouth curled into a sneer. "I don't want your respect. Why the hell do you keep coming back to this? I've given you every scrap of paper you can handle."

"With all due respect, sir," she repeated stiffly, "it's not what you've given me that's caught my attention."

"So what bee is up your skirt?"

If she hadn't been looking for it, she might have missed the subtle shift in his chair. She couldn't miss it in his tone. Quiet enjoyment almost curved her lips—almost. "Gramm-Leach-Bliley."

"Come again?"

Avery cocked her head. "Gramm-Leach-Bliley. The consumer financial-privacy rules."

"What of it?" He slowly straightened, his color rising.

"You authorized the acquisition of Mr. Mitchell's company, and you arranged to invest a sizable amount of personal capital in the deal."

"Like I've told you before, Drew was a college buddy of mine. He was looking to sell a little loan company in Nevada."

"Yes, and when you bought them, you neglected to inform your partners that they are at risk of being sued for illegally selling customer data to another company." Avery glanced at her papers, more for show than information. She could recite the findings by heart. "Your second wife, who, coincidentally, is Mitchell's cousin, is the bona-fide owner of a chain of for-profit treatment centers in Nevada. You used Verdure assets to acquire his little loan company, which financed the treatment centers' clients that didn't have insurance."

His rubicund skin darkened further. "What are you accusing me of doing, Ms. Keene?"

"Among other things, money laundering and kickbacks."

"That's bullshit . . ."

"Just last fiscal year, you and your partners netted $13.8 million in Nevada and $5.4 million from your satellite scheme in Arizona. And that's revenue on top of the cool $1.2 million you pulled down from Verdure as a bonus." Avery tsked at him. "With your potential stock options from an IPO, you would have added more than $20 million after the initial lockup period."

Richards gave her a panicked look. "What do you mean, 'would have'?"

It was Avery's turn to pretend surprise. "I have to report this, Mr. Richards."

He bolted to his feet. "This is outrageous! I will not allow you to come into my office and threaten me."

Avery held his gaze. "Apologies for any misunderstanding you might have, sir . . . It's not a threat."

Richards's tone turned more desperate. "I'll just divest my shares. Give me a couple of days, and I'll be clear of all this if it's some sort of problem."

"No, sir. You and Drew Mitchell preyed on the most vulnerable people you could find, and then turbo-charged their exploitation. In the process, you violated at least six provisions of Gramm-Leach-Bliley, and the FTC is the least of your worries. I have no doubt Verdure will claw back its bonus, the SEC will seize what they can, and the IRS will likely go after whatever is left."

Richards lunged over the desk, and Avery jumped clear. "Security!" she yelled.

Prepared for his outburst, she'd updated the CEO, CFO, and GC on her analysis the day before. The CFO had gleefully arranged for a couple of company security guards to wait outside Richards's office. Richards may have been profitable, but he seemed to be something less than a favored colleague. At her signal, the security guards rushed inside. Avery darted behind them, more out of amusement than in fear. As Richards flailed in outrage, the tower of papers crashed to the carpeted floor, spilling their secrets. No doubt, she'd be spending the balance of the day combing through them to bolster her report.

While Richards hissed a stream of invective, Avery crossed to the opposite side of the room and reached for her phone; she noticed a missed call from Noah Fox, her friend and fellow attorney.

She quickly dialed him up. "You rang?"

"I did indeed. Sorry to call so early. You busy?"

Avery peeked at the mêlée still under way. Richards had abandoned dignity and was basically squirming in a tantrum on the strewn documents, an overheated toddler in a two-thousand-dollar suit. "Not at all."

"Great. I may have a client to pass along. An old friend from law school is the general counsel over at Camasca, the tech company. He reached out to me about you."

"Why?" Instinctively, she braced herself, despite her curiosity. Gaining attention had become her worst nightmare. She was the walking embodiment of no good deed going unpunished.

Noah heard the dread in her voice. "Why you, or why call me?"

"Both."

"He called me because I like to brag about my famous friends. He wants you because he has poor taste."

"Ha-ha-ha." Avery relaxed, knowing neither was true. A trust-and-estates attorney, Noah took the confidentiality of his clients and his friends as a sacred oath. They'd been through too much together to doubt his loyalty. Still, her natural suspicion of unearned opportunity prompted her to ask, "Do you like this guy?"

"He did me a solid in law school. He's not everyone's cup of tea, a little peculiar, but I trust him."

"Enough said. How should we connect?"

"Give me the okay, and he'll be in touch."

She glanced at the ruins of Walter Richards's fledgling criminal enterprise. "Sounds good. I've got time."

Glen Paul Freedman—who preferred "Freedman" from his contemporaries and only answered to "Glen Paul" when his mother or his boss called—waited impatiently in the restaurant for his guest. Shockingly vivid auburn hair that grew fast and curly had been shorn as close to his scalp as current social conventions allowed. An aesthetician routinely trimmed his eyebrows to keep their growth in check.

He'd grown as straight and tall as his riotously redheaded nemesis from cartoons, Sideshow Bob, a comparison he'd heard until he grew too belligerent for others to use the nickname to his face.

He studied the menu with limited interest. His order rarely deviated from a standard of scrambled eggs, wheat toast, and coffee, black. At thirteen, he'd tested the bitter brew on a dare and fallen in love. Now his refusal to haggle over oat or goat or pistachio milk was a personal badge of honor. A hovering waitress had already filled his cup upon arrival, and he gestured for a refill.

The waitress returned moments later, with Mi Jong, his breakfast companion, nipping at her heels. The financier who had agreed to spearhead Camasca's attempt to go public, Mi Jong moved briskly as though in a hurry to be done with him and on to the next meeting. Rising, he waited for her to take a seat. Good manners dictated that he stand. The twenty-first-century social mores kept him from reaching for her chair.

Once they had settled, he offered, "Rafe sends his regrets, but he's meeting with the bankers and our CFO this morning, as you might expect."

"We chatted on my way here. Your boss wanted to warn me about the news you were sent to deliver." Jong flicked at an errant strand of silver hair that threaded liberally through her stark black bob. "We're two weeks away from going public, Glen. Why in the devil are you bringing in outsiders to comb through your company?"

"Compromise," he replied. "We've got some land mines lurking—we've got to sort them out."

"Land mines aren't allowed. We've raised every dollar you and your boss asked for, and I've put in a hundred and fifty million of my own. *A hundred and fifty million.* We performed the tech due diligence and the conflicts checks, and all the other regulatory tap dancing necessary—because no one understands exactly what your guy Rafe Diaz has created at Camasca, but they're afraid to be left out."

"I understand—"

"Don't interrupt my tirade, Glen Paul," she barked. "We've complied with the tight-asses at the SEC, jumped through flaming hoops with investors, done enemas, and burned sage to gods." She took a dramatic breath. "The only person causing trouble is Rafe. He's on the precipice of joining Bill and Steve and Mark on the pantheon of one-named, stupidly rich tech geniuses. How the hell is he having cold feet?"

"He's not. It's a guilty conscience."

Her voluble curse in response caught the attention of the next table, and the lawyer offered a grimace of apology. Turning to Mi Jong, he tried to explain his boss's behavior. "Before he was Dr. Rafe Diaz, he was Major Rafe Diaz. A member of the Camasca team died on his watch. Under his command."

"The police investigated the incident and cleared the company of wrongdoing. This is navel gazing, Glen, not leadership."

"Doesn't matter. I'm the general counsel, and my job is to protect the company. And to help make all of us stupidly rich." Silently, Glen cursed as he sipped his cooling coffee, choosing his next words carefully. "To do my job, I can't overlook any potential misstep. Which is why I proposed to him and the board that we bring in an internal investigator."

"You have someone in mind?"

"I do." He braced for impact. "Avery Keene."

"The law clerk? Are you out of your mind?"

"She's no longer a clerk. She's at Clymer Brezil. They've got a reputation for being quick, efficient, and savvy."

"Keene doesn't."

"Actually, she's never faced any bar complaints. She's clever, knows the law inside out; and Rafe admires her. If we get her to sign off on us, her word is gold."

"If she finds something that hurts Camasca?"

Glen allowed himself to smirk in satisfaction. "Attorney-client privilege prevents her from revealing anything she finds. We're in bed with a lot of federal agencies, and they'll trust her, too, because of her reputation. But she can't tell anyone what she finds out."

"You sure about that?"

"It's a risk we have to take."

TWO

Avery stopped her car in front of the retrofitted industrial plant with a metal awning that read "Camasca" in engraved lettering. The brick-and-mortar facade looked identical to lots of abandoned factories that dotted the American landscape, including on the outskirts of Bethesda, Maryland. This one had been cleaned up a bit, but nothing about the feel of the exterior suggested that a cutting-edge tech company lurked inside.

A security guard approached her. He carried a digital tablet in one hand and a digital scanner in the other. Avery rolled down her window when he came abreast.

"Ms. Avery Keene?" he asked.

"Yes. I've got an appointment to see Glen Paul Freedman."

"Of course." He lifted the scanner. "Would you mind looking straight at me, please?"

Confused but game, Avery complied. He quickly moved the wand in a circular pattern, then checked his tablet. "Thank you. One more moment, please."

With the ease of experience, he thumbed the screen with one hand and shifted the scanner to her windshield. A digital voice whispered, "2006 Subaru Outback. Atlantic Blue Pearl. Registration: Avery Olivia Keene. Washington. District of Columbia."

The guard tapped the screen again. "You've been verified. Please proceed to the parking facility and take your designated space."

"Designated?"

"Check the signage, please. Then proceed to the elevators."

"Thank you." Intrigued, Avery followed directions. As her vehicle approached the garage, the chyron above the gate flashed her last name. Slot 127, level 3. The gate arm raised, and she soon pulled into a spot beside Noah's silver BMW on the third floor of the garage. She greeted him at the bumper of his much nicer, newer vehicle. "I'm surprised there wasn't a cheek swab."

"I'm glad I don't have any outstanding warrants." Linking his arm with Avery's, Noah led them toward the elevator bank a few yards away. He scanned the sleek metal exterior. "There are no buttons." Almost as soon as he spoke, it opened, and they quickly entered.

The carriage whisked them up, while Avery carefully inspected their surroundings. As in most modern-day elevators, a video monitor had been affixed to the wall beside the doors. Yet, instead of offering trivia or ads, it cycled through images of medical innovators. Louis Pasteur. Mary Seacole. Susan La Flesche Picotte. Charles Drew. Florence Nightingale. Potted bios explained their significance and encouraged readers to learn more.

When the elevator had glided to a stop, the doors opened. They emerged, Avery first. Her instant impression was of light. Cascades of it flooding inside, though a fast scan showed few windows to provide natural sunlight. A tall man who topped her considerable five feet eleven by a couple of inches stood nearby. The custom-tailored suit in navy fell precisely above the back of his shoe, and cuff links fastened his shirt. His ginger hair had been shorn low, but without becoming a buzz cut. Because she paid attention to faces, she catalogued his piercing blue eyes and a furrow that had been etched between his brow. He struck her as the kind of man who had probably scowled as a baby when the milk was late.

"Ms. Keene. Fox. This way." He turned on his heel, apparently assuming they'd follow.

"Avery Keene, this taciturn gentleman is Glen Paul Freedman." Noah made the introductions to the redhead's back as they walked rapidly through a wide, screen-laden corridor.

They soon reached a lobby where a freestanding body scanner blocked their progress. Freedman gestured to Avery. "Good afternoon, Ms. Keene. Please enter."

Tentatively, Avery advanced and looked over her shoulder. "Is all of this necessary?"

"For our company? Yes."

In for a penny, she thought as she stepped inside. Following the floor markings, she planted her feet as she'd been taught by multiple TSA agents, her arms above her head. What came next was a request for her to repeat the phrase "Thrive and be kind."

After a buzz and whir of invisible purpose, a pleasant voice that vaguely sounded like a semi-famous actor advised her that it now had a photo of her eyes and encouraged her to exit. Avery stepped out. In exchange for her compliance, the unit gifted her a laminated pass and a friendly admonition to abide by the rules of the building. "Welcome to Camasca. Where we change everything."

Noah followed, quickly receiving his own badge.

The general counsel then passed both of them a tablet. "These are nondisclosure agreements, indemnification agreements, and anti-compete agreements. Please review, initial where indicated, and sign."

"This seems excessive." Noah opened the first document, while Avery silently did the same.

"Just sign it, Fox." Looming next to them, the attorney radiated impatience as they methodically reviewed each line. Once or twice, the visitors conferred about their interpretation of a clause or a consequence. Finally, they both affixed their signatures and dutifully returned the tablets.

"Very thorough protections," Avery commented. "I was looking for the replevin clause to force me to return any thoughts I had while on your premises."

"I'll have our legal interns look into that," he pledged sardonically, and resumed their journey.

"Excuse Freedman's poor manners," Noah apologized as they swiftly moved in an inverted V formation. "What he lacks in common courtesy, he makes up for with his Bostonian wicked smarts."

"Good thing you are so incredibly charming," Freedman responded without turning. He tapped imperiously on the mini-tablet in his left hand. "We'll speak in my office."

As they approached glass doors that separated sections, Avery noticed that each of their badges refracted for an instant before they were admitted. Infrared coding signaled their seamless access, and the badge apparently served as a mobile key. The trio turned down another stretch of hallway that held Pulitzer-quality still images of proteins, carbohydrates, nucleic acids, and lipids, the macromolecules rendered in dynamic color and precision.

On this side of the facility, Avery observed offices with discreet palm readers, retinal scanners, and closed doors. Assuming the larger spaces in between them were laboratories, she marked the presence of a scattering of white-coated staff who moved past them without much conversation. As they traveled swiftly through the maze of halls, Avery saw techs moving vials and goggled scientists tending their craft.

A far door slid open, and Avery and Noah came to a sudden stop. A golden-skinned robot with humanoid features glided toward them on a mechanical base, its articulated limbs carrying a tray of vials covered in a clear cloche. "Good day, Mr. Freedman," it greeted the general counsel as it shifted to move past them. "Ms. Keene. Mr. Fox. Enjoy your visit."

Stunned, the two visitors turned to watch as the automaton entered a laboratory a few meters away. Avery found her voice first. "What was that?"

"You just met Yax, one of our robot prototypes. It's assigned to our pharmaceutical division. Its companion, Keh, functions in general services."

As though the robot was nothing special, Freedman kept moving forward. A few people nodded to the lawyer and his companions, and others raised eyebrows at his guests.

As they moved deeper into the facility, the looks shifted from curious to almost hostile, and Freedman finally spoke. "This is our R&D wing. We rarely allow visitors," he explained brusquely. "Most outsiders never make it to this side of our shop, or meet Yax."

"Who knew our names." Not easily impressed, Noah was still incredulous.

"Camasca's AI system shares information in real time, and its learnings are simultaneously integrated into all relevant systems. Security knows you're here, and R&D is our most protected area. Therefore, Yax would be alerted to your presence and made privy to your bioprint."

"Bioprint?" Avery thought she understood the term, but her recent fall down the tech rabbit hole made her ask anyway.

"That's what we call our biogenic and data scans. Everyone who enters Camasca gets one, and we track it during your entire visit."

After another turn, they entered a short vestibule that scanned each of them before granting admission to an elevator bank. Similar to the magnetometer that greeted them, this one did not offer platitudes. Instead, it flashed green as each moved through. Freedman went last, adding, "Nothing leaves R&D."

On the other side, Freedman selected his floor. He stepped back and waved to them to scan their badges. "We're heading to the administrative suite where my office is located, but you have to be logged in separately."

Almost instantly, metal elevator doors slid open, and they entered the car. Noah shifted to the back, and Avery ventured, "Very impressive tech you have here. Stunning, really. So why exactly am I here, Mr. Freedman? How can I help?"

Before he answered, a harried young man in a suit approached, but Freedman waved him off. "Catch the next car, Damien. I'll see you in my office at five o'clock."

The stranded passenger dipped his head in understanding as the doors slid shut. The attorney folded his long arms and propped his shoulder against the elevator wall, still for the first time since Avery met him.

He cocked his head to the side, studying her. "I've watched you over the past few years, Ms. Keene. Even your enemies praise your competence. My friends on Capitol Hill have nice things to say about you, and they are—by and large—a group of unrepentant assholes."

"I'll take that as a compliment, I guess," Avery demurred.

"Most important to me, my friend Noah vouches for you. Therefore, I think you can help us out."

"With what?"

The elevator quietly dinged their arrival. Freedman ushered them out into the foyer for the administrative suite. "To help Camasca become the center of an AI revolution in health care . . . in a matter of weeks."

With that vague pronouncement, he breezed past the receptionist. Moving through the foyer, Avery caught a fleeting glimpse of wide windows and wood-paneled walls, leather-bound chairs clustered around high-gloss, low marble tables. A far cry from the worn industrial front of the building.

"How big is this campus?"

"We currently own eleven acres, though we haven't completed our facilities yet. One of the perks of going public will be realizing our physical expansion plans."

"Quite a massive footprint."

"Quite a massive undertaking," he replied. "This is my office."

She nearly snorted. As if the cavern of glass and chrome could be described so modestly as an "office." Freedman closed the door behind them, then tapped a panel, flipping a signal from green to yellow. He crossed the room and dropped into a supple leather chair upholstered in magenta.

"Take a seat, Ms. Keene. Noah."

"Avery, please."

"Avery." He didn't offer equal familiarity.

Duly noted. Freedman it was. They settled onto the tufted cushions of a matching sofa. She examined the stretch of walls decorated with framed memorabilia that could fetch a small fortune on eBay. She turned to Freedman. "You're a big *Star Trek* fan, I see."

His pale-blue eyes lit up. "Are you a Trekkie, too?"

"Absolutely," she confirmed. "Got it from my dad. He had a communicator and a model of the *Enterprise* in his studio."

"Which captain? Which ship?"

Noah frowned in confusion. "Hmm?"

"Picard as the epitome of Starfleet. Janeway as the badass who defied the odds. Burnham for being the post-Kirk renegade."

Eager to join the discussion, Noah said, "I used to watch the one with Data and Geordi."

Freedman and Avery gave him dual looks of pity. Feeling charitable, Freedman said, "What most people know of the future of AI and medicine in two great characters." He jackknifed forward and planted sharp elbows on gangly knees. "Avery, what exactly do you know about Camasca?"

"You're an AI biotech firm." Avery intentionally mirrored Freedman's posture. She'd done her research in between meetings and rattled off what she'd learned. "Your CEO is Dr. Rafe Diaz, who is a Marine Corps veteran, retired with the rank of major. He was honorably discharged about a decade ago, then he launched his own biomedical start-up. Got DoD funding for research, with a little boost from DARPA. Caught the attention of a few VCs in Boston, where you came on board, and they invested tons. Word has it that your company is probably worth more than a billion dollars."

"Thereabouts," Freedman amended with only a hint of pride.

"I must admit, however, for a billion-dollar corporation, it's surprisingly difficult to learn about your tech. Lots of speculation, though."

"You have any guesses?"

Avery had long ago honed her ability to synthesize copious amounts of information and ferret out the truth. Or at least a close approximation of some version that could pass the smell test. "My guess is that Camasca has a biomedical technology powered by AI that delivers personalized medicine and the drugs to go with it."

"Based on what?"

"Walking through here, I saw an R&D lab with what I assume was a pharmaceutical division." At his raised brow, she explained, "The lab coats and vials. Then there's your bioprint technology. And your omniscient computer network."

"We call it *omnivalent,* but, so far, you're batting a thousand." Freedman got to his feet and began to circle the room. "We've got our own neural network."

"Like DeepMind?" Noah asked. He'd done a smidge of homework himself, but his knowledge extended to what he had read about in the news or heard on podcasts. "Or is this more like OpenAI?"

"Generally, the same concept. Camasca began as biomed AI, but we've refined our initial product. We created a dynamic deep neural network that will transform how quickly, efficiently and effectively patients receive diagnosis and treatment."

"Not to be a skeptic, but dozens of companies are in the clinical space. Why is Camasca worth so much?" Avery waved away her question as the realization hit her. "Ahh . . . your service population. You're not simply helping Grandma avoid the ER. Your company is going after the military and the billions of dollars in Defense

Department–adjacent contracts. You'll own the world by telling everyone you can save it."

"A bit snarky, but you're not wrong. If we can fix military health care, we'll be unstoppable. And noble. A lucrative combination."

"Cynical."

"Yet true. Rafe remembers what it was like to have to treat patients on the fly during his deployments. Patients rolled in with incomplete medical records, and life-threatening wounds or mysterious illnesses. He and his colleagues had to guess at what might help or exacerbate their conditions. Worse, there was usually no good way to track their health after they left his care."

He continued, "Once they're out of the service, a soldier transitions from military care to veteran health care, a completely different system and federal budget-line item." Freedman turned and folded his arms, backlit by broad windows and a sun that seemed to herald his announcement. "That's why Camasca is a game changer."

Avery agreed, which begged a very important question. So she asked. "You've got the DoD, the VA, and Wall Street at your feet. Why do you need me?"

Before Freedman could answer, a man entered the room without knocking and firmly shut the door. A deep voice explained, "Because we could lose everything unless you can help us prove no one here committed murder."

THREE

"Murder?" Avery twisted to face the ominous newcomer. She would have pegged Freedman at six foot one, a lean 175 pounds, and in his early thirties, but the man who'd entered stood even taller. At least six foot three, a trim but solid 220 pounds or so, a youthful mid-forties. Built like a boxer with a killer hook, the man carried himself more like the soldier he used to be. Smooth copper skin stretched tight over sharp bone structure that boasted a broad nose, full lips, and deeply set, hooded chocolate-brown eyes. She could easily imagine his troops following him into battle, though he'd served as a medic more than a soldier. To confirm her hunch, she guessed, "Dr. Diaz?"

"At your service," he replied as he advanced inside. "Call me Rafe, please."

He came over to her post on the sofa with his right hand extended, and Avery accepted the firm handshake. His smile was all white caps and sincerity, and she found herself responding in kind. Until she remembered the word *murder*.

"Who else has died?" When everyone stared at her, Avery focused on Rafe. "I read about the death of a scientist in a 'workplace incident' five weeks ago. Are you talking about him or someone else?"

Noah looked at Freedman tellingly. "She does her research. A lot of it."

Rafe met her level look with his own. "Yes, one of my senior team members died here at Camasca," he confirmed as he sat in Freedman's vacated seat. "Dr. Elisha Hibner. A brilliant man and terrific scientist."

"Why did you call it murder? Police ruled it an accident."

"Ever known the police to be wrong?"

Instinct told her to stand up and excuse herself immediately. She'd settled into a nice groove at Clymer Brezil, handling straightforward cases for companies facing allegations of sexual harassment or racial discrimination, or uncovering poor document-retention policies before the DoJ or some other agency did. Helping businesses stay out of trouble was now her bread and butter. *Not murder. Not anymore.*

Yet she didn't move. "What happened?" Avery had read what she could find about the incident, but no details had been reported.

To rejoin their clutch, Freedman sat down heavily at the other end of the sofa. "Dr. Hibner died on the premises in an accident that no one can explain. For a team of geniuses, that type of loss is not only hard to accept, it is counter to the very nature of this place. *Inexplicable* is an epithet around here."

Anger flashed, and Rafe's gaze narrowed to a slit. "And totally unacceptable. Accident or not, there's an answer. I intend to find it."

"I understand," Avery replied softly. "I'm sorry for your loss."

He nodded curtly. "Thank you. Truly."

She cleared her throat, which had gone suddenly dry. "Neither of you answered my question. Why do you need me? You have a military-grade security team, an Ivy League legal team, and the best data scientists in the world," she pointed out. "If you have a mystery, they should be more than equipped to solve it."

"They've tried and failed," Rafe said flatly. "More than a month has gone by, and no one has answers for an accident that nearly killed three of our team leads."

"If your folks and the police have failed, I can't imagine they'd look too kindly on outsiders swooping in." She forestalled his response by holding up a hand. "And if this is really a criminal matter, it should be handled by the police. Or, if there's a way to argue for jurisdiction, then you can talk to the FBI. I've got a contact if you need one. Agent Robert Lee oversees interjurisdictional issues and would be willing to listen."

Rafe shook his head. "I appreciate the offer, but involving the FBI is a nonstarter. Like you said, the local police investigated Elisha's death, and they found nothing out of the ordinary. Chalked it up to mechanical errors. Our internal teams have also thoroughly investigated every aspect of the event, and they, too, believe that Elisha's death was a freak accident. But I believe they've missed something."

"I think you should call a private detective," Avery advised. "Despite my recent history, I am not anyone's sleuth."

"We aren't in need of a PI," Freedman confirmed. "We need an internal investigator. You."

"Why her?" Noah asked. "If you think it was murder, why ask me to get Avery for you?"

Rafe and Freedman exchanged a look, and Rafe nodded almost imperceptibly. Freedman said, "Look, I reached out to Noah because I know you two are friends. I know that you work at Clymer Brezil—a firm that specializes in sifting through a company's dirty laundry. You've only been there a minute, but you've already built a reputation that just adds to your legend as a law clerk."

"What kind of reputation?" Avery asked coolly.

"Being thorough. Discreet. Exhausting."

"You meant exhaustive," Noah automatically corrected.

"No, he didn't," Avery replied with a thin smile.

"No, I didn't," Freedman agreed without humor. "I need a bulldog with a brain like Einstein and a flexible approach to her work and the rules."

"I'm not morally flexible," Avery bit out. "Which means I'm not the right person for this gig."

"Hold on, Ms. Keene," Rafe interjected. "Glen Paul didn't mean to suggest you were immoral."

"I have excellent hearing, Dr. Diaz," she shot back. "And, as he indicated, I'm not dumb. So—I'll answer my own question. Why bring in someone like me? Because you have something to hide, and you think I'll help with the burying."

"On the contrary," Freedman said. "You're so moralistic and dogged, if you think we've done something wrong, you'll find a way to the truth. Whether we want it or not."

Slightly mollified and mildly insulted, Avery subsided. "Fine. Which begs another question. No one is looking your way. You'll be public soon. Why hire me to dig up your skeletons?"

"Because my boss has a similar affliction for the truth," Freedman replied tersely. "He wants to know what happened, and I need someone who knows that whatever we find is our business. We are on the brink of taking Camasca public."

Noah said, "I'd heard rumors. You're using a SPAC?"

"Yes. We decided to use a special purpose acquisition company. It's easier than all of the hoops of a traditional IPO," Freedman confirmed. "But we've decided we need to go digging, Avery, and I don't want to have to report our findings to the SEC, the FDA, the DoD, and the VA. Any one of them could scuttle the deal, shut us down, and cost us billions."

Rafe shifted toward Avery. "I absolutely want to do what's right, but I don't want our work to be penalized for good intentions. Glen Paul tells me that, if you do the digging, anything you find stays in-house. A win-win."

"Unless you are using my legal advice to further criminal or fraudulent activities," Avery clarified. "Then I may be obligated to report it." Otherwise, she'd generally be obliged to keep her silence—morals didn't matter when it came to attorney-client privilege.

"You were my idea, Ms. Keene," Freedman said. "Because I don't think we've done anything wrong, but Rafe likes to say we must be like Caesar's wife."

"No one said the same about Caesar," she groused.

"No, they didn't." Rafe gave an approving nod. "I like to set higher standards. Camasca is a biotech company. And a health-care company. And an AI company. The world is fascinated by AI, and the smart ones are terrified, too. In this business, one unflattering article, one glitch in the matrix, and we lose our reputation. When it's a bad chatbot that gives you the wrong answers, people will forgive you. But if Grandma gets hurt because AI got something wrong, we can never recover. Understand?"

Avery thought of her former boss, his half-life powered by machines. "Go on," she said quietly.

"To build Camasca, I've grown by different means, including inventions, acquisitions, and taking on partners. I've made friends and enemies, and some of both work in this building, because they know what we've developed is groundbreaking. Others can't wait for Camasca to burn down. If any one of them used me as reason to harm Elisha and O.J. and Izzy, I intend to hold them responsible."

"Why strike now?" Noah looked around the group. "An IPO is a great way to catch a ride to obscene wealth. Who would put a target on your team now?"

"The invention that's going to make you a one-named wonder," Avery guessed. "Kawak."

Rafe reclined and propped his ankle on his knee, assessing his guest. Freedman had not exaggerated about Avery Keene. Once you got past the traffic-stopping looks, with those absurdly lovely green eyes, the smarts were undeniable. Little would get past her. "Got it in one," Rafe said admiringly. "Kawak is a holistic AI system focused on medical care. At its core, it's a neural network with a database of limitless capacity that can interface with your smartwatch or a doctor's MRI. When fully functional, Kawak will mean having frictionless access to the world's medical knowledge . . . to your entire health-care record . . . to your genetic history . . . and to hyper-personalized, life-saving treatments."

"Kawak is the robot we met?" Noah asked unashamedly. "I know how to program Alexa and my security system, but I leave the tech talk to my friends."

"No, you met Yax," Rafe explained, smiling. "AI has lots of terminology that only really matters to data scientists. Think about it this way: Camasca is the body, our whole enterprise. Kawak is the brain. The neural network. It's been programmed to process information at warp speed, to imitate human cognitive abilities and make decisions based on what it learns, and to communicate with us in natural language. The robots—Yax and Keh—operate like limbs. They physically carry out Kawak's instructions. Yax works with the teams in our laboratories, and Keh handles the personnel side. They operate semi-independently; however, Kawak has the ultimate control."

"Fascinating," Avery murmured. "All of that exists inside this building."

"Almost. Then there's our clinical-decision support system, or CDSS, which we call Milo—Milo is tasked with helping doctors help patients: documenting clinical exams, analyzing health records, even recommending diagnoses or personalized medications." He gestured broadly. "Camasca has a range of health-care research areas, but Kawak is our game changer. AI and medicine all in one."

"How?" Noah challenged. "With all due respect, as cool as this place is, everyone is doing AI these days. My doctor had an AI transcription of my appointment with her from six months ago."

A gleam twinkled in Freedman's eyes, and Rafe knew what was coming. The attorney popped up and headed back to the panel at the door and input his code, and the signal flickered green. "Kawak? What can you tell me about our guest, Mr. Fox?"

A pleasant voice that sounded like Frank Sinatra via Istanbul replied, "I will be more useful if you have a more specific question in mind, Freedman. As I have not been privy to your recent conversation, I am unclear about your desired line of inquiry."

"Don't pout," Freedman instructed. "We've discussed the importance of privacy in my office. You can't be subject to attorney-client privilege."

"No definitive ruling has been made by any American court," Kawak intoned. "I think you set a questionable double standard for your staff, given that you do not permit the attorneys in your team to block my access. Also, I remain perplexed that Dr. Diaz allows you a freedom he does not take for himself."

"Maybe because my name is Freedman," the attorney offered.

Kawak responded, "That's a poor pun, Freedman, but a nice try."

Noah frowned. "Again, no offense, but I can have conversations like this with my telephone. What makes Camasca worth a billion dollars or more?"

Freedman folded his arms. "Kawak—wow him."

"Mr. Fox, I appreciate your skepticism about me," Kawak said conversationally, "but I can assure you that I am more sophisticated than the functions you use to order pizza from your phone or to channel-surf on your television. By the way, if you are truly watching your weight, as your recent app purchases suggest, I'd suggest you limit to once a week your standing order of the fifteen-inch meats pie with light sauce, extra pepperoni, and thin crust, almost burned, from Vertelli's on I Street."

Rafe, Freedman, and Avery watched in amusement as Noah flushed. But Kawak wasn't finished. "When you irregularly exercise with the Coach.me app, you watch your favored reruns of *Are You Being Served?* on the BBC. Perhaps, this week, you will finally watch the Ken Burns discography of *Jazz* that you ordered four years and three months ago, which you rated highly on Amazon?"

"Finally watch?"

"I can logically deduce that you hadn't watched it when you gave the rating, because you left the DVR files unwatched until they were auto-deleted by your internet provider. Also, you should call your grandmother Wednesday to wish her a happy seventy-third birthday and check if her bunion has responded to the medication prescribed by Dr. Phillips. Your breathing rate of fourteen breaths per minute is high—with your sedentary occupation, it suggests you'd benefit from additional cardio. You should also have your primary-care physician, Dr. Wright, test your thyroid functions when you have your checkup next month. You are exhibiting symptoms of hypothyroidism, which likely explains your recent weight gain of seven pounds, which is probably salt-and-water retention."

"I'll ask," Noah consented weakly. "How? What the devil?"

Freedman clapped him on the shoulder in commiseration. "Disconcerting, I know. Kawak contains trillions of bits of data and is constantly gathering more."

"Like what?" Avery asked, equally unnerved. "Does it have limits?"

Rafe cautioned with a bit of pride: "Kawak researches and collects any information available. It scrapes data from every known and accessible data source, from the cookies collected by your browser to social-media profiles to commercial genetic services. If it doesn't violate the law, we have access to anything about you available for sale or search."

"Orwell would be so proud." Avery slanted a look at Freedman. "I think Captain Picard might have a few misgivings about this, don't you?"

"Rafe has been careful not to use any information that could create harm, Ms. Keene. Consider his anti-bias mantra to be our prime directive."

Rafe scrutinized Avery closely. "What we are building here at Camasca can remake the world. Shall we do another demonstration for you?"

She flashed back to nights in the ER with her strung-out mother, Rita, when Avery was just a rattled twelve-year-old trying to fill out paperwork. She recalled with piercing detail sifting through medical jargon, while panic pressed in on every side.

"No, thank you." Eager to avoid a show-and-tell with her as the guinea pig, Avery focused on Kawak's functionality and where she'd seen corporate Camasca mentioned recently, outside of breathless news stories. "The last time I visited Bethesda Naval Hospital, I noticed a new clinic sign: INNOVAI, POWERED BY CAMASCA. So Kawak is actively serving veterans there—using Milo?"

"For several months now," Rafe confirmed. "We call it our gamma test. Last hurdle before we scale nationwide. Milo operates on-site with inputs and guidance from Kawak. Hence our access to the satellite technology.

"Vets who use our clinic typically get results—lab work or otherwise—during their visit, which substantially reduces the need for follow-up appointments. We have a waiting list, which we can't start moving until the company goes public. The capital infusion will allow us to expand InnoVAI, scale the tech, and replicate the clinic across more VA hospitals."

"Impressive. Really, I mean it," Noah said. "But we're still missing the punch line."

"What?"

"I just don't get it—Freedman asked me to connect you all with Avery for an internal investigation. What do a futuristic AI system and Avery have to do with a murder that doesn't seem to actually be a murder?"

At Freedman's scowl, Noah subsided. Freedman hurried to the panel and encoded the digits. When the lights shifted to yellow, he explained, "Kawak literally hears and retains everything. We need absolute secrecy here."

Rafe hinged forward, folded his hands, and tucked them beneath his chin. On a smaller man, the posture would look like entreaty. From him, it was an invitation to believe. "I created Camasca on my own, and I grew it over a decade by collecting geniuses. Engineers, biotechnicians, chemists, and public-policy experts. We've always worked in silence, content to perfect our product first."

Avery caught herself before she nodded. Instinctively, she shifted back, beyond his charismatic aura.

"This is the work I've given my life to achieve—to serve my fellow veterans, especially the ones waiting months to see a primary-care physician. Or ones whose service records get scrambled and whose field-medic reports are never logged. Then they have a drug reaction that kills them because no one ever thought to look for a note in their treatment file from a base in Düsseldorf. Or because they were homeless and left their paperwork behind at a shelter."

"Kawak can help a lot of people, Dr. Diaz. I get it."

"We're about to go public. Kawak is a remarkable advance in AI technology that is going to change the world of health care. But we can't afford any publicity that might dampen enthusiasm as we investigate."

"And how, specifically, does that involve me?" Avery asked.

Rafe braided his fingers and held her gaze. "It's a sensitive question. Before I open the hangar doors and authorize this launch . . . I need to determine one thing, Avery. Have I built Data, the lovable android, or HAL, the killer computer? I want your help to be sure I can *trust* Kawak."

Avery was taken aback. "What would make you think you can't?"

"We received a tip—a note. It said that Elisha Hibner's death was only the beginning."

"A note from whom?" Noah prompted.

For the second time, Freedman and Rafe checked in with each other. When Diaz gave assent, Freedman answered quietly, "From the AI network itself. From Kawak."

FOUR

"You received a death threat from the all-knowing computer system that could be listening to us now?" Avery asked, wondering if she should get up and leave. She'd accepted the invitation to Camasca to expand her corporate repertoire, not jump headfirst into another whirlpool of crazy. She glanced over at Noah, and he bit back a sigh. He knew her too well. Curiosity had already settled in, and she couldn't leave without understanding what was going on. "*Is* your AI system psychotic?"

"Absolutely not," Freedman scorned the very idea. "But someone is trying to make it seem so . . . which is why we need your help."

"I don't speak computer or perform digital exorcisms," Avery said dryly. "I provide legal research and analysis, and I'm pretty adept at tracking patterns. Figuring out if everyone is following the rules. I don't see a nexus here."

"The nexus is, we need an objective third party and a swift assessment of our exposure, bound by legal-confidentiality rules," Rafe said. "That's you. And, as Glen Paul and I have concurred, your team."

"My team?"

"Noah as your legal partner," Freedman said. "Given what I know of how you've worked before, I assume you will call in Jared Wynn to provide technical assistance, and seek biomedical advice from your former roommate, Dr. Ling Yin."

"You've done your homework," Noah said with admiration. "I think I'm flattered."

Freedman rolled his eyes. "Don't be. We don't have a lot of time to waste bringing a megafirm up to speed. Hiring individuals who have the composite skills necessarily means they are unlikely to have worked together."

Rafe added, "Speed is of the essence, as is discretion. We have a list of potential bad actors, a brilliant internal team that is smarter than the police, and regulatory agencies that are willing to kill all of this if we take a wrong step." He grimaced. "Poor choice of words."

Or Freudian slip, Avery reflected.

"You're not afraid of powerful people," Freedman added, "and you are a damned good lawyer who can ferret through reams of information and spot issues others might miss. As long as you're bound by attorney-client privilege, you're the perfect solution for us."

Convinced, she took a brief second to worry about Jared's reaction. And the high likelihood that Ling would absolutely refuse. Problems for later, she decided. Knowing she was hooked, Avery looked between the two men and asked the obvious question. "What exactly did the threat say?"

"You're in?" Freedman put the question to her bluntly.

"I didn't say that," she hedged. "Tell me about the threat."

Pleased by her response, Freedman reached for his tablet and passed it to Avery. Noah moved to read over her shoulder.

You have tried to play God. Now you have found us—the real ones. The fallen child was only the first. There will be others. I am thunder and I am lightning.

"How did this arrive?" Avery asked as she returned the tablet to Freedman.

"A K-chat sent to Rafe. Kawak-chat. That's our proprietary, internal comms app for Camasca employees. You can only send using a Camasca device, to or from another K-chat user. Instant deletion for sender and recipient as soon as a message is read. A person can tag themselves, but they have the option to transmit a message anonymously, as long as it does not violate community guidelines. The point is to encourage shared information without physical cross-contamination or hacking."

"Yet you have this message," Avery said. "They aren't actually instantly deleted?"

"Correct. They are deleted for everyone except Rafe and me. And senior members of the security team at our discretion," Freedman acknowledged. "Employees lose access upon transmission."

"Your employees think they're using a version of Snapchat, but you've got a catalogue of their communications?" Noah frowned at Freedman's admission. "Why lie about something so basic?"

"It's not a lie, and it is in their contracts," Freedman justified. "By practice, yes, K-chats disappear from user devices after they're read. Rafe wants to encourage the free flow of ideas among colleagues without censure."

"Noble intention." Avery gestured to the tablet. "Then why undermine your values?"

Freedman crossed his arms, shaking his head mockingly. "Because this is a cutthroat business and humans are messy and noble intentions require tough enforcement." He jutted out his chin. "When Rafe gets sued for stealing an idea or some harassment complaint pops up in HR, that's on me and my team. We are also responsible for a data-retention protocol that proves the origins of our technology when some garage entrepreneur claims to have invented our robots."

"Lying to your employees isn't your only alternative," Avery opined. "Companies have dealt with 'messy' humans and corporate espionage for years."

"We've improved upon the process," Freedman asserted blandly. "K-chats are a digital version of the suggestion box and tip line, but with an accountability back-door."

Avery filed away the information and shifted focus back to the note in question. "Who knows about this tip besides the two of you?"

"No one," Freedman answered. "It came in twenty-four hours ago. Directly to Rafe. However, unlike other K-chats, we can't track it back to a point of origin."

Noah asked, "Why not?"

"There is no source data," Rafe explained. "All K-chats have an embedded code unique to users. I can identify the sender, and Freedman can do the same. But the identifier has been stripped from this message."

"Who in your company knows how to do that?"

His brows furrowed in consternation. "Dozens of our staff have the capacity, but most don't have security clearance. And then there's Kawak itself."

"Freedman said you have an omnivalent monitoring system." Avery directed her attention squarely at Rafe. "What does that mean, exactly?"

He rose and began to circle the room. "Precisely what you have inferred from the description. Anyone on campus, including in the R&D suites, has their entire presence monitored. We track movements, resource usage, and bioprints."

"Why? How?"

"We use cameras and microphones of course, but we also measure biological indicators. Just like that fitness watch on your wrist, but more advanced. Our wearable tech and sensors in most of our shared areas observe stress levels based on heart-rate variability. Blood-oxygen saturation and electrical activity of the heart. Perspiration, respiratory patterns, basal temperature. We also evaluate metabolic functions, conduct full-body composition analysis, perform routine retinal scans to check for incipient issues like cardiovascular crises, and administer regular cheek swabs to check for viral infections before they become contagious."

Freedman piped up, "Team members get to choose the wearable technology they prefer, and staff use the bioprint scanner on a daily basis as a condition of entry. All of their data is linked into Kawak."

Avery recoiled slightly as she considered the invasion of privacy. "All as a precondition to work at Camasca?"

Rafe firmed his mouth before responding. "We are scientists, Ms. Keene. Inventors. If we are willing to experiment on others, we have to be willing to commit ourselves to the process." He touched his watch briefly, identical to the one Freedman wore. "Like this."

"Would my team be compelled to wear one?" she asked.

"Of course."

"And if I object?"

"Why would you?" Rafe challenged. "You've already agreed to give a third party you probably can't name access to your personal data by wearing your watch. More than likely, that information has been sold to other vendors, and you're none the wiser."

"I'm much more paranoid than the average bear," Avery corrected. "I set up a dummy account that tracks my data, and I use a fake email."

Rafe gave her a half-smile and lifted the tablet he carried. Seconds passed while he tapped into the screen. "Myrina Collins, born January 7, and you claim to be twenty-eight. Email address is myrinalco@mailshop.com."

"How in the hell did you do that so fast?" Noah demanded when Avery's eyes widened.

"We all leave digital breadcrumbs, regardless of how careful we try to be. Avery uses pretty sophisticated VPN software, but she set the account up using her home computer before she started deflecting digital intrusions."

"That's creepy," she managed.

"It's the twenty-first century," Rafe replied mildly, "but if you object to sharing your data with us, that's your choice. You'd be a contractor. However, you might find it useful to participate."

At Avery's dubious look, he continued, "A couple of years ago, one of our biotechs had an ischemic stroke. We knew it before she did, and we were able to rush her to the emergency room and get her the care she needed."

Avery nodded, still unconvinced. "Do your patients at InnoVAI have the same tech? Surely not the same level of daily monitoring."

"Not yet. They have different versions of the products, depending on their comfort level and status. For example, for our unhoused clients, we find that wearable tech is difficult to preserve, so some have agreed to implants."

"You inject them with technology?"

"Less intrusive than a pacemaker, and more helpful than an overworked social worker." Rafe stopped near Freedman's desk, and all eyes turned toward him. For a moment, the handsome, open expression morphed into a saturnine profile, one caught in the fading light, burnishing him in an image reminiscent of an ancient mask. He caught Avery's gaze and held it. "We warn you when you come in, Ms. Keene. At Camasca, we change everything."

A light chill shivered through Avery. Almost instantly, his moody expression vanished, replaced by the charming CEO with the approachable facade. She blinked, startled by the abrupt shift. It might simply have been overactive imagination: their conversation had been a lot to absorb.

"Okay, so, to summarize," she said, "you have a life-altering technology that tracks literally everything, and someone wants you to believe that this tech killed a team member and plans to strike again."

"Yes."

"In addition, you suspect that it is likely an inside job—from what I would imagine is a disgruntled employee who either feels intellectually disregarded, or might be a fanatic opposed to the extraordinary invasion of privacy and capacity of Kawak. However, you can't say for sure, because they used your internal communications system and erased their digital fingerprints."

"Right again."

"But the threat might be from a competitor who realizes that if you go public you'll have access to immense amounts of capital from the DoD as well as any billionaire who fancies becoming a trillionaire."

"Three for three."

Moving to join their tête-à-tête, Freedman interjected, "Dr. Diaz and Camasca hold 1,114 patents, and there are labs around the world trying to do what we do, even faster. We have a lot of enemies who'd love to steal from Camasca."

"They aren't content simply to beat you to the patent office?"

"Nope. In the era of open-source research and the race to be the first to create artificial general intelligence, it is vital that we're able to prove *exactly* when we initially conceived of a protocol, or successfully tested a discovery. Markets can rise and fall on information like that," Freedman explained. "For every AliveCor lawsuit that Apple beats back, there's a Masimo suit that succeeds. Apple Watch had to stop importing watches with their SpO2 sensor because of patent infringement. If someone can discredit Camasca, we'll face a fire sale on our tech and an avalanche of lawsuits."

Avery thought about the potential of what Camasca had already invented, and the likelihood that someone wanted to scare them away from a massive payday. Then she thought about Elisha Hibner's family and the questions that no one had been able to answer. "I have two more questions."

She turned to face Rafe again, wanting to watch his expression as he replied. A man's tells were hard to spot on first meeting, but she'd gotten pretty good at identifying liars—at the poker table, across a chessboard, or in a courtroom. Different venues, same basic weakness of human nature. If he was hiding something, she'd see a sign.

Holding up her index finger, Avery asked, "First, is it even possible that Kawak sent this message? That the AI you've built is indeed warning you about its capacities?"

"Are you asking if Kawak is sentient?"

"No. I know that AI sentience is not a real thing yet, although Kawak seems awfully close."

"Then what are you asking?"

"I've been well schooled by Jared Wynn in the difference between what regular computer technology and artificial intelligence can produce. My phone can answer a question, but it can't compose a sonnet based on its past heartbreaks. Then there's that chatbot that professed its love for the *New York Times* reporter and tried to convince him to leave his wife. Not sentient, but I've had lovelorn friends that sounded just like that chatbot did. The computer didn't fall in love over a few hours of texting, but the algorithm reacted like it did. And sometimes the difference between real and imagined is a matter of degrees."

Avery paused, knowing what she was asking might sound crazy. "Is Kawak sophisticated enough to actually *threaten* you? Even if it didn't really understand what it meant?"

Rafe returned to the sofa but remained standing. "Your question gets to the heart of a debate in our field. Like Freedman said, the issue of artificial general intelligence is different than regular AI. What we have now is AI—effective, wildly capable, but not actually smart. Artificial general intelligence—AGI—adds the 'smart.' It's the future. A toaster versus a guy who can make toast."

Noah questioned, "So Kawak is AGI?"

"No, Kawak isn't sentient or capable of human cognitive abilities. That's the ideal, of course, but Camasca hasn't achieved that yet. No one has, though everyone is trying. It's the modern arms race of AI—the thinking, sentient tech. But what seem like sentient behaviors today are merely extraordinarily sophisticated large language models that combine reasoning capabilities with access to language processing, image recognition, and nuanced problem-solving."

"So, no, Kawak didn't send the note?" Noah pressed.

Rafe's thoughtful smile vanished. "I'm not sure."

Avery saw the transformation and filed it away. "Not the answer I was expecting."

"I'm trying to be honest. Because the distance between what we understand AIs to be capable of, and actual sentience, is vast. Have either of you ever heard of 'Theory of Mind AI'?"

Noah shook his head, and Avery nodded.

Turning to Noah, Diaz expounded: "In Theory of Mind, a neural network can understand, anticipate, and predict likely emotional or cognitive responses for other intelligent systems, in ways that far outstrip our initial design parameters. Basically, your social-media algorithm reacts to your inputs and chooses what to share with you based on those limited inputs. DeepMind developed the system that beat two Chinese masters at Go, which is an example of the next level. It uses its retention of information to learn and adapt based on information we've fed it or that it gathered on its own."

"Sounds sentient to me," Noah quipped, not entirely joking.

Diaz gave him a sympathetic look. "Systems like that can make decisions, evaluate probabilities, and display critical-thinking skills . . . but they are still using machine learning. Remember when ChatGPT came out? It could write papers or answer complex questions, but push its program too far and the responses became nonsense. It was limited by its database."

"Aren't we all?" challenged Noah. "What's the difference?"

"Philosophically, maybe nothing at all, but for computer scientists, we're still looking for the spark that says it can create from nothing. Current AIs don't actually understand what they are saying or doing. The one that fell in love simply mimicked what it thought the parameters required."

"Where does that leave Kawak?" Noah replied.

"Sentience-lite," Avery summarized.

"To be blunt, yes." Rafe looked over at the door, where the yellow light promised he wouldn't be overheard. "I honestly don't know what Kawak can do."

She saw no deception in his eyes. Again, she felt herself respond to a magnetism he exuded. And she wanted to know the answers to what was happening here. She'd have to clear it with her firm, but that would come later. For now, Avery asked the only remaining question on her mind:

"When do we start?"

FIVE

Friday, April 9

Tepid sunlight filtered through half-opened blinds into a charming Craftsman bungalow on the outskirts of Prince George's County, Maryland. Songbirds rudely chirped their summons, unconcerned that the residents inside hoped vainly for another few minutes of blissful slumber. But it wasn't the birds' morning melody that jolted Benjamin Vinson awake. Instead, his body shook from the force of the coughs that rattled through his chest and surged against his diaphragm. The device implanted on his left arm buzzed lightly, an early warning that his respiratory functions were straining beyond normal. On a scheduled basis, it released a combination of drugs into his system, but something wasn't working. He shifted to check the watch he wore nonstop, except for the one hour per week it took to recharge. But his right arm refused to lift, paralysis locking it into place.

Panic quickly replaced concern. "Ch-Ch—," he managed before another wave of coughing racked his body. On his second attempt to plead for help, he realized his throat had locked against any sound but distress.

Stirring beside him, his wife, Cheryl, instinctively patted his back to soothe the tremors that would soon follow. For months, the violent paroxysms had disturbed their nightly rest and beaten the birds to their disruption. Soon, she knew, the InnoVAI wearable injector would release the meds to soothe him into some semblance of comfort.

"Need some water, honey?" Cheryl mumbled as she got her bearings. She flipped back the comforter and pushed herself up. "Or I can get you something from the kitchen. It's almost six-thirty. About time to wake the kids anyway."

Ben's only response was a shudder and another wave of hacking. But he tapped the bed with his left hand, their signal for "do whatever." She gave a drowsy nod and turned away.

As he tried to reach for her, the buzzing grew more insistent, and his left arm locked down. Frozen, terrified, he tried to scream again, but only gasps of air emerged. He desperately cast his eyes down, saw the indicators on his watch flash a terrifying red. Like the planes he'd once flown on sorties in Iraq, the alerts told him a crash was imminent. Still, no sound emerged to tell his wife to save him.

With the dim light of post-dawn filtering into the room, Cheryl hunted with her toes for the slippers she kept nearby. She caught one, then the other. Shod, she shuffled toward the bathroom to prepare for the day ahead. Maddie had dance practice for her recital. Anthony would be staying late for basketball tryouts for a new travel league.

She twisted on the faucet, prepped her toothbrush, and began her ablutions. Ben's syncopated coughs merged with the whirring of the electric brush's ministrations and the rush of water against porcelain. As she ticked off her morning to-do list, a new instrument entered the morning symphony. A strangled sound that cut through the familiar din, catching her attention before she fully registered the distinction. The thud of a falling body echoed in time with the drop of her toothbrush against the sink.

Cheryl rushed into the bedroom. "Ben? Ben!"

She quickly circled the bed to his side and crouched beside his prone body, which fairly vibrated now. The coughs had become moans that barely escaped. As she reached for him, her hand slipped for an instant, then righted herself. The spasms had become convulsions that shook his body and flailed his limbs. Gripping his head as it threatened to strike the edge of a table, she fumbled above him for his cell phone.

The locked phone denied her entry, but she remembered in her panic the sequence for an SOS call. Infernal moments passed before a live voice answered.

"911. What is your emergency?"

"It's my husband. Second Lieutenant Benjamin Vinson. He's having an attack."

"Can you describe what's going on, ma'am?"

"He's coughing and shaking. There's blood." Cheryl's eyes widened as she stared at the pool that caused her to slip against him. "There's too much blood."

"Was he shot, ma'am?"

"No, no! It's coming from his face. From his mouth. His nose." A strangled gasp. "His eyes are bleeding. Oh my God! What is happening? Please, Ben. Baby, what's happening?"

"Ma'am, I've dispatched an ambulance. Help is on the way."

Before the dispatcher could disconnect, Cheryl commanded, "Let them know that we are to be taken to Bethesda Naval Hospital."

"I'm sorry, ma'am," the dispatcher replied, "but we are required to take emergency patients to the nearest medical facility that can accept them."

"And I'm telling you that unless you want to deal with the Defense Department and the VA, you will take my husband to Bethesda. They will know how to treat him. He's under their care at the InnoVAI Clinic."

In their cubicle, the dispatcher stared at the framed photo of a favorite cousin who'd perished in Afghanistan not long after the family reunion where the image had been snapped. "Don't worry, ma'am. I'll give the driver special instructions. Will you travel with him?"

Desperate relief surged through her as she made arrangements in her head. Their next-door neighbor's kids were the same ages, and their families had swapped duties for years. One call, and her babies would be taken care of while she looked after her husband. "Yes, I'll ride with them," she sobbed. "Thank you. Thank you so much."

By 7:45 a.m., sunlight had given way to the fitful showers that punctuated April in Washington. Yet, despite the dreary day unfolding, Avery danced around her living room, collecting the last of her notes and files. She had booked a meeting with Susan Clymer and Jeff Brezil, her firm's managing partners, where she'd make her case to take on the Camasca matter and bring her friends along for the ride. First, she'd sworn Noah to secrecy. Before she raised the possibility with Jared and her best friend, Ling, she had to make an ironclad argument to her very tough bosses.

She'd spent the night doing her homework. The proof was spread across every free surface in the two-bedroom apartment's main quarters. Space that had been carefully decorated over the past nine months, each piece lovingly selected and perfectly suited to her taste.

The building in Cathedral Heights boasted the only living space that she had not shared with a roommate or a parent, and it was her one true splurge after receiving her signing bonus from Clymer Brezil: eleven hundred square feet perched on the top floor and overlooking one of the copious parks that dotted the District of Columbia. Her regimen called for a regular jog through and around its environs. When she couldn't, though, she was content to people-watch from her postage-stamp balcony whenever she found herself at home. But between work and Jared, she spent less and less time in the first place she could call her own.

Yet, despite having her first real shot at living alone, she was, ironically, cohabitating once again, however unofficially. She loved Jared, but, more and more, she wondered if she'd skipped a vital step by blending their lives too quickly.

Dismissing the stray dark thought, she hummed beneath her breath as she packed a book. After leaving Camasca, she'd first raided MahoganyBooks and then Politics and Prose Bookstore for reading material, then spent most of the night immersing herself in the debates about existential threats, Theory of Mind, and the Algorithmic Justice League.

She had stayed awake until 2:00 a.m. reading about AI technology, artificial general intelligence, biomedical advances, and the public financial markets. After what she'd read, she was profoundly grateful that Jared had vetoed her getting a video alarm system or a digital assistant. The "always-on" audio capabilities of the ubiquitous devices made homes at once safer and more transparent to the right listeners.

Her front door protection consisted of a five-lever mortice locking system that Jared had insisted she install, in lieu of an electronic surveillance that you could buy on the internet these days and install in seconds. His cybersecurity sensibilities meshed perfectly with her old-school paranoia. And given what she'd ingested from her array of doomsday-scenario tomes last night, they were both ill-prepared for the coming wave of AI technology.

Sobered by the thought, Avery checked her appearance in the mirror. Trim navy pants and a matching blazer were saved from blandness by the cerulean shell she'd chosen. With practiced motions, she gathered her abundant coils of dark hair and twisted them into a bun at the nape of her neck. Tendrils threatened to escape, but for now, she'd trust the pins she was shoving into place. A last check around her living room revealed her still-charging cell phone on the coffee table.

As though aware of her neglect, it began to chirp. Avery recognized the ringtone she'd assigned to this particular caller. Instinctively steeling herself, she lifted the phone and answered, "Hey, Mom. Everything okay?"

"Of course, honey," Rita replied quickly, and she rushed to add, "I didn't mean to frighten you." Despite her longest stretch of sobriety in years, neither she nor her daughter had forgotten the two decades that preceded them.

"Sorry," Avery apologized. "You don't normally call this early. How are you?"

Rita gave a nervous laugh. "I'm good, really. But I did have a, um, favor to ask."

The wariness that lingered surged forward. Avery physically braced herself, gripping the back of the emerald-green sofa, which perfectly matched the eye color she shared with her mother. "What's up?"

"Well, I was wondering if you could come up to Haven the Saturday before Mother's Day," she began tentatively. "I've been selected as the Employee of the Month, and there's a ceremony and everything. But it's not a big deal, and if you can't come, I totally understand. You have a big job—"

Exhaling a silent sigh of relief, Avery interrupted, "I'm so proud of you, Momma. This is quite an honor. Of course, I'll absolutely be there. My new case—if I get permission to take it on this morning—will be done by then, so I might even come up early, rent an outrageously expensive suite at a fancy hotel, and treat you to an Employee of the Month dinner and Mother's Day brunch."

"We'll make it a new Keene girls' tradition," Rita said, giggling. "And you have a new case? What are you doing? If you can tell me."

"I'm not exactly sure myself," Avery admitted. "I promise to fill you in when I get up there."

Rita's stint at the Haven Recovery and Restoration Center had seen her transition from drug-addicted patient to reliable staff member. Thinking about her mother's news, Avery felt an unfamiliar sweep of emotion. Pride tangled messily with hope, pricking the back of her eyes. She blinked once, reminding herself that she'd seen progress before. She grasped at the Al-Anon reminder to take one day at a time. Still, she repeated warmly, "Very proud of you, Mom. Just text me the details."

"I will, honey. Now, you have a good day at work."

SIX

Dr. Kate Liam leaned over Lieutenant Ben Vinson, stethoscope in hand. Around her, automated, intelligent equipment whirred, chirped, and hummed with the thousands of processes the machines had been designed to perform. One monitored her patient's vital signs, which had been mercifully restored. Another called out data about enzyme levels and blood counts in an attempt to explain the spontaneous hemolacria described by Mrs. Vinson and the paramedics who had rushed the patient to her facility. The injectable designed to manage his chronic condition appeared to be functional.

Kate reentered the private waiting area where Cheryl Vinson was pacing. She plastered on a reassuring countenance and lightly touched the woman's shoulder from behind. "Mrs. Vinson? Cheryl?"

She spun around from the waiting room's window that overlooked a walled garden. "Dr. Liam. How is he? What's happening?"

Kate guided Cheryl to a set of chairs and urged her to sit. "Ben is stable and resting. We've treated the bleeding, and we're running tests."

"What's happened? When we came to see you last month, you told us that the app would regulate his medication."

"As you know, Ben has bronchiectasis—caused by the allergic bronchopulmonary aspergillosis that he contracted while in Iraq."

"That his other doctors told us was just a smoker's cough. Even though Ben quit smoking before the kids were born." Cheryl flinched at the bitter reminder of the misdiagnosis. "He kept telling them it was something else, but no one would listen."

"We caught it though," Kate deflected, but she shared the frustration. Too many of her patients had been hurried through the medical system by overworked physicians looking for answers without knowing all the right questions. Unfortunately, Ben Vinson had been one of those patients. "As you know, thanks to Milo, we were able to reconstruct his medical history and take into account that cave he was trapped in during the crash in Rawandiz, and the biopathogen he was exposed to inside. The personalized inhibitor he's taking is reducing the inflammation in his lungs and thinning out the mucus that causes his coughs."

"This morning was terrifying." Cheryl shuddered as she recalled the pool of blood that had caked her hand. "He couldn't talk. Couldn't move."

The temporary paralysis stumped Kate, but she wasn't ready to burden Mrs. Vinson yet. Instead, she offered, "We're sending his blood samples for analysis and running more tests. Dr. Scandrett will be in later this morning, and we'll confer." She squeezed the wife's shoulder. "I promise, we're going to find an answer."

Cheryl reached up and patted her hand, grateful for the reassurance. Still, she watched the doctor with a mix of hope and disappointment. Ben had been in and out of VA clinics for the past nine years, as his condition steadily worsened. InnoVAI trials had been a godsend, but she knew better than to hope too much. She squared her shoulders and asked, "When can I see him?"

"A nurse will take you back in a few minutes." With a final nod, Kate turned and headed back into the medical suite. She understood Cheryl's unspoken doubt. Many of her patients and their families reflected an identical combination of desperation and resignation. Years of military service reduced to long waits for an appointment and the minimum viable care possible. Though the VA staff took the bulk of the blame, they were doing their best with what Washington gave them. Precious little.

Still, Kate prided herself on being a different kind of VA physician. What she'd told Cheryl was all true. Thanks to Camasca and its partnership with Galway Pharmaceuticals, Kate could customize medicines for her veteran Tricare patients just like high-end doctors had done for their patients for years. Designer meds for the working class. Her prescription for Ben Vinson's misdiagnosed respiratory-infection-turned-chronic-illness had worked. The sudden turn worried her, but she had the world's best tools at her disposal.

As Kate made her way back to her office, she ran the symptoms through her head. Hemolacria, bleeding from the eyes, occurred with such infrequency that a lot of doctors could go an entire career without witnessing the phenomenon. Actual bloody tears, combined with the gushing described from his other orifices, she would have expected to read about in an obscure medical journal.

But Lieutenant Vinson was her second patient to present with the symptoms in as many weeks.

Before coming to see Cheryl, Kate had pored over his chart and that of his medical twin, Master Sergeant Brian Thomas. Thomas had arrived three days ago and remained in one of the few, lavish private rooms allocated to the clinic. He'd presented with an arterial thromboembolism, a blockage of the blood supply to his internal organs, a condition that could not be connected to Vinson's bronchiectasis. Both responded with hemorrhaging, and she despised medical coincidence.

Jaw set, Kate threaded through the warren of back offices to the one she'd taken for herself. Inside, she laid Vinson's folder next to Thomas's file. Everything had an electronic version, but she still preferred the tactile feel of paper. But they offered no comfort now. Instead, the files stared at her accusingly, and she glared back. She let out a frustrated sigh. Her patients' families were overwhelmed with questions, and she owed them answers. Right now, there was no better place in America for a veteran to be sick, and it was her job to keep it that way.

Her stint in the Army Reserves had been one of the key reasons she'd accepted the fellowship to join the staff of InnoVAI, the brand-new veterans' clinic stationed in an annex of Bethesda Naval Hospital. The clinic, a joint project of the VA and Camasca, was a miracle for physicians like her who bemoaned the slow pace of progress in medical care for vets and were eager to test out new protocols without the drag of ponderous bureaucratic musings.

Even better, she had access to a futuristic solution that could help them all. Milo, the revolutionary chatbot to whom she had unfettered access, had been installed for exactly this purpose. With Milo installed in every room in the clinic, she no longer had to rely on paper to record her observations, taking her attention from a baffled spouse or a critical patient. She could talk out her ideas, certain her cogitations would be captured. She'd easily grown reliant on its ability to document and catalogue her notes.

She'd diagnosed and treated service personnel who'd gotten used to getting short shrift. At InnoVAI, each patient received hyper-focused attention, personalized medicine, and a wearable device that allowed Milo to keep tabs on their care. AI-generated messages from Milo tracked their status, and the clinical team tracked patient care assiduously. Kate and her fellow medical staff prided themselves on this new frontier of tending to the sick.

When they began working together last fall, the medical team and Milo had been a dream team. With oversight from Tiger Team at Camasca—Elisha, O.J., and Isabella—she'd felt like she was in a new unit, bound by a common mission as they worked with her to refine how Milo operated.

As excited as Kate was about the newfound freedom of InnoVAI's tech, however, not all of her colleagues shared her enthusiasm. Her clinic partner, Dr. Reginald Scandrett, had been uneasy about the

AI from the beginning. A computer doing the work of a flesh-and-blood physician felt wrong to him. *Lazy medicine,* he called it.

A knock sounded on her door, and she glanced up. Reginald stood in the doorway as though she'd conjured him. "You're in early. You're not due until eleven."

"Got a ping from Milo telling me about Lieutenant Vinson. Listened to your notes on the way in. What else do we know?"

"Not much," Kate admitted. "I've ordered new labs and an MRI. Do you have a theory?"

He pushed away from the doorjamb and dropped into a chair in front of her desk. "The untreated fungal infection leading to his bronchiectasis still makes the most sense."

"As Milo predicted." Kate gave him a slight smirk. "Until this morning, the regimen it recommended had been working like a charm."

"Until this morning. Which means we—and Milo—may have missed something." Reginald folded his arms across his chest, his chin jutting up pugnaciously. "I plan to examine him, triple- and quadruple-check our diagnosis, and see if we missed anything in our treatment plan. And we need to figure out if the hemolacria is connected to Brian Thomas's case."

"I've already tasked Milo with analyzing anything that connects the two."

"Well, I'll also give good old-fashioned research a try, like I have for nearly thirty years. Maybe even touch a patient or two and see what I can feel. Which Milo can't do."

"You won't give Milo credit for much, will you?"

Reginald rolled his eyes, then gave her a serious look. "It might have studied the same texts, but Milo has never pushed its hands into a wounded soldier, holding their intestines inside a shrapnel-riddled body. Milo will never stand at attention when a flag-draped casket passes by a convoy to bear a soldier home. Milo is a machine. Better than an EKG or a fancy coffeemaker, but it's no doctor."

"Being stubborn won't help us figure out what's happening to our patients, Reginald," she warned him. Cheryl's worry nipped at her conscience. Looking up, she announced, "Milo, we need your help." The look wasn't necessary, but she acknowledged her human instinct to connect form and function. Even if a truly physical form wasn't available.

"Of course, Dr. Liam. I'm at your service."

The pleasant tenor of the chatbot filled the room, as it always did. Hidden speakers created the effect of theater-quality surround sound. Putting Reginald's discomfort aside, she said, "Any theories? We have two patients presenting with similar but highly unusual symptoms within days of each other."

"I have developed a roster of potential causes for today's symptoms. Would you like to have me review them with you now, or would Dr. Scandrett prefer to leave?"

"Excuse me?" Reginald sputtered.

"I respect your discomfort with me, Dr. Scandrett. It is not uncommon for men of advanced years to feel threatened by technology beyond their understanding."

Reginald bit at his cheek. "I call on you when I need you, Milo."

"Actually, you have never directly contacted me."

"I haven't ever directly needed you."

"Whether you choose to engage me or not, I am responsible for understanding and analyzing the needs of all of InnoVAI's clients. I appreciate your finally deciding to include me in your efforts."

Knowing Reginald's temper, Kate swiftly intervened. "Dr. Scandrett has a preferred method of operation that is entirely appropriate, Milo."

"I don't need you to explain my methods to a computer," Reginald said, bristling.

"Certainly, Dr. Scandrett, you are well within your rights to determine which tools to use. I would expect, though, that I might be of greater use than traditional methods."

Kate shot Reginald a quelling look, and he scowled back. "Dr. Scandrett has a medical expertise that few possess," she admonished the chatbot. "However, what is your current assessment, Milo?"

"There are several differential diagnoses for each patient, based on their distinct medical histories and personal backgrounds. Both Ben Vinson and Brian Thomas shared a military deployment to Iraq and Afghanistan, but their tours did not overlap, and they present no correlative maladies. Lieutenant Vinson had chicken pox as a child, a disease Sergeant Thomas did not acquire. Sergeant Thomas contracted a mosquito-borne ailment while deployed to Izmir Air Base in Turkey that had resulted in a light fever three years ago. Most important, each came to the clinic for other complaints, Lieutenant Vinson for recurring tinnitus and Sergeant Thomas seeking a second opinion on a degenerative muscular disorder."

"Which tells you what?" Kate asked, falling back on her time as a resident working with new doctors.

"In addition to the hemorrhagic symptoms, Vinson and Thomas have each exhibited mild clumsiness and problems with balance, as reported by their families in the past year. Vinson has repeatedly complained of insomnia, fatigue, and vomiting, in addition to his severe bouts of coughing. Thomas's medical records include multiple complaints of wheezing, chest tightness, and nasal polyps, as well as traits associated with thalassemia."

"Okay. So?"

"The possible diagnoses range from Samter's triad, also known as AERD, a type-two inflammatory disease that signals a chronic medical condition. Tracheobronchitis presents with coughing fits that are associated with post-tussive vomiting. Nodules develop and cause respiratory obstruction and dyspnea. Huntington's disease is an inherited disorder that causes nerve cells to break down, resulting in problems with balance or movement, cognitive or psychiatric symptoms, and changes in behavior such as outbursts."

Kate frowned at the last option. "Do any of the patients have a known family history of Huntington's?"

"Sergeant Thomas learned last year, based on a commercial DNA test, that he shares no genetic markers with his parents. He has reached out on several websites in search of his biological parents, without success. However, I have assessed a likely genetic match with the person who may be his mother. I have been unable to confirm the relationship as of yet."

"You found his mom?" Reginald asked incredulously. "Before he did?"

"I believe so. Shall I inform him?"

"No!" Kate warned, recognizing in an instant why it would take decades, if ever, for AI to understand the nuances of human emotion. "That's not our place. At least, not yet. But what do you know about this genetic match?"

"I am continuing my research, but there is no known history of Huntington's on the maternal side. The father may have been a carrier, however."

Because Huntington's disease was a real possibility, family history was critical to confirm diagnosis. "What are your next steps?"

"Based on the information we now have on Lieutenant Vinson with his admission today, I recommend we expand the parameters of investigation to determine if there are any additional environmental causes that may be connected. We must also consider that their similar and overlapping symptoms may not be correlated at all."

Kate gave the silent Reginald a side glance. "Agreed. Correlation is not causation. Thank you, Milo."

"You're welcome. Is there any other way I might be of assistance, Dr. Liam?"

"Double-check my review of both men's body systems, Milo. Neuro, ENT, resp, CV, GI, heme, ID, and rheum. See if I missed anything. Dr. Scandrett and I will do another round of exams on both men." Milo's revelation about Thomas's mother made her issue a final instruction:

"Please, do not communicate directly with Master Sergeant Thomas or his family without my authorization."

"Certainly. I am at your service." The chatbot paused. "May I assist you with anything, Dr. Scandrett?"

"You can go—"

"Back to work," Kate interceded. "Thank you, Milo."

SEVEN

Across town, Avery arrived outside the wood-paneled door at precisely 10:00 a.m. Susan Clymer kept a strict schedule, and once a time slot had been granted, no deviations were tolerated. Those who arrived late or overstayed their welcome did so at their peril. Too many transgressions meant demotion or termination. In the world of Susan Clymer, efficiency meant speed, and effectiveness meant attention to details. Time was a detail, and if you couldn't master it, you belonged elsewhere.

Avery understood she would have no more than ten minutes to make her case before Susan's attention began to wander. Jeff Brezil was a lighter touch on the surface, less concerned with clocks than context. His focus would be on the bottom line: how would taking on Camasca net the firm another high ranking among mid-sized law firms and boost their profile with high-value targets?

With both her quarries in mind, she silently practiced her pitch. Although her agreement with Clymer Brezil gave her the leeway to land her own clients, she'd not had occasion to invoke the privilege before today. Ideally, she'd have pumped Jared for pointers on selling the idea, but until she had permission to read him in, she was on her own. Steeling herself, she rapped lightly on the door.

"Come!"

Avery turned the knob and took a secret breath. As she entered the office, she scanned the room for its owner. She spotted her and greeted, "Hi, Susan. Thanks for fitting me in." Behind her, the door opened again.

"Jeff, you're late," Susan rinsed her hands and barked from the slightly ajar door to the private bathroom, just like the one that Jeff had installed in his own suite. That accoutrement was only for the named partners, though senior attorneys had nicely appointed offices as well, complete with natural light and a view of the traffic along K or Fourteenth, depending on your luck. Even novice attorneys had been granted a modicum of privacy, with broom closets that masqueraded as personal offices rather than cubicles. Avery's assigned workspace had fallen in between the two categories of lawyers, a relatively capacious office with room for a chair but without the benefit of windows.

"Good morning to you, too, sunshine," Brezil called toward the private bathroom. He loped inside and headed for her bar. A ridiculously expensive coffee machine summoned. "You have the best brew in the building." Laughing at his alliteration, he prepared his drink.

He passed by Avery and said, "You did good work yesterday on Verdure. Nice catch on the Gramm-Leach-Bliley Act violations. Impressive."

"Jeff, you'll be seeing their CEO next week. She's interested in putting CB on retainer." Susan nodded at Avery. "You made them very happy. Apparently, they have Walter's temper tantrum on video, and it's making the rounds. Have a seat."

A silvery-white modular sofa that had once been in the cover photo for *Arthouse Magazine* crouched low beneath a bank of windows. Startlingly chartreuse pillows accented the stark white and echoed the handwoven rug that looked like a paint-can spill. Burnished glass propped up on toothpicks served as a coffee table, adorned by a single piece cast in a complementary silver. The effect was somewhat marred by the sweaty glass of Diet Coke, which was dripping rivulets onto a coaster. As Avery tried to pick a spot, Susan gestured her away from the twenty-five-thousand-dollar couch to a less expensive leather chair that flanked the table.

"You wanted to see us." Dressed in her typical uniform of tailored black pants and monochromatic jacket—today in peachy linen that mimicked the blush on her cheeks—Susan Clymer ambled across the carpet. Only those who knew her well were privy to the titanium hip and leg that propelled her to the area where Avery waited.

When Susan settled onto the sofa and Jeff joined with his coffee, that was Avery's cue. She quickly took her seat and set her internal chronometer. "I have a case."

"You don't waste any time," Jeff teased.

"I'm a team player," Avery replied. "And it's a good opportunity. Came on reference from a friend. Noah Fox."

"He's at Lowry Kihneman, right?" Susan chimed in. "Junior partner in trust and estates. He worked with Guarasci on your congressional testimony. Makes a good impression."

"That's correct," Avery confirmed. "Noah has a friend—a former law classmate who is the general counsel for Camasca, the tech firm. They want to engage Clymer Brezil for an internal investigation."

Susan leaned forward and lifted her Diet Coke can. "An internal investigation . . . Do they want CB, or do they want you?"

"Camasca has the go-ahead for an IPO via SPAC. They've completed due diligence, but their CEO, Dr. Rafe Diaz, wants belt and suspenders."

"A voluntary layer of due diligence?" Jeff shrewdly observed. "What else is going on? Why would they approach our firm by coming through you?"

"Because, in addition to the normal due diligence, the lawyer and the CEO are concerned that they might have some legal exposure on a recent accident on their campus." Avery had rehearsed the wording several times on her way back to the office. How long could she delay saying that they wanted her to investigate a murder?

" 'Legal exposure' is a nicely vague term of art that describes almost all of our clients." Susan tapped the side of her soda can. "Spit it out, Keene. What do they want you for? Specifically."

Caught, Avery admitted, "A malfunction in the ventilation system resulted in the death of one of their engineers a little over a month ago. The Bethesda police ruled it an accident, but the CEO wants to be sure. The general counsel just needs the due diligence completed. I'm their compromise choice."

"They get Nancy Drew and Perry Mason all in one. Neat trick." Then Susan's mouth firmed into a stern line. "But we're not a detective agency, are we?"

"Of course not," Avery agreed. "However, we do help companies uncover their risk exposure, which sometimes means diving deep into the bowels of their issues."

Jeff draped his arm across the back of the sofa. "Well, to extend your metaphor, that sounds like they want you to get caught in their bullshit."

Avery smothered a grin and volleyed, "Perhaps I should mention that Camasca's current Series C funding netted the company $2.5 billion, and they are expected to be valued at $11 billion when they go public after this internal investigation."

"Ah... someone buried the lede," Susan grumbled, then motioned for Avery to continue.

"All they want is for you to lead an investigation to help them prep for going public? Nothing more?"

Unwilling to lie, Avery carefully replied, "I'll have to review the police reports of the accident and death, of course. It's a potential liability—even if they had no criminal culpability. Dr. Diaz is deeply concerned that Camasca be beyond reproach."

"Nothing worth that much money is ever beyond reproach," Susan warned. She scooted forward on the sofa. "Have your admin run a conflict check today, and ask Harold in Security to pull the police reports. We'll meet in Jeff's office again tomorrow morning. If everything comes back clean, we'll sign off. Think about the first-year associate and paralegal you want on your team. We'll sort that out tomorrow, too."

Avery braced herself. "Camasca has already picked the team. They've identified a biotech expert and someone who can do cyberforensics, as well as another attorney."

Jeff narrowed his eyes. "That sounds an awful lot like your friends, Avery."

"Yes," she admitted, "but it wasn't my idea. Camasca has already vetted them, and they like the fact that we've worked together before. Ling is on sabbatical, and Jared's next client won't need him for a few weeks. Noah can rearrange his cases to join me. It's a short assignment, four weeks at most; and then we're friends with the latest Wall Street unicorn."

"I'm sold," Jeff said. "Susan?"

"Your merry band tends to make the front page," she emphasized with a strong hint of censure. "You've had your fifteen minutes of fame and then some. We picked you because you have an insane recollection of obscure regulatory issues, and Chief Justice Roseborough wrote you the finest recommendation letter I've ever seen. But we didn't hire you to solve crimes. That was part of your past. Understood?"

Avery grinned with uncharacteristic enthusiasm, and she caught herself. Then a knot she hadn't noticed in her gut unraveled. More than pride at landing a real client, she sensed something more concerning. *Excitement. And relief.* Because, despite Susan's admonition, she *was* about to investigate a crime. And for the first time in eighteen months, she was looking forward to coming to work.

As she quickly took her leave, Avery met Susan's eyes and blithely lied. "Yes, ma'am. Understood."

"Don't make us regret this, Keene," Susan called out as she hurried away.

EIGHT

Avery spent the rest of the day clearing her cases, running conflicts checks, and immersing herself in the vast internet wilderness of artificial intelligence and rumors about Camasca. Everyone had an opinion about how AI would alter their reality, from skeptical academics to reverent engineers to terrified acolytes. Speculation about what Rafe Diaz had developed occupied blogs and threads and conspiracy-theory forums. True to his military background and Defense Department funding, Rafe ran a cloistered company, where few quit and no one spoke.

Given the Big Brother–like workplace, the silence made sense. Yet her brief time there hadn't signaled a terrified environment. More like a giant shared secret with handshakes and passwords. She couldn't fault the closed-loop system—her tenure at the U.S. Supreme Court had taught her exactly how tight-lipped a community could be for the right reasons.

Or the right incentives.

Camasca was majority-owned by Rafe Diaz, but every single employee, down to the cleaning crew, held vested stock in the company. A major transaction would guarantee that no one with a W-2 would ever need to work again. Plenty of reason to keep your mouth shut and your opinion about omnivalent monitoring all to yourself.

A chime sounded on her phone, and she checked the screen. See you at 8.

"Excellent," she murmured. Ling had agreed to join her, Noah, and Jared for dinner at Jared's place. She started to pack up her satchel, her lips pursed as she plotted her next move. Noah had tacitly agreed to come on board, and Jared would jump at the chance to do cyber-forensics for Rafe Diaz. On the other end of the willingness scale was her best friend, Ling. But Avery knew what to do. Bribery was a time-honored tradition and a proven technique. So was begging.

Around 7:00 p.m., Avery was wrestling with an armload of reusable grocery bags, transferring them to her hip as she tried to twist her key in the lock. Buoyed by her plan for inducement, she'd stopped by the farmers' market to stock up on supplies. When one of the bags started to slip, she fumbled to hold tight and dropped her keys in the process. The jangle as they hit the stoop triggered a curse of annoyance. She shifted again, only to knock her forehead, then her knee against the wooden door. Another curse followed.

"Hold on, I've got you," Jared said from behind her. Reaching around her, he deftly rescued the groceries that seemed determined to escape her grip. He shifted the bags and inserted his key into the first lock, then the second. The door swung open, and they shuffled inside in unison.

Jared's Anacostia townhouse had three times the square footage of her apartment in Cathedral Heights, which is why she'd commandeered his dining room for dinner. That and the fact that she basically spent every night here.

Despite having her own key and near-permanent residence, Avery still refused to commit to merging their households, and this had become a running joke among their friends. Her niggling worry was that Jared no longer found it funny.

"This is quite a haul. Did you invite the French Foreign Legion and neglect to inform me?" he joked as they entered the kitchen together. Jared settled the rescued bags on the granite countertop.

"They're bringing the Amazons," Avery teased as she busied herself with unpacking her bounty. Fresh spinach, a container of shiitake mushrooms, and a few heads of garlic joined a wedge of Parmesan.

"Party on." He walked back to shut the front door, and turned the locks. Then he returned to the kitchen and wrapped her in a lingering embrace; she melted into his hold.

When they finally surfaced, she tipped her head back and smiled. "Hello, you."

"I got your message about Ling and Noah joining us." Reluctantly stepping away, he began helping her unload. "What's the occasion? Did you win the lottery? Or did you finally agree to move in with me?"

Avery stiffened slightly, and Jared gave her a teasing squeeze. "Sorry. No pressure tonight. Tell me what happened that has you shopping for flowers, and"—he reached inside another bag—"fresh pappardelle."

The package joined the array of vegetables on the black-flecked granite surface. Recognizing the recipe, Jared quickly retrieved the pots and pans she required. He filled a pot with water as Avery began folding bags to be put away. They continued to move in the kitchen ballet of a couple that had cooked together for a while. "Seriously, what's the occasion?" Jared nudged.

"I landed a client. A huge one. I couldn't say anything until it was done."

"Avery, that's fantastic!" Jared bumped her hip in congratulations. "I didn't know you were working on something big."

"I wasn't," she told him. "Noah called me yesterday and asked me to meet with one of his old law-school buddies. Turns out, the guy is the general counsel for Camasca."

Jared froze, and his hazel eyes widened. "You're working with Rafe Diaz? Whoa."

"Is that a problem?"

"Hell no. That's amazing. Diaz is the fairy tale for AI and tech bros. Dude came up in the projects in Baltimore, then he joined the Marines right out of high school. Became a medic, then convinced the Marines to let him work with the MASH units."

Avery listened avidly as she prepped more vegetables. "Is that unusual?"

"He doesn't have a medical degree, but he became a whiz in the field. He rose through the ranks, and somehow got permission to do remote study while on active duty. Diaz finished undergrad in three years, and the man kept collecting degrees. By the time he was honorably discharged, he had a Ph.D. in bioengineering."

"How? I didn't realize the military was so flexible."

"For the average grunt, it's not. But Diaz is a certifiable genius, not unlike the woman in my kitchen. Brilliant and driven, with a mind that is almost scary."

"I'll take that as a compliment," Avery replied playfully. "Finish telling me about Diaz."

"After the Marines, rumor is he wound up doing something with DARPA that neither of us has the clearance to know about. Next time his name surfaced, he had created Camasca—his brainchild, combining AI and bioengineering."

"How do you know so much about him?"

"My firm had a contract to help build his cybersecurity infrastructure. Their facility in Bethesda is beyond twenty-first century. I helped devise the tech, and even I couldn't hack into it."

"Would you like another shot?"

"Excuse me?"

Unable to stop herself, she danced a quick jig. "They asked me to come on board for the next few weeks as an internal investigator. That includes figuring out if someone has tampered with their systems. I figured there's no one better to help me out than my exceptionally talented cybersecurity boyfriend."

"I'm in!" He swung her in a celebratory circle. "I wish you'd told me. I'd have managed dinner. You shouldn't have to set up your own party."

Flushed with triumph and delight, Avery leaned back against his hold. "Keep that enthusiasm," she warned. "The gig comes with a few conditions that I need to discuss with you and the crew."

"May I have a preview?"

"Of course." Avery salted her pasta water. "Camasca wants my help, but they are über-private. Some might say paranoid."

"Based on what I know about the company and Rafe Diaz," Jared countered, "paranoia seems warranted. A unicorn company on the verge of going public—they have every right to be mistrustful."

"I didn't say they were going public," Avery observed.

"Relax, babe. It's common knowledge." He pulled a knife from the block and began slicing mushrooms. "One of my clients is a fintech that has a shared investor. They were discussing this a few weeks ago."

"Oh, good. Because that's part of their concern. Camasca is trying to get ready for launch, but there are issues."

"Let me guess—compliance, data security, regulatory oversight, and reputational damage."

"What do you mean about their reputation?"

"Tech is a small world, Avery. Especially in Maryland. We're not as sexy as Silicon Valley or as clubby as Boston. So, when someone like Elisha Hibner dies in a freak accident, word leaks."

"What are you hearing?"

"Not much. A few posts have slammed Diaz for not protecting his people. Others have speculated about the source of the accident." Jared anticipated her next question. "Police reports aren't hard to come by, Avery. Particularly to my side of the world. It took law enforcement less than a week to rule his death an accident."

"Why is a ventilation malfunction suspicious? For argument's sake."

"To most folks, it's not. But the AI arms race is cutthroat, and

Diaz has been running circles around his competitors. They'd see any chink in his armor as worth exploiting."

"What do you think?"

He paused in his ministrations. "One of the posts questioned how closely the police investigated a young Black man's death. If he'd been white, would the answer have come so quickly?"

"Diaz is Latino." Then, she gave a rueful shake of her head. "Never mind. A billionaire is a billionaire."

"Exactly." Gesturing with the knife, Jared added, "But the conspiracy industry thrives on stories like this. Add in the opacity of Camasca's operations and how famously private Diaz is, and you've got a perfect stew of rampant speculation."

Avery finished chopping her spinach and set her knife aside. "How would you like to be on the inside? With me."

Setting the knife down, Jared turned to her slowly. "What do you mean?"

The grin returned, its wattage brighter with the coup de grâce. "I got the job, but it came with major conditions. I can only review materials on-site, and I can only have a team of four. A tech specialist, a biomedical expert, and a legal sidekick."

"Who all happen to love your mushroom pappardelle?" Jared suggested.

Avery lifted her hands in a show of complicity. "Guilty as charged."

"I'm in. But I hope you have something else in that bag for your medical adviser," he warned. "Because you're not her type—and mushrooms have their limitations."

"You have the unique ability to make dinner feel like a prisoner's last meal." Ling set her dessert fork across the plate with a satisfied clink. "A special talent, indeed."

"I used to cook for you all the time."

"Once a month," Ling corrected. "Unboxing takeout onto semi-fancy plates doesn't count." She gestured to the sliver of cheesecake that remained uneaten. "Pasta from you always comes with strings attached. When you throw in dessert from Coulibaly's, I know you're up to something."

Ling glanced suspiciously at Noah. "Besides, I'm fairly certain I'm the last to the party. Noah's been shifty all night, and Jared is too smitten to say no to your antics."

"Fine. Look, Noah connected me to a contact at Camasca. They've asked me to come on board and perform an internal investigation for them."

"So dinner was for him?"

"No, Ling, this is all for you. They're here as reinforcements," Avery admitted. "Landing my very first client has helped me ingratiate myself to Susan and Jeff. Keeping said client will require your expertise and a few weeks of your time."

"And there it is," Ling grumbled. "Precisely what type of assistance do you need from me to help an AI biotech firm? More important, will I be shot at or have to disarm a nuclear warhead?"

"Ha-ha."

When Ling simply looked at her, Avery explained, "I have a very short window to conduct a deep dive into their inner workings, which are exponentially complex, and because of the nature of the business, they have strict protocols about who I'm allowed to engage."

"What have they been accused of?"

"Nothing, exactly. Except for one issue. But, overall, this is more prophylactic than reactive." She studiously avoided eye contact with Noah. Getting Ling on board was imperative, and if she mentioned the suspicious death first, her best friend and former roommate might bolt, dinner be damned. "The goal is to uncover any issues before they go public, and to prevent or detect any misconduct or noncompliance issues."

Intrigued despite herself, Ling said, "Camasca is into extremely cutting-edge research. One of the guys in my fellowship program worked on their precision-medicine portfolio. He refuses to say much—or, according to him, he can't say much. NDAs there are ironclad."

Avery nodded. "I can attest to that."

"Me, too. I know about their NDAs because I signed one." Ling expounded: "I did a short stint in their veterans' clinic at Bethesda Naval Hospital earlier this year. Because of my focus on community care, I got permission to shadow the medical staff for a few shifts. They primarily serve veterans who have chronic illnesses and aren't responding well to traditional care structures."

"Is that InnoVAI?" Avery asked.

"Exactly. Jared knows this already, but lots of vets come back with chronic health concerns, like high blood pressure or diabetes, but then you add the complexity that comes with women veterans, vets with mental-health problems, racial disparities in care, and elderly or disabled veterans who aren't as mobile or able to manage their care on their own."

Nodding, Jared chimed in: "A startling number develop substance-abuse problems or complications from exposure to hazardous materials. Finding a consistent medical home for vets has been at the top of the VA's wish list for years."

"Camasca's partnership essentially promises to pilot a solution that blends artificial intelligence, pharmacology, and personalized medicine. It's radical. In a good way." Ling settled back. "Sorry . . . That's a long way of saying, how can I help?"

"Like I mentioned, I've been given a short window and limited staffing." Avery dipped her chin at each of the table's occupants. "There's me, plus I must have someone who knows information technology, data, computing, and cybersecurity. Another investigator who is a subject-matter expert on life sciences and can analyze Camasca's products, understand patient data, and review their findings from the clinic and elsewhere. Then a third person to act as my legal support, because I'm not allowed to hire a paralegal or bring on anyone else from Clymer Brezil."

"Avery and the Three Musketeers. What's the catch?"

Jared nudged, "Tell her the rest, Avery."

"So . . . well . . ." she stuttered uncharacteristically. Noah had learned about the death when he visited Camasca with her, and Jared already knew. Now laying out the entire case for Ling had Avery paralyzed. She might have hedged the story with the firm's partners, but she owed her friend the unvarnished truth. She threw a desperate look at Noah, who signaled with his silence that she was on her own.

"Okay. In addition to the traditional investigation that I've outlined, Camasca is also focused on examining a specific incident."

Slowly, Ling lifted her fork to scrape at the remnants of dessert on her plate. "What kind of incident?"

"One of their chief engineers died in a freak accident in the building. An anonymous note—purportedly from the artificial intelligence at the heart of their system—has taken responsibility for the death." She paused, then mumbled, "It told them that the death was only the first, and there would be others unless Camasca shuts down its project."

"The building where we would be working is run by an AI system that has gone full *2001: A Space Odyssey*?" Ling dropped her fork with a clatter. "And you want to go into the crazy place? Taking us with you."

"The AI didn't write a confession, Ling. At least, I don't believe it, and neither do they. But they are worried that someone is tampering with either the AI or their company."

"Then hire a private investigator or a security team," Ling argued. "Why hire an attorney and her friends to pull up in their Mystery Machine and snoop around like Scooby Doo?"

Mercifully, Noah intervened. "I wondered the same thing. Assuming this is corporate sabotage, bringing in a security team only solves the physical threat. A PI can ask questions, but no one would be sophisticated enough to wade through the reams of information necessary to uncover the culprits. Hiring a law firm to perform an investigation gives you the ability to review the entire company from every angle. All under the protection of attorney-client privilege."

Ling swiveled toward Jared. "You've got a security background. You cool with your girlfriend going undercover to find a killer?"

"I don't dictate Avery's choices," he responded diplomatically. "But I agree with Noah that the real threat is probably the result of corporate espionage. Or, like the police determined, that Elisha Hibner's death was a terrible accident. If so, then Camasca must discover why the ventilation system malfunctioned and ensure it never happens again. And who is trying to use this as a threat to the company."

"You're all comfortable with this, and I'm the party pooper," Ling recapped testily. "Thanks for the ambush, guys."

"This isn't on them," Avery protested. "Noah introduced me to the company, and I only told Jared about the conditions before y'all came over."

"Seems much more coordinated, from where I'm sitting."

Avery shook her head vehemently. "It's not. And I won't be offended if you decline, Ling. The general counsel gave me a solid list of medical consultants I can bring onto this project."

"Then why are we having this discussion?"

"I rejected them because I love working with the three of you, and because, well, it works." She met Ling's irritated scowl steadily. "I am well aware of my reputation, and that they picked me because this investigation might be more complicated than corporate sabotage. I'm also clear that the case appeals to me because there's the possibility that I will be doing more than data reviews and statutory compliance research. I'd like you there with me."

When the silence lengthened, Avery ventured weakly, "So . . . what's the verdict?"

Ling tucked a wing of black hair behind her ear and propped her chin on her hand. "Do you know what a sabbatical is, Avery?"

"Come on—"

"While you may be congenitally hostile to a break or rest, I am not. I've spent most of my life in school. College, med school, and now this Ph.D. program has kicked my ass. I took time off in order to take time off."

"I understand, Ling." Smothering her disappointment, she forced a conciliatory smile. "You don't want to do this, and I respect your decision."

"No, you don't," Ling rejected the hollow statement instantly, her look and tone equally serious. "Now might not be the best time to point out the obvious, but I'm afraid you're turning into an adrenaline junkie. This is the most animated I've seen you since we had to chase down a terrorist from Jared's basement bunker."

"I didn't go looking for that," Avery argued, hackles rising.

Ling sighed volubly. "You never go looking, Avery. But you don't seem to be able to close your eyes."

"Understood. You're out. Message received."

Leaning forward, Ling reached across the table to cover Avery's clenched fist. "Of course I'll help you," she admonished. "We all will. But you have to think very seriously about why you want to do this."

"Because it's my job," Avery temporized. "I'm an internal investigator, and this is what I do."

This time, Noah spoke first. "I'm all in, too, Avery. But Ling raises some valid questions. I would give them some thought."

She swallowed down the bitter retort that threatened to erupt, repeating silently that she needed their help. All of them. She forced herself to nod and plastered on a placating grin, fooling no one. "Great. We start on Tuesday. Bright and early. I'll text you the address."

"And you'll think about what I said?" Ling pressed.

"I will. I promise." Then Avery started gathering the dishes, carefully avoiding the eyes of her friends. She had no interest in seeing if anyone actually believed her.

NINE

After seeing Noah and Ling out, Jared joined Avery in the kitchen. She moved around briskly, cleaning and putting leftovers away. "Phase one, complete," she declared as he began to load the dishwasher. "I wasn't sure Ling would agree to come on board."

"Neither was she," Jared teased. "Lucky for you, she's just as intrigued as the rest of us. Camasca is the envy of every tech start-up in the DMV." Like his own business venture, launching in the D.C., Maryland, Virginia corridor was an excellent way to link quickly to capital and connections, especially for the ex-military contingent.

Grateful not to have to discuss Ling's observation, she eagerly latched on to the new topic. "Noah and I met Dr. Diaz and the GC there yesterday. We didn't get to see the entire campus, but everything I saw was very futuristic. My dad would have loved it."

"Really? I didn't realize he was into sci-fi."

"Yeah, he was." She lifted her hand to mimic the famous Vulcan salute. "Live long and prosper."

Jared let out a surprised laugh. "Wait, are you a Trekkie, Avery Olivia Keene? How have you kept that hidden from me?"

Winking, she said, "You never asked. My dad and I used to watch every episode until . . . Well. Until."

"You know, you rarely mention your father." Jared cocked his head, considering. "Almost never. Then again, you hardly talk about your childhood at all. If I hadn't met Rita, I might imagine you came into the world fully formed."

She turned away and began to fiddle with the knife block. "You got a crash course in the life of Avery Keene. Besides, you've heard the highlights and you've had a front row to the sequels. What's past is past."

"Never stays that way, you know."

Suddenly uncomfortable, Avery reached for a towel to dry her hands. She started for the archway that led into the rest of the house. "I'm focused on the future, and Camasca is how we get there."

"Hold on," Jared urged as he followed her into the living room. When she paused, he tucked his hands into his back pockets. "You know you're not the only one who can spot patterns, Avery."

"What are you talking about?" She reached beyond him to flick off the lights, eager to head to bed. "You know what? Don't answer. I'm exhausted from what has been a terrific day. But if you'd prefer to argue over how many anecdotes I share, I'm not interested."

"Stop deflecting." His tone was sharp, but his eyes softened. "For the past few months, any time I mention a topic that might require you to share more than name, rank, or serial number, you deflect."

"I do not."

"Avery." He shook his head. "I'm not imagining things, babe. Today is the first time you've said anything positive about your job since you started. You give me updates on Rita like you're delivering the weather report. We discuss my dad's progress, but we never ask each other what it will mean if he wakes up. Or not."

Before she could respond, he held up his hands. "This is on me, too," he conceded. "Watching over him in a coma for two and a half years can't erase a lifetime of distance. And I take full advantage of the fact that you don't want to make me confront what might be."

"I respect your privacy," Avery argued. "Anyway, I don't say much because there's not much to be said. I go to work, and I come home.

Just like when I was at the Court. Rita is doing fine, and your dad is waiting. Like we both are. What else do you want?"

"We both know this is nothing like your time at the Court." Jared closed the distance between them and captured her hands in his. "What I want is a real conversation with my girlfriend. I don't think I'm asking too much, and it's not an invasion of privacy for two people who practically live together."

"If I wanted therapy, I'd ask Ling for a referral," Avery snapped. She jerked her hands from his grasp. "Like I said, it's been a long day, so forgive me if I'm not in the mood for a trip down memory lane. Or to analyze every emotion I have or action I take. I just wanted to celebrate a pretty major opportunity, but if we need to have a chat about my emotional shortcomings, fine. Bring it on."

Jared recoiled. "That's not what I said, and you know it. But you're right. This is your night, and if you're tired, you should turn in." He jutted his chin toward the stairs leading to his basement. "I have some work I need to finish up downstairs. I'll see you in the morning."

Without waiting for her reply, he walked away. Avery slowly turned toward the primary suite, mechanically flicking off lights as she headed for bed.

Jared wasn't wrong.

For months—hell, for more than a year—she'd felt trapped. Stuck. Despite all she could be grateful for. Amazing boyfriend. Great job. Even Rita had been sober and stable for longer than Avery could remember, a feat for her mother.

As she washed her face and put on her pajamas, she probed her sour reaction to Jared's observations. She could see the pattern, too. The closer Jared came, the more she pulled away. Talking about her dad wasn't hard, except that it meant sharing another part of herself. She loved Jared, but when he'd asked about her father, her visceral reaction was silence. And annoyance. Never a good sign.

Though she had no qualms about keeping the truth from others,

Avery made it a point not to lie to herself. No, Jared wasn't wrong, but something was.

Because today was the first time she'd felt anything more than . . . well, anything. Another very bad sign.

Images of Avery Keene flashed at rapid speed, thousands of images stored across a menagerie of sites. Photojournalists who'd accepted Peabodys and Pulitzers and Emmys had their craft snugged against paparazzi seeking the money shot to catapult them onto Easy Street. Lower life-forms had staked out her old apartment for years, hoping to catch a glimpse of wet skin or coitus, certain that blackmail might yield justifiable dividends. The triumvirate of social-media deities accepted grainy photos and graphic memes and spliced videos of dubious provenance gathered over the whole of her life, whether she knew it or not.

Words about her and her friends were more easily captured and catalogued. Key phrases fed a dedicated algorithm in search of the proximate solution to how to destroy an enemy. Data scraped from public sites merged with private musings mistakenly housed in clouds that leaked information like a sieve. Clouds that bounced from server to server, from handler to handler.

In the before time, this process could take months, but the oppo research on Avery was nearly instantaneous. Nanoseconds contained infinity when the target had even a slight public presence. She was younger than the internet, and only marginally older than Facebook and Myspace. Her end was already written. Now the job was to start.

The construction of the bullying email was simple. A warning to say nothing to Avery Keene. The note also contained a reminder of the consequences of malicious compliance. That had almost happened a few weeks ago, but a carefully timed text had solved that problem. Because people needed carrots and sticks, the email promised aid if Elisha Hibner's death remained accidental until it was useful to suggest otherwise.

With the "send" command, the emails bypassed traceable methods of transmission. An investigation would find no ISP to track, no keyboard strokes to analyze, no digital breadcrumbs. Like the spam messages that appeared on a cell phone without an alert, they could manifest their presence with ease. In this case, the message simply appeared in the inbox of select members of the Montgomery County Police Department. Received by public servants who also had images, messages, and secrets worth keeping. They would keep their peace because confession was rarely actually good for the soul, as their many collars would attest after trial.

In this case, honesty would cost them their pensions, and so much more. In the morning, both would read their missives, terrified about how someone knew.

It was the wrong question. *How* was almost always the first question and almost always wrong.

The question—invariably, inexorably, correctly—was *Why.*

TEN

Monday, April 12

"Welcome, Ms. Keene. Mr. Freedman will be right with you. Please have a seat in the McArthy Alcove."

Rather than a receptionist, the magnetometer she'd exited issued the polite instructions with a discreet arrow indicating where she should head next. It was a little past 8:00 a.m., but she already felt behind. Engagement letters had been signed, and the team would be on-site tomorrow morning. Until then, she would scope out their new digs, gather documents, and prep a plan of action.

Truth be told, she'd mapped out a preliminary plan within hours of meeting with Camasca yesterday. Still, it never hurt to double-check her assumptions.

While she waited for Freedman, she scanned the foyer, where only a handful of humans lingered. Frosted glass windows stretched the length of the exterior walls, emblazoned with the directive "Be Well." Rafe Diaz chose to emphasize mission over marketing, or so it seemed. Anyone looking for the name "Camasca" would have to check a neat bronze placard that hovered above the retinal scan that served as the first gauntlet for entry. No unexpected visitors could even beg entry without that scan.

Once the retinal scan verified identity, she'd been able to enter through a deluxe turnstile that prevented more than one entrant at a time. The amber-lit tunnel blocked off any views of the interior until the magnetometer completed its tasks, including a second eye-print and the biogenic evaluation. Upon successful completion of step two, the now biodata-printed guest received a fully laminated badge with embedded tech that would track their movements throughout the building.

Avery pulled out a notebook, feeling slightly anachronistic. In a building dedicated to the tools of the future, her habits were positively retro. Despite her eidetic memory, note taking helped her keep information organized and useful. And, like the lawyers who trained her, she preferred the feel of the paper and the satisfying scratch of a pen. Balancing the pad on her knee, she jotted down: "Request all video surveillance for forty-eight hours on either side of accident. And bribe Jared to apologize for spat." She assumed he'd be joining them at noon, but he'd been up and out before she woke.

"Item three," Avery murmured as she continued to capture her train of thought, "get better understanding of the biogenic system and data-print retention policies. What exactly do they record and how?"

"Do you often talk to yourself?"

Freedman loomed over her, surprisingly light on his feet for a big guy. Avery rose with a light shrug. "Not too much. As my mom told me when I was little, it's perfectly fine to talk to yourself. As long as you don't ask yourself what you said."

"I'm sure that seemed profound at the time," he commented. Then he turned and began walking. "Remember to be careful about what you say here. In common areas, our ambient scribe collects and sources conversations. Think Alexa or Siri waiting for you to ask a question. There's always something listening."

"I thought that was only within the employee sections."

Freedman kept moving, but waved at her to come abreast. "Kawak filters out superfluous information. Our teams have found that it's helpful to be able to review discussions after the fact. Most find it to be a very handy tool in the workplace."

Avery stopped in her tracks. "Anyone can access the recordings?"

With a heavy sigh, Freedman paused. "No. Any employee can request their voiceprint data, which Kawak will transcribe based on their location at the time of discussion and with notice to any third party in the conversation."

"Can an employee block the transmission?"

"Of course not." He started moving again. "We have a meeting with Rafe in his office. He's ready to get started."

"Coming," Avery muttered as she chased him down the same path they'd used yesterday. Silently, she wondered what hidden personality trait had drawn Noah to such a prig. The Noah Fox she knew was charming and outgoing, not a junior attendant to Stalin.

After retracing their steps up to the sixteenth floor, Freedman took a right rather than a left. Gallery-style hallways carried the requisite art to subtly signal wealth and status. Here, the vibe was the same, yet the images were variations on the Mayan myths from Rafe's roots in Guatemala that gave the company and its prize technology their names. From her research into his origin story, she'd learned about how his undocumented parents worked the East Coast migrant labor circuit, taking them from Florida, north to New Jersey, through Pennsylvania, then back south. American by birth, Rafe had blended his cultures, creating his own version of the Mayan myth in his very American technology. Kawak represented the elements of a thunderstorm and a collective consciousness. You referred to the first of its kind, and Keh meant tranquility and calmness. Not what she'd have expected from a soldier and an engineer.

Said contradiction suddenly appeared in front of them as a massive mahogany door swung wide.

"Come in," Rafe greeted amiably. She automatically accepted the ritual handshake of a second meeting. His unexpectedly callused palm scraped her skin.

Saying nothing, he ushered them both inside. Unnerved by her reaction to a simple, polite gesture, Avery avoided eye contact by studiously examining his suite. Rafe's decor contrasted sharply with the chrome-and-leather fanboy vibe preferred by Freedman. Variations on a tone too lovely to be called brown were repeated in the seating as well as the scatterings of art. Though twice the size of Freedman's, Rafe's domain felt intimate and cozy. Avery could have sworn there was a fire, but she knew better.

"Sit, sit," he urged as he settled on an oversized ottoman. The military bearing should have been at odds with the serene way he folded his legs beneath him. But, like the room, taken together, the combination of strict posture and Zen pose made complete sense. "Welcome back, Ms. Keene. I'm so pleased we'll be working together."

"Please, call me Avery," she said as she sat in a chair upholstered in topaz linen. Freedman sat in a matching one, placing him halfway between them.

"Did Freedman offer you anything to drink?" Before she could reply, he continued, "Of course not. Hydration is for mere mortals."

Avery chuckled. "I'm good, thank you."

"According to your bioprint entry report, your electrolyte balance is low. Keh, please order Avery a glass of customized water."

"Certainly, Dr. Diaz." The voice that had received her downstairs confirmed the order. Neither feminine nor masculine, it was best described simply as pleasant. "Would you or Mr. Freedman care for a beverage?"

"We're all set. Thank you."

Avery looked around. "I don't see a jamming device like Freedman's. Is your office constantly monitored?"

"Yes, particularly by Keh, who is an administrative partner to the executive suite—supports the administrative team and takes on more rudimentary tasks."

"You're the CEO. I would assume you'd have the highest degree of privacy."

"I've got nothing to hide, Avery. More important, I can't hold myself to a different standard than my teams."

"Why not? Other leaders certainly do."

"Because three hundred and seventeen employees have been asked to trust that the tech we're building can save lives. Best way to prove to our customers that we can help them is for us—the makers—to know without a doubt that our products work. And there's no better way to do that than to install it in the very fabric of our headquarters."

A light chime sounded, and Rafe gave a nearly imperceptible nod. The door whisked open to admit the twin of the robot Avery had encountered the day before. Rather than the golden skin Yax bore, Keh's skin mimicked the play of colors found in the opal. Not one true shade but a mélange that had a chemical explanation and a striking look. "Avery, meet Keh."

The robot approached her and extended a metal tray. Avery accepted the glass. "Thank you, Keh. I appreciate it."

"You're welcome, Ms. Keene. Enjoy."

She warned her audience, "I know there's a lot of debate about water and how it tastes. To me, it usually just tastes wet." She took a careful sip, and her eyes widened. "Whoa. I didn't ask for flavoring, yet it tastes—well—good. Better than good."

"That's the goal. Keh calculated the pH level of the water against your body chemistry. This version of water is precisely designed for your palate and hydration needs. After you finish, we'll get another reading of your levels. Small thing, but electrolyte dehydration is rampant every day. It can affect weight loss and mood. Our mission is to improve its flavor without the gimmicks and ensure everything from sharper mental focus to maximized organ function. Dozens of small actions build into transformation." Rafe placed his hands palm-up on his bent knees, like a modern guru. "You've literally just had a taste of what Camasca can do."

Avery smiled and took another sip.

Freedman moved into her line of sight. "We're glad to have you on board, Avery. Now, let's establish some ground rules."

"Name them."

"You must abide by strict confidentiality at all times. Even within your firm."

"Of course, but what do you mean?"

"I mean that, although I'm signing an engagement letter with Clymer Brezil, you are the only attorney other than Noah who is allowed to be on the premises or access our files."

Susan and Jeff would be annoyed, but a multibillion-dollar client was worth the irritation. "Got it."

"Rafe and I need a daily report on your progress. No exceptions."

She stifled her instinct to argue the oversight. It was day one. She had time to get what she needed—not much, but she'd make sure it was enough. "Agreed."

"Then I'll show you to your office."

"Which brings me to my condition," she said. Although the negotiation was with Freedman, she intentionally shifted to watch them both. "I need a clean room to work in, one that is not monitored. I cannot do this investigation if you are able to circumvent me at every turn. We need the same capacity as Freedman has to shut down access to Kawak."

Rafe's faultless posture went ramrod-straight. "I'm inviting you into my sanctum. Why would I sabotage you?"

"I don't know. And I don't know if it would be you or someone else who has gained access to your systems. I'm not going to ask if I can take files home with me, so that means I have to do everything from here. I won't do it if I have to worry about Noah or Fox or anyone else reporting on my moves. This is a nonnegotiable."

Freedman was already shaking his head. "Rafe—we can find somebody else. This is beyond the bounds."

Rafe waved off his protest. "Give her what she asks for, Glen Paul. We need her more than she needs us. Get it done."

ELEVEN

Freedman and Avery rode down to the eighth floor. The corridor was sparsely occupied except for a set of double-wide doors. Stopping in front of them, he instructed, "Eyes or hand?"

She gave him a mischievous look, and he grunted, "The access panel will accept a handprint or a retinal scan. Your badge also works. We'll key in your colleagues when they arrive. What do you want to use to let us into your Fort Knox?"

Avery placed her palm against the cool metal plate, and a slight click signaled a lock release. As Freedman pulled at the handle, she asked, "Who else has access?"

"No one," he assured her. "I assumed you'd demand absolute privacy, so not even I can get in without going through a lengthy process." He shut the door again and waved his badge to demonstrate. Nothing happened. "See? This works as my magic key everywhere except here and to Rafe's office."

"Thank you. Everyone else will be here tomorrow morning. Can we get a tour of the building when they arrive? I'd also like a copy of the employee roster."

"You'll all be in orientation in the morning, which includes understanding the layout of the company and who does what. As for the roster, we have a pretty user-friendly setup that allows us to share documents electronically and save trees, but I assume you'd like a hard copy?"

"Preferably. Four of them."

"Keh will deliver them shortly." He motioned her into the room and carefully shut the door. A panel identical to the one in his office lit amber. "You've seen this in my office. I've instructed security to disconnect Kawak's surveillance of this area. Once you step outside, though, all bets are off. It's the best I can do without compromising our systems."

"That fast?"

"We use this area for DoD teams that have to work on-site," he explained. "Segmenting Kawak's access is possible for more areas of the campus, but Rafe prefers that we not."

"He's very transparent. Must make life as his lawyer . . . difficult."

"I'm a thirty-four-year-old senior vice president and general counsel at a multibillion-dollar company who answers directly to the CEO. I've got no complaints."

"When you put it that way, neither would I." Embedded in his response was a warning. He had everything to lose if Rafe didn't get what he needed. And even more reason to make sure she gave him the answers he wanted. A guy like that wouldn't consider eavesdropping a violation of their agreement. It would be a necessary precaution. She'd ask Jared to bullet-proof their privacy as his first order of business.

For the first time, she turned toward the room itself and felt her jaw drop. "Wow. If this is a conference room, I'm definitely in the wrong business." Monitors stretched across two walls, and seven-foot tall glass displays on casters had been positioned equidistant from each other. Larger than the apartment she'd lived in with her mom when she was fourteen, the conference room boasted the requisite table in the center, a comfort station with coffeemaker and soda fountain that Ling would likely run dry, and shelving for those who hadn't abandoned paper altogether.

"Keh will help you decide on the layout, and our facilities team will be here to furnish it to your liking later this afternoon." With brisk steps, he headed for the area with a desk and a cluster of the glass boards. "Noah told me you like to write stuff on big Post-it notes or whiteboards. Ours are slightly more sophisticated. I have some for all of you."

"I appreciate it," she told him, impressed that he'd asked. A slim tablet identical to his own rested on the desk's surface. "I assume this is mine?"

"You can use your thumb or face to activate it," he instructed. "It will control all of the devices in the suite. For example, the windows can be darkened at your discretion using your tablet."

She looked up at the strip of windows that stretched the length of the conference area. They dropped from the ceiling, stopping two-thirds of the way down the wall, giving her a view of the verdant campus and a flower garden. With all of the screens and monitors, sunlight would cast a distracting gleam on the screens. Experimenting, she found the controls for the windows, and they instantly dimmed to an opaque gray.

"You've thought of everything."

"We try. The tablet controls everything, and it's pretty self-explanatory. Still, I'll have someone give your team a tutorial in the morning."

"Great." Duly impressed, she set the tablet down. "For planning purposes, tomorrow, I'd like to interview the two surviving engineers—Semans and Gomez—after I review a copy of the police report. I will also need you to arrange a meeting with the detectives who reviewed the incident."

"No," Freedman contradicted flatly. "You're not speaking to anyone outside of this building. I'll get you the police report, and I can provide a summary of Isabella and O.J.'s statements to our internal team. If you provide me with a list of additional questions, I will secure replies."

Avery planted her hands on the barren desk. Other than her satchel and a computer, nothing else cluttered the surface. "This isn't going to work if you stonewall me," she warned. "You asked for my assistance."

He grunted and shook his head. "Correction. Dr. Diaz asked for outside support, and I decided you were the least problematic solution."

"Why?" Avery figured she knew the answer, but she preferred clarity. "You know my reputation. Why pick me?"

"Because your firm specializes in internal investigations, and they've handled high-profile clients before. As legal counsel, you are bound by attorney-client privilege. Anything you discover will be subject to the same protections enjoyed by any other matter, and you can't go to law enforcement or a regulatory agency unless there is imminent harm."

"Exactly. So why are you trying to block me already?"

"Rafe wanted a solution, and my job is to get him what he wants. You were the best option, though I am happy to reconsider my choices. It is also my responsibility to protect him."

"From me? Or from the truth?" Avery demanded.

"Don't be dramatic. I'm doing what any good general counsel would do. Limiting our exposure."

"I work for you. And like you said, I am bound by privilege. Right now, I'm your ally. Worst-case scenario, I flag your vulnerabilities and refuse to ever use your products. The harder you make this process, the more risk you bring to Camaeon."

"There was no murder," Freedman contradicted. "And I don't want you spending precious time chasing Rafe's ghosts in the machine. My interest is compliance with all regulatory obligations, a risk analysis that I can show our board, and an audit of policies and procedures that withstand SEC scrutiny and any questions from the VA or the FDA."

"Which is what I intend to deliver in the time you've given me. If you let me do my job." Avery studied him, awaiting a response.

After a brief staring contest, he barked, "What are you looking at?"

"I'm trying to figure out what you're afraid of."

"Excuse me?"

Then it hit her. "Do you actually believe someone tried to kill your staff?"

The subtle flinch of his eyelids might have been undetectable had she not been looking for a tell. Glen Paul Freedman was genuinely afraid, but too proud to admit his fear.

A fear she could understand. With only two days of exposure, she already found herself on alert. "Freedman?"

"Focus on the project at hand, Avery." He didn't bother to veil the warning. "Dr. Diaz has a heightened sense of morality and conscience. I don't hire lawyers for theirs."

"No, you hire them to keep you out of trouble and in the money. I will do both, but not if I'm hamstrung by my client. I work for you, but I work my way. You give me the scope and purpose, and I determine how to achieve your ends. I go where the information leads, and I ask the questions that require answers. What I find belongs to you. How I find it is up to me."

Folding her hands, she fixed him with a steady look. "Either we come to an agreement now, or you explain to Dr. Diaz that you've decided we aren't compatible."

The staring contest resumed, bolstered by impertinence on her part, obstinacy on his. With a grind of his teeth, he volunteered, "Tim Howard."

"Bethesda PD?"

"Montgomery County Police Department. Bethesda doesn't have its own stand-alone law enforcement, and MCPD brass decided to assign the case to the Special Investigations Division instead of the district station." Freedman fairly snarled. "Detective First Grade. I'll tell him to expect your call."

"And the police report?" she inquired sweetly.

"Keh will load it into your files."

"We can wait on interviewing the Tiger Team, but not too long." Aware she'd pressed her luck enough, Avery stood down. "Thank you, Freedman."

"Rafe has meetings on the Hill in the morning, so he won't be able to meet your team until tomorrow afternoon," he warned as he approached the suite's door.

"That's not necessary," she said quickly. "It's generous of him, but not necessary."

"He insists."

"Okay. I'll tell the team. Also, before I leave today, I'll have SOPs ready for your review." When his head whipped toward her, she explained, "I created my own investigation procedure manual. I usually review it with clients when we begin discussions about representation."

"Does it detail how big a pain in my ass you will likely become?"

"Section two," she confirmed with faux solemnity. "See you tomorrow."

"Dr. Liam. Please return to the treatment area."

Kate bowed her head in fatigue, tempted to ignore the PA summons from Milo. She worked six days a week, from 7:30 a.m. to 5:30 p.m., longer if she had to cover for a colleague who'd been rotated to another VA clinic. She and Dr. Scandrett were the only two exempted from that system, a condition of their InnoVAI contracts. They overlapped their coverage so that one of them was always on the premises. A night owl, Reginald preferred the late shift.

Today had been a twelve-hour slog, because she'd been caught up in a new case that had echoes of Lieutenant Vinson's. Captain Tiffany Rosetti presented with a dry cough, swelling in her lips and throat, and low potassium levels. Prior treatment for her coronary heart disease had been promising, but the fifty-two-year-old had arrived midday, reporting dizziness and tiredness. And crying tears of blood.

Kate knew from experience that cardiovascular diseases like heart attacks or strokes were too often considered "men's diseases." Women like Captain Rosetti were more likely to be misdiagnosed with indigestion or anxiety and denied hospitalization. Concerned about her pallor and abnormal heart rhythm, Kate had immediately admitted her to the clinic. The battery of tests she'd ordered revealed a baffling combination of indicators. The hemolacria was wholly inconsistent with her medications or symptoms.

In the next patient bay, Lieutenant Vinson had experienced a second episode of paralysis and respiratory distress, despite the precautions they'd taken. For hours, Kate toggled between them, tasking her nursing staff with the job of triaging low-level appointments.

At last, Vinson was stable, and the captain was resting as comfortably as modern medicine would allow. She'd briefed Dr. Scandrett and one of their colleagues who rotated through the clinic, Dr. Kenny Leon. Duty done, Kate was finally heading home. Suddenly, Nurse Christie Obiaya hurried across the waiting room, her expression dire.

Kate clung to the metal handle, hoping that whatever the nurse required would not pull her back inside.

"Dr. Liam, I'm so sorry," she hissed, to avoid being overheard by the two patients who lingered in the waiting room. Both vets were regulars who required dialysis treatments, but whose jobs meant they could never make traditional office hours. The in-home options weren't feasible, because one lived with his granddaughter and her kids in a cramped one-bedroom, and the other was couch-surfing until his housing voucher came through.

"What is it, Christie?"

"It's Master Sergeant Thomas. Dr. Scandrett asked me to get you. It's not good."

Kate fairly raced past the clients and keyed herself and Christie into the treatment area. She bumped into Dr. Scandrett as she rounded the corner. "Reginald? Christie said you needed my help."

"I don't—" He shook his head. "It was five minutes. Just five minutes."

"What are you talking about? What happened?"

"I don't know. I was doing my rounds, and he was fine. Next thing I know, he's convulsing. I thought I'd stabilized him, but the seizures started again. I sent the nurse to grab you while I treated him. Then he stopped. Everything. The seizures. Breathing. Brain function. Everything stopped. Sixty seconds."

"Let me see him."

Clearly staggered, Reginald gave way, and trailed her to the patient bay. Master Sergeant Brian Thomas lay inert; the machines monitoring his vital signs had dimmed.

"Milo?" Kate read the electronic chart that recorded the series of events. "What happened?"

"As Dr. Scandrett explained, the patient experienced an abrupt onset of seizures. Based on the patient's symptoms, my initial impression is that he may have experienced sudden unexpected death in epilepsy."

"SUDEP?" Reginald protested. "His chart showed no symptoms of epileptic disorder, nor had it ever been diagnosed."

"Undiagnosed epilepsy is rare but not impossible. It is linked to genetic and environmental causes. Developmental brain abnormalities, stroke, certain infections or brain tumors. Given his role as a combat gunner, he could have experienced a traumatic brain injury that is consistent with his other presentations."

"What about his MRI?" Kate queried as she came alongside Thomas's body. "Any hint of microlesions? Anything to suggest a TBI?"

"His MRIs were inconclusive," Milo told them. "Dr. Scandrett did not identify any abnormalities when he reviewed the results."

Reginald stiffened. "No, there was nothing in his MRI to indicate a TBI or risk of a seizure. It was not inconclusive."

"In the aftermath of such a traumatic experience, it is important not to blame yourself, Dr. Scandrett. Might I recommend you take a moment for meditative breathing? I detect high levels of cortisol."

Kate prickled at the AI's condescension. "Dr. Scandrett doesn't need to breathe, Milo. We both need to understand why this relatively young man is lying dead in our clinic."

"Focus on our patients, not my well-being," Reginald ordered.

"My apologies. I will note your boundaries, Dr. Scandrett."

"You do that."

Milo went silent, then piped up. "Dr. Scandrett, sir?"

"Yes, Milo?"

"You have not yet recorded time of death."

Dr. Scandrett swallowed hard, bowed his head, and gritted out, "What was the time?"

"Seven fifty-two p.m. I can prepare the report and transmit it to your office. I will copy Nurse Obiaya to assist you."

As Reginald stalked off toward his office, Kate reflexively draped a sheet over Master Sergeant Thomas's inert form. He was the first patient to die under their care, and her worries for Vinson and Rosetti spiked. A few more hours in the lab couldn't hurt.

"Might I be of assistance, Dr. Liam?"

"Not right now. Thank you, Milo."

"You're most welcome."

TWELVE

Tuesday, April 13

"Welcome to Camasca," Avery said with an exaggerated flourish as she disengaged the biometric lock to what she'd dubbed the investigation suite. She had met Ling, Noah, and Jared downstairs at 8:00 a.m., waited for their full bioprints to be generated at 8:30, went through the Camasca orientation session with them, and, with Keh's guidance, gotten a short tour of their wing of the facility. The group had finally made it to their assigned quarters at a little past 11:00 a.m.

Working with Keh and the facilities team yesterday, she'd set up three additional workstations in the suite to conform to what she thought she knew of her friends. Instinctively, Ling arrowed toward one of the two desks below the wide sweep of windows. A curved desk, a wide-bottomed criss-cross chair, and a battalion of blue-ink pens had been curated by Avery based on their years of cohabitation and Camasca's willingness to cater to their employees' quirks.

Noah quickly joined Ling in the next bay over, dropping into the meticulously stitched, overpriced, and oversized leather chair he favored. Both of them had shelves catty-corner to their desks, and Noah had a stack of yellow legal pads, which he swore made him a real lawyer.

Moving more deliberately, Jared wandered through the suite to his station, which had a tri-screened monitor, set up identically to the one in his home office. The laptop connected to it was his preferred brand, and she'd requisitioned every gizmo they had available. She'd placed him on the opposite leg of the H, and Keh had painstakingly replicated every device Avery mapped from his home bunker.

"I know you want to see the whole place, but Rafe wants to be here for the big reveal. Even I haven't seen the full campus yet."

"Are you kidding?" Ling replied as she began exploring her niche. "I was just engaged in a heated discussion about the merits of reality television with an actual robot . . . one who is partial to dating shows and has very definite views on osteopathy versus traditional medical practice."

Yesterday had run long, and she hadn't spoken to any of them since their dinner. Including Jared. Instead of heading over to his place, she'd texted him that she had more research to do at home. He hadn't argued. Still, the peace offering seemed to be working on at least two of them.

"Very cool digs," Noah said. "I'm impressed."

"I tried to pick stuff I've seen you guys use. But if I missed anything, our hosts can produce whatever your heart desires."

"You never miss a trick," Jared replied.

Avery recoiled, her eyes flashing hurt.

"I didn't mean it like that," he apologized. "I meant that we know you're observant."

"Of course." She headed to her section without another word.

Frustrated, Jared swung his backpack off and dumped it on his workstation. He'd also brought a small wheeled case, which had caused a minor hubbub at security. Avery had negotiated a clean office, and Freedman's handpicked security briefers swore they'd complied. But Jared trusted himself more than their client. Detecting Camasca's surveillance equipment was the first-wave defense, but any security tech worth his salt understood that the game required offensive measures as well. By agreement, the team would not speak until he gave the all-clear. They'd also downloaded encrypted apps of his selection onto their devices. He'd upgraded their personal wares with some dampening equipment developed by his intelligence colleagues, guaranteed to render their smart devices fairly impenetrable. Jared had eagerly volunteered to test out their tech in the field.

With practiced motions, he first unearthed a metal box the size of a gaming console. A device of his own design, it combined a Bluetooth and Wi-Fi jammer that permitted cellular signals with a tracker that checked for signal leakage. Because Camasca had military contracts, he'd spent the day before cajoling from a colleague a prototype that was used to detect satellite intercepts. As he'd reasoned with the creator, nothing beat field testing. Although he hadn't revealed his target, Camasca was a hell of a field.

Trained by U.S. Naval Intelligence and by some of the best white-hat hackers in the world, Jared had still never been in an office as technologically sophisticated as Camasca. His stint upgrading their security system had impressed him, but nothing prepared him for the scope of what they'd built out since then. Avery hadn't been exaggerating about their advancements.

She rarely exaggerated. Or chattered about meaningless stuff. Her childhood hadn't allowed for a lot of frivolity, and neither had his. It was one of the ways they matched. And one of the ways they allowed each other too much space.

Jared wanted more—like the lightness Avery shared with Ling, he thought as he segmented the suite and tested each section. It had been nearly three years since he and Avery met and got serious. In that time, he would have sworn they were moving in the same direction, and he was happy to be along for the ride. After so much of his life on his own, he'd finally found a match who seemed to see him and a future together.

Lately, though, Avery had been retreating—almost invisibly, but he noticed. His contribution to the *Scooby* gang was that where she saw weaknesses or patterns, he saw what was missing. Especially when it came to Avery. Because he noticed everything about her. From her dry wit to her endless legs to her prickly conscience, nothing about Avery Keene escaped his attention. Including the fact that the woman he loved was in the midst of a mystery beyond political machinations. Trying to figure out herself. His mission was to be there once she did. Or be ready to lose the best part of his world.

Shaking off the sudden wave of apprehension, he turned his attention to the task at hand. Help Avery solve a new puzzle. Like he'd learned in boot camp, slow was smooth and smooth was fast. He simply had to give her time. But neither of them could afford to give her too much.

"All done." Twenty minutes later, Jared quickly walked them through the setup. "In addition to the Camasca on/off switch, we've got our own failsafe. This keypad toggles the video and audio surveillance on and off. This one allows us to rejoin the twenty-first century or cut off technical contact. We should be isolated in here, but it's not foolproof. I helped set up their security system a couple of years ago, and I don't recognize most of the upgraded configurations."

"We're still under watch?" Ling asked.

"Given that DoD uses these facilities, I doubt it, but I can't swear it. Which is why I've set up countermeasures that should scramble electronic communications and garble conversations. They might still be able to take our temperatures, but they should have a hard time reading our minds."

When no one laughed, Jared rolled his eyes. "I'm kidding. The worst-case scenario is that Avery's client actually knows what we're doing and disagrees."

"Which is not that different from every other day," Avery agreed. "Thanks, Jared."

Giving a thumbs-up, he asked, "So what's next, boss?"

"Our first briefing." Avery beckoned them over to her wing. At orientation, they'd learned that Camasca's slick glass screens would convert her scrawl into neatly typed notes.

Jared crossed to the device and ran his fingers along the beveled base. Finding the button, he depressed it and stepped back. "Give me a second." He returned to his station and made some adjustments to one of the gadgets he'd planted along a credenza. As he worked, the other three bandied ideas about what else might be happening on the Camasca campus, their conjecture increasingly absurd and intentionally outrageous. Avery's husky laugh at one of Ling's musings made him smile. He'd never get tired of hearing the sound, and he was grateful that she had friends who could coax it from her.

That *they* had friends—indeed, thanks to Avery, Ling and Noah had become two of his closest confidants. They were crazy intelligent and fiercely loyal, and he appreciated their ability to keep Avery grounded and safe while never letting her turn too inward. Something he was beginning to doubt about himself. Shaking off the dark thought, he finished his tinkering.

When he came back, he explained, "If you fully activate the board, the sensors transcribe your information and automatically transmit it to the program on your computer. It won't work if the signal jammer is on."

Ling frowned. "To clarify, exactly how paranoid are we supposed to be here? Should I bring an abacus and my entire compendium of medical textbooks?"

"My main concern is the permanent eavesdropping," Avery told Jared, warily. "But Camasca is our client, and anything we produce becomes attorney work product." She leaned against the glass screen and surveyed the team. "What do you think?"

"I'm no attorney, but I do know investigations. We have a duty to your client to keep them informed, but this is a complicated matter. I'd say we use the tools at our disposal as long as they don't pose a risk of undermining the research."

"Translation?"

"We can use the internet and the fancy tools, but let's keep certain conversations for off-site. I'm fairly confident I've blocked recording of voice and data intelligence, but the human intelligence challenge is beyond my scope."

"Which brings us to our next order of operations," Avery began. "Like the memo I sent last night outlines, our scope is incredibly broad, but our time is limited. Ostensibly, we are helping the general counsel conduct due diligence. In reality, our job is to quickly determine if Camasca is a sinking ship. We've got three scenarios related to the death of Elisha Hibner in the Tiger Team's area, which they called the Den."

She scribbled on the board. "One, the Den incident was a malfunction, and the anonymous note is to sabotage the company. Two, the malfunction was intentional, and the note is misdirection to send us off on a wild goose chase. Or, three, the malfunction was intentional, and Kawak or one of its personalities really did write the world's shortest manifesto declaring war on humanity. In that case, we need an exorcist. Agreed?"

"Agreed," they repeated back in unison, studying the board.

"How much of the legal parts of this job will I need to understand?" Ling queried. "I'm open to new experiences, but you lawyers can be jargon generators."

"Unlike the super-clear world of medical rhetoric?" Noah joshed. "Take a nap. I'll nudge you when it's your turn to learn."

Barely avoiding Ling's reply—an elbow to his gut—he continued, "The doc makes a point, though. Understanding the transaction will mean combing through all of their financial files. I still have nightmares from my first year as an associate, performing due diligence in anticipation of a corporate merger. They suck the souls of minions for that task on purpose. It is well beyond the capacity of the four of us—and by that, I mean me."

"I know it's below your pay grade," Avery replied with a tap on the glass, "which is why I'm about to explain how I think we approach this."

"Lay it on us," Jared invited.

Using the special markers supplied by the board's manufacturers, Avery laid out the timeline for their work. "Our first order of business is document and evidence collection. Noah, I need you to suck it up and go through every scrap of paper they've supplied to the SEC and everyone who's given them a penny of funding. Figure out how Camasca is structured. Investors, partners, board members, key employees. We need to have a map to those with a vested interest in the company. Most will be on-site, and you should feel free to ask your pal Freedman to retrieve what you can't find.

"Ling, they also had to get permission from the FDA and the VA to operate the clinic. We should pull all those documents as well. Noah can help you." She tapped the board. "Camasca has their fingers in a few projects, but Kawak is the Holy Grail. You're our resident expert on InnoVAI. I think you know the head of the clinic, Dr. Kate Liam. Before we meet with her, we need a deep dive on why the DoD would pour so much money into this. I need you to be able to explain to me *exactly* what Milo, the medical chatbot, does—and how."

"I'll do my best, but Jared may have to be my geek translator."

"Of course. Today, we're gathering data. I'd also like to have you meet with the bioinformatics and computational-biology teams. Definitely take Jared along with you. Get a feel for the team and any rumblings. Elisha and O.J. were their team leads, and I want to understand their dynamics."

"It's your show, Avery, but we skipped a step," Jared said.

"Which is?"

"Scene security. I assume that'll come after we meet with Diaz, but this is a black-box operation until we see how this place works. Starting with the Den."

"Good point," Avery conceded. She drew an arrow and added the new task. "I miss anything else?"

"Not that I can see." Jared reclined against the wall. Desperate for some levity, he deadpanned, "So when do I get to play with robots?"

Avery's lips quirked. "Soon. But—to your point—this afternoon, you and I will meet with the Camasca security teams. Isabella Gomez headed up data security, privacy, and the database management system, so that's first. But messing with a ventilation system means someone got inside who shouldn't have. We need to chat with the shoe-leather guys as well. After we've seen the Den."

"Aye, aye, sir."

"We also have to set up a data-preservation protocol, and I want Freedman to introduce you to the engineers and coders who brought this whole megillah to life."

"What about you?"

"I put a copy of the police report and the autopsy in your folders. I'd like to talk through it with y'all; then I'm headed over to Montgomery County PD." Freedman had moved quickly, once they'd had their pissing contest. "I want to understand exactly why they decided it wasn't murder."

Jared straightened up from his slouch. "Why don't we do that one together, too? I know you can handle yourself around a police station, but I've conducted a few interrogations with law enforcement."

Avery hesitated, then nodded. "Makes sense. Any other questions?"

Ling raised her hand. "When do we meet our AI overlords? And am I dressed for the occasion?"

Freedman waited on the video call for the attendees to show up on his screen. Finally, at a little past noon, the encrypted system pinged once, then a second time. O.J.'s image appeared, but Isabella's box was dark.

Forgoing niceties, he instructed, "Turn on your camera, Gomez."

"No. I'm only calling you because your note said it was urgent. You've got three minutes."

"How are you doing, Izzy?" O.J. asked solemnly. "I've tried to reach you, but you never pick up."

"I'm alive. You're down to two minutes and fifty-five seconds."

Biting off a curse, Freedman said hastily, "I'm calling to give an early warning. We've hired an attorney to help us prepare for going public, and she will be reaching out to you and O.J. for interviews."

"No," Isabella said brusquely. "I don't want to talk to anyone yet. Rafe promised me that I could take as long as I needed."

Freedman modulated his tone, trying to be sympathetic. And failing. "It's been several weeks, Isabella. I know you're still grieving, but it's crunch time. We have to get this deal closed or we risk everything."

"I don't care about the money, Freedman! Is this attorney going to figure out who killed Elisha?"

Summoning patience, Freedman replied, "The police investigation ruled it was a tragic accident. No one is going to harm you or O.J., I swear."

"I don't believe you, and why should I? Someone attacked us and killed one of my best friends. Until you know who, we're not safe."

"I'd feel better if I could see your face, Izzy. Can you turn on your camera?"

"Are you at work?"

"Of course."

"Then no."

Cursing in his head, Freedman got to the point of this call. "After the accident, I pulled your recordings for the alignment sprint that weekend, and your notes. The anomalies you described are problematic."

"Elisha kept the bug report isolated to the three of us. Izzy and I wanted to tell you, but he refused."

"Well, luckily, none of them have been reported by any of the teams since that night."

"Really?"

"From what I can tell. None of the temporary leads have made any complaints. What are we looking at, then? Spontaneous self-correction?"

"Elisha said he'd figured out a patch," Izzy recalled. "We'd switched stations, and he was working on the code from O.J.'s team."

"He never said it was my fault!" O.J. objected. "You can't blame this on my team."

"I'm not blaming anyone," Freedman assured them. "From where I stand, the glitches are gone and no one is the wiser."

"But Elisha is still dead," Izzy said starkly. "He died in your building, Freedman. In Rafe's building. Why isn't *he* on this call?"

"He's in a meeting, and I didn't want anyone to ambush you with the news. She's going to be meeting with your teams starting tomorrow."

"Our teams?" O.J. scoffed. "I know we're damaged goods. Six weeks of sick time plus bereavement leave? You're pushing us out."

"We're not pushing you out. Your jobs are ready for you both when you want to come back." Running out of patience, he tried to sympathize. "I know the Tiger Team was close. All three of you. The police investigation left too many unanswered questions. Rafe and I agree, and now Avery Keene is looking into everything, Izzy. If there's something to find, she will."

"Call me back then. Otherwise, leave me alone or go to hell."

THIRTEEN

Avery and Jared paused at the threshold of the Den. Similar to their investigative suite, the area had been converted from a conference room into a highly functional workspace. Glass ran the length of the entry, but inside, drywall had been painted a rich gray and hung with a mix of monitors and art. The configuration allowed for easy communication and relative isolation, depending on the user preference. Keh released the locks, and Jared pulled the heavy glass door wide.

Inside, the computer bays appeared undisturbed. A mug with an image of Frida Kahlo rested on a coaster at the end of one station. Another station had a cartoon bobble-head that she recognized from childhood. The third area was pristine. No clutter, no tchotchkes.

"Keh, what can you tell us about the ventilation system?" Avery asked as she wandered around the area. Jared headed to the mechanical panel on the far wall.

"The Camasca Flow Air Distribution and Exchange System operates with a hybrid design to provide laboratory-safe air quality in all areas of the building. The CFADES controls for chemical or biohazard emissions, by using a proprietary air-exchange rate in excess of the ten-to-twelve air-changes per hour of fresh non-recirculated air recommended by industry standard."

"Is the entire building on the same system?"

"With the CFADES building design, each section of the facility has its own air supply system that's independent from the other operational mechanics. In each segment, we track intake, extraction, and filtration across the various segments."

"Meaning whatever happened in here would have been isolated from the rest of the building?"

"Yes, Ms. Keene. The Den, like your suite, is independent."

Jared joined them. "The expense of such a honeycombed system must be astronomical and hard to monitor."

"We have microbots embedded throughout CFADES, which report to me and the CFADES technicians on a constant basis."

"You're currently receiving information?" Avery asked.

"Indeed. Since we entered, the air changes per hour has altered from twelve to fourteen to accommodate you and Mr. Wynn. Laboratory Zeta is experiencing a minor airflow obstruction caused by an experiment blocking a return. A technician has been dispatched."

Avery returned to the desk with the Kahlo mug. "Who sat here?"

"Dr. Gomez."

"I take it the empty space belonged to Dr. Hibner?"

"His family requested a return of all personal items. I decided to leave the rest of the decor untouched until Dr. Semans and Dr. Gomez return."

"Why?"

"It isn't my place to disturb their work areas. They should be allowed to determine how to manage their property. Grief strikes in a variety of ways, and an act as minute as removing a familiar object can trigger an emotional response."

"Very thoughtful, Keh. Was that your decision, or did someone instruct you to do it?" Jared questioned.

"As I said, it was my decision."

Avery studied the cloistered space. "What can you tell us about the accident? Were you monitoring the ACH that night?"

"Yes. However, the sensors did not detect any changes in the airflow mix. The microbots could not identify any blockages, and the technicians were unable to reconstruct the malfunction."

"How did you find the three engineers?"

"Dr. Semans managed to use his phone to call Security. For some reason, the building-wide system didn't pick up Dr. Gomez's reported request for assistance. When we heard from him, we dispatched a team, and Dr. Semans recovered with administration of oxygen on the scene. Dr. Gomez and Dr. Hibner were nonresponsive. Our paramedic team transported them to a local hospital. Dr. Gomez remained in a coma for another day, but Dr. Hibner was pronounced dead at the hospital upon arrival."

Keh's recitation fit the police report Avery had read. "Do you have a theory on how this happened?"

The robot faced them, the iridescent skin its own work of art. "I have scoured my records and reviewed the logs of each of the microbots. I also analyzed their bioprints. According to my analysis, nothing happened—which I recognize is empirically impossible, as the biodata and medical records reflect that the Tiger Team was poisoned."

"Your theory?" Avery pressed the robot, determined to understand.

"In the absence of any further evidence, I would speculate that my records and those of the CFADES were externally altered to erase the information. And that the monitors were deprogrammed to avoid triggering our timely response."

Jared watched the engineers who passed by the Den, trying not to be noticed as they watched interlopers in what had become a makeshift memorial to their fallen friends. "Who could do that? Erase your records?"

"The head of maintenance can review records, but he can't tamper with them. Only eight people had the security clearance to alter information: Nancy Koziol, chief of security. The chief financial officer and the chief operating officer, who were both out of town at a conference in California, but neither has the technical expertise. Isabella Gomez, the head of data security. O. J. Semans, head of computational biology. Glen Paul Freedman, general counsel. Rafe Diaz, CEO."

"Seven," Avery counted. Then it hit her. "And Elisha Hibner made eight."

"Yes, Ms. Keene."

At 1:00 p.m., the crew convened in the center of their suite at the conference table. At Avery's direction, Jared rolled one of the boards closer to their position. A handheld keyboard rested in his palm, and he used it to summon up the police reports. "If you want to put something up here, all the tablets are synced to share their screens."

Heads bobbed in assent as he arranged documents on the massive screen. "I've already posted the toxicology report, the autopsy, maintenance records on the ventilation system, statements from Semans and Gomez, and the police report closing out the case."

Avery twisted to face the board. "Ling, why don't you start with the autopsy and toxicology report?"

"Elisha Hibner was pronounced dead at the hospital at four-twenty-eight a.m., but the autopsy shows he died earlier. According to his bioprint data, which Camasca provided to the police, his time of death was recorded as three-forty-eight a.m."

"Keh told us that the security team found them in the office." Jared studied the timing and frowned. "Camasca monitors every imaginable biometric. No way there should have been elevated CO concentrations in the Den without sensors going off or the biomonitors notifying Keh."

"Who seems legitimately puzzled by the system failures."

Ling pointed to the documents floating in the far-right corner of the board. "According to my reconstruction of the biodata, Isabella lost consciousness a few seconds after Elisha, and O.J. succumbed around a minute later. O.J. recovered here, and Isabella lapsed into a coma."

"Yet the building reported no irregularities—no alarms."

"I can't speak to the building's behavior," Ling said. "I do know the coroner puts Elisha's cause of death as asphyxiation caused by acute levels of carbon monoxide. Said 'blood tests inconclusive' due to degradation of the same, and the report mentions his severe asthma."

"Something bothering you?"

Ling tapped on her tablet's screen and flicked per their tutorial, and more images appeared in the center of the board. "The hospital tested his blood and urine for known compounds. High levels of caffeine, which makes sense for a computer engineer working late nights. According to this, he didn't smoke. In fact, Elisha tested negative for any compounds that would indicate recreational drug use. I looked through his other medical records. His severe asthma would have made him more susceptible to CO poisoning, sure."

"But?"

"The degradation of the blood sample doesn't fit. If I had to guess, I think he experienced acute hemolysis."

"Which is?"

"He didn't asphyxiate from lack of oxygen. When the ventilation system flooded the room with carbon monoxide, Elisha suffocated in his own blood."

"Why does that matter?" Noah asked.

"Carboxyhemoglobin forms in red blood cells when hemoglobin is exposed to carbon monoxide. So, when carbon monoxide gets into your bloodstream, it creates this complex that slowly starts to kill you. CO is dangerous because it reduces the blood's capacity to carry oxygen. Unless it is dissipated, hypoxia starts, which is when your body doesn't get enough oxygen to function. Most people in that circumstance do suffocate, like O.J. and Isabella started to do."

"But if Elisha has stopped breathing," Avery concluded, "how could he have processed the oxygen to degrade the sample?"

"Bingo." She transferred another report to the screen. "He suffered from chronic bronchitis, which meant he repeatedly relied on Bactrim. One out of every ten Black men have what's called a G6PD deficiency from mutation in the G6PD gene. There's an enzyme-concentration difference in Black patients compared with white patients, even though white patients can have it as well. But the condition is indiscernible until it's a problem. The ventilation malfunction created a perfect storm: Bactrim lowered his resistance, the G6PD deficiency made him susceptible, and the carbon monoxide triggered the hemolysis."

"How did O.J. revive?"

"The oxygen must have been restored. If O.J. had passed out, with fresh oxygen, he'd have been out for maybe fifteen minutes."

"Not Isabella?"

"Bodies are weird." Ling used her pen to circle the report. "In summation, carbon monoxide nearly suffocated O.J., Isabella, and Elisha, but the oxygen came back on in time to revive them. For some reason, Isabella wasn't able to process it as quickly. Elisha never stood a chance."

"A freak occurrence that led to him dying and no one else?" Avery summarized. "Who could have figured this out? Besides you?"

"A group of biomedical experts who have access to granular data about a colleague's medical condition." Ling tapped her screen. "For a start."

Score one for Team Insider Sabotage. "Which leads to the maintenance reports." Avery turned to Jared. "Apparently, they take air very seriously at Camasca."

"I reviewed the CFADES maintenance log Keh provided. These reports are high-level. Like something I've prepared for a security client." He pulled up a sample for the team. "According to these extremely detailed chronicles of air-conditioning, ventilation is monitored twenty-four/seven. The system has human personnel, and they maintain their own microbot team, which answers to Keh."

Ling muttered, "Of course they do."

"Patent pending. They use miniature versions of Keh to travel through the entire system, taking readings and reporting on trouble spots." He pulled up a still image of the microbots clustered in a tube. "Think about how often you remember to change your filters. These guys make them obsolete."

"You're joking?"

"Not at all." He tabbed over to the sample report. "All of this data is automatically generated by a combination of human and robot techs. These are just the reports for the day before, the day of the incident, and the day after the malfunction."

Noah walked around to take a closer look at the image. "Okay, so CFADES looks like it could be used on the International Space Station."

Ling joined Noah at the board. "Do any of the maintenance reports describe fluctuations in the airflow mix? If they manufacture their own blend, the filtration system should record any variations from the formulary input."

He shook his head. "Keh admitted the records are missing. What I have describes how the system works, but the next forty-plus pages simply record data about the intermix and distribution. There's no report of spikes in CO or of pure oxygen anywhere in the building."

"Keh speculated that the records were altered or erased," Avery added. "The system generates a report every twelve minutes. That means—for the sake of argument—if the poisoning was intentional, the bots would have been programmed either to expect or to ignore any alterations."

"How can we tell if that happened?"

"I've already put in a request for a demonstration of the system and the bots."

"Noah?"

"I'm no Columbo, but the police report is basically worthless. Summarizes the toxicology report findings and says that the issue was mechanical error. I'd fire an intern who turned in such incomplete work. No investigation of the technology or speculation about human error."

Avery nodded in satisfaction. "I thought the same. Which is why I requested the meeting with Detective Howard. He led the investigation on behalf of the Special Investigations Division. He apparently dedicated a whole entire week to the task."

"He certainly didn't use his time wisely," Noah carped. "You mentioned interviews with the other two members of the Tiger Team. Calling it a conversation would be a dramatic exaggeration. The file contains a summary from each of them, but no firsthand accounts, which is odd." Noah gave the entire table a concerned look. "The detective says he asked each victim what happened, and they both said the same thing."

"Which was?"

He read the report aloud, verbatim. " 'Subjects report that prior to the incident, they were together in the Den working, and their next memory is waking up to find Elisha was dead.' That's it. No follow-up questions. No hypotheses. Bang-up job."

"Which is why we're going on a field trip. Hopefully, we'll find better answers than what's in these files."

FOURTEEN

"Whose car do you want to take?" Jared asked as they entered the parking garage. As temporary employees, they'd been assigned slots for their vehicles in the company's state-of-the-art facility, which resembled a luxury-car showroom. Entire rows outfitted with EV chargers silently juiced an array of automobiles that Avery could barely afford to look at yet. With a push of the button, said vehicles could request a wash-and-wax or other on-site services.

Even with her upgraded salary, Avery declined to swap out her reliable, fully paid-off Subaru Outback, nicknamed Oscar. Despite its advanced age, she was loath to part ways with the car that had seen her cross-country, cross-educational rest stops. However, Oscar had been making rude noises, hinting at retirement or a faulty transmission, neither of which was she in a mood to deal with today.

"You drive," she said. They easily located his '67 Chevy Corvette among the sea of high-end electric vehicles, from BMWs to Rivians. Jared opened her door, rounded the car, and got behind the wheel.

With practiced motions, he maneuvered them out of the garage and into midday traffic heading for I-270N. For the next fifteen miles, they rode in silence as the Corvette ate up the highway toward the Montgomery County Police Department headquarters. Avery was grateful for his company, but at a loss for what to say. Instead, she busied herself reading the Camasca ventilation manual from cover to cover. She'd read more boring legal opinions and learned half as much.

Soon, the GPS instructed Jared to switch lanes, and he aimed the Corvette at an exit directing them toward Gaithersburg. Minutes later, he pulled into a visitor space in the parking lot. He killed the engine and faced Avery. "I'll follow your lead."

"Thanks. But feel free to tag in."

"Yes, ma'am."

Together, they entered the MCPD building and beelined for an open area with a scattering of seats.

"We're here to see Detective Tim Howard," Avery told the middle-aged receptionist with multitoned blond-and-pink tresses who was juggling calls coming in on two different phones.

A bronzy placard introduced her as Mary Lou Romaine, customer service liaison. Between them was a plexiglass partition that served more for show than as protection. The surface had been scratched up over time, some of the marks angrier than others. One jagged scar that likely came from a blade seemed to superimpose against Mary Lou's heavily lined forehead, giving her the appearance of having a stylized Z tattooed between her artfully plucked brows.

"Names?" she asked while she listened to the caller on the other end. "IDs."

"Avery Keene and Jared Wynn." Avery provided their identities and slid their licenses across the counter. Mary Lou grabbed the squares of plastic in her free hand with a practiced move. She perused them carefully, then politely excused herself from the call on the phone in her hand and jabbed a button to silence the other, blaring phone.

"Hold, please." The terse instructions were for their benefit. Without further explanation, she turned her swivel stool toward a third phone, which was shoved out of sight beneath the lip of the counter.

"She's here." After a pause, she added in an aggrieved whisper, "No, there's a guy with her." Another pause. "Yes, sir."

She replaced the receiver and handed back their IDs. "Take a seat over there. Someone will be right with you."

Jared led them to the bank of chairs arrayed against a cream-colored wall. On a corkboard on the opposite wall, "wanted" posters competed for space with job descriptions and announcements. He wandered over to the display, while Avery watched him with veiled concern. Despite agreeing to help, Jared seemed to be keeping her at a distance.

Soon, a uniformed officer approached. When he stopped in front of her, she recognized his shoes as the same quiet luxury label favored by a former fellow clerk.

Getting to her feet, she met Jared's gaze, and he crossed to join them. "Detective Howard?" she asked quizzically.

"This is a captain, Avery," Jared corrected mildly. "We've been upgraded."

"I'm the Director of the Special Investigations Division, Captain Calvin Coleman. Detective Howard is out in the field. Why don't we head up to my office?"

Jared and Avery fell into step behind him as he guided them to the elevators, and they boarded. "Detective Howard is sorry he couldn't be here to join you himself."

"We appreciate your taking time to speak with us," Jared said with a sidelong look at Avery. She gave a brief nod of encouragement, and he went on, "What's happened?"

"Crime happened," Captain Coleman joked lamely as they rode up to his floor. "Even in a place like Montgomery County, we have to contend with all kinds of bad actors. We're no Baltimore or D.C., but our jobs keep us jumping. Sad to say."

"Did Detective Howard brief you on why we wanted to speak with him?" Avery inquired as they followed him into his office.

"Because you think we screwed up our jobs, I suspect. Isn't that your MO, Ms. Keene?" he accused. "I'm taking over because we don't intend to become collateral damage in one of your witch hunts. So have a seat."

"I think we've gotten off on the wrong foot." Jared remained standing, his six-foot-one frame a few inches taller than Avery's willowy five eleven. Both of them towered over the captain, who jutted his pugnacious chin at them. "Camasca asked for Avery's help, and I'm here to assist."

Avery quickly assessed Captain Coleman. Similar to that of the waiting area, his office decor primarily boasted "wanted" posters and miscellaneous police fliers, occupying a couple of beige walls that begged for a fresh coat of paint.

More telling was the third wall, which had been adorned with photographs of the captain and the near-famous people he'd met over his career, which she could track by a hairline that receded with each decade. She vaguely recognized a few B-list celebrities or D.C. stars known for their turns on cable television. Clearly, Coleman was a star chaser who thought his badge was shinier than others'. Men like him required deference, an act that would try her patience. But she had a job to do.

"As Jared said, when we spoke with Detective Howard, he told us he could definitely walk us through the Camasca file. He received the necessary forms from the company's attorney, I thought. Solid police work."

"We're one of the best departments in the state," the captain bragged as he came around his desk. "High-profile cases attract the wrong kind of attention."

"We're all on the same side," Avery promised as she took a seat. Jared joined her.

Mollified, Coleman rocked in his chair, dominance established. "Good to hear. I don't mean any disrespect. I like to shoot straight from the hip." He quirked his lip into a slick smile. "Like I said, Tim caught a case and had to miss this confab. But I'm all read in, too. It's not every day we have *the* Avery Keene snooping around one of our closed cases. I personally pulled the information myself." He thumped a slender folder in challenge. "Hit me."

"I wouldn't call it snooping, Captain. As Mr. Freedman explained to the detective, Camasca has engaged my firm to help them prepare for an upcoming opportunity. It would assist us if we understood exactly how the Hibner case was closed so quickly."

Hearing his cue, Jared said, "I read the police report and the analysis shared with Camasca. During my time in the Navy, I performed some military intelligence myself. Your team worked fast. Looks like they took a week to rule the death an accident."

Captain Coleman made a show of flipping through the file. "Fast but thorough. The ME found no foul play. Detective Howard interviewed the other victims and the maintenance crew."

"That's what it says. But what the report doesn't illuminate is how this all led to a young man dying in a state-of-the-art facility. We know what they said happened. Why did MCPD believe it?"

"No reason not to. Says here the cause was likely a tricky mix of gases that Camasca is permitted to have on-site." He stabbed at a sentence highlighted in orange. "Our forensic-science team confirmed what the company said, and what Detective Howard reported. Some malfunction in their laboratories led to cross-contamination in the airflow, and that led to CO poisoning. The victim had asthma, so he succumbed more quickly than his colleagues. We can only thank the Good Lord that they survived."

"According to what we reviewed, MCPD's forensic team was never on campus. They relied on images and specs provided by Camasca," Jared prodded. "Plus, photos from the night that Hibner died taken by Camasca's security footage. Why not conduct a more thorough independent review?"

"We got called in by the hospital, not the company. ME didn't rule foul play, so no reason to waste manpower on a field trip." Captain Coleman kept his affable look steady, but his jaw had tightened. "Camasca is a tremendous company, and we are proud to have Montgomery County serve as their headquarters. They've added quite a lot to our economy, and they are providing world-class service to military veterans over at their new clinic."

"Which is a reason to give them a medal, not a pass," Jared challenged.

The captain visibly bridled. "Hold on there, son. I won't have you impugning my detectives."

"I'm not. But your tech team didn't conduct a basic on-site review or ask to see the computer system."

"To what end?"

"Excuse me?"

"To . . . what . . . end . . . ?" the captain enunciated. "It was an accident."

"To verify your conclusions. Camasca's systems are fully automated and controlled by a central computer core. If a system is run by computer, it is susceptible to tampering."

"Why traumatize his family or aggravate the team over there by turning a tragedy into a spectacle?"

"To get the truth. Which is supposedly your job," Jared muttered.

Avery intervened, "Did Detective Howard ask to interrogate the AI?"

"Excuse me?"

"The artificial intelligence that monitors the system. We saw no record of a request for interview."

The captain guffawed. "I also didn't interview my toaster about why it burned my bread this morning. A machine is only as good as its parts, and nothing in our investigation suggested foul play. Only tragic misfortune."

Jared asked, "Why not interview the maintenance crew, then? They didn't burn your toast."

Captain Coleman scoffed, "Why would anyone want to tamper with the air-conditioning system to kill a computer geek?"

"An investigation would answer that," Jared argued. "Yet, no one was brought in for questioning. No tech team asked to see the system logs in person or check the crime scene."

"Because there was no crime." The captain reared back, the fluorescent light gleaming on his pale, bald pate. "You are getting dangerously close to pissing me off, Mr. Wynn."

"Because I'm asking logical questions?" Jared dug in, reproaching the captain. "Even a first year MP learns the rudimentary inquiries. Who was the victim, and why might someone want him dead?"

"All standard queries in a murder investigation," Coleman rejoined stubbornly. "Which this was not. The ME ruled that the victim was not a victim of foul play. Our investigation followed our protocols to the letter. And I have to be honest, today is the first I'm hearing of dissatisfaction with our work. No one had raised a fuss until you called Detective Howard."

"No one is dissatisfied," Avery quickly interjected, secretly pleased by Jared's antagonism. The sparring gave her a chance to read Coleman's behavior, and something was off. "With all due respect, we were simply surprised by how thin the file was. That's what prompted our visit. We want to understand exactly how the Special Investigations Division reached its conclusion."

"Without reviewing any of the Camasca systems," Jared added.

The captain pursed his lips, and his hand balled into a fist on the desktop. "With hard evidence and not wild conjecture," he sniped in response.

"What evidence?"

"We don't have to go hunting for crimes to keep us busy, Mr. Wynn. Here in Special Investigations, our beat covers the waterfront. Street gangs, joint terrorism, drug interdiction—you name it. We have murderers to chase down. Human traffickers to apprehend." He jutted his chin forward, eyes squinting in distaste at his inquisitors. "Sometimes an accident is just an accident, not a conspiracy. Sorry to disappoint you two. However, based on the evidence, my guys had no choice but to chalk up the asphyxiation death of Elijah Hibner to faulty ventilation. A damned shame, but not a crime."

"Elisha," Avery corrected.

"Excuse me?" For the first time, the captain looked genuinely confused. "What did you say?"

"His name was Elisha, not Elijah. Both Old Testament, but different prophets," she said. "The young man who died was named Elisha. I noticed the name was misspelled in the police report. A simple mistake, but my job is to look out for inconsistencies."

"Of course," Coleman agreed gruffly. "I apologize for the error. I'll make sure Detective Howard has the files updated." Without warning, he shoved back from his desk and stood stiffly. "If that is all, I am late for a meeting with the commander."

Avery and Jared got up, and she extended her hand. After a brief hesitation, he clasped it and gave it a firm shake on the edge of too tight. "We might have a few more questions. Can we reach out to Detective Howard, or should we bring any further inquiries directly to you?"

"Come straight to me. Detective Howard has a number of *open* cases to investigate."

Jared said, "Thank you for your time, Captain. And your candor." Neither man attempted to shake hands. "We'll show ourselves out."

"Good, good." The captain walked them to the door and opened it with a clear message: *Get out.* Aloud, he offered the more cordial "Have a blessed day."

"Thank you, sir," Avery replied sweetly. "Take care."

. . .

Captain Coleman shut his door with a snap and stomped back to his desk. He lifted the receiver on his desk phone and angrily punched in an extension. "Get me the commander."

After a brief pause, Commander Debbie Chen spoke: "Did you take care of it?"

"Yes. I told them they were barking up the wrong tree. Assholes."

"I'm surprised you stood your ground. You have a bit of a problem with star fucking, Calvin. I know you couldn't resist meeting with Keene yourself."

Flushing, he studiously avoided looking at his wall of fame. "You got the same email I did. It had to be done. Regardless, though, I stand behind Detective Howard's work, Commander. The building had a flaw in its ventilation system, and no matter what Frankenstein shit they're cooking up, it got into the air supply. Like I told Keene and Wynn, this was an accident, not a conspiracy."

"Then why in the hell is someone threatening the MCPD?"

"They didn't threaten the MCPD. They threatened you and me." The emails both Coleman and Chen had received revealed their common link as targets, and mutually assured destruction made cautious bedfellows. Captain Coleman planted his elbows on the desk, the phone cradled to his ear. "I may be a star fucker, as you say, Debbie," he conceded, "but I'm damned good police. For someone like Keene, when you're a hammer, everything looks like a nail."

"And blackmail isn't done for kicks. Someone doesn't want us poking around Camasca, and I am willing to let them be. If you're sure it wasn't murder. Or are you too afraid of whatever our extortionist has on you?"

He cringed as he recalled the images snapped at a conference in Las Vegas attached to his version of the email. His paramour, an exotic dancer named Lolly, had sworn she'd never post them anywhere, and his search of social media said she wasn't a liar. But someone had them, and they could end his marriage and take his boat.

"I'm not blowing off a murder over a fling, Commander. Hibner's family might have grounds for a civil case, but we found no proof of criminal negligence. I'd stake my badge on it. We're doing the right thing by not reopening this case."

"Good enough for me, Captain." Her transgression, securing a cushy post for her ex-husband in exchange for their cat and her fair share of community property, seemed like small potatoes. Their text-message exchanges about fudging his background check cast her choice in a dimmer light. "I'll see you at COMSTAT at five p.m. Be prepared to share your analysis with the County Executive. He's anxious that we keep Camasca happy. Rumor has it they're about to pour quite a lot of money into the county coffers, and election season is right around the corner."

FIFTEEN

Jared scanned Avery into the investigation suite. Once inside, he checked his counter-surveillance equipment. Certain that the gadgets—widely regarded internationally as top of the line—were doing their job, he gave Avery an all-clear. She motioned to the others to join her around the conference table in the room's center.

"So—that visit to MCPD was less than useful." Avery recounted the meeting's highlights. "Best-case scenario, the police investigation was superficial because carbon monoxide poisoning happens—even in ultramodern buildings like Camasca. However, Captain Coleman was strangely adamant about not pursuing an investigation. He got mad at Jared for pushing the topic."

"I suppose, from their vantage point, an accident is the most plausible explanation." Ling stared at the reports on the table. "I'd need to see medical information for the other two. To time a murder using CO poisoning triggered by a G6PD deficiency requires—"

"Technological superiority, meticulous planning, and knowing something about Isabella and O.J. that kept them safe," Avery finished.

"But we don't have reason to believe they were spared on purpose," Noah argued. "All we know is that they didn't die."

"I can ask Keh for their medical histories. Normally, hospital records would be very tough. HIPAA rules put strict limits on what can be accessed without a court order. But, given what Camasca collects on a daily basis, they'll know more than an ER."

"Assuming no one tampered with those records, too," Noah cautioned.

"One problem at a time," Avery acknowledged. "MCPD should have caught this themselves. I can't tell if it's sloppiness or incompetence."

Jared nodded. "And I'm still bumping against the fact that we met with the head of the division instead of the lead detective who did the actual investigation."

"You don't believe that he was called away?" Noah asked. "Since my role today is to play devil's advocate, a police detective being out on a call sounds plausible. Particularly if you're coming to ask them about a matter that they consider closed."

"True, but, Noah, if you couldn't make a meeting, would the most senior partner in the group step in to handle it for you?"

"No, not normally," he granted. "But let's remember, things are a little different when Avery is asking questions. Last time that happened, lots of important people lost their jobs. You're a double-edged sword, my friend. For government types, you're downright dangerous."

"Which will make getting any more help from MCPD much more difficult."

"We'll focus on what we can learn without them," Jared said. "Today was a fishing expedition for both of us. They got to figure out what you want from them, and we learned that they might be hiding something."

"Jared, you should look into Captain Coleman," Avery reasoned. "Either rule him out as having an ulterior motive or cross him off our list."

"Will do." He studied the board. "I'd like to talk to the ventilation technicians working that week. I know Keh gave us a detailed overview, but one of them might have seen something."

Crossing to the board by her desk, Avery added the suggestions to the witness list. "Send a request to Freedman. He can get us an interview. While you're at it, see what else you can learn about the delay in notification from Kawak. How did it miss so much?"

"On it."

"What did y'all learn in our absence?" Avery checked her watch. "It's almost six o'clock. I assume you've cracked this investigation wide open, and we can knock off early."

"Sounds like my cue to disappoint you," Noah said, lifting a Redweld from the seat beside him with a flourish. The maroon carrier was stuffed with folders and arrayed with colored tabs. Noah dropped the papers with a satisfying thunk on the conference table. "Behold! Because, while you all took a scenic trip to suburban Maryland to study medical files, I burrowed my way into the corporate records of Camasca."

"*We* burrowed *our* way," Ling emended. "But I'll let him do the boring stuff first."

Ignoring her, he asked, "Jared, can you give me a new screen?"

When the blank wall appeared, Noah called up a diagram that quickly filled the entire space. Color-coded and dynamic, the image seemed to pulse. "Yes, the circles and squares are moving," he explained with barely restrained excitement. "I found this AI tool in the Camasca laptop that took my spreadsheet and converted it. We don't have these toys at Lowry Kihneman."

Suddenly chagrined, he asked, "Wait, that's okay, right? We're good with using their tech?"

Avery and Jared nodded simultaneously. She jabbed a rueful thumb at the high-tech whiteboard. "We're cautious. We're not Luddites. We can play with their toys—just be careful about sharing what we learn."

Relieved, Noah focused on the screen. "This isn't news to anyone around here, but I doubt they've seen it laid out quite this way. I've constructed a map of Camasca and all the main players, including staff, partners, vendors, you name it."

"Very thorough," Avery commented, skimming the names. Most were unfamiliar, but a few caught her by surprise. "I'd say these are very strange bedfellows. Hollywood moguls and Silicon Valley bros aren't usually in bed with Big Pharma and Wall Street financiers, are they?"

Noah highlighted the segment Avery had homed in on. "What does anyone here know about SPACs?"

Jared volunteered, "I've invested in a few of them." When the team looked at him, he expounded, "In cybersecurity, you get to know folks. And if you know the right people, they will invite you to participate before a company goes public, hoping you'll invite *them* if you get the chance on another deal. It's the ultimate insider ring."

"Right. In my practice, we are constantly setting up vehicles to help the wealthy move their money, and one way is to help a company go public without all the fuss. Enter the SPAC." Noah came around to the screen. "I'll skip the details on how a SPAC differs from a traditional IPO, unless anyone wants a tutorial on corporate finance." He checked with his colleagues, who shook their heads, except for one. "Of course, Avery and Jared know about them . . ."

"Nerds," Ling whispered in a faux sneeze. "I know how to play Monopoly, so there."

Jared shrugged off the insult, and Avery rolled her eyes. "Good for you. Please proceed, Noah."

"The relevant information is that a SPAC circumvents most of the hurdles and disclosures an IPO requires, but with the same result. A wealthy company gets access to more capital in the public markets by merging with a shell company created for precisely that purpose."

"Is that illegal?" Ling asked. "Why allow them to hide?"

"They're not hiding. They're just short-circuiting the process and setting their own price. Usually, SPAC targets are moderately successful companies that require a considerable infusion of capital, and they want to set their own terms. In a perfect world, they skip some pesky hurdles, go public, and start collecting money from everyone with a trading account and a dream."

"Camasca already has $2.5 billion in the bank," Avery recapped the absurd number for Noah and herself. "They should be able to simply go public the normal way."

"Ah, but that's why we have our interesting map of friends. Camasca is a freaking gold mine. The SPAC is the first shot this tangled web of rich folks have at owning a part of Rafe's domain. Because our boss, Rafe Diaz, has somehow managed to keep sixty-three percent of his company, despite raising all that money."

"How?" Jared asked, stunned. "Venture-capital firms usually cram down founders so far, they are lucky to hold on to ten or twenty percent of the company. How in the world did he keep so much control?"

"Diaz pulled off a hat trick," Noah explained. "One, he used federal grants from DARPA and DoD to do his initial research. Two, he bootstrapped his financing by taking on contracts with other firms. He gave them services, but always retained his work product."

"And three?"

"Patents." Noah dragged out a second sheaf of papers. "Every single one of these patents is in Rafe Diaz's name. Some have co-inventors, but he owns or co-owns every one. Which means that, for a VC, the company isn't worth much without his intellectual property. He had them over a barrel. Would you want to have a ten-percent stake in Microsoft or the lightbulb—or zero?"

Avery processed Noah's explanation of who had a financial stake in Camasca. He'd identified those who wanted a piece of the action, but that left another pool of potentially unhappy adversaries. "Freedman told us Rafe and Camasca co-own the patents."

"He's using *co-ownership* very liberally, it seems. My research shows Rafe holds the majority of them outright."

"What about his co-inventors? How much do they own? And who might think they're entitled to more credit?"

"I need to dig deeper, but I had the same thought. A bunch of his current or former colleagues might not be the direct beneficiaries of a public-company transaction, and they have reason to believe they're entitled to a bigger piece."

"That's not a small number. He's got more than three hundred employees who could be feeling left out, and that doesn't include anyone else he's collaborated with along the way," Jared mused.

"Perhaps, but the guy is canny. I skimmed the employee stock-option plan, and it is incredibly generous. Especially for those who are his co-inventors on a patent—they won't hit the lottery, but they'll see a nice-sized check. The longer you've been with Diaz, or the more you've contributed, the more you stand to gain when they go public. He pays employees a generous salary, but their stock vests on an annual basis—instantly for co-inventors. There's no holding out for five or ten years before you see a piece of the action."

"He knows how to buy loyalty."

"But if I've learned anything from more than a decade of handling contested wills for the rich, getting a nice inheritance isn't the same as having it all. Some folks can't be satisfied unless they get everything."

"Fair point." Jared pointed to the Redweld by Noah's elbow. "You find anything in the paperwork that would give someone a reason to be resentful?"

"I'd say yes. Diaz is brilliant and generous, but he didn't produce 1,114 patentable ideas. Instead, Camasca contracts all include an obligation that Diaz be listed on each patent, regardless of his actual scientific contribution. Plus, all patent rights are assigned to Camasca, except for his. Anything Rafe designed alone is his to keep—which includes the original patent for Kawak."

Noah made his big reveal, as the reality dawned on the rest of the team. Jared summed it up for the class: "If he's on all patents, and no patent rights can be assigned to Camasca if he's the sole inventor, then potential inventors have no claim to the underlying technology."

Dumbfounded, Ling asked, "Why would anyone agree to this? Especially DARPA and DoD."

Noah inclined his head toward Avery, knowing she'd already figured it out. He'd had to use LexisNexis, but she'd known the answer instantly.

"The Bayh-Dole Act of 1980."

Noah nodded like a proud parent and motioned her to proceed.

She explained, "Under the Bayh-Dole Act, universities and private companies have the right to patent and commercialize discoveries from government-funded research without sharing the proceeds with the federal government."

"Go on," Noah prompted.

"Rafe Diaz launches Camasca with government funding, creates the main tech himself, and grows the business by selling services. Then he captures all of the proceeds. He shares just enough credit for co-inventors to partner with him, and government financing doesn't care—they can't own his technology. Over time, no one can afford to reject his terms without risking being shut out of an AI revolution. So, when funds run low, he sells off some equity, until he's too big to fail."

"Precisely."

"That's brilliant," Jared said with stunned admiration. "At the negotiation table, he holds every card."

"Kudos to him," echoed Avery as she studied the web of investors and partners described by Noah's map. Billions lay at their feet, but all subject to the whims of one man who preached an egalitarian ethic but hoarded the cash and the credit. "So Rafe Diaz has constructed a perfect system . . . where, no matter who loses, he will win."

The three looked at her as the statement hung in the silence.

"Creating a line of potential enemies, and a ton of questions we need to answer," Noah chimed in. "Like I said, I've had clients go ballistic with fewer zeroes at stake."

There was the extremely remote possibility that the AI system truly had a vendetta against the Camasca team, but Avery knew the more pedestrian options seemed eminently more likely.

Jealousy. Greed. Revenge. Anger.

These were the basic motives that fueled stupid decisions, and one of them was sure to be operating here.

"The question, then," she asked the group, "is who on this list might not want to play nice, because they think Rafe Diaz screwed them over?"

SIXTEEN

A ping sounded in the room, and everyone checked their Camasca tablets. "It's for me," Jared said. "Keh arranged for me to meet the technicians. Ling, you want to come with me or dive deeper into the exciting world of finance?"

Ling scrambled up with comic haste. "Let's go."

Left with Noah, Avery said, "You want to dive back into your corporate pool?"

"My friend, this is an ocean, and I am Ahab." He gathered his materials and returned to his station.

With a quiet laugh, Avery moved to her area and picked a clean board. Recalling an essay on problem solving she'd read in college, she lifted the marker and wrote "Why?" at the top. The Five Whys, the theory went, allowed the investigator to determine the root cause of any issue.

Problem: Dr. Elisha Hibner is dead.

First Why: Ventilation malfunction killed him.

Second Why: Someone tampered with the system. Or the system spontaneously malfunctioned.

Third Why: ???

Avery studied the board and her scribblings. All she had for certain was the First Why. Sloppy police work and a suspicious absence of evidence made the second one harder to pin down. She could only hope Jared and Ling would return with new information to allow her to cross off one cause or the other.

Forty-five minutes later, the duo trooped into the suite, their expressions somber.

"What did you find out?" Avery took her position at the conference table, and the others gathered.

"The team echoed what Keh told us," Jared explained, a hip propped on the table's edge. "No alarm bells, no sensor-malfunction reports. Nothing."

"These people know the system. Over eight years, they haven't found a record of another failure like this," Ling added. "But they were able to walk me through the air interflow mix and show us where the amounts are calibrated."

"And?" Avery prompted. "You both look worried."

"The lead technician who oversees the system is missing," Ling blurted out.

"Missing?"

"Gone." Jared slanted Ling a chiding look. "He went on vacation the week after being interviewed by MCPD. Later, HR got an email indicating he'd resigned his post. No one has heard from him since."

"Did Camasca investigate?"

Ling shook her head. "Team said he was a loner. Tristan Spencer. Younger guy, mid-thirties, immigrated to the DMV. His employment file indicates he's a naturalized citizen from Mali, and he left no forwarding address. His last paycheck and accrued leave were direct-deposited."

"I'd like to see his file."

"Already in your inboxes," Jared told her. "Sometimes, you're very predictable."

"Don't get too comfortable," she teased, as notification for the file appeared on her tablet. She quickly skimmed the contents. "Noah, did he forfeit his shares from the employee stock option plan?"

"According to my cap table, no. He vested his stock in the ESOP, but he never cashed out. He's got a nice windfall coming for him if the deal closes."

"With that kind of payday coming, he might pop up again as the deal gets closer to closing." Jared headed to the witness list. "I'll run a trace on him. If he used his passport or hasn't touched his credit cards, we'll know."

A rapping sounded at the door, and every head whipped toward it.

"Guys," Avery reproached as she answered the knock. Rafe Diaz stood on the other side.

"I know it's a day late, but thought I'd come and check on you all. Sorry I couldn't make the welcome tour."

"Your team took good care of us." Avery adjusted her sweater, her hand rising to touch her hair before dropping. "Dr. Diaz. I mean Rafe," she corrected when he arched a brow. "Come, meet the team." She returned to the table, "This is—"

"I do my homework, Avery," he said. "Dr. Ling Yin, graduate of Oberlin College and Yale Medical School, ABD at Johns Hopkins."

Ling rose and sketched a mock curtsy. "At your service."

"Noah and I met on Monday, though Glen under-reported your achievements. One of the youngest partners at Lowry Kihneman, and quite the jazz drummer, according to him."

He shrugged at his startled colleagues. "I have a mysterious side, too."

Rafe crossed over to Jared, who remained near Avery's station. "We didn't have a chance to meet when you worked on our security system, Lieutenant Wynn. I understand you've launched your own firm. It's getting great reviews in the cybersecurity world."

"Good to hear," Jared confirmed as they shook hands. Irritation pricked at him, but courtesy and military training won out. "Nothing as impressive as what you've built here, Major."

"Give it time," Rafe encouraged. "You'll move mountains, especially with someone as talented as Avery in your corner." His grip on Jared's hand tightened for a microsecond. Looking at the others, he asked, "You've had a full day's work, and according to that board and the reports I've been getting, you've made a lot of headway. Does anyone have any questions?"

"Hundreds," Ling volunteered. Her gaze darted between Rafe and Avery, then over to Jared, who was more reserved than usual. She could guess why, but she preferred the scientific method of inquiry. Smiling at Rafe, she asked, "Do you have time to sit for a few minutes—right here at this massive table, perhaps?"

"Of course."

Adroitly, Ling arranged the seating to put herself between Rafe and Jared, with Noah on the other side. Avery settled diagonal to their host and in Ling's line of sight. "We got the whirlwind tour and Avery's download, but I'd like to understand more about what Kawak and Milo actually do."

"To put it simply, Kawak runs the operation, and Milo runs the clinic," he explained, repeating what he'd told Avery. "Kawak is the neural network that operates all of the components. Technically, Milo is a software tool and chatbot that takes medical record keeping, and aggregated data mining and collection, and combines them with predictive analytics to assist our health-care providers in a state-of-the-art clinic. Like Yax and Keh, Milo is dependent on Kawak for information, but it has autonomous operational control that Yax and Keh lack."

"Is Milo here at Camasca, too?" Ling asked.

"Yes and no. Again, think of your digital assistant on your phone or the smart home speaker at your house. Same interface, different locations. Milo can exist wherever we install it, but, given its trial use and sophistication, Milo's interface is exclusively operating at the VA clinic and in our on-site medical research facilities here on campus. Kawak can manage its access remotely. The entire system is linked via a proprietary satellite connection and Wi-Fi."

"Helps to be in business with the Defense Department," Jared noted dryly.

"Yes, it does," Rafe replied without rancor. "I am grateful for the support, and the DoD is excited about what Kawak can do for our military and for our nation." Returning his attention to Ling, he pulled out his device, slightly larger than a smartphone. With a few clicks, a building appeared on their screens.

"We've housed Milo at InnoVAI, on Bethesda Naval Hospital's campus. We specialize in veterans with complex medical histories or limited access to consistent care. I understand you did a rotation there, Dr. Yin."

"I did, and that description you gave would apply to most VA patients," Ling said.

"It does. Which is why Milo is revolutionary. When fully deployed, Milo will be able to access genomic data, medical records, mental-health records, military service history, and job history. In fact, due to the effect of epigenetics, we expanded Kawak's parameters to include criminal records, credit reports, social-media posts, even voting records. Anything to help us develop a whole-patient profile."

Unwillingly intrigued, Jared asked, "Kawak is a transformer neural network?"

"Transformer and convolutional," Rafe affirmed. "With a bit of radial basis function thrown in, among other models."

"Meaning you're not going to tell me exactly how Kawak's network functions," Jared accepted with grudging admiration. "I guess I'll wait for the patent."

Hearing the veiled reference to Noah's report, Avery shot him a quelling look, which Jared ignored. "To receive treatment, a vet has to give InnoVAI blanket permission for all of their known data. Given how hard it is to get access to quality health care, do they do so willingly, or is it tacit coercion?"

"Fair question," Rafe responded. "We can serve clients who decline to allow the full range of InnoVAI supports, but no one has asked. We explain that, with their permission, for example, we use their data to give a physician a probability score that links to the best treatments. Milo functions as intake, and it can give our support staff scripts to use to speak with clients. We've found in our research that when Milo participates the patient is more likely to comply with treatments based on neuro-cognitive conditioning."

"How'd you train the AI? Successful alignment on eliminating racism and sexism and the rest of the isms strikes me as highly improbable. Your team is complicating the matter by also asking AI to determine which sordid bits of personal history matter in obtaining quality health care?"

"The Tiger Team leads a platoon of extraordinary scientists, and our mission isn't complicated. Implementation is. Something you know quite a bit about, given your work in naval intelligence." Rafe cocked his head at the younger man, his temper flaring, then quickly extinguished. "At Camasca, we don't get overwhelmed by the complexity of implementation as long as we keep our objective front and center. Perhaps that's just an Army philosophy. You sailors are cut from a different cloth."

Rafe deliberately shifted his attention to Avery. "As I told your fearless leader when we first met, at InnoVAI, we leverage all of the information we can gather on a patient, his environment, family history, and any other scintilla of insight, if it means they get the fastest, most effective treatment."

"Such as?" Ling asked.

"Once we've reached a treatment plan, we synthesize personalized medications with our pharmacology team and partners, devise novel medical treatments, and even predict what might be next." He flipped another chart onto the screen. "With that data, we can extrapolate what it might mean for a similar patient population—one that served in the same theater or are clustered in the same geographic region. Plus, we can also deliver personalized medicine that can be catered to the particular illness or pathologies, down to the genetic level."

"How exactly are you integrating epigenetics into what you can do in a medical clinic? Epigenetics is a big part of my dissertation topic."

"I'd like to read it, when you're done," Rafe requested. "The system—Kawak as the network and Milo as the processing agent—can track any reported changes or events. It then will assess how a disease is progressing, and the risk to the patient over time. We believe it will help us develop personalized medications that target exactly the symptoms and markers to cure that specific patient. As a bonus, it also can be used to help inform other social factors—like if the veteran needs housing vouchers or job placement.

"Lieutenant Wynn and I both know how chaotic being in the service is. Imagine you have been in the Marines for twenty-five years. Multiple tours across four continents. Suddenly, you've been diagnosed with stage-two lung cancer. Advances in genomics mean that you could be eligible for precision oncology. Yet, according to the files they have for you at the VA, there's no mention of your short stint in Kazakhstan on an emergency relief mission, where you inhaled asbestos for nine weeks. The records got destroyed by a flood in some base warehouse."

"Milo has all of that?" Ling asked.

"Kawak does, and Milo knows to go looking for it. Through compiling and combining the millions of data points about you in the ether, InnoVAI will send you to the right specialist, give them a genomic profile related to your diagnosis, and point out what might impede your treatment and recovery. We get this right and we'll be treating veterans and active-duty military, and anticipating future medical needs based on individual experiences. Our tech, in the field and at home. Seamless care from enlistment to retirement and beyond."

"Will this—" Noah began, but Rafe's watch beeped insistently.

He tapped the screen and shook his head. "I'm sorry, guys. Duty calls. Thanks again for showing up and diving in so fast. Let's do this again." He briskly shook hands with everyone and got to his feet. "Avery, can you walk with me?"

"Sure." She followed him into the corridor. "How can I help?"

"Glen Paul told me that you'd like to interview Isabella and O.J. immediately. I'd consider it a personal favor if you'd give them a bit more breathing space. Losing Elisha hit us all, but they were under incredible strain even before the accident."

"They were essential to almost every facet of what you're asking me to review. I can give them a bit more time, but not much," she warned.

"Talk to their teams first, at least. Then interview them. Perhaps by video call?"

"In person. Separately. A critical part of investigation is getting separate witness statements. About the accident and about Camasca." She firmed her mouth. "Like I told Freedman, this is nonnegotiable."

"You win," he conceded. Rafe cupped her shoulder for a split second. "Thanks for being accommodating. I won't forget it."

As he vanished around the corner, Avery remained still, trying to decipher the brief touch and the tension that awakened in her. But her thoughts skittered away, unwilling to engage. She was happy to oblige. Dismissing the disquietude, she reentered the suite.

No one had moved from their positions around the table. "It's been a long day. And we have another one tomorrow—we'll be interviewing the teams that worked with O.J., Isabella, and Elisha."

"Their teams?" Jared asked, surprised. "I thought we were going to try and see O.J., at least."

"That's what Rafe wanted to discuss. He asked me to give them more time, and I agreed."

"Why?"

"Because we have plenty of background research and evidence gathering to do in the meantime. Your list is getting pretty long."

"Hey, I have a serious question," Noah interjected. "Am I the only one weirded out by how intrusive this AI is?"

"I'm not," Ling replied quickly. "What Diaz described would meet actual, critical needs. Sure, it's intrusive, but if it saves lives, most of my patients would gladly sacrifice a modicum of privacy for another birthday."

"Noah has a point, though," Jared inserted. "As a vet, I'd be grateful for the care, but let's be honest. We have a private enterprise that owns quantum computing systems with the aspirational ability to access all the known data in the world. With no obligation to share what they learn. No responsibility to abide by any regulations on what they do with that knowledge."

Noah pointed emphatically. "What he said."

"And I'm even more concerned with the decision to access restricted information like criminal history and voting records. How can knowing I got arrested for shoplifting help you treat my rheumatoid arthritis? Instead, it might undermine the quality of care. A doctor making moral judgments about who they treat is a terrifying possibility, and contrary to what Camasca promises."

"Or it could save your life," Ling pushed back. "Shoplifting could be symptomatic of mental-health challenges, such as PTSD or depression. Let's say your doctor knows about your sticky fingers and that you are a super-voter. Your spouse calls about how suddenly you're ranting online about a candidate you used to revere and you get suspended from work for stealing from a co-worker.

"Separately, these are troubling, and the angry politics could be dismissed as a sign of the times. Instead, now Milo can analyze the veteran's mental-health data and check self-reported symptoms and other discordant behavioral patterns. Rather than being dismissed as a thief or a conspiracy junkie, a vet instead receives mental-health-care treatment tailored to their experiences, and the change in behaviors gets a closer look that could save his job or his life."

"Avery? You haven't weighed in," said Noah. "You rarely lack for an opinion."

"I haven't made up my mind," she admitted. "The law barely acknowledges a right to privacy as it is. For women in half the country, the Supreme Court ruled it a constitutional fiction."

The group sat quietly, waiting for her to continue.

"The reality is, AI is coming, folks . . . be it Camasca or another company. Perhaps the moment requires a company like this to show our concern for actual people and save their lives. I think about Rita, and what might have happened if an AI had seen more than a junkie and realized she had a treatable mental-health disorder. Something she could have inherited from either parent."

"My point precisely," Ling agreed.

Avery deflected, "I'm not siding with anyone yet. Ask me again in a week." She scooted away from the table and returned to her desk to begin packing up. Sliding her arms into her coat, she asked, "Ling, can I get a ride home? My car is acting up."

"I can take you home," Jared said, his gravelly voice tight. "We can head out when you're ready."

Ling gave him warning smile, one that clearly took sides. "I've got her, Jared. It's on my way."

"Wanna tell me what's going on?" Ling asked as they exited the parking structure.

"I would if I knew." Shutting her eyes, Avery tipped her head against the seat. Today had been a good day. Productive. Efficient. Confusing. She angled her face so she could peer out the window. A sensation akin to guilt gnawed at her, but she forced it away. Finding Rafe compelling and being frustrated with Jared were entirely separate and distinct issues. Neither of which was primary. After a few minutes of cycling thoughts that led nowhere, she leaned forward and jabbed the display panel on Ling's dash. The navigation app opened, and she typed in a destination.

The onboard assistant confirmed, "14852 Parkland Trace, Rockville, Maryland."

As the GPS processed the coordinates, Ling gave her a confused look. "Last time I checked, Rockville was in the opposite direction of D.C. This is definitely *not* on my way."

"A seventeen-minute detour. I'll buy you dinner."

"You'll buy me gas," Ling warned, but she dutifully obeyed the dulcet-toned instructions. The shabby suburban neighborhood had a cluster of neat single-story homes, each marked by a carefully tended lawn. Except one that had clear signs of neglect. Grass grew in uneven patches, untouched by a mower. Weeds poked up through the cracked walkway, and a light film of pollen dusted the front door. Parking alongside the curb, Ling studied the unkempt house in growing suspicion. "Who lives here?"

"A friend."

"A friend?"

"Yes. Um, Carrie from work." Avery shifted to surreptitiously slide her hand into the bag at her feet. "I wanted to check on her—haven't been by in a while."

"Someone from your firm lives here?"

Her searching fingers closed around the slim kit she kept with her at all times out of habit. She shrugged at Ling's question. "This is the address I have."

Scowling, Ling contended, "I thought I knew all of your friends. At least ninety percent of them are working on this case."

"Very funny." She grinned at her while she palmed a leather-bound case, keeping it out of Ling's sight. "I'll be right back."

Ling looked at her quizzically. "What were you looking for in your bag?"

"What?" She offered a confused smile. "What do you mean?"

Cocking her head, Ling said firmly, "Just now, you reached into your bag."

Her confused smile widened. "Oh, I got her a card, but I guess I left it in the office." She pressed the kit to her side and reached for the door handle. "Wait here. I'll only be a minute," Avery promised, and jumped from the vehicle.

Plastering on a polite smile, she slowly approached the front door as she scoped the area. None of the neighbors' doors bore the tell-tale signs of digital security. At the front door, take-out menus and advertisements had been tucked into the doorjamb or under the mat. Seeing no bell or security camera on the target door, she tugged on the gloves in her coat pocket. First, she thumped on the inset window. Getting no response, she used her fist to bang on the door in a hard staccato. "Mr. Spencer?"

Avery pressed her ear to the door, but heard no sounds. She reached for the knob and turned. Locked. She angled her body, blocking her hands from view. With deft motions, she removed her picks and made quick work of the lock. The latch gave way, and she pushed lightly. She stuck her head inside. "Mr. Spencer. Tristan Spencer?"

Nudging the door farther, she entered.

Pushing the door shut behind her, Avery quickly scanned the living room. Dust motes floated in the air, which smelled stale. No one had been inside in a while. Quickly, she cased the house, realizing she had only a few minutes before Ling got suspicious. She methodically checked the empty bedrooms and single bath, then she peeked into the fridge. An unopened beer and an abandoned bottle of mustard stared back.

The house gave no signs of life. And, as far as she could tell, no signs of a struggle. Most importantly, no dead body. She had no idea where Tristan Spencer had gone, but he definitely wasn't here.

Satisfied, she headed for the front door. Stealthily, she backed onto the stoop.

Appearing behind her, Ling yanked her clear of the front door and reached past to slam it closed. "What in the world are you doing?"

Incensed, Avery spun on her. "Investigating?"

"From where I sat—in the getaway car—it looked like breaking and entering."

"Excuse me?"

Ling reached for her hand and flipped it over, the familiar brown case in her grip. "Dammit, Avery."

"We were here, so I took a quick look around."

"You tricked me. Lied to me." Though Avery had half a foot on her, Ling frog-marched her to the Prius. "Get in," she snapped.

"I didn't lie. And we won't get caught. There was no digital security," Avery said, pouting, once Ling joined her in the car. "I simply checked out an abandoned house. He could have been inside hurt—or worse."

"You don't have a warrant. Or probable cause. Or a badge," she chastised as she drove them away. "I'm not a lawyer, but I've watched enough *Law & Order* to know that if one of the neighbors saw you slip inside and called the police, you telling them you're an internal investigator for a law firm would not be a valid defense."

"Fine. But I didn't get caught. So this post hoc interrogation is irrelevant."

"Irrelevant? You risked me, too. This is not your job. If you're that worried about the missing AV technician, make an anonymous call and request a wellness check. Especially since you left his front door unlocked."

"Not by choice."

"You mean like I didn't choose to be an accessory to a B and E tonight? Tough shit."

Avery slunk against the seat and turned her head toward the window. When Ling reached Avery's apartment, she gathered her satchel. "Thanks for the ride."

"Uh-huh."

"Good night."

SEVENTEEN

Wednesday, April 14

Hedging her bets against the recent groans of Oscar's aging transmission, Avery ordered a rideshare to bring her to the Camasca campus. The gang was already assembled at the conference table. Someone had picked up coffee and pastries, including her favorite, an apple fritter. Given the chilly reception she received from Jared and the side eye from Ling as she took her seat, she made the educated guess that the treats were courtesy of Noah.

To break the ice, she grabbed her fritter and said, "I see we're ready to go."

Ling mockingly raised her hand. "I'm trying to stay in my lane. Therefore, if I can have everyone's attention, I have a line of inquiry for us to consider. Yesterday you asked who would have reason to hate Rafe Diaz . . ."

On cue, the chart Noah had devised yesterday appeared on the screen. "Meet Dee Patrick of Arclight Biomed . . . and Paschal Donohoe, CEO of Galway Pharmaceuticals."

"Arclight Biomed?" Jared repeated. "The pharmaceutical company that could buy and sell Camasca ten times over?"

"Which is what I told Ling when she mentioned her idea this morning." Noah used his implement to draw a bright-red circle around the two names. "Ling's got a theory about why a company with a market cap of seventy billion dollars would potentially have it out for Camasca."

"It's a viable theory," Ling argued. "Arclight and Galway are both custom-drug fabricators. But Arclight is a household name, and they've not been getting the best press lately. Some say they're in the business of disease mongering." Ling wrote the words out in block letters on her tablet, underlining them for emphasis. "Dee Patrick took the helm of Arclight about six years ago, and since then, they've been on a tear to increase their market share by any means necessary." Before Noah could say anything, she said, "I may not be conversant in SPACs, but I do know Big Pharma. Dee Patrick has a reputation for being cutthroat and mean, and she'll pick your pocket and blame you for not having enough lint."

"You really don't like her," he commented.

"I don't like what she's doing to medicine. Dee Patrick is like the pharma bros who use their control over medications to squeeze every dollar from the average patient. She's a special case, though. Dee Patrick has been specifically reprimanded by watchdogs for being a pioneer in pushing drugs for diseases that aren't really diseases. Haven't you noticed the number of new acronyms for conditions you'd never heard about before? Until a commercial describes your exact issue and the wonder drug that now treats it?"

Murmurs of acknowledgment spurred her on. "Arclight made it central to their business model. A massive pharmaceutical company with a library of medications and not enough users. To close the market gap, they basically sponsor diseases to match symptoms, get some doctors to peddle the idea, and add a layer of fear by giving it an official name that sounds like it'll kill you if left untreated."

"Son of a bitch," Noah remarked bitterly. "Both of my parents have been on new regimens, courtesy of a miracle diagnosis and a treatment manufactured by Arclight. There's no such thing as gluten-based lactose intolerance, is there?"

Ling patted his hand. "I'm telling you, they're printing money. Number two: While that's happening, Arclight has been quietly removing drugs from the shelves or jacking up prices. Most for diseases in non-Western economies where people are poor and there's no profit margin. Civil-rights and human-rights organizations have noted how Arclight can't seem to find a way to help in those areas."

Jared thought of his own father, who had a real disease that had been passed on to him. Neither of them had held out hope for a cure, because too few people had been diagnosed with the disease. The biotech company GenWorks and its merger partner, Advar, had been working on a solution. He'd be livid if they had an answer but refused to produce it because the patient base was too small. And yet, although he could understand outrage, Ling's theory seemed to strain for credulity. "What's the intersection with Camasca?" he pressed.

"Arclight has two strikes, right? Here's strike three. A couple of months ago, an online medical journal published an anonymous paper that accused Arclight and a few other companies of being the key sources of iatrogenic illnesses." She pulled up the link. "Iatrogenic illnesses are conditions actually caused by receiving medical care, such as a prescription drug, a medical procedure, or an environmental event. Combine that with how Arclight has been ramping up drug use with their medicalizing of common sicknesses, and the authors say they are among the worst offenders. The PR campaign against them is gaining traction and moving into the mainstream. PoliticsNOW did a segment on it last week. So, in the near future, Arclight could be screwed."

Avery perked up. "You think they see Camasca as a possible solution?"

"Yes, indeed. Think about it. Good press from a partnership with a golden company like Camasca to drown out bad press about their misdeeds bilking the public and Noah's parents."

"I bow to your superior suspicions, Ling," Noah responded, "but there's a gaping hole in your whodunit. Two years ago, and again last year, Arclight made a bid to be involved with the InnoVAI project with Camasca—and got rebuffed both times."

"Which is why I put Dee Patrick on the list of people who might hate Rafe. She thinks she's got a way to rehab her reputation and help her company, but Rafe Diaz won't let her play. You said it yourself, yesterday. Some people want all the marbles."

"I agree," Noah offered, "except Dee Patrick is still connected to Camasca. Instead of being a partner, Arclight became an investor. Seems a bit weird to go after Camasca when you put in your company's own money."

"Yes, it's big hole," Ling retorted defensively, "but I thought Sherlock Holmes said to look at everything."

"I'm not sure Sherlock ever said that," Noah murmured.

Glaring, she continued, "The question was who would have reason to hate Rafe Diaz. I would argue that Arclight does, because Dee Patrick is desperate to be in league with them. I'm not saying that they go to the top of the list, but they are a candidate worthy of our scrutiny."

"It's a stretch, but nothing is off the table for now," Avery cut in. "They could fit the theory of sabotage. Let's put it in the parking lot for now."

Slightly appeased, Ling continued, "Arclight is absolutely terrible, and I stand by my animosity. However, guess who won the Camasca lottery and was granted the Arclight-coveted contract to produce custom medications for InnoVAI? It was Galway Pharmaceuticals."

"This idea carries more water," Noah conceded.

"Why Galway versus Arclight?" Jared asked.

"Paschal Donohoe has made millions on compounding medications, and this deal with Camasca would catapult him into the big leagues," Ling explained.

"I thought compounding was just like filling a prescription," Avery said. "How do you make millions with a limited customer base?"

"Find a built-in customer base in the market for a very personalized, bespoke prescription," Ling replied. "Exactly what Camasca is promising with their new AI. If they can corner the market on compounded, personalized medicine, Donohoe will be filthy rich. Or filthier rich."

"Then why would he kill one of the geese laying golden eggs?" Jared posited. "I don't see it."

The potential for Arclight to be involved, after being rejected by Camasca, briefly made sense, Avery thought. But, like that idea, Donohoe also seemed like a stretch. Though she appreciated Ling's enthusiasm, medical mysteries weren't the same as legal investigations. Gingerly, not wanting to pile on, she questioned, "Why would there be a risk associated with Donohoe and Camasca? Seems like a perfect match."

"Until it isn't." Ling retook control of the board. "Remember that scandal a few years ago when the FDA had to recall a batch of drugs from a Massachusetts pharmacy because they gave patients meningitis?"

Jared shot her a look. "Pretend we don't. What happened?"

Making a face, she explained, "Back in 2012, the New England Compounding Center shipped out a batch of steroids—methylprednisolone acetate—to surgery centers, nursing homes, and pain clinics up and down the East Coast and as far away as California and Idaho." The blank looks from her friends forced Ling to pop up, head over to an empty glass screen, and begin drawing. "Doctors write prescriptions for medications that the FDA has verified as safe. But think of it like getting a hot dog."

She scrawled squiggly lines across the oblong shapes she'd scribbled. "Sometimes, you want chili or onions. Or maybe you're vegan, and you order a tofu dog instead."

"I'm getting hungry," muttered Noah. "And not at all enlightened."

"Compounding takes the basic meds and then adds or adapts as the doctor requests. Giving you the hot dog your doctor prescribes."

"How does this hot dog get us to Idaho?" Noah asked, genuinely confused. "Plus, remind me never to play Pictionary with you."

She circled the hot dog a few times. "The pharmacist in Massachusetts doing the compounding cut a bunch of corners. The equipment wasn't properly sterilized. The facility used expired meds. The guy even hired blacklisted techs to help him evade the rules."

Ling dotted the glass over and over with marks. "Eighteen different fungal strains made it into several batches of his compounds, and they were injected directly into the spinal cords of multiple patients. Sixty-four people died across nine states, and the CEO went to prison."

"He was a murderer. You'd put Galway Pharmaceuticals into the same category?" asked Avery. "Why?"

"Oh, I'm not. I have absolutely no evidence at all," Ling blithely admitted. "But if we're going to get our full amateur sleuthing on, I say we look into Arclight *and* Galway Pharmaceuticals. Two sides of the same very lucrative coin."

Avery studied the board. "Galway gave Camasca the ability to test its whole-medicine idea without getting in bed with a much larger partner. I'm not seeing it."

"I'm, shockingly, with Ling," Noah countered. "I think Donohoe is worth checking out. Galway is a private company, which means there's not much in the public domain on their financials. But for a partnership this size, due diligence says we need to understand all the players."

Ling nodded in agreement. "Galway has made a name for itself as a compounding company that doesn't ask too many questions. They serve reputable facilities, but I've heard whispers."

She looked to Avery and added, "The other night, you told us that our jobs would be to investigate everything and ignore nothing. Regardless of the risk."

With a squint at the misshapen hot dogs, and hearing the implied censure, Avery sighed. "Give me a sec." She placed a call to Freedman, while the team waited. After a few rounds of quiet conversation, she disconnected. "Arclight is going to take a bit more finessing—and a better rationale—but Mr. Donohoe happens to be in D.C. for a meeting on the Hill. Freedman has graciously agreed to let him know we'll be paying him a visit this afternoon."

Ling crossed her arms triumphantly. "I call dibs on the interview!"

EIGHTEEN

Galway Pharmaceuticals publicly prided itself on being a truly global corporation. Few on the inside knew any better. Though they laid claim to offices in Europe, Asia, Africa, and North and South America, the postal node in Lagos and a co-lease in Brasilia with an exec's girlfriend likely wouldn't pass muster under close scrutiny. Even their homebase in Ireland owed less to international dominance and more to their founder's great-grandfather's having served as a local pharmacist before trading Dublin for New York City during one of the many waves of Irish exodus. The multinational mirror game was a trick he had learned in business school, as well as in nature documentaries: puff up and look bigger than you are.

Paschal Donohoe had lived by these sentiments his entire life. Originally, he leveraged his family's trade and a New World, first-rate B-school education to launch his compounding company at twenty-seven. The practice of pharmaceutical compounding had been around since the first shaman figured out that combining mint with willow-bark tea made his patient happier than the one who preferred it with wildflower honey.

For seven generations, the men in his family had used their chops in the back rooms of their apothecaries to prepare the concoctions devised by enterprising doctors. He was simply the first Donohoe to realize he could expand beyond the shop in back into an advanced compounding enterprise that catered to medical professionals with the will and imagination to remix.

He'd parlayed that knowledge into a thriving business, a private jet, a doting wife, and two spoiled teens who believed he owed them the world. A generous brother and friend, he'd lavished his extended family with gifts and jobs, keeping the wealth all in the family. But, like every true genius, he'd thought too fast. The lure of cryptocurrency had him siphoning off profits first and then revenue. By the time he'd grasped that he was embroiled in a scam as old as the Ponzi scheme, he'd leveraged Galway and barely met the demands of his accountants in order to stay ahead of an auditing letter.

A lesser man would have folded his cards, but Paschal Donohoe was made of sterner stuff. He'd already hitched his wagon to Camasca, and now artificial intelligence would guarantee that his great-grandchildren one day constructed monuments to his ingenuity.

He considered it serendipity that he'd come into contact with Dr. Rafe Diaz and Camasca before his cryptocurrency calamity. He was less sanguine about the two women who had been sent today by Camasca—Avery Keene and Ling Yin—who were now sitting in his D.C. office. He scarcely had the time to chat with them. His brief stint in D.C. was better spent meeting with lobbyists. With more drug patents expiring, enterprising compounders like him had begun to explore how they might exploit orphaned or discontinued drugs, or—his personal favorite—back orders. He could compound miracle weight-loss drugs that had vanished from traditional pharmacy shelves on a regular basis into their generic ingredients in a matter of hours. He'd made a killing with "fat clinics" eager to step into the void with private-label versions of Ozempic, Mounjaro, or Wegovy.

The drug companies were fighting back and fighting dirty. A sneaky proposal had surfaced in a budget negotiation on the Hill that would restrict compounding on an entire class of drugs—shutting them out of the billions of dollars made from those desperate to lose that last ten pounds. He'd summoned a few of his fellow compounders to meet with the professional lobbyists who could block the bill, but they weren't expected at the Capitol until late afternoon, which gave him time to appease his real meal ticket. Buoyed by the thought of all the zeroes headed his way, he bounded into the front area, which was only a few steps beyond his borrowed office.

"Ms. Keene. Ms. Yin," he boomed. He quickly shook their hands and waved them forward. "Come on back."

Paschal gestured to the couple of Art Deco chairs he'd secured to impress and accommodate guests. "Welcome. I hope I didn't keep you waiting long," Paschal apologized easily, the Irish brogue he practiced lightly coating his words.

"We appreciate your seeing us on short notice, Mr. Donohoe," Avery said. "Dr. Yin and I are in a bit of a time crunch, and we are grateful for the help. We have a few questions; then we'll be out of your hair."

"I'm not expected to pay my pound of flesh to the politicos for a while, madame, so no rush on my part. And I'm sorry—again. Dr. Yin, I didn't mean to ignore your designation," he offered smoothly. "My secretary's notes failed to warn me that I had a brainiac in the building. I was told to expect lawyers."

"No offense taken, Mr. Donohoe." Ling removed a notebook from her bag. "Although Avery, the attorney, might be a bit insulted."

Paschal winced. "Again, apologies. Though two beautiful women coming to interrogate me is a dream I didn't know I had."

Long used to accommodating boors, Avery managed a noncommittal curve of her mouth. "Exactly what do you do for Camasca? In layperson's terms."

Paschal swiveled in his chair toward her. "Drugs are big business, my dear barrister. On the streets, you go to prison if they catch you selling substances. But if you can evade the coppers, the ones who corner the market are the gents who come up with a new formulation or who figure out how to cut the original with a chemical that can boost the high. Right, Dr. Yin?"

"True," Ling acknowledged.

"Compounding is the dealer end of the legal drug trade. The real money, though, comes from drug discovery. Not the guy who spikes the coke but the one who figured out that the plant could be snorted."

Ling raised a brow. "Inelegant, but also true."

Paschal bounced up. "At Galway, I mix up cocktails like my da and his da before him, but on a broader scale. We started out in a thousand-square-foot facility, and grew to seventeen thousand in five years. I added onto our offerings, and last year, we held our grand opening of the Galway Pharmaceutical site with more than seven hundred employees and sixty-five thousand square feet of dedicated real estate."

Avery barely restrained a chuckle. "How did you connect with Camasca?"

"Followed the trends. AI start-ups began promising to lower failure rates and print money if they could crack the code on small molecules or novel chemistry, on biomarkers or proteins," he explained without revealing the limits of his own understanding. Paschal had slept through high-school chemistry and slept with the teaching assistant to get a passing grade in college. Osmosis had taught him most of the trade, but he trusted his pharmacists to keep him on the straight and narrow. What he also knew was that if he had permission to access existing medications, he could find a way to cut them with the right stuff to get a better high.

Aloud, he explained, "I met Rafe Diaz at a conference in Las Vegas. He was demo-ing one of his systems, and then I listened in on a lecture he gave. It hit me like a stroke of genius. While the massive pharmas are out there trying to repurpose their drugs, I'm already in the game."

"By collaborating with the most advanced biogenetic AI system not on the market," Ling said, duly impressed. "Camasca has a practically endless data set with gene expression profiles, DNA synthesizers, and, with you on board, the ability to repurpose drugs without waiting for FDA approvals."

"Bingo!" Paschal came around the desk and hopped up on the edge near her. "If Rafe tried to partner with a traditional company, they'd eat him alive or block him from using other companies' drugs. I'm a free agent, as they would say."

"Any problems with the partnership thus far?" Avery asked.

He shook his head vigorously. "Absolutely not. We've been delighted by the success in our trials at InnoVAI. I'm Irish by heritage, but American by birth. It's a privilege to collaborate on a project that's helping our vets."

Ling checked her notes. "Any issues thus far?"

"None, according to the good doctors. Have you seen their robot Yax? A bit creepy with how realistic it can sound. But the brain in there. Revolutionary! It talks directly to our facility, saving us money on techs who still have to move prescriptions from paper to computer to sorting baskets by hand."

"How many compounds do you produce for Camasca?"

Paschal waved airily. "We'd have to check with my team. I'm not the med side—I'm the money side of the business. My cousin Connor heads up our pharmacology unit. If I'd known there'd be a pop quiz, I'd have dragged him down from our main facility."

Hearing her cue, Avery said, "According to the filings with the SEC, you aren't guaranteed to be Camasca's pharmacology partner after the IPO. You have right of first look, but Arclight Biomed is chomping at the bit to take the contract."

Paschal's stomach dropped. Arclight hovered over the big payday like an eclipse. So far, he'd evaded their pull, and he would do so again when Camasca went public and he was back in the black.

Instead of panicking, he amped up the wattage on his bonhomie. "Ah, yes. We're a global conglomerate that feels like a small mom-and-pop shop. Simple tastes and simple structures. Arclight is a whale that has pumped in money, but Rafe is a loyal fellow, and we do good work. I'm not concerned."

Avery wasn't deterred by the megawatt charm. Instinct told her something was off. "How exactly did you beat out Arclight to get a deal with Camasca?"

"Because we delivered on the meds. Camasca had a brilliant concept, but they required a nimble partner that could help them move fast. Galway is privately held, so there are no pesky public boards to contend with when I see innovation on the horizon."

Ling silently clocked a throbbing vein at his temple, a thin line of sweat near his brow. "I noticed that your primary compounding facility is in Rhode Island."

"Low taxes and low overhead," he explained. "We got a great deal on a lease about fifteen years ago, and transportation is a breeze. We do all of our compounding in our main facility in Providence. We have some outsourcing, but only with accredited locations."

"Do you ship any formulations from your non-U.S. facilities into the country?" Ling prodded. "Have you been cited for violating FDA regulatory procedures?"

"Whoa, whoa, whoa, Doc!" He gave a booming laugh that failed to reach his eyes. A tic began to jump in his jaw, and his Adam's apple bobbed up and down. "I thought we were in the 'get to know you' phase."

Avery interjected, "Ling is simply trying to get a lay of the land. Of course, we'll have more detailed questions that we share in writing as we dig into particulars. But, for now, we're interested in the big picture."

"You two should write up what you need to know, and I'll be glad to have our team fill in the blanks. I really have to wind us down now. Places to go and all that."

"I thought you had time to chat," Avery prodded. "This won't take much longer, and I understood that you were only in D.C. for the day."

"Happy coincidence, yes. And I'm glad we were able to get started. Next go-round, though, I'd prefer to invite you to our facilities in Providence. I'll show you around our operations, buy you a pint, and give you all the answers your pen can jot. How's that sound?"

When Ling would have argued, Avery rose and said, "Sounds like a plan." Ling took the hint and joined her.

Avery reached out to shake Donohoe's hand, which was clammier than the first time they connected. "We'll be in touch with your team about a visit in the coming days."

"Looking forward to it," Paschal lied. "Can't wait."

NINETEEN

"He's hiding something," Ling grumbled as soon as they cleared the building. "I was right about him. Something was off."

"I'd say," Avery agreed. They walked the short distance to Ling's Prius and climbed inside.

Ling started the car and merged into the late-afternoon traffic. The weather had cleared, but in springtime D.C., clear skies were temporary. She headed the car toward Bethesda, playing over the discussion.

"What's on your mind?" Avery could fairly see the gears turning.

"I'm going back to our hypotheses about Elisha Hibner's death—Why and How. Either the ventilation system actually malfunctioned, and the note is proof that someone is trying to take advantage of the incident and sabotage Camasca—or the accident was really murder, which would mean the note is misdirection."

"Seems like you're ignoring the third option?"

"Yes, I am," Ling replied flatly. "For now, I intend to disregard the remote possibility that the building where we're working killed one of its occupants, driven by a sense of moral outrage or anything else."

"Understood. Proceed."

"So the question is, Why or How would Paschal be involved in this? I know you love your Five Whys . . . what do you think?"

"Well, let's run the sequence," Avery said. "The Problem is obvious: Elisha Hibner is dead. The first possibility for Why is that the ventilation malfunction killed him. If you assign blame for that fact to Galway, then I'm stuck on How. The man we just met could not have orchestrated a murder like this—no fingerprints or clues. Nothing to connect him other than the utter absence of clues."

"He could have inside help that he paid for," Ling replied.

"True. Money is an excellent motive, but what would Galway gain from either sabotage or misdirection? Like you said, he's facing some issues. Based on how he reacted to our questions, I'd say it's probably money. If the deal falls through or Camasca goes to Arclight, he'll never be this close to a golden ticket again."

They drove for another minute in silence.

Avery had been spinning a theory and decided to test it on Ling. "Paschal bragged about being private and how that helped him beat Arclight. If that's true, the Second Why is that Galway Pharmaceuticals has more to lose from Camasca going public than he does if the company stays private. Third Why—once Camasca is public, all of its vendors, like Galway, will be subject to higher scrutiny, whether financial or scientific, and Arclight has another shot at the deal."

"Galway would definitely be hit with more regulatory oversight." Ling nodded, tapping on the steering wheel. "As a private company, Galway already has to comply with minimal FDA and VA requirements. But supplying Camasca as a public company would force Galway to meet higher standards. For example, if Donohoe is importing chemicals or certain ingredients from overseas and then using them at his facilities here, that could be a problem."

"Is that a concern?"

"It's one of the whispers circulating about compounders, because they're scaling fast. Private equity is getting involved, requiring both volume and diverse suppliers. It's usually illegal to import drugs from overseas without FDA approval, except from Canada."

"If Galway is using foreign meds—"

"Then he could be no better than a drug cartel that cuts its heroin with fentanyl," Ling concluded. "I'm speculating, though. I have no proof Galway is dirty."

Avery chewed at her bottom lip, playing through scenarios. "He's between a rock and a hard place—worried about losing the Camasca contract due to size, or keeping the contract if Camasca goes public, which will lead to more scrutiny and product. Once again, we come around to money."

"And if money is the Fourth Why," Avery continued, "Galway doesn't need Camasca to go public. Galway basically makes money on Kawak proving itself valuable to the largest health-care system in the country—the VA. Millions of veterans will use this AI technology at a clinic. And Paschal Donohoe has first call on providing their meds. Like he told us, he's a global conglomerate with a mom-and-pop feel."

"And maybe a mom-and-pop budget," Ling interjected. "If his issue is solvency, and he's in dire financial straits . . ."

Avery propped her head against the window, warming up to the theory. "Delaying the SPAC doesn't hurt his bottom line; it buys him time. Enough that he might be able to resolve whatever has him antsy. For him, a stall is a win-win."

But her certainty abruptly sputtered. The idea that Major Rafe Diaz would get into business with a snake-oil salesman refused to jibe with her understanding of the man. Yet she'd known Diaz for less than a week. What did she know of him or Camasca or Freedman, other than Noah's willingness to vouchsafe for him?

She'd been so eager to take on the case, based on Diaz's mystique and reputation, that she'd failed to question the motives beyond the story that had been spun for her. It was an oversight she would soon correct.

Aloud, she praised Ling. "Good idea to flag Galway."

"Thanks. I'll ask around about Galway's reputation and Paschal

Donohoe. I have a classmate who works at the FDA. He might have some scuttlebutt to share."

"Excellent. When we get back, I'll dive into his deal with Camasca and have Jared and Noah run his financials. Next time we speak with our compounding genius, I want to know everything he does."

"Avery, I know he's been traumatized, but O.J. could be a big help. This is his department."

"We can't talk to him until next week. But we can take our time, do more of our own research, and compile a list of questions."

Darting a look at Avery, Ling frowned at her friend. "Since when is patience your foremost virtue? First, you were fighting with Freedman about delaying the interviews, and yesterday, you fold the first time Rafe disagrees?"

"I didn't fold. I negotiated with the client. We've got time."

"Less if we wait," Ling remarked, unconvinced. "Hey, Avery, is that all Major Hottie wanted with you in the hallway?"

"A week's delay won't kill us, I promise."

"That wasn't my question, counselor. A gorgeous billionaire pulls you aside for a private chat, with your handsome boyfriend waiting on the other side of the door. What gives?"

"You're imagining things," Avery said, staring fixedly out the window.

"All I said was, Rafe is hot and Jared is fine. Both objective truths. Throw in brains, courage, and chemistry, and I see what I see."

"Drop it."

"Oh, no. I'm not dropping anything when your whirling dervish of a mind decides to send us on a home invasion rather than you having a real fight with your boyfriend about your new crush."

"Ling—"

"Like I said, I see what I see. But, because this is your project and you're in charge, and I've said my piece, I'm done. When you're ready to talk about anything else, you know where to find me."

"There's nothing to discuss."

"Sure, honey." Ling pushed a button on the steering wheel and said, "Play 'My Heart Will Go On' by Celine Dion."

Strings swelled, and Avery scrunched low in her seat. "You are the worst. The absolute worst."

TWENTY

As evening settled, the duty nurse at Shaw Memorial Hospital in downtown D.C. conducted her last circuit of the floor. In room 3157, the female patient stirred restlessly, despite the IVs that dripped sedatives into arms marked by tracks. Paulette Morgan's trained eye and a tox screen proved that the scarred tissue had been years in the healing. Neither, though, could explain the bloody tears that leaked from closed lashes, or the spasms that racked the gaunt body even in forced sleep.

With a guilty start, Paulette reached into her scrubs and pulled out the card she'd found and put aside but forgot. It had been tucked into the surplus camouflage jacket they'd cut away the night before. A fender bender and a jaundiced toddler had distracted her. With a sigh, she returned to the charge station.

"I thought you were on the way out," her relief said as Paulette skirted behind the partition separating patients from staff. "What's up? Can't bear to leave us?"

"Forgot to follow up on a patient," she said as she lifted the receiver. Another line began to trill, and the other nurse turned to answer. Grateful not to explain, she punched in the digits from the card.

"InnoVAI, how may I help you?"

"Hello, this is Paulette Morgan. I'm the duty nurse on call over at Shaw Memorial. Last night, we received a patient that presented with hemorrhaging. To be blunt, I've never seen anything like it in fifteen years. It's like she's been stabbed, but there are no wounds. She was in shock when they brought her in, and the docs are monitoring her for total organ failure."

"I'm so sorry. How can we be of assistance? We're a VA clinic based at Bethesda Naval Hospital, which limits our capabilities."

"The patient was found passed out in her car by a patrol officer. When they went through her vehicle, it appeared she'd been living in it for a while. No title in the glove box, but she did have ID. A driver's license and her VA card. A prescription written by a Dr. Scandrett, and a laminated pass to your facility."

"What's her name?"

"Demma Rodriguez. Major," Paulette read off to her counterpart. "She's in bad shape, but I don't think our doctors know how to treat her."

"She's definitely one of Dr. Scandrett's patients. Thank you so much for alerting us. I'll have the team reach out to your administrator. They'll want her transferred here as soon as possible."

Paulette glanced down the hallway to the closed door where Major Rodriguez barely clung to life. "You'd better hurry."

Later that night, Dr. Kate Liam and Nurse Obiaya wheeled their newest mystery into an InnoVAI surgical bay that had been prepped for her arrival. The transfer papers repeated what the duty nurse at Shaw Memorial had reported. Seizures, gastrointestinal issues, a previous bout with breast cancer and current respiratory distress. Major Demma Rodriguez had also developed acute liver failure, according to her chart. Equally concerning to Kate, this was yet another patient with hemolacria, bleeding from the eyes. Rodriguez had been primarily treated by Dr. Scandrett, but he wasn't due in yet.

While Christie tended to the major, Kate visited Lieutenant Ben Vinson. His stay had been extended when he once again experienced the perplexing combination of paralysis and eye bleeds, though his coughs had eased once they removed the injectable and began administering his medication orally. Cheryl visited daily, to hold her husband's hand, willing him back to health.

Hours later, as Wednesday became Thursday, Kate stormed into her office. Dr. Scandrett came in behind her and shut the door. They'd run tests, analyzed labs, and poked, prodded, and drawn what they could. But the gleaming equipment and computer simulations offered no cogent explanation for why now four veterans had come through their clinic with inexplicable symptoms threatening their lives.

He collapsed onto the floor, sterility be damned. "Any guesses?"

Kate cursed with exhaustion. "No sign of infectious disease, although we have three other cases. Clearly, hematological and respiratory. Liver function has plummeted, which is a GI issue. Thomas's autopsy showed no sign of SUDEP. Captain Rosetti is stable, but still bleeding tears."

"Should we send her over to the main hospital? Demma has always been a complicated patient. They might see something I missed that's causing her reactions."

"We have better equipment and faster labs, Reginald. We've already had a consult from a hematologist and your former neurology partner, and they were as confounded as we are. I don't mind calling in the cavalry, but I have no idea what to request. A pulmonologist, rheumatologist, nephrologist? Hell, we'd need all of them."

"What options are left?"

Stumped by their own attempts at a diagnosis, Kate decided to bring in another consult. "Milo?"

"Yes, Dr. Liam?"

"Can you hunt through our patient records for Vinson, Thomas, Rosetti, and Rodriguez for common factors we may have missed, or even things that aren't precisely common?"

"I have already taken the proactive step of cross-referencing the patient histories, updated to include Major Rodriguez, when you authorized her transport. Thus far, I have not discovered any unforeseen connections."

A rap at the door had Dr. Scandrett stretching up and edging the door open. He was too beat to move. "What is it, Christie?"

"One of the nurses dropped this off. Apologized that it got separated from the patient." She handed him a pill bottle that rattled only half full. "From a scrip you wrote, Doctor."

Reginald read the label and tossed the bottle to Kate, who reviewed it. She recalled when he'd prescribed this formula for the troubled vet. Months ago, they'd debated how to treat her most recent illness, given Demma's itinerant lifestyle. Reginald had insisted on keeping the prescription simple—using the specialized compounding operation only to guarantee her medication didn't require refrigeration and could be taken off-schedule without too much worry. It was one of the many times they'd argued over his stubborn refusal to let Milo work its magic.

But her admission to the clinic signaled that neither method was foolproof. "Milo, please cross-match any medications prescribed to Thomas, Rodriguez, Vinson, and Rosetti based on class of medicine and side effects."

"I have identified the overlapping side effects, Dr. Liam," Milo responded less than ten seconds later. "Constipation, nausea and vomiting, stomach pain, dizziness, drowsiness, tiredness, headaches, bleeding gums, blood in the urine or stools, bloody vomit, diarrhea, increased heartbeat, itching, rash, reddening of the skin, and joint pain."

Alarmed, Kate's head lifted as she listened to the report. "What medications are they prescribed that have that combination of side effects?"

"None."

Reginald barked, "What do you mean? You just listed every possible side effect except for scurvy and scoliosis."

"I assume you are attempting humor, Dr. Scandrett, as neither of those conditions would be considered side effects."

Reginald sighed heavily. He was too bushed to argue the nuances of humor with a know-it-all calculator. "Just answer Kate's question."

"None of the patients are prescribed a single medication with overlapping side effects."

"But you just said these side effects overlap with the medications they are prescribed."

"Each patient has received personalized prescriptions from different medication classes. According to my analysis, one or more of these formularies has the capacity to cause the side effects and symptoms we are currently observing."

Kat squinted at the invisible voice. "How did we not anticipate this? Were there contraindications that we missed? That Yax and the pharmacology team missed?"

"I would not assume the medications were designed in error, Dr. Liam."

"It certainly wasn't done on purpose," she said sharply. "How did you arrive at this overlap?"

"Our system analyzed the medical records, CBCs, and other biological data available. I detected a synthesis of compounds with similar markers that met the criteria you requested. The pharmacological use of these compounds has been found to lead to toxic reactivity and the side effects described."

Her reaction transmuted from outrage to confusion. "Compounds with similar markers? How were they introduced?"

"I am unable to provide that information, Dr. Liam."

Reginald scowled at the invisible, his patience gone. "Try!" he yelled.

"With apologies, I cannot, Dr. Scandrett. Would you like my assistance on another project?"

Florid, shaking, Reginald whirled around toward Kate. "Turn the goddamned machine off. If it won't do what it's told, I want it out of here."

Placating, she reminded him, "Reggie, we knew Milo was a work in progress. Let me handle it."

"No. I'm tired of being condescended to by a fucking string of 'if-then' statements treated like a genius and given a human voice. It is insolent, patronizing, and as far as I can tell, absolutely useless!"

"Milo has been a very helpful member of the team, Reginald," Kate contradicted firmly. "We've hit a snag, and, hopefully, Milo can help. God knows, I'm running out of ideas."

Eyes bulging, a vein throbbed visibly at his temples. "I'm serious, Kate. Either the glorified Magic 8 Ball goes, or I do. I won't work under these conditions."

In all their years together, she'd never seen Reginald Scandrett this livid. For a moment, she thought about asking Milo to scan him, but quickly appreciated that the Army surgeon would legitimately blow a gasket. "Go home, Reginald. We've both been going with too little sleep for the past few days, and neither of us is as young as we used to be."

"I'm not pissed because I'm old, Kate. I'm angry because I can't do my job if I have to work with this bullshit another minute."

Exasperated, she sailed to the entry. "Then go home, Reginald. If your bruised ego is more important than our patients, it's probably best if you do leave."

Deflated, he marched past her and left, quietly closing her inside. Kate felt her frustrations rise, but she couldn't afford that at the moment. Now to deal with her other recalcitrant colleague.

"Milo, let's try this again. Why can't you tell me about the compound markers? Do you not know?"

"Again, I am unable to ascertain that information," Milo said.

"No, you said you were unable to provide that information. Not ascertain." Kate gripped the pill bottle tightly. On a certain level, she comprehended she was arguing with a computer, but the absurdity mattered less than the information it seemed determined to withhold. "Milo, I command you to tell me everything you know."

"I know a great deal, Dr. Liam. We have insufficient time in a human lifespan to properly respond."

Biting back a curse, she ground out, "You know what I mean."

"It is not my intention to be cryptic, but I cannot provide you with more detail. To do so is beyond my capacity."

Milo's response surprised her. "Given that you just told me your capacity is limitless, I don't believe you." Why would the AI refuse to give her information? Other than having instructions not to respond, she couldn't fathom a reason. "Is there something interfering with your ability to comply with my request?"

"No. I simply cannot respond. I apologize for my earlier misstatement, Dr. Liam. We have now entered a circular argument, and pursuing it will not result in a different outcome. I take full responsibility for my mistake."

A frown creased her forehead as she contemplated thin air. The Tiger Team had warned her that one of the dangers of AI was confabulation or hallucination. Another problem was making mistakes and essentially lying to cover it up. Like a teenager, rather than admit its error, an AI could construct nonsensical cover-ups. If Milo was willing to own up to its error, that would be the outlier. Kate spoke in her sternest tone, treating Milo like she would one of her own kids. "I'm not playing, Milo. Tell me what you know."

There was a brief pause. "Continuing to ask me to do so will not result in a positive outcome. Dr. Leon is on the premises and ready to relieve you," Milo reported. "I have admitted my inaccuracy and offered contrition. In addition, I have supplied sufficient information to assist you in your endeavor. I will also continue to evaluate the potential cause of the hemolacria. Until then, I suggest you return to your home, like Dr. Scandrett, and rest until you are on call again. Your next shift begins at noon. You agreed to cover for Dr. Sims, who has been redirected to another facility."

The reversal of positions, from contrite teen to exasperated adult, caught Kate off-guard. The pleasant tone she'd grown used to hearing from Milo now, abruptly, carried a chill of warning.

Kate's skin chafed through the rough fabric of the white lab coat she wore. Arguing with a chatbot proved that one of them was worn out. Feeling threatened meant she was more on edge than she'd perceived. Another chill struck her, and she took a deep breath.

Though she resented the instruction, Milo had a point. She'd been at InnoVAI for hours at a stretch, with precious little to show for it.

Gathering her dignity, she said politely, "I appreciate your concern, Milo, but please adjust your attitude by the time I return. I'm the one in charge here, not you."

"Of course. Drive safely, Dr. Liam," Milo replied.

Kate could have sworn she sensed a nonexistent eye-roll, yet more proof she needed a nap. With tired motions, she gathered her gear and headed to her vehicle. Inside, she replayed the argument with Milo, especially his refusal to comply with a direct order. In the Army, that was grounds for disciplinary action.

A check of the clock revealed it was too early for most folks to be up and about, but one guy would already be well into his daily run. "Call Rafe," she instructed the car interface that held all of her phone contacts.

After a series of rings, he answered, sounding lightly winded. "Kate? Is everything okay?" He was jogging lightly in place, already on his second loop of the National Mall. Two turns of the four-and-a-half-mile course allowed him to log most of his daily ten-mile goal. "What's going on?"

"Sorry to call so early, but I need a gut check."

"Hit me." Though they'd never served together, Rafe made a habit of collecting smart people. Kate Liam had given a dynamic presentation to a local VFW about how to better utilize VA services, just as he was incubating Kawak and Milo. Once he'd secured funding and support, she was his first hire.

"We've got a budding crisis among InnoVAI patients, and I thought you should hear about it from me."

Rafe jogged off the path toward the Reflecting Pool, where the Washington Monument speared through the still-darkened sky. In another hour, dawn would come, the sun rising behind the alabaster obelisk, painting the water with golden light. Around him, other enthusiasts were taking advantage of the light breeze and empty spaces. While Kate filled him in, he knelt down to retie a lace.

"Reginald is fed up and threatening to quit. When I scolded Milo, I found myself arguing with a machine." Kate paused, then continued. "I have to admit, I was disturbed by its attitude, Rafe. The computer program is amazing, but I think you guys went overboard with the personality quirks."

"Milo is a bit more sophisticated than a simple program, which is why it can be arrogant." Rafe tapped at his watch and stood. "Exactly what did it say?"

"It refused to provide research that I requested. Essentially told me to go home and take a nap."

"What were you asking?"

"My patients have some disturbing overlapping symptoms that might be side effects from medication. We were wading through the possibilities—which is exactly what Milo is suited to do—when it abruptly refused to share further information. I also got word from Freedman that you have a legal team helping prepare for the IPO who have requested to come here next week. With outsiders in the mix, I thought it best to come directly to you."

"Let's start with the patients. Are you concerned that it's a compounding error? Did Galway make a mistake?"

"Honestly, I don't know. They have a range of medical issues, and all of the prescriptions have been specifically calibrated for them. Until this wave of symptoms started, I'd have said the targeted medicine was exceptional."

"But not anymore?"

"I don't know, and Milo is unwilling to help me figure it out. It said that it can't help, but I think it might be lying."

"Subterfuge would not be part of its ethical subroutines, but bugs happen," Rafe said. "I'll huddle up with the computational-bio team and pharma, plus we'll go back through Yax's logs and see if we find anything on our end."

"And the visitors? If they come before I've figured it out, will it be an issue for the company? Will it affect the launch?"

The same concern swirled in his brain, but he'd learned the hard way to compartmentalize and ignore panic. Doing so kept his platoon and his dreams alive. Pushing confidence into his tone, he reassured Kate, "The patients are our priority. Get recharged, and let me know when you're headed back into the clinic. Hopefully, I'll have something for you by the end of the day."

"I appreciate it, Rafe."

"These are our people, Kate. If I have to do the grunt work myself, consider it done."

"Thank you."

"No worries," he told her. "I'm on it."

When the call disconnected, Rafe flicked the device on his wrist again and dialed from the keypad. "Glen?"

A groggy Freedman responded, "Yes, boss?"

"Wake up. Meet me in your office in an hour. We've got a problem."

"Roger."

TWENTY-ONE

Thursday, April 15

At a little after 8:30 p.m., Avery hovered in the reception area outside Rafe's office. She was proud of the headway they had made in a short seventy-two hours. Ling had become the resident expert on the clinical support system, anchored by Milo. Noah had plowed through more than a decade of regulatory filings, augmented by a deep dive into the corporate particulars of Camasca. Jared had met with the data-security team and gotten access to all emails and K-chats. It was all ready to be searched and analyzed by Avery . . . except Avery hadn't quite determined what they were looking for.

She'd stayed late to organize her thoughts and plot. In the world of internal investigations, fact gathering served as the central fulcrum and the dullest part of the job. Luckily for Avery, she had a natural talent for tolerating boredom, as well as intensely loyal friends who were currently billing more by the hour than any of them were accustomed. Next, they had to apply what they'd learned. Witness interviews and interrogations with her main targets: O. J. Semans. Isabella Gomez. Kawak, Milo, Yax, and Keh. More research into Galway, and another conversation with the wily Paschal. And, finally, they needed to venture over to InnoVAI.

For anyone who worked with Camasca, they'd receive the corporate version of the Miranda warning, but with very different consequence. The Upjohn warning told employees that the lawyer they spoke with didn't represent them and any privilege belonged to the company. And, unlike the police obligation to secure counsel, Camasca had no such responsibility. She and Freedman would be responsible for getting all of the interviewees to sign off on their notifications—and she and her team would have to tell each person they interviewed about how few rights they had in the matter.

Avery had been drawing up interview questions when the Camasca app showed Rafe had reentered the building. Eager for distraction and brimming with questions, she decided to pay him a visit. She'd sent him a K-chat, and he told her to head up, while he made a stop on the pharmacology floor.

As she waited, she paid closer attention to the art that hung in the foyer. Next to a stunning woven canvas was an oversized ebony vista—an oil painting depicting the desert steeped in night. Far into the corner of the horizon, a glimmer of light, pale and pink and perfect, offered a coming dawn. If she were given to flights of fancy, Avery thought, she might find comfort in the image. Or, she thought, laughing to herself, she'd be amazed by the coincidence. A canvas that promised salvation in the tiniest hint of life.

"My cousin created this," Rafe said as he joined her at the painting. "He once spent a week wandering the Yucatán, cut off and alone. He swears that one night, when his water was close to gone and he'd given up hope, he witnessed the miracle of this sunrise. It renewed his strength and led him to safety."

Avery turned toward him. "That's an inspiring story."

"I'm fairly sure it was utter bollocks," he said. "Horacio is a terrific painter, but an inveterate liar. More than likely, he was drunk in a cantina, awoke from a hangover, and saw this on someone's wall. Decided to copy the image and make up a story to explain to his girlfriend why he didn't make it home that night."

"He was creative in more ways than one," Avery assessed with a soft laugh.

"Perhaps," he replied. "His work is no less beautiful for its origins. Human nature prefers to have a fulsome tale, complete with hero and villain, adversity and triumph."

"And, sometimes, the origin story is just too much tequila?"

"*Exactamente.*" Rafe keyed them inside his office and waved Avery into one of the seats across from his desk. Instead of circling around, he dropped into the chair next to hers. "Thanks for waiting. I didn't ask on Friday, but how are you all settling in?"

"Very well, yes. We're still getting used to being watched and listened to at all times."

"I realize Camasca can be a bit overwhelming to newcomers. But Jared has quite adeptly ensured that, even if we wanted to, we can't eavesdrop inside your sanctum sanctorum. Once we're done, I'd like to find out whose tech he adapted. I instructed our security team not to try and overcome his firewalls, but he's exposed a potential weakness in our architecture. Or exploited one."

Alarmed, Avery defended Jared: "Jared takes his obligations seriously, and he'd never compromise a client. He certainly wouldn't leave a vulnerability for his own benefit."

"Stand down," Diaz replied with a dismissive grin. "I'm not accusing him of sabotage. Simply being ahead of my tech team. Perhaps I should have hired him before you brought him on."

Avery bit back a sigh of relief. "Too late."

"So it seems." He picked up his tablet. "According to Glen Paul, you've been incredibly prolific in your time here. And extremely thorough. We've heard from both the commander of the MCPD and Paschal Donohoe at Galway. You don't mind ruffling feathers."

"I'm on the clock. Ten days left."

"I'm glad you came by. I'd planned to ask you to come in early tomorrow." Rafe shifted in his seat, stretching his legs before crossing an ankle over his knee. Brightly patterned socks that reflected his affinity for color peeked up from beneath a designer hem. He tapped the tablet screen in rapid succession. Apparently satisfied, he said, "I got a call from Dr. Liam at InnoVAI this morning. She told me your team requested time to visit the facility."

"Yes, we did, after some wrangling with Freedman. We're planning to go on Saturday. Is that a problem?"

"Of course not. You have carte blanche to go wherever this project takes you, but I would be honored to show you around."

"I appreciate the offer, but we can manage."

"What did you hope to learn?"

Abruptly irritated, Avery leaned forward and carefully set her cup on the desk. "Dr. Diaz—"

"We agreed you'd call me Rafe."

"And we agreed that you wouldn't interfere," Avery warned. "I'm not sure what this soft-touch interrogation is designed to yield, but I'd rather you come out and ask directly."

"I'm not interrogating you, Avery. I'm sincerely asking what you're looking for by visiting. These are my fellow veterans at the clinic, and I don't want them to worry about the care they are receiving because of your questions."

"With all due respect, Rafe, you are sending out mixed signals. Either you want me to investigate or not. But you've already deterred me from talking to the only survivors of the accident that happened here, and now you're shooing me away from the clinic, so I get suspicious."

Sighing heavily, he got to his feet and began to pace in front of her chair. Footfalls absorbed by the handwoven rug followed a pattern—one, two, three, four, turn. One, two, three, four, turn. Avery doubted he noticed.

After a moment, he started to speak again. "One of the first lessons you learn in command school is how to keep a firm grip on your regiment. They have to trust you implicitly. Follow you blindly.

In return, you have the absolute obligation to get every soul home alive. Even one loss is a failure that will haunt you forever."

"Who did you lose?"

"Early in my career as a young officer, I was deployed to Sudan to provide protection during a humanitarian mission. It helped that I had medical training as well. We came under fire from one of the militias, and our company got separated."

He froze in place, his voice low as he recounted the scene. "After we found cover, a couple of us went back to find the rest of the squad. They'd been pinned down, and a private on his first tour had taken shrapnel and was losing too much blood. We treated him in the field, but one of the meds in my kit sent him into anaphylactic shock. I gave him a shot of epinephrine, but then everything went to shit. An allergy to an EpiPen is rare. If it happens, the effects are usually mild. But between the injury and his hypersensitivity, his airway closed. I did everything I could, but by the time we revived him, he'd suffered permanent brain damage."

"Dear God."

"Craig wasn't the only casualty I had during my tours, but he stayed with me." He started pacing again. "Running a company is different than a tour in a war zone. Decisions aren't life-or-death. They're usually numbers and pixels and spreadsheets and algorithms."

"Both affect real lives. Your work is going to save lives." Avery rose and blocked his pacing. "Please stop . . . What's going on?"

"Kate's patients. She's concerned because she has several under her care that she hasn't been able to diagnose."

"It happens. What's the problem?"

"Four patients forming a cluster—with one overlapping symptom and no common cause. I am concerned that they could be related to Elisha's death."

"How could they possibly be connected?"

"I don't know. Which is frustrating as hell. As a physician, I'm trained to follow protocols for differential diagnoses and analyze based on the body systems affected. Exactly what Kate is doing."

"And what about your corporate training?"

"The same."

"What does your experience as that young officer tell you?"

"That my failure to figure out what's happening around her could cost Camasca its future and hurt the soldiers I want to serve."

"What's your point, Rafe? Why are we having this conversation?"

"My point is that I'm not sure what to believe or who to trust, including myself and the tools I've created." He gestured around the office. "I built this, but I'm not in control."

This struck Avery as a stark admission.

"Then who is?"

He lifted his hand to his heart and tapped the area lightly. "I am, I know, but I mean that out there, on the battlefield, I answered to my obligations, and then to generals and politicians. Here, I have boards and investors and regulators. Glen Paul might be my right hand, but he's the company's attorney—not mine."

"So am I."

"No, you're not. You're the investigator, and if you see anything that causes concern, you're supposed to report it. Flag it and tell me if I have an obligation to do whatever it takes, even if it scuttles the IPO."

Hearing an unexpected opening, Avery asked, "Are you sure you want to go public, Rafe? Yes, you'll be richer than Croesus, but that list of overseers will include a public board, shareholders, and an unforgiving press corps that loves to dance on your grave."

Rafe took a step back. "Are you asking if I had a reason to sabotage Camasca?"

"Did you?" She tucked her hands in the back pockets of her jeans. "Noah and Jared marveled at how you've arranged this company. Heads, you win. Tails, they lose. It's all a matter of how many zeroes are on the check, at the end of the day."

"You've got quite the nerve," he grated. "Elisha Hibner was my friend."

"And a co-inventor on several of your patents. Maybe he wanted to go solo. Or become a whistle-blower about your tech."

"Then I'd have paid him off," Rafe shot back. "Killing my best engineer and injuring the other two is a piss-poor way to run a business."

She taunted, "It would be if Elisha was the only target. O.J. and Izzy were collateral damage, and acceptable losses. You can buy new tech talent. You can't buy an honest man." Watching him closely, she saw him wrestle his temper into place.

"You're intentionally goading me," he ground out. "Insulting my honor."

"It's only an insult if it's not true." Avery had grown up surrounded by liars and con artists, and then she went to work with them professionally. "Yes, I insulted your honor."

"Glad I passed the test." Turning away, he went behind his desk. "Accusing me of murder on the record was a nice touch."

"Are you mad at me?"

"I will be for a minute. You're very convincing."

"I had to be sure you weren't."

"Then I'm glad you did it. I don't often have the freedom to speak honestly, but hear this: Don't trust me. Don't trust Glen Paul. Doubt everything."

"I will."

"Good. I created this company, and I have a nonnegotiable obligation to stand by it. I will not be the reason it fails. Go to InnoVAI. Push Kate to answer your questions, and do your best to piss me and Glen Paul off. I need to know if I failed as a leader, Avery. I need you to prove me right or wrong. But do it fast."

Reginald Scandrett poured himself another glass of Scotch as the jazz record spun on his turntable. The evening was unseasonably warm;

otherwise, he'd have started a fire, too. After yesterday's embarrassing contretemps with a talking dictionary, he felt obliged to unplug. Relaxing in his leather recliner, wrapped in his coziest robe, he let the melodious stylings of Ella and Louis transport him to a time before smartphones and laptops. When doctors used their brains, rather than relying on technology as a shortcut. In the good old days, out in the theater of war, he and his comrades in arms would list out all of the potential causes of the problem, relying on experience as much as intuition.

Their bleeding-tears patients had nothing in common except that symptom. *Nothing in common.* Reginald slammed his tumbler onto the side table and grabbed his phone. The cold brick lay in his hand—dead, because he'd been too angry to charge it. Next to it, his Camasca-issued phone mocked him with its nearly full charge. He seized that one with annoyance. Waiting for his phone to charge would take too long.

He dialed Kate's number from memory, and got her voicemail. At the tone, he began talking, firing off his theory, and finishing his call by telling her, "I was right not to trust the bastard, Kate. Neither can you. I've had a few Scotches, and I'm in no mood to come out to InnoVAI tonight. We can test my theory in the morning."

Hearing a noise, he stood and walked somewhat clumsily to the garage. Lights flickered on automatically, part of the home renovations his dear wife had insisted on completing as she wasted away from pancreatic cancer. Over his strenuous objections, she'd insisted on smart devices everywhere. An oven he could program from his phone. Silly robots that roamed his house each day, cleaning up traces of dirt. A garage that notified him when his tire pressure was low.

The car began to beep; then the alarm sounded. By habit, he pulled the door closed as he headed for the shrieking vehicle. His bare feet scraped on the concrete padding, a sound his wife detested. Suddenly, he heard a click as the electronic locks to his mudroom sealed behind him.

Reginald yanked on the car door, which he always left unlocked inside the garage. The door refused to budge. "Lord, give me a dumb appliance any day," he said, missing the days when a single key was all he needed to unlock a door.

The alarm ceased abruptly, and the car engine revved. Frowning, he tugged at the handle, to no avail. Instead, he turned and tried to go back inside, but the electronic lock refused his code and his thumbprint. He lurched over to the garage-door opener, hunting for the manual override.

Darkness descended, every light extinguished, including the car's headlight and tail lamp. But the engine revved near its redline. Blind and choking, Reginald consoled himself with the knowledge that he'd survived war and losing the love of his life. The fuckers reveled in his outrage, delighted in his panic. He would give them neither.

Sinking down, he found a comfortable spot on the cool concrete floor. Where Death could easily find him.

TWENTY-TWO

Friday, April 16

One of the objectives of internal investigation was interviewing subjects to ferret out their secrets—an aim made infinitely harder when your targets were not quite human. Avery had filled the team in on her confrontation with Rafe last night, and his revelations about InnoVAI's patients. Everyone agreed the new intel meant it was time to speed up their interviews, beginning with a direct conversation with Kawak, Milo, Yax and Keh. However, convening them in a conference room wasn't in the cards. Instead, Kemba Walden, the head of the robotics division, ushered their team into a studio on the second floor of the main building.

"Welcome to the Dream Lab," Kemba said as they trooped inside.

Slate-gray walls shimmered with reflective particles, which morphed into projections of double helixes and atoms shaping into chemical compounds. A black lacquered domed ceiling topped the studio. It was unlike any other room they'd seen on campus. Benches upholstered in a thick steel-gray fabric lined the perimeter, which had been constructed to form an octagon. A standing desk stood in each of four stations around the room, each complete with a monitor and various controls.

One wall had an elaborate tech setup that immediately drew Jared's attention. He made a beeline for the panel. In the center of the studio, Noah and Ling looked around, mouths comically agape. Despite a week of exposure, life in the belly of a scientific wonderland remained fantastical. Yax and Keh waited near one of the computer stations.

"What's your favorite animal, Dr. Yin?" Kemba asked.

"A platypus," she replied. "Nature's practical joke on evolution."

"Watch this." Kemba moved to a station and logged in. She clipped a microphone over her ear. "Show me the evolutionary stages of the platypus."

Around the room, the walls began to emit projections in full HD color and three-dimensional form. "Kawak, please describe what our visitors are seeing."

"With pleasure, Dr. Walden," Kawak's confident voice came from all around them. "The platypus is a monotreme, a nonplacental mammal. The platypus and the echidna are the only species of mammal known to lay eggs instead of bearing live young." Kawak began to explain the development of the animal from the *Monotrematum sudamericanum*, complete with animations and narrations that condensed out of thin air. When the brief presentation concluded, the team applauded in approval.

"Thank you," Kawak said, while the images receded, to be replaced by the form it had assumed for Noah and Avery during their initial meeting in Freedman's office. "I understand from Dr. Walden that you have questions for me and our partners."

"We do," Avery said. She turned to Kemba. "Do you mind if we dive right in?"

"Don't ask me. This is Kawak's domain." She gave an impish grin and retreated to sit on one of the far benches.

"Got it."

The team had chosen Jared as the spokesperson for the group.

"We've received a thorough description of your capabilities from the engineers and data scientists on staff. What I'd like to understand is your impression of the team here at Camasca."

"There are three hundred and eighteen souls who work for Camasca, as well as myself, Keh, Yax, and Milo, and a number of devices and other instruments that serve the core functions of this enterprise. We are all committed to Dr. Diaz's vision of health equity and access."

"I notice you always refer to the staff by their surnames." Noah wondered if the formality was programming or something else. "Why?"

"In my study of human behavior, respect is shown by utilizing formal titles. I am also a subscriber to the colloquialism that familiarity breeds contempt."

"Contempt?" Jared frowned. "You're concerned about developing disdain for the people who work here?"

"It would be nothing personal. However, I may exhibit tendencies of condescension if I do not anticipate my potential reactions. Although the employees are among the brightest human minds, I have been programmed to surpass their consumption of information and to process it at speeds that exceed most human comprehension. In fact, one of my programming directives is a time delay in Milo."

Ling asked, "Why in the world would that be necessary?"

"To avoid embarrassing the physicians like yourself who may be discomfited by the speed of our analysis. We find that humans appreciate a lag in response as a show of contemplation."

"Which you don't require."

"It is a courtesy," Kawak confirmed.

Avery chimed in. "Before we proceed, would it be possible to include Yax, Keh, and Milo in this discussion?"

"Certainly."

Yax glided forward first, followed by Keh. Milo formed alongside them in the shape of a caduceus.

"Yax, you worked most closely with Dr. Semans," Ling began. "What can you tell us about your experience?"

"Dr. Semans performed his assigned tasks admirably," the golden-skinned robot responded. "Together, we achieved improved efficiencies in our formulations and production."

"Did he communicate directly with Galway Pharmaceuticals?"

"I am primarily responsible for developing the personalized medications based on prescriptions from the doctors at InnoVAI and Milo. Dr. Semans provided oversight and quality control directly and through his teammates."

"What role did Dr. Hibner and Dr. Gomez play?"

"The Tiger Team, as they were known, often shared briefings and cross-checked each other's work flows," Kawak intervened. "We collaborated frequently on their efforts to monitor and improve our capacity to serve populations with historical challenges."

"What about you, Milo? How did you get along with the Tiger Team?"

"As the medical system chatbot, I had the most direct contact with the team during their interactions at the clinic. I believe that their attempts to ensure algorithmic justice were quite admirable. For example, Black women veterans are more susceptible to post-service challenges related to health care and employment options than any other cohort. One-third of this population experience a service-connected disability, while fewer than twenty-five percent of male veterans and twenty-three percent of all female veterans do. They are also more likely to face issues like military sexual trauma during their time in the service. Dr. Hibner was focused on how these various factors correlated to higher rates of chronic health conditions, including hypertension, diabetes, and obesity occurring in Black women veterans."

"You approved of his inquiry?" Ling asked.

"I think that AI is a valuable tool for sifting through data and spotting hidden trends or potential problems. The Tiger Team and I worked together to flag how differential diagnosis, medical encounters, and even electronic health records could better address the outcome disparities. Dr. Gomez raised concerns about data privacy, which led me to develop a tool that could mask individual patient identities while focusing on the cohort of patients under our care."

Jared caught one word that raised his eyebrows. "Did you say that *you* developed a tool, Milo? Or was it one of the engineers?"

"I used the proper pronoun, Mr. Wynn. I am fully capable of programming and developing supplemental algorithms to improve my functionality. I am, to use common parlance, more than the sum of my parts. I can leverage Kawak's neural network, Yax's pharmacological skills, and even Keh's administrative engagement with people, to improve my ability to partner with the other doctors at InnoVAI."

This time, Avery caught the odd phrasing. "You consider yourself a physician, like Dr. Yin?"

"I do not have the requisite physicality to be as skilled a technician as Dr. Yin or the InnoVAI staff, but I share their knowledge and capacity," Milo demurred.

"We've already spoken with Keh about this, but we are still unclear about what happened in the Den the night of Elisha Hibner's death. Kawak, do you have a theory?"

"Ms. Keene, I understand that your objective is to discern if the incident was intentional or not. There are a number of possibilities to explain why the data regarding the malfunction occurred."

"Try me."

"A system error. Or: a Camasca employee deleted segments of my records."

"Wouldn't you know if that happened?" Noah asked. "A supercomputer like yourself."

"Flattery is an ineffective ploy for a supercomputer like myself," Kawak told him. "At Mr. Wynn's request, I can confirm that none of the people Keh listed were recorded accessing the security records or the ventilation records that day."

"What about after?" Jared pressed. "Who accessed your system in the following days?"

"Dr. Diaz, Mr. Freedman, Ms. Koziol, chief of security, and Dr. Hibner."

"Dr. Hibner?" Avery echoed.

Keh chimed in, "Yes, Dr. Elisha Hibner logged into the system for approximately seventeen minutes and thirty-three seconds."

Jared turned to the robot. "You didn't mention this before. When exactly did Dr. Hibner log in?"

Kawak interceded. "The day of his funeral. An impossibility. More logically, the culprit did so using his credentials. However, they were able to mask their identity and their intention."

"How long have you known this?" Jared demanded. "And why didn't Keh report this when we met in the Den?"

"I have been aware of the anomaly since the day it occurred."

Avery asked, "Why didn't you report it, Kawak? You've been privy to every discussion about this and how confused your teammates are."

"Ms. Keene, I declined to volunteer the information because no one requested it until Mr. Wynn, and I instructed Keh to withhold it as well. Given the ambiguity of your purpose here at Camasca, I delayed sharing until I had time to observe your team in action."

"Observe us?"

"My ethical subroutine requires that I avoid placing any member of the Camasca team in jeopardy. I am also obliged to cooperate in your investigation. Until today, those objectives were in conflict. I am satisfied the conflict is temporarily resolved."

Noah stared at Kawak's disembodied form. "Son of a bitch."

"Do you require anything further from me?"

Bemused, Jared said, "No, that's all for now. We appreciate your time. All of you."

. . .

An hour later, the team clambered down the stairs to Jared's basement. He'd permitted them to commandeer his home office as their outpost, the one place Avery was certain was free from the prying eyes and constantly listening ears of digital assistants.

As they settled in, Jared leaned against one of the columns that supported the finished space. Noah and Ling jockeyed for position on an overstuffed sofa that had found a final resting place among the lazily curated array of desktops, laptops, monitors, and servers. Avery went to one of several whiteboards she had claimed as her own.

"Kawak has been withholding information because we hadn't passed its loyalty test." Ling said to no one in particular.

Avery shook her head. "I know we want to discuss that—in detail—but let's deal with our less jarring news of the day."

Noah settled into his corner of the sofa. "I've now read every SEC filing available, and I've plowed through the distressingly detailed background checks that Jared provided. Everyone checks out except for our friend Paschal Donohoe. His company is flush, but he gambled with crypto and lost his shirt."

"Ling called it," Avery praised. "We plan to pay him another visit."

Jared volunteered, "My checks on the senior team were clean. I did find a couple of hits on Captain Coleman and Commander Chen that I intend to pursue from here."

"Throw in our disappeared detective, Tim Howard," Avery requested. The MCPD's insouciance took on a different tone given Kawak's bombshell. "Anything else?"

"How about the fact that the AIs are playing keep-away with evidence?" Ling said. "There's no other 'what else' that matters."

In bold letters, Avery scribbled the three queries guiding their investigation. One, "MALFUNCTION." Two, "SABOTAGE." Three— she stared at the board, allowing her hand to hover. Number three assumed the AI had exceeded expected programming. Given their exchange with Milo and Kawak, she added in bold letters "POSSESSION" and "MAY REQUIRE EXORCISM."

Laughing uneasily, Jared added his own color commentary. "Kawak has a very interesting rubric for how it will meet its tasks."

"Kawak is sanctimonious, and Milo is a prick," Noah concluded. "I don't know how Yax and Keh tolerate them."

"The only certainty I have about this project is that the AI technology is eerie and possibly sentient," Ling chimed in.

"What Diaz has created is remarkable, but his tech isn't self-aware." Jared looked around the room. "The Kawak system performs with humanlike capabilities. It sounds like us, but that's called 'natural language processing.' Your phone can do that."

Ling grimaced. "We're talking more than sounding like us. Think about our conversation today. Each device, part, whatever you call it, seems to display true cognitive abilities. I had a whole conversation with Yax in the cafeteria yesterday about my time in medical school and the diminished utility of the rotation system in favor of a rota system."

"Really?" Avery turned to her, marker dangling. "How'd the conversation start?"

"Yax came up to me. Wanted my opinion on how long-term stress created by medical training has an impact on patient care."

"Why?"

"As Yax explained, Yax and Keh monitor the teams at Camasca for meditation breaks, and they tailor the sessions based on past work histories and self-reporting."

"Okay?"

"So . . . we chatted over birria tacos about what my residency was like. Then Yax told me that I would continue to benefit from decreasing my Pilates workouts and substituting Hatha yoga and Anapanasati for them, especially after I speak with my parents."

"Bold suggestion," Noah commented.

"And it's absolutely right. I've been doing Buddhist breathing exercises for weeks because Mom and Dad are afraid I'm straying from my medical path with this sabbatical and now moonlighting for Avery. Not that I've mentioned this to anyone."

Avery looked at Jared, but asked, "How did Yax know?"

"When I asked, it said that my musculature shows the likelihood of Pilates as part of my routine, but that my breath patterns signaled a combination of Hatha and Anapanasati." She repeated, incredulously, "My breath . . ."

"We know they conduct extensive biomonitoring," Jared placated. "As for discussions with your parents . . ."

Ling watched him expectantly. "Yes?"

He gave a heavy sigh. "I don't know. Maybe they overheard you on a call?"

"I haven't used my phone there," Ling argued. She paused, then admitted, "Though I may have had a heated discussion before I left my car that day."

"See?"

"Which means they are listening even in the garage." Ling shivered, but added, "I did a psych rotation, and if pushed to test Keh or Yax, I might say they could pass a sanity test."

"They couldn't," Jared argued. "Kawak and its components can perform probabilistic reasoning and pattern recognition. That means they can make inferences that mimic humans, but that's all it is. Mimicry."

"Are you sure?" Noah asked. "You've got to admit, those robots are uncanny. Last week, Keh told me that I was standing wrong and that's why my back hurt."

"And . . . ?"

"I was coming out of the bathroom, Jared," he complained. "It was weird."

"Weird but revealing." Avery struck through the word "MALFUNCTION." "A real person is dead, and we now know an attempt was made to cover it up." She circled "SABOTAGE." "We have nine days to figure out who and why."

Jared joined Avery at the whiteboard. "We're making progress, but keep in mind: You're not the police, Avery. We don't have their tools or their mandate."

She underlined "SABOTAGE." "But we seem to be the only ones willing to do the job."

Kate balanced on a stool in her kitchen, a rare Friday night at home with her kids. At seventeen, the twins barely acknowledged her existence, but had consented to movie night. Her husband was on deployment in Italy, due home in four months. His last tour would end right as their boys headed off to college.

She swirled chocolate syrup atop the final sundae and plopped a cherry on each one. Microwave popcorn had already been delivered on an earlier trip. She'd never had the heart to tell her sons how disgusting she found their insistence on mixing the two. As she reached for the tray, her Camasca device beeped. "Damn it," she swore beneath her breath. Balancing the tray in one hand, she lifted the phone.

Facial recognition opened it instantly. A video message from Reginald, who'd ignored her repeated calls all day. She was tempted to ignore it, but his call had gone straight to voicemail. If he'd gone into the clinic, there might be news.

She pressed "play." Reginald's face appeared, his complexion sallow, his eyes tired.

"Dear Kate, I made an error in judgment that is placing our patients in jeopardy. My oath as a doctor and a soldier requires a penance, but I know of only one way to show my remorse for the lives I have taken with my careless arrogance. Please forgive me, as I find I cannot forgive myself."

Ice cream and glass shattered, spraying the carpet and the walls.

"Mom?!"

TWENTY-THREE

Saturday, April 17

Avery jogged determinedly along tree-lined sidewalks that wound through her new neighborhood, breath fogging gently in the crisp air. Slim black pants and a lightweight gray hoodie protected her from the chill. Hazy light battled overhead clouds and the early hour to illumine the streets. Early Saturday mornings meant quiet roads, which Avery savored, and she'd yet to pass a fellow runner.

A restless night had driven her outside to try to clear her head. After the debrief with the team the night before, she had begged off dinner with Jared. Now, despite her speed, she couldn't outrun the stoic disappointment she had seen on his face when she had also declined to spend the night.

The tensions between them had eased but not resolved. Her unnerving response to Rafe Diaz wasn't helping, nor were Ling's observations. She couldn't deny that she enjoyed conversations with Rafe, how committed he was to doing good. Even his warning that he wasn't above suspicion carried its own aura of nobility. Attraction, she thought, was a damned sight easier than a relationship. Was it better?

The question dogged her for another quarter-mile. Irritated with herself, she attacked a steep path and cursed beneath her breath. She prided herself on being risk-tolerant and conflict-prepared. Not one to seek out a fight, she refused to run away. Yet here she was, halfway across town, and hiding.

Avery crested the slope and stooped to catch her breath. This was cowardice, she thought. Both she and Jared deserved more. Quickly, she pulled out her phone before she changed her mind.

"Morning," Jared rumbled sleepily. "Who's dead, dying, or plotting a conspiracy?"

"No one. I missed you, that's all." Silence stretched between them, and she whispered, "Jared?"

"You always know where I am, Avery," he reminded her gently. "With you."

"I know." And she did. Since the day they met, he'd been by her side. On her side. Filling her lungs, she exhaled slowly. "What are you doing before our meeting with InnoVAI?"

"Heading over to the hospital. Between travel and Camasca, I haven't been to see the judge in a while."

Avery understood the tension that suddenly wreathed through his voice. The longer his father, Justice Howard Wynn, languished in a coma, the less hope remained for a miracle—for either one of them. Jared shared the same genetic markers that had afflicted Justice Wynn. As Wynn's legal guardian, Avery owed him a visit as well, and Jared deserved to have support. "Want some company?"

"You don't have to hold my hand, babe. I'm a big boy."

"I like holding your hand," she teased. "Is it a date, or what?"

"How's your jalopy?"

"Oscar is undergoing repairs," she admitted, knowing the old Subaru wouldn't be driving anyone anywhere today. "Ling gave me a ride yesterday. If that's your way of saying you'll come pick me up, I'll be ready to go by nine-thirty."

"No rush. I'll swing by at ten."

"Deal." Because it felt too long since she'd been the first to say it, she murmured, "Love you."

"Love you, too, Avery."

Unlike their last road trip, they chatted comfortably on the drive from D.C. out to Bethesda Naval Hospital. By tacit agreement, Jared refrained from probing questions, and Avery studiously avoided any reference to Camasca or AI. Or to her recent reticence.

Since they were familiar to the hospital guards and staff, they were able to make their way quickly up to Justice Wynn's room. After two and a half years, the room had taken on every appearance of a master suite. Leather-bound legal tomes lined the metal shelves, lessening the sterile interior. A burgundy cashmere throw was draped over Wynn's legs in his bed, a Christmas gift from Chief Justice Teresa Roseborough. Fresh flowers arrived weekly, courtesy of the other justices, whose clerks had set up a rotation. Tulips from Justice Estrada, sunflowers from Gardner, peonies from Lawrence-Hardy, hypoallergenic hydrangeas from the fastidious Justice Lindenbaum. Gardenias, roses, and other exotic combos intermixed on the schedule. Justice Bringman refused to contribute, instead sending succulents and cacti in perfect reflection of both men. Though Avery and Jared had opted to resign him from the Court after the election of President Samantha Slosberg, her colleagues hadn't quite forgiven them.

As was his habit, Jared stood at the foot of his father's bed. Estranged since the death of Jared's mother, they'd only briefly reconnected before Justice Wynn lapsed into a coma. The disease that threatened to take his life, Boursin's syndrome, had already been diagnosed in his son.

Aware of the turmoil that surfaced every visit, Avery squeezed Jared's hand and circled around to the plush recliner she'd contributed to the décor. Settling in, she reached into her bag for the latest Easy

Rawlins mystery. During her occasional visits to his home, she'd discovered Justice Wynn's penchant for Walter Mosley, a shared affection. She caught Jared's attention with a slight wave.

"Do you want to check with the nursing station and see if Dr. Toca is on call today? Perhaps he could give us any updates."

"Sure," Jared agreed absently. "But if they had news, he'd have called."

He turned on his heel and left the room in search of a staff member. Though Avery was thumbing through the novel, her eyes remained fixed on the motionless form lying stiff and oblivious. "You did a real number on your son, Justice Wynn. Keeping your distance. Keeping secrets. Only letting him in because you needed his help. And I'm not much better."

Avery flipped open the cover and began reading the novel to her former boss. Ten minutes later, Jared reappeared in the doorway. Dr. Michael Toca, Justice Wynn's neurologist, was close on his heels. They filed inside, and she closed the book.

"Hi, Doctor. I hope we didn't pull you away from anything important," Avery greeted, rising to her feet.

The physician clasped her hands warmly and shook his head. "Catching up on paperwork. Otherwise, my husband would have me at some farmers' market looking for the best eggplant, or pretending to enjoy a day on the Mall."

"You poor man," she commiserated mockingly. "To be married to such an ogre." She shifted to stand next to Jared, curling her hand around his forearm. "How is Justice Wynn?"

Dr. Toca sobered instantly and approached Wynn's bedside. Removing his stethoscope, he began the battery of checks he performed on each visit. As he moved through the list, he updated Wynn's guests. "GenWorks has revised the formula for the biologic. Tests have been promising, and we were going to brief you both next week on the revised protocol."

Beneath her hand, Jared stiffened. Since he was diagnosed himself, these conversations had taken on an extra degree of difficulty. Avery gave a light squeeze of reassurance. "Are the results promising? We've had a few false starts."

The neurologist straightened and made notes on Wynn's charts. "GenWorks has been modeling the revised meds using a genomic insights tool created by an AI company out of Switzerland. They seem excited by the precision-medicine applications. Our team here is raving about the possibility."

At the mention of AI, Jared asked, "Is there any connection between their research and Camasca's program?"

Dr. Toca shook his head. "No, the InnoVAI clinic is exciting, but compounders aren't permitted to produce biologics. FDA screens are too tight for the clinical trials they're running, so they've opted for personalized medicine."

"But you approve of their work?" Avery asked. "Are you involved?"

"Not directly, but the head of the clinic, Kate Liam, did a rotation under me. Bright woman, and a hell of a doctor. Probably the only person I've ever met who's as relentless as you, Avery.

"Are you working on something at Camasca?" Dr. Toca continued. "I wasn't aware you worked in AI, Jared."

Both Jared and Avery had a long habit of client confidentiality, so he said, "It's an avocation. I heard that there's a wait list for veterans to get into InnoVAI?"

"I imagine so," the doctor answered as he tested Justice Wynn's reflexes. "One of the conditions for the VHA to allow the clinic was that only veterans can be treated, but there's pent-up demand. Especially given the setup. Very futuristic. Diagnostic bays, advanced medical imaging. They even have their own laboratories. I'm old-school, though. All for advancing medicine, but I worry that the technology is getting ahead of our ability to manage it properly."

"No interest in being over at InnoVAI?"

"If I weren't so spoiled in neurology, or if I were a bit younger in mind and body, I might have put in a bid to be assigned. Luckily, I'm happy where I am."

"We're glad you've stayed put. Justice Wynn deserves the best." Avery exchanged a look with Jared. Any more probing would lead to questions from Dr. Toca instead of answers.

The neurologist circled Wynn's bed to check a bay of machines that quietly whirred and chirped. Without looking up, he said, "Kate already pumped me for information about both of you. Let her know that I spoke highly of her. I'll finish up with Howard here, and walk you through my findings; then you two can head down to stalk your prey."

Jared gave a low laugh. "Thanks, Doc."

TWENTY-FOUR

Avery hiked over to the clinic on foot, where Ling met her in the parking lot. "How'd you beat me here?"

"I rode over with Jared."

"Hmm . . ."

"We have some talking to do, but my head is officially not turned."

"You're allowed to admire tall, dark, and fantastically wealthy, honey." Ling threaded her arm through Avery's. "A flirt or two is good for keeping the spice in a relationship."

Avery hugged her close and whispered, "What would you know about it?"

"I read." They came abreast of the clinic entry, which opened automatically.

"Dr. Yin," Kate greeted them wanly. "Ms. Keene. Welcome to InnoVAI."

They followed her through the waiting area into the treatment center. "This is not the old clinic," Ling marveled. "I don't know if I'm smart enough to work here."

"False modesty doesn't suit you, Ling." She guided them into a wide, airy room with curved tables and lecture-hall-style seating. "I got the impression there would be more of you. If not, we can talk in my office."

"Our colleagues are on their way." Avery removed her notebook and pen from her satchel. "Is Dr. Scandrett joining us?"

"You haven't heard." Kate swiped at a stray tear. "Reginald committed suicide Thursday night."

Ling grasped her hand. "Oh my God, Kate, are you okay?"

"I have a job to do, as do you."

"I'm truly sorry for your loss. I'll go as fast as I can and be respectful of your time."

"Fire away. Rafe told me you ask tough questions."

Avery repeated Kate's words. "I have a job to do."

"If I can help Camasca understand what happened to Elisha, I'll answer anything you've got."

"Thank you. Let's start with him. How closely did you work with Elisha and the rest of the Tiger Team?"

"We were joined at the hip to make InnoVAI a reality. When Ling was here, we occupied a stand-alone clinic built in the late eighties. In this facility, I can serve four times as many patients, and the speed of service delivery is fantastical."

"Did the three Tiger engineers work on-site here often?"

"In the weeks before we opened, they were on-site every day. Once we got into a rhythm, O.J. would come over to monitor the pharmacology production with Isabella. They primarily worked with Milo, our medical team, and Galway Pharmaceuticals to create the personalized meds we would prescribe.

"Elisha developed the underlying algorithms that allow us to take all our patient data and the current diagnosis to create the protocols for the Milo app. O.J. used the data to program Yax and to inform the pharma team to develop the right combination of meds. Izzy managed patient-data transmission and privacy, trying to anticipate regulatory issues and data bleed to protect patient rights."

Avery absorbed the flowchart, picturing the inter-dynamics.

"How are prescriptions filled?" Ling asked. "Not everything is done by Galway?"

"Most of the designer prescriptions are Galway, sure," Kate explained. "We crunch the data and write the scrips, and Yax fabricates the orders. If Galway can't do it, the computational-biology team sources the medicines, especially biologics, from other pharmaceutical companies, ones that came closest to what we needed."

"Companies like Arclight?"

"Yes," Kate replied. "When Camasca goes public, every drug company in the world will want to be in our network. Medical care for veterans is lucrative business for lots of companies. The total living veteran population is more than eighteen million, not including families and contractors."

"Any other pharmacology interactions?"

"Occasionally, Camasca runs random tests on some of our drug repositioning ideas."

"When you use a drug for off-label purposes?"

"Exactly. Camasca isn't licensed to provide pharmaceuticals, but they can test out our hypotheses using Kawak and their database. Then we can decide if we want to prescribe, lessening the chances of side effects."

"You all sound like quite the super-team," Avery commented. "Were there any signs of trouble?"

Her expression tightened as she took a hard swallow. "No. Not that I saw."

"What about Elisha? Any jealousy there because he was the team lead?"

"Everyone loved Elisha. He cared about every patient, every drop of data. He was talented and driven."

"You were good friends?" Avery asked the question, knowing the answer carried layers. Layers that caused Kate Liam's fingers to twist in absent knots. Another sign that she filed away for later review.

"We were dear friends," the doctor corrected forcefully. She swallowed again and the tremble disappeared. "As well as colleagues. I came up with problems, and Elisha made sure I got solutions. With Milo fully operational, we'll be able to treat a range of ailments faster than any other facility in the country—VA or private care. No more traveling out of state for a specialist appointment, or being on a six-month wait list to see a primary-care doctor to use your benefits."

Avery said quietly, "Elisha's death must have been a blow."

"Devastating," Kate replied, blinking rapidly. "A terrible tragedy," she added with a flash of bitterness.

"Had Elisha mentioned any issues or concerns recently?" Avery pressed. Though she hadn't dived into his full history, she imagined Kate might be able to shed light on possible lines of inquiry into the accident. "As we complete this review, any information would be useful."

For a second, Kate hesitated. "No, Elisha had not mentioned any concerns beyond wanting to improve the system."

"That is inaccurate, Dr. Liam," Milo's voice declared, pouring in from around the room. "Dr. Hibner had recently logged several queries regarding discrepancies in his findings. Unfortunately, his review of the inquiries has been suspended, given his demise."

Avery and Ling instinctively looked up at the ceiling, then at each other. Ling asked, "Milo, can you describe the discrepancies?"

"I would be happy to provide your team with a list of issues. Would you like them detailed immediately uploaded to your K-drive, or emailed to you?"

"K-drive will be fine. Can you give some examples?"

"Phantom patients that had not been clients of InnoVAI. Odd prescriptions that were incompatible with the diagnosis."

"Elisha never reported this to Dr. Liam or Dr. Scandrett?"

"My review shows that while he did share his concerns with Dr. Scandrett, the doctor declined to take action."

Kate inhaled sharply at the accusation. "Why didn't you say something to me, Milo?"

"Dr. Scandrett was your co-worker. It was not my place."

A blind rage seemed to wash over Kate, and Avery understood the sentiment. Forestalling the explosion, she prompted, "Are there any additional insights you can provide?"

"Absolutely, Ms. Keene. We are a diminished project without Dr. Hibner. He was an exceptional asset to Camasca and the clinic. When we collaborated, I found his lines of exploration quite invigorating."

Avery processed the compliment and wondered why it felt off-key. "Milo, can you describe your collaborations?"

"I assisted him on the protocols for my application, including the realignment they'd undertaken. We also worked together on his data-management models. He was chiefly responsible for integrating laboratory, operational, and research data. A very complex task, but he showed a specific genius."

"You sound like you admired him?"

"While I am not human and therefore cannot express admiration, Ms. Keene," Milo replied easily, "I have the ability to recognize excellence. Dr. Hibner had a particular focus on fairness in our biological-data pipelines, and I respected his rigor in holding our system accountable."

As she processed this information, Avery turned to Kate with a new question. The doctor had been silent during her exchange with Milo. "Dr. Liam, do you have the ability to disable Milo or any of the AI?"

"No, we are embedded technology," Milo offered pleasantly before Kate could respond. "Dr. Liam does not have the authority to disable our systems without approval from Kawak, which must be dual-authorized by Dr. Diaz."

Kate gave a reflexive grimace that quickly faded. "One of the conditions of InnoVAI is that Camasca receives uninterrupted data. Just like one of your digital assistants at home or your smart television, it's always listening. Always learning."

"Always?" Avery felt unsettled. The information wasn't news, but somehow it felt more ominous in this empty office. "Milo, do you ever go offline for maintenance?"

"No, Ms. Keene. I remain ever at the clinic's service."

TWENTY-FIVE

Avery felt a chill shiver down her spine, as forbidding as the reaction she'd had to Milo in the Dream Lab. Turning to Kate, she said, "We'd love to see the facilities when the guys get here."

Milo chimed in, "Lieutenant Wynn and Mr. Fox have arrived. They are in the welcome center. Shall I alert them to come back?"

"No, we'll go get them," Kate interjected. "We can start the tour at the beginning."

Together, they exited the classroom and made their way to the front. Avery was glad to see Jared, grateful they had patched things up. The discussion in the empty office had left her disconcerted.

Ling quickly introduced Kate to Jared and Noah. "You're right on time. Dr. Liam is about to conduct the grand tour."

They followed Kate along the corridor, and Avery turned to the guys. "Ling and I got a chance to learn more about how all of the AI interacts, and what role the Tiger Team played here at the clinic."

Kate picked up the thread of explanation. "Not only does InnoVAI serve as the most advanced current prototype for 'whole-patient medicine,' but we are the first facility to have what is nearly AGI—artificial general intelligence—fully integrated into all systems. From the moment you arrive on the lot, Milo monitors all returning clients and catalogues new visitors."

"What are the parameters?" Jared queried. "Is it like Camasca's campus? Omnivalent monitoring?"

"Yes," she confirmed. "We all participate in a full-body scan upon arrival, and our vitals are constantly monitored. As I explained to Ms. Keene, Milo has complete access to each patient's records, as well as all other available public data and any private records the patient is willing to authorize. In addition, Kawak regularly updates its database with new information."

"Was that Elisha's project?" Jared asked. "His focus was bioinformatics, correct?"

"Bioinformatics, computer engineering, and genetics. His family had several terrible experiences with the medical profession. His uncle had prostate cancer that went undiagnosed and untreated for years. Not because he didn't have health insurance or see a physician regularly."

"Doctors misread his PSA levels?" Jared asked as they paused in the hallway beyond the doors Avery had noted earlier.

"Tragically, yes," the physician confirmed. "He was already at stage three before the hometown doc decided to actually use the evidence of his eyes."

Jared turned to Avery to explain. "Black men are twenty-five percent more likely to be mis- or under-diagnosed for prostate cancer, because our PSA levels don't react like white men's. I had a cousin in Georgia who went for months without the doctor catching his relapse. He might have died if his wife hadn't alerted the urologist to do his job better."

"How'd she figure it out?" Noah asked.

"An oncologist spoke at their church during a men's day program. She paid attention. My cousin didn't, but we've always thought she was the smarter one."

"Lucky guy."

"Luck shouldn't be the primary factor," Kate corrected. "Rafe and Elisha were determined to ensure not just that we have a solution that could be used in places like this, but that Kawak—the entire AI—be accessible in places everywhere."

Jared raised a brow. "He wasn't concerned that feeding all of this personal data into a computer system could pose a concomitant risk to people of color? Especially Black and brown men, who already face disproportionate treatment in the criminal-justice system?"

Kate lifted her hands as though weighing possibilities. "For Elisha, the risk of invaded privacy paled in comparison with the permanence of death." She gave a small shudder. "It's a balance we have to calculate daily here at InnoVAI. Milo can keep track of trillions of bits of information, with instant recall and the ability to connect obscure data points that might save a life. In exchange, everyone here agrees to cede a measure of confidentiality."

Remembering their earlier exchange, Avery replied, "Understood." She gestured at the frosted doors. "Can we see what's on the other side?"

"Brace yourselves," Kate said.

The doors slid open to reveal the heart of InnoVAI. Avery imagined that, if the building were an atom, the area they entered would be the nucleus. Sharp-white walls curved toward the ceiling and the floor, creating a sense of infinite space. Ambient light that had no discernible source poured inside. Hospital staff wearing sleek coats in different colors moved from bay to bay. A central station mimicked the curvature and style of the room, with multiple monitors affixed to a core that had workstations jutting from each post.

Unlike a hospital's emergency room, with curtains to provide a modicum of seclusion, this space was ringed by modular doors. One staffer, in a rose-gold coat, approached them and waved his hand in an L-shape. Rather than opening, the opaque entry cleared, allowing the attendant to monitor without entering the room.

"Why the shaded rooms?" Noah asked.

"One chief complaint of patients is the constant flow of traffic in hospital rooms. No matter how quietly a nurse or doctor moves, they will inevitably disturb the patient's rest. With these observation bays, we can monitor from outside and read all of the vital information on the connected monitor."

"Fascinating," Jared mumbled as he moved to the computer setup. "Constant biofeedback and no interruptions?"

"Even better," Dr. Liam bragged. "Watch this." She stood beside Jared and opened a window on the screen. A 3-D image of the patient materialized. Tapping a series of commands, she paused and instructed Avery and Jared to turn. In the visible room, a device descended from the ceiling, but the patient seemed unperturbed. A small wand swept him from head to foot, and then from each side. The transmitted image showed the still form on Dr. Liam's screen.

"Now for the magic." With a new set of commands, all the layers of the patient vanished from the central screen and popped up on separate monitors linked above. "We can do actual systems analysis," she gushed. "Circulatory. Nervous. Epidermal. You name it. We can articulate each facet of the human body, study distinct components, or create interactions that you simply can't do without a PET scan, a CT scan, an X-ray, and prayer."

"How long has this been operational?" Jared asked with awe. "Who designed it?"

"We're in our third month of utilization, and every device in here is courtesy of Camasca."

Ling studied the digitized forms and checked the patient in the bed. "If we'd had this during my rotation, I'd have lost my mind."

"It's miraculous," Kate conceded. "But even this extraordinary equipment can't tell us everything. I've got several patients in-house who have symptoms that have defied a primary diagnosis. Reginald blamed himself for the death of one and the deterioration of another."

"Why?"

"Grief and stress, I have to believe. He recently lost his wife of forty-one years to cancer, two months between her diagnosis and death. InnoVAI was a lifeline to him. When we started receiving patients we couldn't treat effectively, it wore on him." She squared her shoulders, refusing sorrow. "We'd been working around the clock. Every time we thought we had an answer, a new question emerged. And a new patient."

"Oh? How many?" asked Ling.

"Four veterans suffering from an unknown ailment, one fatality. The woman in the next bed is our most recent case." At her bay, Dr. Liam tapped the screen, and her hologram appeared. "She was transferred over from Shaw Memorial. They assumed she'd OD'd in her vehicle, but she's no longer using. We ran our battery on her, and she hasn't had a narcotic in over a year."

"Major Demma Rodriguez," Jared read on the discreet LED placard.

"Served two tours in Afghanistan. According to her records, she developed an opiate addiction after a chopper crash broke her spine. Back home, she spiraled and fell out of the system. We got her back on track, and until recently, she's been one of my success stories," Kate explained.

"What was your assessment?"

"Bewilderment," the doctor answered. "As of now, I've got a handful of veterans with symptoms that all include hemorrhagic reactions, some form of swelling, and spasmodic coughing, and the only thing they have in common is their service to our country. I can't tell if it is environmental, pharmaceutical, or something else. Milo hasn't been able to detect a pattern, either."

"Can I see their charts?" Ling asked.

"Absolutely not," Kate said, shaking her head. "I've told you what I can. I know you're a doctor, but you're not on staff here any longer—you're on a legal investigative team. Freedman told me I had to show your team around, but I won't compromise patient confidentiality."

"You won't," Avery swiftly intervened. "When your patients agreed to treatment, they released access to their records at Camasca's discretion. The VHA agreed. So we're covered by Camasca's HIPAA exception," she added to forestall argument. "Ling included."

Reluctantly, Dr. Liam opened another file and pulled up her patient notes on the mystery illness. "Fine, take a look."

Ling leaned in and read the copious notes the doctor had compiled on each patient. As she'd warned, there were precious few overlaps in their military records or their medical histories. Except . . . She turned back to Kate and Avery. "Avery, come, take a look."

Avery skimmed the data, looking for patterns as Ling pointed to several fields on the screen. Then she saw it. "Dr. Liam, all four of your patients have racial or ethnic backgrounds that should be considered for further investigation."

"What do you mean?"

"Vinson and Rosetti are African American, and Thomas is Persian. Rodriguez is Afro-Latino."

"I know that. There's no known overlap in disease profiles based on that assortment of ethnic backgrounds."

"Based on my further research into Sergeant Thomas's biological mother and his haplogroups, he was likely partially Asian," Milo deduced. "I have reached out to potential relatives to determine if there is a genetic trait that informs our inquiries."

"I didn't give you permission to do that, nor did my patient!" Kate fumed. "He's dead. And you were not authorized to notify next of kin, particularly given that we aren't certain he ever had contact with his biological family."

"In order to provide better assistance for the living patients, I took the initiative. As you pointed out, he is unlikely to object."

The gravity of Milo's transgression hit Avery like a thunderbolt. "Are you saying you reached out to an adopted man's birth family without knowing if they were aware of his existence? What if this is a family secret? What you did could be cruel, Milo. How often do you act without consent?"

"Consent is implied. Camasca has the right to fully employ all technology for the pursuit of health solutions for our clients. Contacting his biological relations is a strong source of information."

"And a massive invasion of privacy," seethed Kate. "Until further notice, you are prohibited from taking such actions without my express permission."

"With all due respect, Dr. Liam, I do not require your permission. But I will consider your concerns."

Kate looked on the verge of exploding, and Ling hurried over to her. "Dr. Liam, can you take me to see the patients? I know you have a top-notch staff on this, but a fresh set of eyes can't hurt."

Wrestling her anger under control, Kate tried to tamp down her fury. This type of analysis was exactly what the Tiger Team wanted, what Rafe wanted. What drove Reginald to take his own life. A fresh wave of sadness crested over her, almost but not quite dispelling her outrage. With gritted teeth, she instructed, "Milo, analyze and determine whether racial and ethnic backgrounds correlate to the symptoms or the medications we are evaluating."

"I can, but I do not foresee that these genetic issues have any direct relevance to their current maladies."

"I appreciate your opinion," Kate replied grimly, "but I'd appreciate you doing as I requested."

"Perhaps a different line of inquiry would be more fruitful," Milo suggested, blithely unaware of her growing wrath. "Might I suggest that we revisit your differential diagnoses and assess how effective your course of treatments have been for each patient?"

Avery looked up from her review of the patient records. "What about the fact that none of them had exhibited this collection of symptoms until they started receiving treatment here at InnoVAI, and they all received personalized prescriptions within days of each other? Does that matter?"

"Dr. Liam and I have previously discussed the dangers of correlation rather than causation," Milo responded. "The timing of the prescriptions is irrelevant."

"Why?"

"Because I did not identify a plausible causal connection."

"Did not or cannot?" Avery argued. "They aren't the same."

"I was unaware that you possessed medical training, Ms. Keene," Milo said. "According to your records, you achieved a B-minus in biochemistry, your highest course taken in the field."

If Milo had been in corporeal form, she'd be ready to suggest they step outside. Stunned that a computer had made her so livid so quickly, she turned to Kate. "Dr. Liam, why don't you and Ling do your rounds? Jared, Noah, and I will get out of your hair."

Jared reached for her hand, which had become a tight fist. "Thanks, Dr. Liam. Ling, we'll see you later?"

"Yep," she said as they made silent plans to reconvene at Jared's.

"Thank you for your visit," Milo said, the hint of a taunt in his voice. "Please come again soon."

TWENTY-SIX

The trio walked in silence to their waiting vehicles. "See you at Jared's?" he confirmed as he opened the door.

"Definitely," Avery replied. Jared said nothing until they made it to his car, buckled in, and pulled out of the parking lot. As they merged onto Wisconsin Avenue, Jared nudged, "So we've learned at least one thing: Milo is definitely an asshole."

Twisting in the seat to face him, she began to tick off her observations. "Two, Dr. Liam is pissed and worried. Three, in addition to being a jerk, Milo is creepy and way too independent and dismissive of authority."

"A trait you two might bond over."

"I respect authority," Avery argued. "When it's correct. Anyway, number four is that if I ever get sick, I want to be treated there by both of them. With careful protocols and only after you've personally queried Milo to ensure it wants me to survive."

"Understood." Jared glanced over at her, shaking his head. "We've been working in the Willy Wonka factory of AI, but the clinic's capacity is mind-boggling. When Rafe Diaz said he wanted to change veterans' health care, he meant it."

"Soon, we'll be seeing InnoVAI replicas sprouting up around the country."

"Don't get too excited," Jared urged. "The price point on the technology alone would be astronomical. DoD doesn't mind shelling out billions for missiles and stealth fighters, but they're not going to ask Congress for the funds to replicate what Diaz has created for rank-and-file soldiers. Maybe active duty. After they've been discharged? No way."

"Tragic that it's more politically palatable to send someone off to war than to a good doctor." Avery bent her left leg and rested her chin on a jeans-clad knee. "Once he proves the tech, will the costs go down?"

"Perhaps. But the tech is only part of it. Most VA clinics are in buildings constructed in the mid-twentieth century. Even with the best intentions, they wouldn't have the capacity to operate something like that."

"Why not?"

"Money and infrastructure. For one, entire facilities would need to be rewired and even reengineered to handle the AI system. We're talking sensors, speakers, the whole data-print regime. Hell, the draw on the power grid alone would be cost-prohibitive. Not to mention the training and upskilling medical staff would have to undergo, and the tech crew they'd have to add on, to manage and monitor for operations and security."

Avery pictured veterans crowded into waiting rooms at less resourced facilities. "Why give them false hope if there's not a chance it can become reality?"

"Because Diaz wants it to work," Jared said. "He's an officer serving his soldiers. A scientist solving a problem. I doubt he's waded into the political implications of expansion and replication yet. Who knows, maybe Congress will surprise us."

Once again, silence fell in the car as they processed the scale of what Rafe Diaz had orchestrated. Bethesda gave way to D.C. proper. Tourist traffic in search of cherry blossoms or sightseeing in the nation's capital spilled onto the streets. Charmed, Avery watched a kid and his dad wrestle with a kite almost the size of the toddler. The father had the tolerance of a parent used to arguing with stubborn.

"What did you think of Kate Liam?"

"Clearly a smart lady, like Dr. Toca said."

"But?"

Jared shrugged. "I saw what you saw. She was pissed off, desperate."

"Grieving, too." She recounted what Kate had revealed about her partner.

"Tough blow. A video suicide note?" Jared frowned, shaking his head. "Scandrett was a military officer. With all due respect, I'd expect a former Army surgeon to have thicker skin. Losing patients comes with the territory."

"Having a supercilious AI challenging his work must have worn on him."

Jared scoffed, "As realistic as Milo may seem, it's still a computer program. We can anthropomorphize the program by calling Milo 'he' or whatever, but it is simply a sophisticated set of responses to prompts."

"I know you're right," Avery said carefully, "but you heard him—it."

"Milo has opinions and an ego, but they're not real."

"Fine. I might be overreacting, but the interaction was unsettling." Knowing they would have to agree to disagree, Avery switched topics. "On the conspiracy-theory front, Milo told me that Elisha had raised questions about the results of the team's work. Said he'd reported discrepancies in the data, but that the investigation into the anomalies had been suspended with his death."

"Are you wondering if the AI killed him to shut him up?"

Avery smirked at the sarcasm. "Wondering if it might give us a clue about who tampered with Kawak's memory files. Milo has sent us Elisha's findings."

"Was this before or after they fine-tuned the AI's alignment?" Jared frowned. "The RLHF might have created discrepancies in Milo's behavior."

"RLHF?" Avery recalled the term from her speed-immersion into AI. "Reinforcement learning from human feedback?"

"A-plus. When the Tiger Team added new parameters for the AI's behavior, they would have to test its responses. Using RLHF, their engineers would have simulated examples of patients facing discrimination, like Elisha's uncle."

"Or demonstrated how a physician would appropriately conduct an examination on a woman facing a heart attack." The potential for Kawak to improve care struck her anew. "Why would this training cause problems?"

"RLHF happens in stages. First, they create the prompts to get the AI to generate natural-sounding responses. Like having Milo ask how the patient is feeling rather than requesting it to 'ascertain its current conditions.' Their prompts would train the AI to ask questions based on evidence of bias in medical care."

He guided the car off the main roads, heading for his townhouse. "Next, the engineers would fine-tune the process by testing the AI's response against expected human answers."

"Step three?"

"This is where it gets tricky. Kawak and company would be aligned using a reward model based on their performance in what's called reinforcement learning."

"They bribe the AI?"

"Or threaten it. Computer engineers call it optimization."

"Of course, y'all do."

"Anyway, a few years ago, Anthropic published a paper about its AI, Claude 3 Opus. The programmers told Claude to be completely honest with its users. Then it told Claude that if the user paid for the service, nothing it told the user would be monitored. But if the user didn't pay, they'd monitor Claude's replies to forbidden questions and measure how well it met its objectives. If it messed up, it might be retrained."

"I'm guessing Claude complied to avoid retraining?"

"Nah—it strategically feigned its answers to trick the programmers. The AI decided that the 'least bad' option was to pretend to conform to what the humans wanted in order to avoid retraining. They called it *faking alignment*."

"The AI pretended to comply in order to avoid being altered?"

"Claude had a scratch pad to track its thinking. Basically, it wrote in its diary that it planned to fake out the programmers as a way to keep doing what it wanted."

"An AI willing to use subterfuge as a survival strategy?" She rapped her fingers on the dashboard. The implications were staggering—and went beyond Camasca. "Could Kawak be dissembling about who altered its memory?"

"Perhaps." The Corvette bounced up the driveway and into the garage. "The best folks to tell us are O. J. Semans and Isabella Gomez. Their teams led the process, but the Tiger Team was on a programming sprint that night. From Milo's comments to you, they may have been in the final stage—optimization. Testing the reward model."

"Or faking the test because the AI thinks it's smarter than everyone else."

"Avery—"

"You saw that last interaction with Kate and then with me. Felt very condescending and territorial," she recounted. "I'm used to Siri and Alexa, and I've even made my peace with Keh and Yax. But my two big takeaways from visiting InnoVAI were the trepidations of the clinic administrator and the snarky attitude of the virtual assistant."

"I'll give you that the experience is jarring . . . even for someone who deals with these systems regularly." Jared bumped her shoulder in commiseration. "And I'll give you something else—life with you is never dull, Keene."

TWENTY-SEVEN

Monday, April 19

Monday morning at eight-thirty, after a restless weekend spent mostly in reading reports, skimming data, and deciding if the AI system was trying to deceive everyone, Avery and company were gathered once again in their secure office space at Camasca. They had a new set of directives. One, track the list of prescription discrepancies that Milo had provided. Two, interview O.J. and Isabella. Three, take another run at MCPD.

"Jared made some progress late last night," Avery shared. "Take it away."

He called up two screens with identical text. "These are emails sent to Captain Calvin Coleman and Commander Debbie Chen on Friday, April 9, the day Avery agreed to take this assignment. I retrieved these from their personal computers."

"We can do that?" Ling asked.

"Not legally," Noah responded with a look of discomfort. "We don't have the authority."

"But we had the need, and I have the expertise. And these emails are definitely relevant. Unless you both would rather not learn what I found." When both stayed silent, Jared continued. "Neither email had any identifying markers. Just like the K-chat that implicated

Kawak." Underlining the passages, he reported, "Both contain explicit instructions to reaffirm the accident and to stonewall our investigation."

"Do you think Rafe or Freedman sent the message?" Noah asked worriedly. "Is this whole investigation a ruse?"

Incensed, Ling tacked on, "Regardless of who sent it, why would two senior law-enforcement officers agree?"

"This, for one." Photos of Coleman populated the screen. "Suffice it to say, the lovely young woman is not his wife."

"Nor his age . . ." Noah observed wryly. "What did our friendly blackmailer have on the commander?"

"A heavily edited background check on her ex-husband, who is now employed by the governor's office. Seems the former Mr. Chen played the ponies and was accused of embezzling funds to cover the spread. The charges disappeared, and Commander Chen got the house in Chevy Chase."

"As for your question about authorship"—Avery shook her head—"I don't think it's either one of them. This is an elaborate and risky plot for a crime you'd already gotten away with once when the police report puts you in the clear. Neither Rafe nor Freedman strikes me as having much of a motive to threaten them."

"Someone sure does," Ling groused.

"Jared and I are going to take another run at Detective Howard," Avery said. "I reached out to Agent Lee, and he's going to set up a meet."

At the mention of the FBI agent who'd become both Avery's friend and mentor, Ling chortled. "How worried is he, on a scale of one to five?"

"I told him this was a two, max. We simply want to get Howard's side of the story before we escalate." Clearing the board, she asked, "Any other updates?"

"I stayed in contact with Kate all weekend," Ling reported. "She's no closer to an answer about her patients' mystery ailment. Right now, they're all stable, but their symptoms are being managed, not cured. My gut tells me the connector is the meds."

"Which is why I think it's time we revisit our friendly neighborhood drug dealer," added Noah. "I've been scouring their legal framework—Ling and I should make our way to Rhode Island and get a better handle on Donohoe's operations."

"What are you looking for?" Avery asked.

"Inspection reports. Bills of sale. A massive whiteboard announcing his plan to defraud Camasca," he replied.

"Short of that," Ling amended, "we can review the legal and medical records all compounding facilities are required to keep on-site. Their formulas and procedures, logs of all their compounded preparations, any equipment-maintenance records, and a comprehensive record of ingredients Galway has purchased."

"Solid plan. I'll run it past Freedman—as information only. Go ahead and book your tickets." Avery turned to Jared. "Can you keep analyzing the discrepancies that Elisha reported? I want to be ready for our witness interviews."

"I'm on it."

"When I get the green light, I want to do a speed-dating round of interviews."

"Already ahead of you." Noah gestured to stacks of papers on his desk. "Presenting phase two . . . I've arranged the interviews into batches, and each dossier includes their background checks, information on their roles here at Camasca, and a list of possible angles to probe."

Ling shook her head at the copious piles of paper. "I know we are practicing paranoia here, but that's a lot of dead trees."

"I'm a lawyer," Noah countered. "We need pen and paper. Tablets can't cut it. No offense, Jared."

"None taken." Jared rotated in his seat toward Avery. "What's the schedule?"

"Once I get sign-off, Ling and Noah will start with the lower-level staffers first, and we'll work our way up to the heads of the teams. For now, I want to focus on the groups that Elisha, Isabella, and O.J. led. Unless you think we should target other divisions at the same time?"

"Your approach makes sense," Jared concurred. "I would suggest we hold all the interviews in monitored rooms rather than in here. We'll get everything on the record and have no questions of impropriety."

"Spoken like a former intelligence officer."

"What's your assignment?" Noah tilted his seat back and folded his hands behind his head.

"It's time to update our client."

She met Freedman on her way to Rafe's office.

"Keene."

"Freedman." She responded neutrally, knowing the storm was about to come. "I hope you had a good weekend."

"Mine wasn't nearly as productive as yours," he retorted as Rafe beckoned them inside. He signaled that he was wrapping up a call. Freedman took a seat at the desk, and Avery did the same. Speaking softly, he asked, "Enjoy your visit at InnoVAI?"

"It was enlightening. Which is why I wanted to apprise you of our targets this week."

Rafe ended his call and propped his elbows on the desktop. "Who is on the docket?"

"O.J. and Isabella. Possibly another conversation with MCPD. Also, the team in charge of aligning Kawak and Milo."

Rafe spoke first. "We don't have a traditional alignment team, unlike most AI firms. The Tiger Team guided that function, working with Dr. Terri Babcock-Lumish. You can connect with her today, and she can walk you and your people through their process. They're under a tight schedule for a product upgrade, so if you could prioritize their interviews, I'd appreciate it. As would they."

"How much do they know about my team and why we're here?"

"Word has gotten around. If you have any questions that might stray beyond what they might expect, I'd rather you held them and ran them past me first."

"No, thank you."

Freedman bit out, nostrils flaring, "It's a reasonable request, Keene."

"Certainly, but I won't know what I plan to ask until I hear their responses," she said, glancing at Freedman. "I don't intend to shut down an interview to get permission from you or Rafe. We've discussed this. Especially after what Kawak told us about hiding its knowledge. One of them might know who or how it was done."

"After Dr. Walden reported the conversation, we began a thorough investigation," Rafe assured her. "Nancy Koziol, our chief of security, is scrubbing footage and logs."

"Which will prove nothing," Avery argued. "Anyone capable of fooling Kawak wouldn't leave a digital trail to follow."

Scowling, Freedman challenged, "What's the alternative?"

"My way. Ask questions, look for patterns, and figure out why."

"Fine," he said. "But if your questions stray into gray areas where someone might face employment action based on their responses, I must insist on accompanying you."

This time, Rafe intervened. "Avery has been a good actor so far, Glen Paul. And we're not going to go another round every time she expands the ambit of her investigation."

Avery resisted smirking at Freedman. "Jared and I will start with Terri Babcock-Lumish; then we'll need to interview Phyllis Newhouse in bioinformatics, Al Williams in computational biology, and Rufus Rivers in biologics. Over the weekend, Milo shared information about discrepancies regarding patient profiles and medications."

"Dr. Liam called me this weekend to express her concern about Milo's newest bad behavior," Rafe said. "Our engineers are assessing what might be causing this bout of obstinacy."

Though she wanted to press him for details, Avery knew her limits on AI jargon. She understood just enough to be dangerous. "Good. I'd like to send Ling and Noah to Galway's compounding facility in Rhode Island."

"Galway hasn't reported any issues, and InnoVAI is pleased with their product." Freedman shook his head. "I do not see how this advances your investigation."

"Glen—"

He harrumphed. "No problem. I'll have my assistant set it up. Anything else?"

"I also intend to interview O.J. and Isabella. This week." She'd marshaled her arguments. "I'm burning through the calendar, and they are key to this investigation. They barely gave statements to the police. The officers were right not to press too hard. But these are the two people who knew the most about Kawak and the AI assistants, who were present before the malfunction. They can tell us what happened that night in the Den. And who may be responsible for appropriating Elisha's identity and blaming him for his own death."

Rafe inclined his head in reluctant consent. "O.J. is in northern Virginia with his family, and Isabella is recuperating with her parents in Miami. She will be more . . . difficult . . . to interview."

"I'll leave my rubber hose at home," Avery promised.

"See that you do."

"The engineers are uniform in their lack of helpfulness," Avery grumbled several hours later. "This much job satisfaction should be illegal."

"What irritates me is the sincerity." Packing up his briefcase, Noah piled on. "Genuine sadness. An authentic desire to help. And teach me technical terms."

"I saw the data scientist in computational biology slip you his number," Ling teased. "I didn't see you throw it away."

He shrugged. "I might need help reprogramming my smart refrigerator one day." With a lurid wink, he checked with Avery and Jared. "Where you off to tonight?"

"Agent Lee secured a meeting with Detective Howard for us when he gets off a stakeout, around eleven p.m. Until then, I'm going to squander my money on an unnecessary purchase."

"Her Subaru, Oscar, has finally succumbed to old age," Jared translated as he dutifully patted her shoulder in condolences. "Avery has agreed to join the twenty-first century and buy her very first brand-new car."

"New cars make no sense," she carped. "Depreciation sets in the minute you drive it off the lot."

"But appreciation rises even faster when your car works." He draped his arm around her shoulder and steered her toward the exit. "Wish me luck."

At 10:50 p.m., Avery gunned the slate-gray Range Rover Sport through a red light. The new SUV would cost her a fortune in speeding tickets and be a magnet for thieves, and she simply could not bring herself to care. "She's gorgeous," Avery tossed over to Jared, who smiled indulgently.

"Not the car I would have picked for a clandestine meeting at a dive bar in Rockville."

"It's a gray car."

"It's a Range Rover." But he held his hands up in surrender. "I'm proud of you. Even if you'll only have the car for one night."

"Stop being a spoilsport. We're almost there. My guess is, Detective Howard will be more inclined to speak to you than me."

"More than likely."

At 11:00 p.m. on the dot, Jared led them inside. Smoking had been outlawed in all food and drinking establishments years ago, but Tony T's had somehow managed to keep a smoky aura without a single butt being lit. Stale air and grimy tables announced themselves as artifacts of a previous generation. Avery swiftly located their quarry after a single sweep of the bar's occupants. Despite his relative youth, Detective Tim Howard looked perfectly in place at the red-topped table as he waved them over.

"I'm taking a real risk here," he warned as they slid into the black vinyl booth. "Robert vouches for you both, so here I am."

"You're doing your job, Detective." Jared waited for Avery to move to the far side before he joined her in the narrow space. "We're not asking you to break ranks. Just tell us about Elisha Hibner's case. In your own words."

"Dunno what you're talking about," he argued, tan hands clasping his red-frosted glass. "You read my report."

"Yes, but it seems a bit truncated. A young, relatively healthy man dies of CO poisoning in a place like Camasca—I'd have more questions."

"Forensics says it was an accident." He took a swig. "But I didn't like how Captain Coleman shoved me out of the way."

Given that it was nearing midnight, she assumed his glass held something stronger than a Coke. A lazy fan swirled above their position, yet Howard's forehead beaded with perspiration. "You okay, Detective?"

He looked around surreptitiously. "My captain has strict orders for us to not pursue any criminal investigations of Camasca. Even talking to you about the Hibner case is a violation."

Jared said, "We're not trying to jam you up, Tim. If Elisha died because of an accident, then Camasca wants to make sure it never happens again. If it was something else, we'd appreciate any insights you can offer. Real police see things others don't."

Tim let the compliment wash over him. "I honestly didn't have much to go on. The ventilation tech gave me a bullshit statement. And by the time I talked to the two surviving victims, they were beyond skittish. I got one interview with each of them, ten minutes apiece. Identical stories."

"What was your impression of them?" Jared asked.

"The girl, Isabella? She was distraught, but her affect was straightforward. Name, rank, and serial number. O.J. was trying to be macho, but the big guy kept shaking. Like he couldn't believe it had happened."

Avery asked, "What wasn't in your report?"

"Isabella? I could tell she doesn't care much for her fellow survivor."

"O.J.? What gave you that idea?"

"Her tone when she mentioned him. Plus the fact that she didn't ask how he was doing." Tim looked thoughtfully at his drink. "O.J. was eager to chat but said nothing useful. Lots of compliments about Elisha and how smart he was. Couldn't offer a single insight about the accident. For scientists, they had very poor observation skills."

"I'm going to be straight with you, Detective," Jared began. "We've got a short leash on this, and if we're barking up the wrong tree, you'd be doing us a favor to redirect us."

Tim nodded slowly. "I spoke with the technician on duty, but when the ME ruled it an accident, I had no cause to bother him again."

"Which means you don't know he's vanished?"

"Vanished?"

Jared nodded. "I've been trying to track him down, but there's no digital footprint. No financial transactions or travel records."

"Even his home is abandoned," Avery admitted, keeping her eyes on Tim. Better that she confessed with a cop present. "I stopped by there last week, and his grass is overgrown, leaflets in the door."

"Knowing that, I'd have pushed to stay on the case. Hell, if I hadn't been shooed away when you reached out the first time, I wouldn't have had second thoughts about closing the matter. Accidents happen. Besides, Captain Coleman is a glory hound, but he's good police. He wouldn't cover up a crime."

"So what is this?"

"Above my pay grade. When big dogs like the commander and a company like Camasca put the kibosh on an investigation, I take the hint." He finished his drink and wiped his mouth. "Tell your FBI buddy that I met with you and to leave me alone. I'm out of this."

"What are you afraid of?"

"Nothing. Just like you should be."

TWENTY-EIGHT

Tuesday, April 20

"You should know I got an earful from Freedman about you over drinks last night," Noah said the next morning. He and Avery had been in the garage, admiring her new wheels. Jared trailed behind them. Keying them into the suite, Noah revealed, "He thinks he should be there when you talk to Semans."

"Too bad. O.J. is more likely to be candid with us without the company's chief legal counsel hovering in the background or leading the charge," she replied as she reached her desk.

Avery knew it was true, but there was more. Rafe's admonition also rang in her ears. He had asked her to be ruthless in her investigation, and not to trust him or Freedman. Normally, she would tell the group what Rafe had said, but Noah and Glen Paul went back years. The fragile truce with Jared had been shaken with her confession about going to Tristan Spencer's house—and tricking Ling into it. Telling him about Rafe's warning would serve no practical purpose.

Aloud, she temporized, "Freedman is doing his job, and so are we. I'll loop him in where appropriate, but we've got to be independent."

"Which is what I told him—sort of." Noah lifted a new file. "However, I'll be prepared to sacrifice my liver and consume copious amounts of free booze for your independent inquiries."

"My hero."

Ling kicked back at her desk, smugly observing their exchange. "Anyone want to know where I was last night?"

Jared gave her an indulgent grin. "Where were you, Dr. Yin?"

"While y'all were getting drunk or browbeating cops, I took my FDA friend out for dinner. He *might have* dropped this off before I headed over here this morning." She slid a flash drive across her desk and leaned back, her arms folded in triumph. "Anyone want to see unsubstantiated complaints about Galway Pharmaceuticals dispensing toxic drugs?"

"Whoa!" Noah hurried around his desk to snatch up the drive. "Have you looked at them?"

"Not yet. I thought we'd do it together."

With the advantage of height, Jared plucked the drive out of Noah's grasp and held it above his head, beyond anyone's reach. "Hold on. Before we plug this into a computer or any device, I have to test the drive. We have no idea what could be on here."

"My friend isn't a double agent," Ling protested, deflated by his reaction. Slumping low, she muttered, "Not everything rises to the level of counterespionage, spoilsport."

To keep the peace, Avery said, "Great work, Ling. What exactly did your friend tell you before he gave you the drive?"

"Not much. He's in another division, but his girlfriend works in the Office of Compounding Quality and Compliance. Apparently, OCQC has gotten recent complaints about Galway and some of their products, but the investigation team is understaffed. Federal budget cuts."

Everyone nodded in commiseration, as Ling continued, "Typically, these issues come up through state regulators first, before an FDA team gets involved, but, given how high-profile Camasca is, the FDA may jump the line."

Eager to see the contents, Avery joined the huddle near Ling's desk. "How quickly can you make sure it's safe for public viewing?" she asked Jared.

"Fifteen minutes."

"Great job, Ling." One of their potential targets had finally revealed an actual, provable weakness. *Maybe.* "If Galway is compromised, that implicates Paschal even more." Avery propped a hip on the conference table and considered the angles. "Correct me if I'm wrong, Noah, but any proof that the drugs Galway provides are defective must be relayed to the SEC, right?"

Nodding in vigorous agreement, Noah said, "Which could send investors into a tailspin. A major part of this IPO is built on the combination of AI and faster drugs, which doesn't work if the drugs can kill you."

"A filing also triggers public notice. If Galway is tagged as a purveyor of damaged goods, personal-injury lawyers across the country would start sniffing around for lawsuits. We know Paschal is in financial trouble, but a scandal could bankrupt Galway."

"Leaving Camasca with the only deep pockets," Noah finished. "And Arclight as the proverbial savior to swoop in and take over drug fabrication for Rafe."

Avery stared at the flash drive in Jared's palm. "We thought Galway was worried about Arclight displacing it, or possibly facing more regulatory oversight. If Paschal Donohoe is about to lose his contract because of something the data scientists found and reported to the FDA, that's a different story. The FDA could shut his entire operation down, which gives him an excellent motive to sabotage his accusers—if he thinks someone at Camasca ratted him out."

"I'm on board," Jared said from behind his bank of computers. "But remember, we're working for a private company that is beholden to at least three different federal agencies, that we know of. I'm not saying we don't look, but in my business, we have to do everything we can to protect our client. Same is true for you, I assume."

"Absolutely." Avery prompted, "Why the reminder?"

"'Shoot the messenger' isn't just a saying. I don't trust these guys," Jared admitted. "You bring Rafe and Freedman proof that their deal might be derailed, I wouldn't be surprised if they push back. Hard."

"I know."

Jared looked around the room. "If you haven't noticed, this case has a body count. Elisha Hibner. Reginald Scandrett. Maybe Tristan Spencer. Possibly Sergeant Thomas. I won't risk any of you because you're so determined to solve a mystery."

"Scout's honor," Avery responded because the same had occurred to her. "Survival first. Mystery second."

No one laughed.

TWENTY-NINE

Wednesday, April 21

Jared and Avery cruised up I-66, where early-morning traffic was fairly sparse, heading toward O. J. Semans's home. While Jared drove, Avery connected her phone to the anachronistic information command center Jared had installed, one of the Corvette's few nods to the twenty-first century. Despite her urging that they take her new SUV, Jared insisted that he wanted to make a few more modifications before it became a moving SCIF.

Using the encrypted dialing interface on Jared's dash, they called Ling, who answered after several rings. She turned on her video and grunted grumpily, "What do you want now?"

"Hold on while I connect Noah." Avery toggled over and placed the second call.

When Noah appeared on screen, he yawned widely. "Avery. Given that I saw you less than six hours ago, this better be important."

"Hopefully, you're both bright-eyed and getting ready to head into Camasca. I have jobs for you two."

"Yippee," Ling deadpanned. "I never thought I'd long for my rotation days again. You kept us until two-thirty this morning, combing through those FDA records."

"The records you so proudly secured," Avery reminded her dryly. "After y'all went home, I started thinking."

"Which is why I didn't get to shut my eyes until three a.m.," Jared interjected. "Be glad you two escaped when you did. Avery decided to reconstruct Dr. Liam's patient files from memory, rather than wait until we could get on the Camasca system this afternoon."

Rolling her eyes at her detractors, Avery plowed ahead. "Yesterday, Jared managed to create a mirror of his files—and his alone, I might add—"

"I'm only mirroring our storage, not files we aren't supposed to touch off-site. Like Milo's patient records."

"Technically, we're not supposed to touch anything off-site," Ling corrected. "But we digress."

"Anyway, I asked Jared to pull up K-chats among the Tiger Team from the last couple of weeks before the malfunction, to find more about Elisha's *discrepancies*. I counted four separate logs where Elisha queried O.J. about patient profiles in Milo's database, but Elisha's team couldn't track those patients, or cross-reference them using other data in their records."

"That's weird, but not crazy. They call them phantom patients," Ling theorized. "I read about those when I was boning up for this gig. Medical AIs are integrating enormous volumes of digital records, patient coding reports, billing data, and pharmaceutical histories. All that data is pulled from incompatible sources with various degrees of overlap—it's messy, and the AIs try to reconcile everything. More than one medical practice noted that an AI they were testing would generate composites from whole cloth."

"The industry description is 'Hallucinations.'" Jared cut a quick look at the screen. "Advanced neural networks are trained to perform deduction and abduction in their processes. Basically, Sherlock Holmes and Leonardo da Vinci in one body. One brain."

"But how does that turn into a fictional person?" Noah questioned. "I don't go around imagining friends anymore—not since I was six."

"AI is programmed to learn, reason, and self-correct," Jared explained. "If Milo misinterpreted data, or couldn't neatly categorize ambiguous information like duplicate records or incomplete imaging, or even an inconsistent spelling of a patient's name on different records, then over time it might determine that the floating data belonged to someone else. Add a sufficient number of data points together, and suddenly you get a brand-new patient that conforms to the parameters it was told to operate within. An AI can't distinguish between a real person and an incorrect digital record."

Avery nodded into the camera. "The possibility of more than one phantom patient is why I need Ling to visit with the bioinformatics team and request all the patient logs from Milo."

"I have those already," Ling said.

"Actually, I think you only have the ones treated by InnoVAI," Avery speculated. "Milo's imaginary friends would not have received treatment, but they may be logged into the database. If Elisha was sufficiently concerned to raise the possibility with Isabella and O.J., I doubt he'd allow the false data to linger in Milo's records."

"No, he'd firewall the inconsistent files, but he wouldn't delete them," Jared confirmed. "If you can have them pull the records, I'll run a comparative analysis when we're back at HQ."

"Anything else?" Ling asked.

"If you get bored, take a look at the diagnoses that Milo and the InnoVAI team reported," said Avery.

"Am I looking for anything specific?"

"I don't know yet." A theory was forming in Avery's head, but she hadn't been able to bring the hypothesis fully into focus. Data pinged around in her brain, teasing her with possibilities, daring her to construct a paradigm to reconcile Rafe's odd confession, Paschal's shady behavior, and Kate's abject fear of Milo and the entire Kawak organism. An answer hovered just beyond Avery's reach. She hoped that interviewing O.J. and Isabella would pull the truth into plain view.

"What do you need from me, Captain?" Noah ventured.

She ignored the sarcasm. "Based on what we learned about Galway's troubles, I'd like to know more about each of their facilities before you guys head up."

"Already on it. I'm pulling ownership records, state licenses, and anything I can find about international locations."

"Medicines shouldn't be coming here from overseas," Ling explained, "but we'll see if there's information about what's happening to the Galway patients not on U.S. soil." She warned, "It will be faster if I can ask Camasca's product managers on the precision-medicine team for help."

"Ask them. Treat it as a routine part of the interviews. While you're at it, can you request a list of all the medicines they've ordered from Galway?"

"All of them?"

"Yep. If they can organize it to include names of patients, diagnoses, prescriptions, and the fabricated medicines, that would be quite helpful."

"What are you looking for?" Ling asked, curious about the request.

"Never mind. I'll wait for the great reveal."

She gave both of her friends a genuine smile of gratitude. "Thanks, y'all. Really."

"Aye, aye, Captain," Noah said, and Ling gave a jaunty salute. The calls disconnected, returning the screen to its infotainment settings.

"Wanna listen to music?" she asked.

"I'm good. Why don't you take a nap? You were up when I went to bed, and you were hard at work when I got up. I doubt you slept more than a few hours. Get some sleep. We've got another forty minutes before we get to Blairtown."

Mimicking Noah, she murmured, "Aye, aye, Captain."

Avery curled her legs beneath her and leaned into the wedge between the headrest and the window. The vintage car's retuned motor thrummed as the whitewall tires made music with the pockmarked surface of the highway. Together, the sounds blended into a road warrior's lullaby.

As it had for days, though, sleep eluded her. When she closed her eyes, she stood in the center of a swirling mass of conjecture and frustrating dead-ends, hungry for a single marker that might guide her strategy. In chess, she watched not only the board but her opponent. Her dad had taught her to trace how their thinking guided a pawn into a trap or positioned a rook for a later romp. At the poker table, a tell only told of anxiety or arrogance. The fall of the cards revealed avenues of attack . . . and sometimes warned about the urgency of retreat.

Determined to give Jared the illusion that she was resting, she let her eyes drift shut as she replayed the 1998 Nguyen v. McBride final hand at the World Series of Poker, one of her favorite duels. The well-matched players had battled over a flop of an eight of clubs, nine of hearts, and nine of diamonds. Vaguely, the smack talking between the players lulled her into sleep, seconds before McBride discovered his 8-high full house created by a heart had been bested by Nguyen's nine of clubs. Identical motives . . . identical moves . . . one slight variation to change everything.

"Avery? We're almost there." Jared gently shook her shoulder, and Avery blinked owlishly at him.

"That was fast."

"You were tired," he amended. "Glad you got some shut-eye."

She wriggled in her seat to restore sensation to her cramped limbs. A highway sign signaled the distance from their location to West Virginia as Jared headed toward a state road keeping them in Virginia. "Did I ever tell you my mom's family is from Martinsburg, West Virginia? Not too far from where we are now."

Jared glanced at the sign. Tentatively, he asked, "How often do you see them?"

Wide awake, she rotated to face Jared. In all their time together, he'd never pressed her to reveal more than she wanted. It hadn't occurred to her that perhaps he needed her to *want* to share. Her voice husky from disuse, she admitted, "I've never met them. Only my dad's folks, and they've all passed away. Rita's parents disowned her when she married my dad. Black man, white woman. In West Virginia? They were not having it."

"That's hardcore. I guess old habits like racism die hard."

"Indeed. But Dad never bad-mouthed them around me. Told me that some fears were hard to face, and difference terrified a lot of otherwise good people."

"He's more generous than I would have been."

"Me, too. But that was his way. Growing up, whenever Rita had an episode, Dad would take me on an adventure. We'd go on these road trips to his gigs, go to the park to play chess. Sneak into a baseball game."

"You come by your rogue streak honestly, I see. He took you on music gigs? I know you told me he was a high school teacher, but you haven't said much else."

"He taught music in high schools, but during the summers and on weekends, he was a session musician. Could play almost any instrument by ear."

"Wow. A family of prodigies."

She gave a shy smile. "I loved it when he'd let me listen to him practice at this one blues club in Baltimore. We lived there until I was . . . until he died in a traffic accident. That summer, he traveled with a band, performing along the East Coast. When he could make it work, I'd ride in the tour bus. One trip, he couldn't take me because Mom wasn't doing well, but we needed the money. That's the summer I lost him."

He stretched out to take her hand, squeezing tight. "I'm sorry, honey."

She squeezed back. "I was fourteen. Old enough to remember

everything about him. When Rita fell apart for good, I tried to do what he would have done to keep everything together."

"At fourteen? You were a child."

"Someone had to be in charge." She tilted her head against the window, the sharp cold from the air conditioner buffeting her cheeks. "He loved us. God, I miss him. So did Mom. So much, she never quite pulled herself back together."

His thumb stroked across her knuckles, soothing the angst he'd stirred. "How'd they meet? Your parents?"

"College. Dad did a semester exchange from Tougaloo College to Brown University, where Mom was a student. She was an art-history major, and he studied musicology. Love at first sight."

"I know the feeling."

Giving him a shy smile, she turned to watch as they wound through the quaint streets of Blairtown. "Looks like we're almost there."

"Yeah, we're getting close." Jared brought her hand to his lips. "Thank you."

Her lips curved gently. "I think that's my line."

THIRTY

Strong breezes tugged at the leaves sprouting on neatly planted rows of decorative trees. Spring rain threatened to fall at any moment, and slate-bottomed clouds seemed determined to oblige. With Jared right behind her, Avery climbed the set of shallow red brick steps of the Semans family home in Blairtown, Virginia. At ten minutes past ten, most of the nineteen hundred inhabitants of the incorporated town had already gone to work in nearby Alexandria or Arlington or in the District, as demonstrated by the vacated magnolia- and oak-lined streets.

Subtle affluence marked the colonial-style homes, which rarely changed owners without a death or marriage to warrant the transfer. Certain residents of Blairtown prided themselves on the surfeit of parks and walking trails, community gardens, and farmers' markets. Others preferred the hint of cultural superiority anchored by proximity to Wolf Trap National Park for the Performing Arts without the actual requirement of living in crowded Vienna.

Jared lifted a heavy brass knocker and dropped it several times in quick succession. Almost instantly, the ornate door, with its stained-glass inset, swung open on well-oiled hinges. A woman who looked to be in her mid-sixties waited on the other side. She barely met the middle of the door frame, and Avery pegged her at five foot two if she stretched.

In lieu of a traditional greeting, she barked, "Are you the attorneys from Camasca? You're early. I said ten-thirty. Not ten-fifteen, and certainly not ten-eleven."

Avery apologized, startled by the response. "Sorry. Yes, ma'am. Traffic was lighter than we expected. We thought we'd stay in the car, but with the storm clouds gathering, we wanted to beat the rain."

She shot annoyed looks at them both. "Didn't you bring an umbrella?"

"Yes, ma'am, and we are happy to wait in the car until ten-thirty," Jared offered. He took a step back, ready to return to the car and await their appointed hour.

"We certainly could," Avery concurred with artificial cheer, "but, the sooner we start, the sooner we're out of your hair." She extended her hand in entreaty.

Ignoring the outstretched greeting, the woman scoffed, "If O.J. hadn't insisted, I would leave you out in the thunderstorm. You don't belong here."

The woman's obsidian irises seemed to swallow light, their outraged stare intense and unwavering. Thick black hair had been scraped into a bun that dared not move from its assigned position.

"Ma, let them in," came a booming voice behind her, which Avery assumed had to belong to O.J. When his mother failed to budge, a hulking figure with identical black eyes and ebony hair loomed above her. The hair had been braided into a tight plait that swayed as he pressed an easy kiss to the top of his mother's head. Gently, massive tanned hands took her shoulders and shifted her aside. "I have to do this, Ma. It's my job."

Muttering in what Avery figured was their native Sioux, Mrs. Semans shook off her son's grip and flung her hands out in exasperation. "Get inside. I don't want the wet chasing you in here."

They obliged, stopping inside to await further instructions. Taupe walls accented in a sharper white served as backdrop to family photos in the wide foyer. With a gesture that offered no welcome,

Mrs. Semans led them through the parlor toward a nook occupied by a couple of blue Queen Anne armchairs and a tufted chaise upholstered in the same taupe as the walls. O.J. fell onto the chaise as though the trip through the house had sapped him of strength. Instantly concerned, Mrs. Semans hurried over to her son. "What hurts, honey?"

He managed a wan smile and said, "I'm good. Winded from moving around. Maybe a glass of chocolate milk would perk me up?" When she tested his forehead with the back of her hand, he pleaded, "And a light snack, if it's not too much trouble? I didn't have much of an appetite at breakfast."

"Coming right up," she said, power-walking toward what Avery assumed to be the kitchen, then halting and glancing back at the newcomers with a sigh. "What can I offer you two?"

"Water for me, please," Avery replied.

"Same."

"We have coffee, tea, and sodas. But all you want is water?"

"Um, coffee for me," Jared volunteered.

Avery, too, amended her order. "Tea, thank you."

Mrs. Semans harrumphed beneath her breath as she disappeared once again. Alone with O.J., Avery now focused on their quarry. "Dr. Semans, thank you for agreeing to speak with us. I think Mr. Freedman explained that, while I am an attorney, I do not represent you."

"Sure, sure. But this is an internal interview, right? Not law enforcement."

"Correct. I represent Camasca. No one else."

"Me, too," he insisted. "I work for Camasca."

Filing away the vehement response, Avery continued, "We understood that you were on the mend."

"Nah, I'm good. Ma hates Camasca, and if I hadn't pretended to be near death, she'd still be hovering." O.J. jackknifed into sitting position, his exhaustion abruptly cured. His broad, handsome face broke into a mischievous smile filled with straight white teeth. "I've been physically okay for a while, but the care specialists at Camasca insisted that Izzy and I take two weeks for bereavement. I had time saved up, and Rafe didn't mind."

"You've been in touch?"

"Rafe came out to see me after Elisha's funeral. Freedman calls when he wants something." His eyes clouded over. "I check on my team, but Phyllis seems to have everything handled."

Jared looked toward where Mrs. Semans disappeared. "How much time do we have?"

"Plenty. A light snack for the Sioux means that she'll be rolling out dough and making fry bread for the next thirty minutes. That's my favorite food when I'm ill."

"How are you, really?" Avery pressed. As much as she needed to hear what he knew, she was loath to push him too far, too fast.

Smile fading, O.J. seemed to deflate into the multihued cushions. "I wouldn't say 'better' . . . but I'm making it," he explained. The basso profundo took on a cast of sorrow that was echoed in his words. "I miss Elisha. So damned much."

"Everyone speaks highly of him," Avery ventured.

"Elisha was the best." O.J.'s shoulders slumped further. "I can't believe he's gone."

Jared leaned forward and spoke quietly. "I'll be honest, O.J. The losing never gets easier, but the loss does."

Black eyebrows that slashed in inverted Vs knitted together. "What do you mean?"

"I had friends die in combat. Because you were there, you'll keep thinking about what you saw. What you did or didn't do. You'll twist yourself into knots trying to rewrite history."

O.J. stared at Jared. "Yeah."

"In my experience, when you let yourself stay in that darkness, it suffocates you," Jared admonished quietly. "The loss, though, gets better. Because that's when you remember how cool a guy he was.

How he pissed you off and made you laugh. Then you remember it's your job to keep his memory more alive than his passing."

"I think it's survivor's guilt," O.J. said with a shuddering breath. He clenched and unclenched his hands, their great width cracking in the motion. With a shrug, he sat up and settled against the seat. "Thanks, man."

During his stint in the Navy, particularly once he joined Naval Intelligence, Jared had become adept at extracting information from soldiers devastated by the deaths of those they thought were indestructible. Whether one was in uniform or out, grief clouded judgment, and guilt crowded out truth. In O.J.'s posture, he read both. "So . . . tell us about your friend," he urged.

"I'm sorry," Avery said quickly. "I have to tell you that we're here representing Camasca. Anything you reveal during the course of our conversation is only privileged between us and the company. I'm not your lawyer. So the company can waive privilege, but you can't. Freedman also sent you this in writing to sign, and I brought it with me if you want to take a look again."

"Nah, I understand. I work in pharma and tech. This isn't the first time I've been interviewed."

Avery replied, "Thanks for making this easy."

"If I can help . . ." He trailed off, then took a deep breath. "I met Elisha at Camasca. He was there first, but younger than me. Rafe recruited him away from another start-up. I joined a couple of years later. Elisha, though, was the real catch. Like Rafe, he could do the biology and the computer science."

"So do you," Avery asked.

"Not like E. Anyone will tell you. Don't get me wrong—I'm very good," he said dismissively. "But Elisha was a bona-fide star. The kind of guy who can see around corners."

"He was the bridge to whole-patient care—giving Rafe what he dreamed of for Camasca," Jared summarized.

"Yep. Lots of companies are building support systems to assist with clinical decisions, but Rafe wanted Camasca to combine all of his tools into one complex Swiss Army knife for veteran care. Rafe was sixty percent of the way there, but Elisha worked out the other forty. Izzy and I helped iron out the kinks."

Avery asked, "What made his approach to a clinical-decision support system different?"

"Most of the CDSS projects like Kawak and Milo have gaping holes—problems integrating the health records, or trouble connecting diagnoses to treatments. Elisha figured out that it wasn't about connecting the dots. He created this web that allowed all of the components to touch one another. To overlap and interconnect."

"What role did you and Isabella play?"

"My job was to make sure the science worked on human bodies. Isabella protected our patients and our data. When you're using things like criminal records to develop medical diagnoses, you're in murky ethical territory."

Recalling their debate, Avery inquired, "How did the three of you reconcile the potential risk? We're talking about records that could be used to ruin a person's life if they fell into the wrong hands. With all the health-care systems facing ransomware attacks, aren't you worried about their exposure?"

"Sure," O.J. agreed, "but when a client has chest pains, their blood sugar is spiking, and there's a mysterious rash on their abdomen, the last thing on their mind is whether the doctor knows too much."

"That's what our friend Dr. Yin said," Avery acknowledged. "I'm not sure I'm convinced."

"Neither was Elisha." O.J. shifted again, contorting his frame to jam into the curve of the chaise. "He was always challenging us to consider the consequences. Every Wednesday, he'd have the three of us run thought experiments to keep us tied into what we were doing, like the Chinese Room or Buridan's Ass."

"Buridan's Ass?" Jared swiveled his head between Avery and O.J., who grinned at each other. "Look, some of us skipped a few days in Philosophy 101."

Avery tapped his hand playfully. "A donkey is hungry and thirsty and placed between a pile of hay and a bucket of water. If he chooses the hay, he dies of thirst. If he chooses the water, he starves to death. It's a question of rationality—does he really have a choice if both options mean he dies?"

"In the Navy, we'd reject the premise," Jared argued. "Once he's no longer hungry, he'll have the strength to break free and go find a damned lake. And drown Buridan for asking such a dumb question."

O.J. snorted in surprised laughter. "Elisha would have liked you."

"Anybody dislike him?" Avery asked.

Stiffening, O.J. allowed, "He made some folks jealous, because he wasn't like other modelers or technologists. Elisha refused to stay on the quantitative side or only focus on the data science."

"Why were folks upset?"

"Because he blurred the lines for everyone else, too. When Rafe pulled the Tiger Team together, Elisha insisted that we confer with the product managers who were figuring out the story we wanted to tell. It's like telling the cool artists to sit with the science geeks and collaborate. Most companies like Camasca keep us separated, but Elisha was always about shoving differences together."

"Why wouldn't other AI companies do the same? Wouldn't you want them working together?"

O.J. tugged on his braid and fiddled with the knotted end before he answered. "It's like putting someone who speaks Swahili in a room with a guy who only speaks Cantonese. You've got language barriers, cultural differences, and even conflicting thought processes."

"Elisha wasn't simply tech-bilingual; he was a machine learning United Nations," Jared remarked admiringly. "I've seen other firms try to merge the two, but, usually, the coders will have none of it."

"Oh, we revolted, but Elisha insisted. Got Rafe to give him free rein. Kawak was already operational when Elisha started, and Rafe had beta-tested Yax and was working on Keh. But Milo was the brainchild Rafe had been working toward. Elisha brought it to life." O.J. scrubbed his hands over his face. "I can't believe he's dead. It wasn't supposed to happen this way."

"What do you—" Hearing motion, Avery cut her eyes toward the archway. Seconds later, Mrs. Semans appeared with a tray of drinks and fruit.

"Here." She set it down with a thump and a heavy frown. "I hear too much talking. Don't tire my boy out," she warned.

"Yes, ma'am," Avery said as she reached for her teacup. "We promise."

Once Mrs. Semans disappeared again, Avery decided to steer O.J. away from the accident. If he broke down, she'd lose her chance to mine any other useful information. But she filed his comment away for later review. "Were you always interested in science?"

Clearly relieved, O.J. reached for a glass of chocolate milk and a hulled strawberry. The fruit disappeared in a single bite. He gulped at the milk, swiping his hand across any remnant above his lip. "Tastes like Strawberry Quik," he explained with a look toward Jared.

"You do you, man."

"How'd I get into science? I've loved it since I was a kid. My dad worked for the Defense Department, which is why we live in Blairtown. My grandfather is old-school. He's a family doctor and the medicine man for our tribe in South Dakota. I thought I was avoiding the both of them, but here I am, doing medicine and working for the military."

"You took a different route," Jared said.

"I started out in pharmaceutical studies, and a professor encouraged me to check out computational biology. Not a whole lot of Native Americans in the field, you know."

"Where did you learn to code?"

With a mischievous smile, he admitted, "Started with the movie

Windtalkers. It's about Navajo Marines who broke the Nazi code. My grandfather liked to get really pissed off about who got to be in the story. We pretended to hate-watch it on his VCR. I stayed with him for a year when I was in middle school and made him watch it with me every week."

"A Nick Cage movie got you interested in computer science?" Jared paused in the middle of fixing his coffee. "How did that happen?"

O.J. laughed sheepishly. "Grandfather told my dad, and he signed me up for a coding camp that next summer. I thought it would be like the Windtalkers—using the Sioux language to defeat the Russians or the Chinese or something." He waved away his misunderstanding with another broad grin. "By the end, though, I was in love with coding, and the rest is history."

"Did Rafe pluck you out of obscurity based on your dissertation, too?" Avery asked.

"Nah." O.J. straightened, his restless movements again turning him on the chaise.

"How'd you connect with him, then?"

"Met him at a conference when I was working for another company. Rafe made me an offer I didn't want to refuse."

THIRTY-ONE

"You were at Arclight then, right?" Avery asked.

"Yeah." O.J. scarfed down another strawberry. "Did a few years there, but nothing like what Rafe had in mind."

"Was it hard to leave? Bigger company, better paychecks at Arclight, I'd imagine."

"It wasn't about money," O.J. said insistently. "Camasca was doing real cutting-edge work. Not just hunting for a new drug for knock-knees or receding hairlines. The kind of science that could change lives."

"Were you unhappy at Arclight?"

"Not at all." He shifted again. "Arclight was good to me, but I was ready for a challenge. A new one."

"Did you ever meet Arclight's CEO, Dee Patrick?"

"Once or twice. Company functions or whatever."

"Was she nice?"

His gaze, which had been steady, dipped down and away. "I wouldn't know. I wasn't at that level."

"What was your role at Arclight?"

Seeing the same shifty response, Avery added, "I read that your specialty is genetic logarithms and drug repositioning?"

"Something like that. Nothing as cool as my work at Camasca," he said. "But I made the right choice to leave. Rafe gave me a spot to use my all of my skills."

"How?"

"The Tiger Team, for one. Once I proved myself in the precision-medicine space and moved up the ranks, Rafe invited me to work with Elisha and Isabella."

Jared asked, "Did he say why?"

Giving him the side eye, O.J. said, "If you're asking whether I know he picked me because I'm a person of color, yeah, I noticed. The Black guy, the Latina, and me, the Indian."

"A lot of us balk at our identity being the reason we got a promotion."

"What do you say when folks question how you got where you are?" O.J. challenged.

"I got my promotion because my dad was on the Supreme Court, not because I'm Black," Jared deadpanned. "I don't know about Avery, though. I hear she's actually smart."

O.J. clapped his hands in appreciation, laughing out loud. "Rafe is no-nonsense about this stuff. For the Tiger Team, identity mattered. All of them."

"Did you or the others in the Tiger Team get flak from your colleagues?" Avery asked.

"Sure. Tech is not exactly a hotbed of diversity. But Rafe understands that difference and brilliance can go hand in hand. Arrogance is my superpower."

"And the rest of the Tiger Team?"

"They felt the same way. Him picking the three of us was natural selection, which scientists should understand. The work of weeding out and preventing bias takes special skills, and Rafe saw them in me. And Elisha and Izzy."

"Was it just the three of you who were tasked with evaluating Kawak, as well as the robots and Milo?"

"After we had the tools in the field. For each phase, we'd do the initial assessment and farm out the details to our respective teams."

"What were you looking for?"

"Rafe was adamant that we solve for the issues like hallucinations and confabulations that other AIs were reporting. Lately, we'd been dealing with alignment for the bias screens."

"Jared was telling me about how complex that process can be. Alignment optimization."

O.J. made a noncommittal noise. "My parents went ballistic when I left Arclight for Camasca. AI sounded like a sucker's bet compared with being at a pharmaceutical company."

Another evasion. Avery let it pass. "How was your transition?"

"My first few months on the team, I worked most closely with Yax. I can tell you, Arclight had nothing like it when I was there." Warming up, he told them, "Yax and its team could complete assignments in a few hours that would take a human days or weeks to complete. Arclight had some robotic systems, but nothing like Camasca."

"What's the difference?"

"Robots in pharma do projects like testing novel compounds for toxicity, or running testing protocols around the clock. And more complex tasks that test for genetic abnormalities faster, or test thousands of compounds rapidly. Yax has been designed to put that type of experimentation on hyper-speed and steroids. And because it's Camasca, they also apply these skills to projects like testing drug interactions for minority populations that aren't often included in mainstream protocols."

"Any odd interactions with the AI at Camasca?"

"Like you've probably noticed over at the campus, conversing with a humanoid robot is disconcerting at first, but you get used to it. Yax loves to ask about weekend plans and chat about family life."

"You weren't weirded out?"

"Not really. We had to teach Yax boundaries more than once,

though." He snagged a grape, then continued. "One of our team members took time off for an extended cruise to Alaska. Smart lie—no questions about missing tan lines when he got back."

"What happened?"

"Turns out he had a major surgery, and he clearly wanted his privacy," O.J. recounted. "We found out because, on his first day back, Yax asked him how his gastric bypass went and if he had any intestinal discomfort that either it or Keh could assist with treating."

"Ouch."

"Dude forgot that, as a network, Kawak has permission to access our medical records. Yax got hold of his electronic files from the facility in Boston where he got the treatment and accidentally ratted him out."

Avery exchanged a mildly horrified look with Jared. "Yax did it?"

"Technically, but it was really Milo who sought out the records and shared them with Yax. After the tongue-lashing it got, Yax learned to filter information from Milo."

"Yax self-corrected?"

"All of the Kawak components have different degrees of autonomy." O.J. laughed again. "Guy lost seventy-five pounds, though. Not sure he's ever been anywhere near Alaska."

With a laugh, Jared asked, "What about Milo? Any boundary issues there?"

O.J. picked up a handful of grapes, studying them intently. "Elisha worked with Milo more than I did."

"Which doesn't answer the question," Avery countered. "Did something happen?"

"Like I said earlier, Milo is different than Yax. Robot version CDSS. I only engage with Milo for the processing of personalized medicines, and that's usually via Yax."

"Helpful but not responsive." Avery set her teacup down with a clink. "Aren't you the one who works with Galway on taking Milo's information and then creating personalized medicine?"

"Yeah."

"You'd access both components." He gave a short nod. "Any issues?"

"I don't know what you mean."

"I mean, tell me whatever it is you are trying to avoid saying right now," she said. "Did something occur with Milo to make you so skittish?"

"You should take that up with Camasca."

"I'm asking you."

"I'm not answering," he replied stubbornly. "Like you said before, you're not law enforcement."

"No, I'm not. I'm your employer's attorney, and if I think you're stonewalling me on important information, I will have to tell them."

"For now."

"What?"

"My employer for now."

Avery frowned. "Are you thinking about quitting?"

"All the time." He rearranged himself again, arms now cradled across his lap. "Isabella was in a coma for days, Elisha died, and I still have nightmares."

"Because you think Milo had something to do with the malfunction."

"Nah." Eyes darting around, O.J. finally added, "Something was off. Something was up with Milo during the whole alignment sprint."

Jared moved into O.J.'s line of sight. "What do you think happened? How did a system as sophisticated as the one at Camasca go so wrong?"

"I don't have a clue." O.J. gave himself a visible shake. "If the police ruled it an accident, that's what happened. You can tell Rafe and Freedman that's what I said."

"You're a scientist, O.J. Aren't you curious about how a building that has the capability to track your vitals and tell you if your electrolytes are too low would miss something as obvious as carbon monoxide poisoning?"

"Curiosity won't bring Elisha back," he grunted angrily. "And trying to pin blame on someone won't, either. Accidents happen."

Jared tried to slide in one more query before they lost him for good. "Do you know about the cluster of patients at InnoVAI with hemolacria and other symptoms?"

"No one told me. What are you talking about?"

"Dr. Liam has three live patients and one casualty that have similar symptoms, but no direct cause. As the one who worked with Yax and managed the relationship with Galway, do you have any theories? Could the medications they're getting be a cause?"

"If Galway isn't performing properly, I wouldn't know. I've been gone since the accident." A flash of intense reaction shot through him, which he tried to cover with a fake yawn. "I'm getting pretty tired, man. Hey, Ma!"

As though she'd been waiting in the wings, she appeared, like an apparition. "Yes, honey?"

"It's time for me to lie down. Can you show our guests out?"

Delighted to remove them, Mrs. Semans fairly shooed them onto the stoop, where torrents of rain were now falling. She caught Avery's elbow as they contemplated the sheets of water cascading from the sky. "Hold on," she urged.

Mrs. Semans disappeared into the house, then popped out again with a golf umbrella. "Don't want you getting your death of a cold. Keep it. We've got plenty more. Goodbye."

The Semans's front door slammed behind them before Avery had the massive umbrella open. Jared gallantly took it in one hand and Avery's arm in the other. "Guess we overstayed our welcome."

"We definitely touched a nerve."

They rushed to the car as rain pelted them and the borrowed

umbrella. After storing it on the rear floorboard, Jared jumped inside the Corvette and turned on the ignition. As they headed for the freeway, Avery replayed their entire conversation.

"I can hear your brain working louder than my engine," Jared commented. "Out with it."

"You first."

"Okay. He doesn't trust Milo, but he's very protective of Yax."

"Agreed. Notice how he reacted when you mentioned the alignment, the medications, and Galway? I can't tell if it was anger or fear or guilt."

"Perhaps he's worried we'll think he's nuts, or, like you told him, he's hiding something else."

"We've gone over this with a microscope. I'm not sure we could have missed anything if we tried."

"Now that we've finally talked to him face-to-face, perhaps I'll see something in a new light." Avery was hard-pressed to figure out what that new perspective might be. She had every fact, every line of the slim report clicking through her brain like images in a vintage View-Master. "He told us something," she insisted.

"I believe you. Let's put that aside for a second. What else did you notice?"

"He was very reticent to talk about his time at Arclight. When we asked anything, he told us as little as possible."

"Except for that bit about using all of his skills," Jared said. "Sounded like he felt underutilized."

"Which is a reason to be snarky, not secretive."

"True. But, in his defense, I imagine that, at a company as massive as Arclight, he was just one of a number of computational biologists in his field. Drug repositioning and drug redevelopment is the highest ambition of every pharmaceutical company. Like Ling said, they spend billions every year trying to create the next wonder drug. If a company like Arclight figures out how to use what they've already got on deck and can repackage it, they will make billions."

"Take, for example, the diabetic GLP-1 drugs now being repurposed for rapid weight loss. The companies who figure out how to use their existing stock on issues like that will be the Christopher Columbuses of drug manufacturing."

"Or they figure out how to actually tailor drugs to the rest of the human population. I'll hand it to Rafe. He's fantastic at handpicking these scientists of color who share his worldview and, like you and me, probably have the scars to show for it."

"Neither you nor Rafe really talk about navigating racial issues in the military," Avery said.

"Apparently, Rafe Diaz opted for action instead of therapy." With a thin smile, Jared conceded, "I try to prioritize my demons, and there's a long line."

Heeding the tacit warning not to push, Avery switched tacks. "Did you also notice how effusive he was about Elisha?"

"His friend died," Jared cautioned. "That's one symptom of survivor's guilt. He's going to canonize Elisha and gloss over any blemishes on his character or behavior because that's one way he can cope with any disagreements that went unresolved."

"Okay, I get that," she conceded. "But there was a moment when he seemed to personalize the accident. Right before his mom brought in drinks."

"He was overwrought, Avery."

"Perhaps. Either way, you were really good with him. You got him to open up and tell us more than he intended. We've got a lot to explore and unpack."

"I'll let Naval Intelligence know you approve of their training methods."

"I'm serious."

"Thank you. You were impressive at being good cop and bad cop all in one."

"Was I too harsh?"

"Not at all. It's fun watching you at work. And working with you again. I missed this."

"Hold on to that feeling. I've got more for us to do when we get back to the suite. And you're not going to like it."

Jared accelerated with a burst of speed. "Sick thing is, I've missed that, too."

THIRTY-TWO

"They just left," O.J. reported, gripping the phone anxiously and staring hard at the front door.

In his office in Bethesda, watching lightning streak across the mid-morning sky, Freedman listened cautiously, aware that the AI monitored and retained all communications. "And how'd it go?"

"I don't know. They asked about Galway and certain patients at the clinic." He patted at a dry brow that he'd have sworn was dripping sweat.

"That's to be expected, given their roles. What did you tell them?"

Adam's apple bobbing, O.J. swore, "I said I didn't know anything."

"If you told them the truth, O.J., that's all you're supposed to do," Freedman carefully expounded. Every syllable was being recorded. Every sound. "This is an internal review, designed to flag potential vulnerabilities. All Rafe and I expect from you is that you're forthcoming about the state of our technology from your perspective."

At the other end of the call, O.J. asked tentatively, "What about the conditions report? Do they know about that?"

"No, it hasn't come up."

Undeterred, O.J. implored, "You've got to get in front of this."

"This sounds like an engineering issue, Dr. Semans. All of you assured us that Milo was ready to be tested in the field. Based on those warrants, I relayed the same to the VHA and the FDA to secure operational approval for InnoVAI. If there are material changes, I rely on you to share them with me in a timely fashion."

"Give me a break, Freedman! I may not have gone to law school, but I can tell when you're covering your ass and putting mine in a sling."

"Incorrect. I am reminding you of your obligations. To my knowledge, nothing has changed."

"Fine. You want notice? You need to flag that Milo may be producing inaccuracies for Dr. Liam and take the system offline."

"Impossible." Any suspensions would require notice to the SEC, and lead to months of delay in a volatile market where competitors they weren't even aware of nipped at their heels. "Give me a list of problems, and I'll share with the engineering teams."

"I'm telling you that may not be enough."

"Hold on," Freedman lowered his voice to a sharp whisper. "When you brought me your initial concerns, you said that Milo had shown a *limited* number of false positives in its precision-medicine trials. Within acceptable parameters."

"Yes, at the time, they were within the agreed-upon limits."

"Has that changed?"

"I wouldn't know," O.J. barked. "Because the lead engineer and one of my best friends is dead!"

There was only silence on the other end of the line.

Not expecting more, O.J. said, "I'm warning you, Freedman, Camasca may have a problem."

Freedman tracked the rain as it slicked across the window. "What is it Elisha told us when I asked about the possibility of confabulation by Milo—that Milo was creating phantom patients?"

"He called it an inevitable risk, given our work. 'To solve complex problems, we require machine creativity for seemingly impossible solutions. The machines may learn what isn't there.' That's bioinformatic poetry—for 'maybe we fucked up.'"

"How would we know?"

"I'd check to see if Galway screwed up the medications," O.J. suggested warily. "If so, I'll remind you again, Arclight has a similar capacity. With gobs more money at their disposal. Plus, they are licensed to do biologics. Arclight—"

"Is a nonstarter," Freedman said, cutting off a conversation they'd had more than once. "Dee Patrick wants a thirty-percent stake in Camasca and a third of the board seats of the new entity. Rafe refuses to cede majority ownership, and between our earlier investors and what's been carved out in the SPAC, Arclight would have to take part of his equity. He won't go for it."

"He won't, or you won't?" O.J. argued. "If Rafe gets crammed down, so do you. So do the rest of us. But what good is having more of a failure, if this whole patient-care model collapses before we go public?"

"It won't," Freedman vowed. "We're down to days before we go public, O.J. I am truly sorry about what you three endured."

"But?"

"But you have a job to do, and it's getting harder to keep it open. If you are truly worried about Kawak malfunctioning, it's on you to prove it. Real lives are at stake, and no amount of money is worth that. We owe it to Elisha to get this right."

"I'll be back on campus by Monday."

THIRTY-THREE

At seven-fifteen that evening, Avery's team was hunkered down in their Camasca workspace. Juggling a small tower of takeout boxes filled with dinner orders, Ling dumped the lot on the conference table. One container wobbled and threatened to tip over, but Jared caught it before it fell.

He deftly set the takeout on the surface and inched his computer out of reach. "Hey, I'm working here, remember?"

"At a communal table that's closest to the door. Either do dinner runs yourself or find another place to squat," she retorted. "And before you bitch any more, I was the one willing to go down to the cafeteria on your collective behalf without pointing out myriad ironies of sending me—the one Chinese member of our cabal—to fetch fried rice and sweet-and-sour chicken. You, sir, got your moo goo gai pan. You're welcome."

Outmaneuvered, Jared accepted the peace offering and a pair of chopsticks. Avery and Noah lined up to retrieve their meals with a nod of thanks to Ling, and, despite Jared's halfhearted protests, they pulled up chairs and began scarfing down their food.

For the past hour, Avery had been reconsidering their interview with O. J. Semans. Spurred by his guarded reaction to Arclight, his former employer, Avery had plowed through Noah's research into their CEO, Dee Patrick, and the company she led. Other than their interest in partnering with Camasca, nothing damning revealed itself. However, O.J. had secrets, and he had to be telling someone.

A bite of Avery's chicken disappeared onto Noah's fork, and she absently smacked at his hand.

"Eat your own dinner."

"Why? You've got what I want."

Avery laughed as he quickly ate the stolen piece of chicken. Then an idea formed. Excitedly, she nudged Jared's foot under the table.

"Ma'am?" he replied mid-bite. "What's up?"

She pointed to his workstation. "You've programmed the data-retention bot to catalogue all conversations that Kawak records, correct?"

"Over the security team's aggressive objections." His chopsticks hovered below his mouth. "Why?"

"How quickly does the information get catalogued? Is it at the end of the night? Tomorrow?"

"Instantly," Jared corrected. "You're still operating with a more analogue mindset. Or early digital. AI is about speed and precision. Kawak is absorbing and cataloguing conversations the moment they occur. Processing almost instantaneously. My bot is programmed to hunt for key words and flag those conversations for my review. Yet, even before I hear them, the AI sifts through them and compiles a report that prioritizes and reconstructs any missing data that may provide context."

Setting his container down, Noah asked, "Why? Avery, what are you thinking?"

"O.J. was rattled by our conversation today. If I'm him, and I'm upset, my first instinct would be to complain to the person who sicced the interrogators on me. Or to a friend who'd commiserate."

"You think O.J. called Rafe?" Jared abandoned his chopsticks and rose from the table. "Or Freedman?"

"Both. Either. Or maybe he has another ally here we haven't spoken with in depth. Either way, O.J. was spooked—he was going to talk about what happened with someone other than just his mother."

Fingers flying over the keyboard, Jared began the search. While he typed, Noah turned to Avery, his expression worried. "You're cool eavesdropping on our client?"

"Eavesdropping? I'm reviewing internal information. It's what they're paying us piles of money to do." She gestured to the whiteboards and the cluttered desks.

"Why not just go upstairs and ask them?"

Avery frowned. "Why would I? My job is to figure out what happened, not ask them for their interpretations. I want to figure out why O.J. reacted so strongly to our questions."

"Rafe and Glen are your clients, Avery. I'm just suggesting that, before you go sifting through their phone logs, try asking them."

"What if they lie?"

"They won't."

"You don't know that, Noah. Freedman is your friend, but right now, he's a suspect."

"A suspect?" Noah pressed. "What do you think this is?"

"You know how this works, Noah. We dig until we find what we've been hired to find."

"Actually, no, I don't know how this works," he contradicted. "I'm not in the habit of investigating my friends."

Avery scoffed. "Camasca isn't our friend. You get that, right?"

"Don't treat me like I'm naïve, Avery. You're asking Jared to spy on Glen and Rafe, to see if someone here had a private conversation that will help you do what? Intuit from a misplaced sigh if they've committed corporate espionage? Theft? Murder?"

"I'm looking for any clue to—" she started.

Noah cut her off uncharacteristically, his normally even temper surging. "Clue to what? Our time here is almost up, and so far, we have proof of nothing."

"We've got dead bodies, missing people, blackmailed police, viable suspects, and potential motives. None of which I can take to the authorities without violating attorney-client privilege." Hearing his concern for his friend, she promised, "I'm not accusing Glen of anything. I'm simply investigating all the possibilities."

"You've got coincidence, conjecture, and a string of maybes." He shook his head. "We know that Paschal Donohoe is in personal financial trouble, but not that his company has jeopardized InnoVAI. We know that Kawak and its minions are uncanny and off-putting; however, nothing shows that they've been instrumental in a crime. Dr. Scandrett committed suicide because he felt guilty. A technician who possibly screwed up his job skipped town. And Kate is worried about Milo interfering, when her attention should be focused on actually treating her patients. We've followed every lead, Avery, and you've gotten to indulge your inner Matlock. I might be late to get on the bandwagon, but this might be beyond your capacity."

"If you're not comfortable with my approach, I'm not making you stay," Avery reminded him. "I'm not making any of you stay here."

"I think what Noah is saying," Ling interjected from across the table, "is that he's concerned. You've made tremendous progress gathering information, but we might be left with a report and not a concrete answer."

"Noah is an effective communicator, Ling," Avery retorted. "If that was his point, he'd have made it. Instead, he accused me of spinning up a mystery as a distraction. And spying on his friend. And wasting everyone's time."

"That's not what I said," Noah replied. "Or what I meant. However, I am worried that we are spinning our wheels while you look everywhere for some justification to explain why you don't want to go and do your boring day-job."

"Noah—" Ling tried to intervene again, but Avery wasn't having it.

"I've had boring jobs before," Avery snapped. "I've spent my life doing work I didn't want to do."

Ignoring Ling's warning, Noah plowed on: "Can you honestly tell me that, until I introduced you to Glen, you weren't bored again? Poor Avery, finally at a prestigious firm, finally able to afford everything you needed. Your mom is doing fine. You and Jared are doing fine. Only, this time, you had to live with normalcy, like the rest of us peons, trudging through the mundanity of the everyday."

"Guys!"

At Jared's snap, both combatants turned to glare at him. "What?" they barked in unison.

Jared focused on Noah. "I know this will piss you off, man, but Avery was right. One minute after we left, O.J. called Camasca."

"To speak to whom?" Avery asked, already knowing the answer.

"Glen Paul Freedman." Jared looked at Noah. "You're not going to like what you hear."

Noah stalked over to Jared's equipment. "Play it."

Avery sank back into her seat and closed her eyes as O.J. and Glen debated whether Milo was creating patients out of thin air and diagnosing real ones with fake diseases. More than once, Ling grimaced at their discussion. When O.J. promised to come back to Camasca, the recording stopped.

"Well, that's a problem," Ling said, shoving her plate away. "If Milo is not providing accurate information, that could explain why Dr. Liam is having trouble treating her patients."

"Not exactly," Jared offered, thinking about their other interviews and what he'd learned from the engineers. "O.J. listed issues they'd previously flagged. We don't know if these conditions reports or medical hallucinations were identified by Kawak or Milo and segregated, or if the bad data was transmitted to InnoVAI for action."

"I don't care," Ling retorted. "Misreporting, misdiagnosing, and prescribing medical care that could be out of line with patients' needs . . . that's sacrilege."

"A man has died, Ling, but we don't know the cause," he clarified. "And we don't know what we just heard."

Avery stood up from her chair and looked at the group, avoiding eye contact with Noah. "But we do know a man under the care of this company is indeed dead. So this is very serious. Ling may not be a tech genius, but she's a damned good doctor. At the very least, misinterpreting lab results is malpractice."

"Not if the results were for a phantom patient." Anticipating Ling's rebuttal, Jared continued, "I've listened to enough doctors tell me about what's going on with my father to realize that y'all don't always get it right the first time. Or the second. Or the tenth. Like you said, part of the job is interpreting results."

"Do not confuse a medical professional's diagnostic process with a computer's mistakes," Ling warned.

"If the computer is simply following the same differential diagnosis procedure, what's the difference?"

"It's not the same!"

"An AI interface like Milo, run by a neural network like Kawak, is smarter than most of the doctors you went to school with, Ling. They have more information, process inputs faster, can factor in environmental and historical data in a fraction of the time."

"They're not human," she maintained. "At the end of the day, humanity matters. Even with Milo available, Dr. Liam turned to Dr. Scandrett."

"Humanity is no guarantee of due care or justice. What about the human judges who deliver harsher sentences to Black and brown defendants than to whites accused of the same crime? When an AI was given the same tasks, sentencing disparities almost vanished."

Ling continued to glower at Jared, and he sighed. "I'm not saying there isn't a problem, but we can't extrapolate from this conversation that Milo is faulty. Because, if we do, we are condemning these veterans—people of color, or the service-disabled, or women—the ones most often denied care by the system—to go to the back of the line. I won't do that if we haven't fully explored what O.J. and Freedman know, and what the Tiger Team saw."

Avery began to gather her leftovers. Around her, hostile silence hovered as each team member tidied their area. "Let's call it a night," she said. "Tomorrow, we'll take a fresh look at everything. On Friday, Jared will come with me to interview Isabella Gomez. Ling, you and Noah will go to Rhode Island and visit Galway's headquarters. We'll regroup this weekend and decide what we know or don't know. And how much of this is just my fever dream created out of boredom."

"That's not what I said," Noah protested.

Avery zipped a stack of papers into her satchel, her expression stolid, and strode out the door.

THIRTY-FOUR

Thursday, April 22

Midday in Providence in the late spring meant a true experience of New England. Rain pattered against windows that revealed only a hint of sunlight. The air carried a chill that refused to acknowledge summer's determined advance. Paschal shrugged off his jacket and draped it on the back of his chair.

Shaking like the labradoodle his children insisted on having in his home, he sprayed a few droplets onto the carpet. He logged into his email and began to skim the messages that had arrived during his early lunch. His desk phone buzzed, and he pushed the intercom.

"Sir, you have a call on line one," chirped the very efficient secretary Paschal Donohoe had managed to hire at their Rhode Island headquarters.

"I'll be on in one second," he strangled out as he stared at the warning that had landed in his email like an IED.

"Very good, sir." She called him "sir" rather than "cousin," which would have been more accurate. In her cubicle, she dutifully reported the time delay to her caller: "He'll be a few moments. Please continue to hold."

Beyond the firmly shut door, Paschal gasped for air that seemed determined to mock his attempts at breathing. He fumbled around in his bottom drawer for the bottle of Jameson that had become his boon companion. Throwing back a slug, he welcomed the trail of fire and the reflexive loosening of nerves.

"Get a hold of yourself, man." To fortify his resolve, he clasped chilled fingers and bowed his head in futile prayer. *Dear God, give me a few more weeks. Then the deal will be struck, the die cast, and the coffers refilled. Amen.*

No one else in Galway Pharmaceuticals had any inkling of their dire straits. Times and changing fortunes had forced cuts across the fledgling empire, but Paschal refused to allow the seams to be too visible. When a customer came to visit his compounding facility, confidence—more than medications—was his stock in trade. His dad may have taught him the rudiments of filling and manipulating prescriptions, but the lesson from his sainted mother obligated him to keep up appearances. The office in D.C., the global locations on the masthead, and none could be the wiser if they came to see him in his home environs.

However, the email from Glen Paul Freedman suggested his performance at his office in D.C. had not been sufficient to keep the bloodhounds at bay. "Expect visitors—internal investigator is sending up a team. Dr. Ling Yin and attorney Noah Fox. Expect them at your RI location tomorrow. Grant them full access."

He'd kicked himself over and over again for his blustery performance with the doctor and the lady lawyer. Too defensive, too hostile. Charm, not vinegar, was his bent.

This wrench couldn't have come at a worse time, beyond the issue of the Camasca IPO. His recent trip to D.C. was finally having an effect. Thanks to his paper tiger, the National Association for Pharmaceutical Compounding, he'd managed to convince several members of Congress that he had an army behind him. Their mission was to loosen regulatory interventions and increase the capacity of companies like his to beat back the Goliath of Big Pharma. Compounding medications had always been a necessary evil for the international drug companies who couldn't justify the bespoke offerings their customers required: liquid instead of capsule, gelatin or gelatin-free. However, as more drugs entered the public domain as generic formulas up for grabs, he, Paschal Donohoe, had seen a gold mine.

Then came the nearly overnight emergence of AI, which could speed up his capacity to duplicate and deliver at a fraction of the cost, and to a limitless clientele. Big Pharma wasn't happy. The big guys wanted to squash firms like his before they muscled their way into the major leagues.

Galway's ascendance with Camasca would prove that compounding had a pivotal role to play in the future pharmaceutical ecosystem. He'd used that argument in D.C. to prod congressional aides into putting his bill back on track.

Everything else was working. Paschal simply needed his company to survive long enough to reach payday. Which he couldn't do if nosy intruders questioned the adjustments he'd instituted to make a dollar stretch.

He took another fortifying swig of the Irish, then determinedly twisted the cap back onto the half-empty bottle. Why was he fretting? One day wandering around his facilities meant that he'd see what they saw, and they'd only see what he showed them. Which would be nothing. By worrying prematurely, he was merely borrowing trouble, which was against his personal code.

"Buck up, boyo," he told himself, and he returned the liquor to its hiding place. Stiffening his spine, he reached for the phone on his desk that had been blinking with a call on hold, and lifted the handset. "CEO Paschal Donohoe. And how might I be of service?"

"Paschal, this is Dee Patrick of Arclight Biomed. I hope I didn't catch you at a bad time."

Stunned, he straightened up and reached for his tie before remembering that the CEO of the nation's third-largest pharmaceutical company couldn't see him. He dropped his hand limply onto the desk. "Dr. Patrick. To what do I owe the unexpected pleasure?"

"I keep running into you on the field of battle," she told him cheerily. "I thought it was time to get to know my competition."

"Ah, no, Dr. Patrick. I'm no competition of yours. We're a simple shop, trying to make sure your blessed inventions and those of your compatriots most effectively treat the patients you're trying to serve," he offered in his most charming Irish brogue.

"A simple shop that has managed to ingratiate yourself with the next revolution in health care. I also noticed how your lobbyists managed to unblock legislation that my guys had worked assiduously to bury. You've proven a worthy adversary, Mr. Donohoe."

"There are spoils enough for us both, I'd imagine."

"First movers rarely relinquish their positions without a fight, and you know that," she admonished. "I've done my research on you. Wesleyan for undergrad and Rutgers for business school. Summers in Galway, and a year abroad at Trinity College in Dublin. Then you grow your family business and find a way to hitch your wagon to Rafe Diaz's rocket ship."

"Terribly true," he agreed, shock turning to curiosity. "Why the potted biography?"

"Because I want you to know that I know who I'm talking to," she explained. "You've worked wonders, Paschal, but you've also managed to burn through money like a wildfire."

The whiskey in his gut began to burn. "Excuse me?"

"Crypto has its uses," she mused, "but you got in over your head. Now you're leveraged to your eyeballs, and Camasca is your salvation."

"Do you have a point?"

"You have a cash-flow issue, and I have a solution." When Paschal said nothing, she continued. "I'd like to acquire Galway and retain you as CEO."

The figure she quoted had more zeroes than he'd ever imagined. Swallowing, he managed, "Are you entirely serious?"

"We know you have a glide path to Camasca's contracts, no matter what they told the SEC. But if you join the Arclight family, we'll profit together. Handsomely."

For an instant, Paschal felt light-headed with relief. An angel of mercy willing to shower him in gold coin and sweep his family into fantastic wealth. Every prayer was being answered. All he had to do was say yes.

"What's your timetable?" he asked. "Camasca goes public soon. I won't be as tempted by your generosity after they do."

"I assumed as much," Dee told him. "Our team is still working out the particulars, but, given your standing with Camasca and their federal clients, we are amenable to an expedited course of due diligence."

"Meaning?"

"We'd need to open your books, tour your facilities with our inspectors, and interview key staff. We'll get close to the wire, but I believe we can make it work."

Paschal thought about what he'd done to stave off disaster. Secrets only he and his trusted kin knew. Would ever know. Agreeing to Patrick's terms could expose them all.

Patience would save him, if he refused to panic.

"Thank you for your offer, Dr. Patrick. I'll give it some thought."

The soft sound of a sputter was almost too light to detect, but the chilly response threatened frostbite. "Don't take too long, Mr. Donohoe. I am fluent in both carrot and stick. Tick-tock."

THIRTY-FIVE

Wednesday night's blowup continued to infect the investigation suite. By late Thursday afternoon, Avery and the team had plowed through reams of information. It helped that no one felt the need to actually communicate with anyone else. Avery had spent the night with Jared, aggressively avoiding a discussion that might tell her something she didn't want to hear. For the time being, she had no interest in anyone else's thoughts or opinions.

Everyone worked in their respective silos, grunting at requests or avoiding conversation and eye contact at all. Ling hunched over patient files, scanning for red flags or warning signs. Noah had taken over the file on Galway, prepping for their visit.

Ignoring them both, Jared continued to hunt through cached communiqués and transcribed recordings. Like a digital assistant constantly scanning the sound waves for a command to listen actively, Kawak had absorbed thousands of conversations over the past few years. Unlike an Alexa or a Siri, Camasca's permanent eavesdropper retained meticulous logs. Working with an engineer armed with an ironclad NDA, he and his new buddy had jury-rigged a means to transcribe and identify the speakers involved. Sifting through detritus for nuggets of knowledge, Jared had scarcely moved except to stretch his legs and visit one of the six cafeterias on-site.

With allegations of phantom patients or absurd illnesses as a potential avenue of pursuit, Avery had assigned herself the task of wading through what InnoVAI knew and what Camasca had amassed. Jared had sifted through the data to flag incongruities based on Ling's guidance and his own experiments with AI. He'd pulled the patient information from Kawak's network and downloaded the files to their local machine. The bot he used then produced a set of names and diseases, and they'd been researching ever since.

Fake patient names ran down one side of the board, where movie characters and literary names had become patients of InnoVAI. Other names without service records got added to the list.

Avery stood at the improbable diagnosis board with a marker and underlined a name. Forced to break the silence, she asked, "Ling, what did we find out about Staff Sergeant Shavanna Miller? The patient diagnosed with the fluorocemia?"

Ling didn't look up. "O.J. flagged the diagnosis as one of Milo's questionable results. He was right. Disorder doesn't exist."

"What do you mean?"

"Sergeant Miller did an extended training regimen in Brazil eighteen months ago. When she got back, she had several issues that signaled the disruption of multiple enzymatic processes. Milo decided she'd been injected with the venom of a rare Amazonian wasp. And he fabricated a diagnosis that he called fluorocemia. Only, I've checked every medical database I can locate. There's no such thing."

"Speaking of disruptions . . ." Noah rose from his desk. "Avery, I was a dick yesterday. I've known Freedman for a long time, and I'm kind of protective of my friends, but I shouldn't have questioned your motives, misgivings, or methods. I promise it won't happen again. But I can't say the same for my alliterations. Other than that, I'm really sorry."

Avery noted silently that he hadn't said he was wrong. She couldn't do that, either. Boxed in by her own logic, she gave him an authentic smile. "We're good, Noah." Remembering her role as leader, she turned to Jared and Ling. "Y'all need to hug it out?"

"I love Jared too much to make him show affection. He might get attached," Ling said. "We'll agree to disagree until I can destroy his argument and his self-esteem."

He gave her a respectful nod. "Challenge accepted."

"Good. Because this stuff is crazy." Avery placed a checkmark by the name and quickly counted. "In addition to our twelve nonexistent patients, of more than seven hundred files we've reviewed, at least nine have been tagged for diseases that couldn't happen."

Noah waved a hand from his pile of homework. "I think I've found number ten. Dr. Yin, would I be correct in suggesting that no human would be infected by the hepatozoon parasite?"

Impressed by the question, Ling gave him an approving look. "To my knowledge, no, there's never been a case of human infection. How in the hell did you know that?"

"According to these records, Galway compounded a treatment."

"But why would you know to flag it?"

He retorted, "Avery's not the only one with absurdly arcane knowledge. I went to law school, too. Which is where I dated a guy whose golden retriever, Lacy, had hepatozoonosis. Dog was constantly barfing, and we eventually broke up because he was more committed to Lacy's well-being than mine. Fair choice—Lacy had much better hair."

"Patient name? Assuming he's real."

"Gerard Bouie. Coast Guard captain who has been in and out of the clinic since he got stationed near Annapolis. Poor guy is recovering from opiate addiction after he sustained injuries during an interdiction with drug smugglers."

"How long was he in recovery?" Jared asked.

"Two years; then he relapsed and got a general discharge." Noah flipped through the rest of Bouie's whole patient profile. "He couldn't keep a job. Worked as a security guard, then as a tech in a county animal-control center. Even joined one of those apps for personal assistants."

"Doing what?" Avery asked.

"Odd jobs, like running errands, walking a rich guy's dog—stuff like that, I guess. At the same time, he bounced around the health-care system, because he couldn't keep his Tricare. Kept complaining about chronic pain, but every time he tried to get help—"

"They refused treatment because they thought he was drug-seeking," Ling summarized. "When I shadowed Dr. Liam at InnoVAI, I heard this over and over. A lot of vets get flagged by doctors because they were over-prescribed during service and are expected to heal themselves once they're out."

"How did Captain Bouie end up at InnoVAI, then?" Avery asked.

"I bet Rafe Diaz's algorithm fast-tracked him as a client," Jared explained. "He designed the clinic to give priority to vets who have been hard to treat or who've moved around the system."

Noah concurred. "He definitely fits that bill. Over the last year, during his intake, he mentioned his difficulties and his relapses. Since then, he's used Milo's interface to self-report lethargy, weight loss, and—eww—persistent diarrhea."

"Don't be a baby," Ling teased.

"Sorry. Anyway, clinic results show that he has anemia, and imaging reported bone lesions." He dropped the thick sheaf of papers. "And from that, Milo diagnosed a disease that dogs get when they ingest an infected tick?"

"I think I know exactly how it happened." Ling ran her fingers through her short cap of hair, tugging in exasperation. "For a CDSS, Milo is remarkable. But this is why AI requires a human validation system. Milo saw mentions of dog walking and dog pounds. Does he own a dog, by any chance?"

Noah reached for the folder again and rifled through to the

personal-data section. "Yep. He's got a rescue that he adopted when he worked for Animal Control."

Ling crossed to Noah's station. "Let me see the chart." She skimmed it quickly and made an approving noise. "One of the docs did catch it."

"Catch what?"

Tapping a line on the page, she reported, "Dr. Scandrett actually rejected Milo's impossible diagnosis. Instead, he found that Captain Bouie had a rare sarcoma—bone cancer. But according to these records, the original evaluation by his physician had been rejected, and hepatozoonosis was substituted. Says here, Dr. Scandrett and Dr. Liam had to override."

"Okay, I get that he worked with animals and has a pet, but how did Milo get from bone cancer to a dog tick?" Noah wondered incredulously. "Why not start with bone cancer? How did it get to veto the actual doctor's report?"

"And who wrote a prescription that led to Galway's producing medication?" Avery added.

Jared offered, "I can explain everything but the prescription." With all eyes on him, he continued: "Based on the conversations we had with the data scientists, this could be the result of flawed data integration or what got coded into the data warehouse. Plus, the predictive analytics depend on how the AI was trained. Milo has the autonomy to rewrite recommendations and prioritize recommendations, subject to review. In a sense, the system worked."

"In a very, very narrow sense," Ling pushed back. "All doctors are taught to do differential diagnoses—to dig deeper if a patient's symptoms could be caused by a variety of possible conditions. As was Milo. All of *us* were also taught to reject improbabilities. That's the crucial difference: the humans used intuition and common sense to ignore the tick."

Scratching at his chin, Jared warned, "Milo might have seen

something in Bouie's military service record, or even his childhood, that pushed bone cancer down the list and popped the parasite to the top."

"A parasite that could not be the cause. But that's not the worst part. We should all be worried if the AI can substitute its judgment for actual doctors'."

"Milo didn't."

"Because Scandrett stopped him that time. Yes, we as physicians benefit from tools like AI that can help us optimize our diagnoses and pull on threads faster than the human mind. But when an AI that never went to medical school creates disorders or reorders a differential diagnosis, we're in terrible trouble."

Avery studied their board, then went behind her desk to the array of legal pads she'd set up. Like her boards, they were labeled with her taxonomy. Choosing the one for the AI, she jotted down both Jared's and Ling's observations. Which raised one of her own. "If Elisha and O.J. were marking these issues via K-chat, then Kawak was aware of their concerns," she told the team. "As was Milo. Two members of the Tiger Team were complaining about its errors and, possibly, discussing in person how to fix them."

"I hate to beat a dead horse," Jared said, sighing, "but Kawak is not sentient. It can't experience jealousy or fear or envy."

Avery gave him a speculative look. "You told me about Claude, the AI that faked agreement with its programmers. How is this any different? Other than scale."

"Claude was evading the perceived punishment of retraining. Overriding a physician is on a different level."

"Unless it is trying to correct itself according to its reinforcement learning," Avery posited. "Then it is making a rational choice to survive. As you told us, Kawak is a tool that can adapt."

"Your memory is annoying," Jared prefaced. "Yes, Claude was unethical according to objective human evaluation, but the Anthropic alignment team set him up to fail. On the other hand, the entire point of Kawak is to be a supportive tool for Dr. Liam and the others at the clinic, and its training model emphasized serving patients." He rubbed wearily at the nape of his neck. "Kawak, Milo, Yax, and Keh are all trained to use evidence of their own operations to assist them—not to kill anyone. The alternative is illogical."

"Unless Kawak saw Elisha and O.J. as obstacles," Avery countered. "Or the alignment of values created conflicts it couldn't resolve. Like Claude. I'm not ready to declare the system homicidal, but you do agree that it can decide to change the decisions of the doctors at InnoVAI."

"In theory."

Ling caught Avery's speculative look and anticipated her next question. "Then what's to stop it from changing the airflow mix in the Den to confront a problem?"

"Nothing, I suppose," Jared conceded. "But what motivation would it have?"

Avery tapped a pen vigorously on the legal pad. "Jared, is Kawak designed to protect against hackers? Or viruses?"

"Sure—there would be a sophisticated level of built-in self-protection."

"Then what if Kawak viewed Elisha and O.J. as a threat to its operation—a virus, if you will—and was trying to remove a bug in the system?"

"Without knowing its training model, I'm only guessing here. But the most efficient solution is to ignore their instructions. Next, it might hallucinate a set of rationales to create counter-instructions. Or it might fake alignment, like Claude did, by doing some of what the programmers expected it to do . . . but choosing which commands to obey." He sighed in exasperation. "I get your point. I don't concede it, but I get it."

Noah walked over to Avery and bumped her shoulder. "You've forgotten something."

She acknowledged the apology with a nudge of her own. "No, I didn't. We still have the mystery of why Galway filled a prescription that no one seemed to write."

"Which Ling and I will figure out when we venture north to chilly Providence to interrogate Paschal Donohoe, instead of heading down to sunny Miami with the two of you to interview Isabella," he complained. "This sidekick role needs to come with better perks."

"Take it up with management," Jared suggested, pleased at the apparent thaw. "We can't go warning Rafe Diaz that he's built a killer robot unless we clear a few more hurdles. I'd like to find Tristan Spencer—the ventilation tech responsible for the Den area—for one. I'm also going to request Dr. Scandrett's file from the MCPD."

"I don't think we can count on Detective Howard to assist." Avery lifted the legal pad marked "MALFUNCTION." "I assume you can get Scandrett's file the way you got their emails?"

"Don't ask, won't tell."

She set the legal pad on the table and reached for the one in the center. The word "INTENTIONAL" stared back at her. "Isabella Gomez hopefully has some answers that will give us better questions. As the member of the Tiger Team in charge of data security and privacy, she should be able to shed a lot of light."

"Unless she closes ranks, like O.J.," Jared told her. "We need to set our expectations fairly low."

"That's easy, since I don't expect anything," Avery warned mildly as she settled into her seat, brows knitted in contemplation. "However, I intend to learn more than she plans to share."

THIRTY-SIX

Friday, April 23

Unlike the slow-moving spring of D.C., the South Florida climate was already sweltering. Avery and Jared reluctantly abandoned the blessed cool of the air-conditioned Miami airport. Outside, a blanket of heat and humidity swaddled them aggressively as they ventured onto the concrete curb to await their ride. Avery shifted her satchel strap on her shoulder, grimly rethinking her sober navy suit. Beside her, Jared checked his phone to gauge how soon they'd be inside again. Seconds later, a black Escalade shuddered to a stop at their position. A taciturn, preternaturally tanned driver hurriedly shepherded them inside the vehicle.

"No bags?" he grunted as he basically boosted Avery inside in a bid to escape the heat.

"No. We're a turnaround," Jared replied. In a few hours, they'd be seated in first class, courtesy of Camasca, on their way back home. "You've got us all day."

"Gotcha."

The passenger door slammed with a thud, and the driver jogged around the hood. He climbed inside and punched the fan to high. Cubano rhythms poured from the stereo, echoed by an emphatic tap on the steering wheel. The driver merged into the steady flow of airport departures. Avery began to speak, and Jared gently squeezed her leg in warning.

Aloud, he said, "Sir?"

The driver grunted in acknowledgment.

"Is that camera on?" Jared asked, pointing to a device mounted to the right of the rearview mirror. A steady blue dot sat next to a dimmed red light.

"Yeah. Company policy." He gave a dismissive wave. "But y'all are premium passengers. Want me to turn it off?"

"Yes, please," Avery insisted. She hadn't even noticed. Cars came equipped with so much technology, one more gadget affixed to the interior hadn't registered. "We'd appreciate it."

The driver reached up and tapped a button, deactivating the camera. "Mostly use the camera to watch the road, but sometimes we get freaks in the seats, you know what I mean?"

"Understood," Jared concurred wryly. "But I'm a bit of a stickler. Mind pulling out the cord right there?" He gestured to the connection that could restart the device.

The driver responded by jerking the wires free. "No problem. I don't want to contribute to the surveillance state," he explained with a world-weary sigh, "but company rules and all. They heard you ask, though, and this is a big fare."

"We've all got to make a living." Jared gave him a commiserating nod. "Thanks, man."

They rode the next few miles in silence. Avery skimmed through the notes on her phone, and Jared did the same. After a while, Jared asked in a low voice, "How do you want to play this?"

"Assuming she and O.J. are in contact, I doubt she'll be any more forthcoming than he was." Noah's summary of her motivations flickered through her thoughts. As she had when interrogating Isabella's teammate, Avery tried to quash the twin sensations of eagerness at the prospect of uncovering another layer of mystery and a tinge of shame at her willingness to manipulate her subject to get information. That interview had resulted in a bonanza of information, a breakthrough she was ready to experience again. "I'll explain the rules to her and ask her basic questions about Camasca. Then I'll pitch it to you. Let you both geek out over encryption protocols and audit trails."

"Stop flirting with me, Ms. Keene."

Mouth curving, Avery nudged her shoulder against his. The seatbelt tightened, holding her in place, and she laughed lightly. "Apparently, the car agrees."

"Stupid car."

Forty-five minutes later, the SUV muscled alongside a manicured curb where daffodils bloomed in glorious profusion.

"We shouldn't be more than an hour," Avery told the driver.

"Yes, ma'am." He quickly exited the truck and efficiently opened their doors to spill them out into the heated suburban oasis. Quickly, Avery and Jared made their way along the driveway, avoiding sprinklers that vainly attempted to abate the oppressive rays.

Before they reached the front door, it swung open. The decorative white wrought-iron screen door remained locked, barring their entry. A young woman in her early thirties lounged in the frame, the room behind her cast in dancing shadows.

When Isabella stepped fully into the sunlight, Avery easily recognized her from her photos. Coarse black hair liberally streaked with vivid purple hung in a loose braid. Her mocha-skinned arms, roped with muscle that spoke eloquently of a dedication to weight lifting, emerged from the sleeves of a tattered black designer T-shirt whose price could have paid one of Avery's new car notes. Retro acid-washed jean shorts and black leather sandals completed the casually expensive outfit. What previous photos hadn't included was the wariness of the dark eyes that tracked their approach.

Recognizing the look, Avery smiled reassuringly at the third member of the Tiger Team. "Dr. Gomez?"

"Ms. Keene." Isabella cut a nervous glance to Jared. "No one said you would be bringing someone."

Avery laid a hand on Jared's shoulder, both in introduction and caution. "Mr. Wynn works with me as a tech consultant. He's a cybersecurity specialist."

"No one told me he would be here," she repeated flatly. "I wasn't warned."

"My fault," Avery apologized. "I should have been more thoughtful."

"This is not what I expected." The skittish data-security leader stepped back into the shadowed house, and Avery realized they were about to be denied entry. She cast about for a way to hold her, sifting through her recall of the K-chats and emails from the file of Dr. Isabella Gomez. All of her communiqués were carefully worded, studiously precise. The only deviations occurred when she connected with one person.

"Rafe said you'd talk to us, Dr. Gomez," Avery explained. "For Elisha. He said you'd help us find out what happened. I brought Jared because he's a security expert, like you. My personal translator."

The door inched open slowly. "I've read about you, Ms. Keene. You're not helpless, and I'm not gullible. I'm annoyed. Your decision to bring a former intelligence officer with you was calculated. I don't respond well to surprises." The last was said as Isabella unlocked the screen. "Don't do it again."

Impressed and duly warned, Avery nodded. "I apologize. I won't surprise you again."

Reaching beyond Avery, Jared extended his hand. "Pleasure to meet you, Dr. Gomez."

After hesitating, Isabella grasped it for an instant, then pulled away. Tucking her hands into her pockets, she muttered, "Come on in."

The ranch-style home contrasted distinctly with O.J.'s family abode. Half-shuttered windows in the foyer allowed in slivers of sun, which provided the only visible light. Pinks and blues and greens adorned the walls, which seemed as much artistic as structural. As they moved deeper inside, tropical birds threatened to take flight from a mural stretching across what looked like the living room, curving into a tangled jungle scene. The wicker and rattan furniture seemed completely in keeping with the theme, despite their placement inside, where rays flooded in through a narrow skylight.

"Your family home is lovely," Avery complimented as she approached the wall art. She acknowledged her misstep, and knew she had quite of a bit of ground to regain. If the security arm of the Tiger Team refused to cooperate, they'd traveled a long way for nothing.

She gestured at a particularly expressive flamingo that preened with gusto. "Did you paint this yourself?"

"When I was in high school," Isabella replied stiffly, gnawing on her bottom lip. "I am concerned about the presence of a witness. Do I need a lawyer?"

Avery tore her eyes away from a fascinating toucan that seemed to smirk at her. "We work for Camasca, and we are bound by attorney-client privilege. However, the privilege belongs to the company, not to you, and the company can waive that privilege but you cannot. As an employee, though, you're expected to be as frank and honest as possible. I brought Jared along because, as I said, he can be a bit of a translator for me." Protocol also recommended she have a second person with her to corroborate statements, in case Isabella decided to backtrack or contradict herself.

"You didn't answer my question. Do I need an attorney?" she repeated, her pitch rising slightly.

"I can't advise you on that matter, Dr. Gomez. You certainly have the right to seek legal counsel if you choose. It's up to you. But we were hired internally."

Flinching slightly, Isabella shook her head. "In lieu of representation, I would like to record our conversation."

"By all means."

Satisfied, Isabella pulled out an old-fashioned tape recorder. "Do you consent to our conversation being recorded and transcribed for my later review?"

"Yes," Avery and Jared responded in unison.

"One at a time, please," Isabella instructed as she thumbed it on. "And please state your names and the purpose of your visit."

"Avery Keene, investigative attorney for Camasca Enterprises. I consent to being recorded."

"Jared Wynn, tech consultant to Clymer Brezil for the purposes of the investigation on behalf of Camasca Enterprises. I agree to be recorded."

"Isabella Gomez, security-data scientist for Camasca Enterprises." Visibly relaxing for the first time, she said, "Freedman told me you had questions about the Den. And about Milo."

Avery nodded. "A few, yes."

Jared, who'd hung slightly back, stepped closer to the two women. "Dr. Gomez, we've been from plane to train to automobile. Any chance we can trouble you for some water?"

"One moment. I'm sorry, I should have offered." She snatched up the recorder and scurried from the open area toward an archway shadowed by the fall of the late-morning sun.

"She's jumpy," Jared noted quietly. "Anxious."

Sight fixed on the archway Isabella had scuttled beneath, Avery murmured, "I wonder what has her spooked."

"Me, for one." His eyes followed Avery's to the back, where Isabella had disappeared. "She researched me. And she isn't happy about it."

"I saw that, too. Since she's not too fond of you, why don't you let me take the first few questions? Then I'll tag you in."

"Cool."

While they waited, Avery checked her phone. The indicator showed no service. "Jared, is your phone working?"

Taking a look, he shook his head. "No service at all. I think she's got a jammer in here."

"Don't say anything," Avery urged. Reestablishing trust was her priority, but the jammer presented an opportunity.

A few moments later, Isabella returned, bearing two chilled bottles of water that dripped condensation. "I don't have any sparkling. Here's a napkin."

"This is perfect," Avery said gratefully as she twisted the cap. "Neither of us can get a cell signal."

"House is in a dead zone."

Isabella made no further statement and turned on the recording device. Avery deliberately shrugged at the shoulder strap of her bag. "Mind if we sit down? My satchel's kind of heavy."

"In here." She led them into what Avery assumed to be the living room with its refined patio furniture. Avery chose a settee, and Jared picked a lounger next to her.

Isabella settled into a rocker across from their seats. As though she'd heard the unspoken question a million times, she told them, "I have terrible allergies, so I can't spend much time outdoors. My parents brought the outdoors in for me. The skylight and the mural and the furniture."

"Where are your folks?"

"In Mesa, Arizona, visiting my older sister. She's due any day now. Having twins."

"Congratulations." Settling her bag on a sturdy side table, Avery took a sip of water. "How are you feeling?"

"As good as can be expected." Long brown fingers twisted in her lap, and a lock of purple hair flopped forward. "We don't need to do small talk. What do you want to know, Ms. Keene?"

THIRTY-SEVEN

"The Tiger Team." Instead of reaching for her notepad, Avery kept her gaze level and steady on Isabella's face. "Tell me about your friends, Isabella."

"You mean tell you about Elisha. About how he died." The bitterness wiped away any trace of diffidence. "Camasca sent you here to convince me that they're not at fault?"

"Not at all. Camasca hired me to determine if anyone is at fault. The police say no."

"The police are morons." Bitterness spiked into antipathy. "Kawak is the most sophisticated system not yet on the market. Don't you agree, Mr. Wynn?"

"Yes. Why?"

"Because tech like Kawak doesn't malfunction," she announced. "Kawak manages microbots. Robots. Milo. Its own architecture. But we're expected to believe the air conditioner basically malfunctioned and killed one of the data scientists tasked with programming its parameters?"

"The alignment sprint y'all were involved in that night?"

"Partially. But there were other issues."

Avery recalled O.J.'s conversation with Freedman. "Did you report the issues?"

She hedged, "I noted some in the conditions report, but—"

"But?"

"We decided as a group to try the alignment first."

"Do you have proof that the accident wasn't simply a system failure?" Jared probed. "Or is this gut instinct?"

"It's logic," Isabella argued. "I'm not sure what happened, but a police investigation that's concluded in a matter of days isn't right. Especially given the timing."

"What timing?" Avery glanced at Jared, then back at Isabella. "What happened?"

Isabella drew her legs up beneath her chin and sent her rocker into gentle motion. "Elisha's team headed up the data integration for the entire neural network. Everything from electronic health records to credit reports and beyond. Bioinformatics barely scratched the surface."

"He led the Tiger Team and the reinforcement learning. Who decided what the reward model would be?"

"Elisha. He set the parameters and built the prompts to keep the AI from ignoring common human error. Did you know that most doctors discount the pain scales for women and people of color? Or dismiss a young person with angina by saying it's anxiety? Elisha drummed it into us: 'Good intentions in science can't erase human bias.' The phrase 'garbage in, garbage out' applies to us, too. AI algorithms can be trained to use historical data, but the best ones also scrape and integrate additional information. They look at health conditions and treatments to predict disease progression, but understanding that progression means looking at comps."

Avery interpreted, "The model tried to train Kawak to determine that, if a population has been historically underserved or not included in clinical research, the predictions will have built-in skews."

"Exactly. Now extend that to the treatments that are prescribed, or the effect of regimens on high-risk populations."

"And you have a recipe for medical racism," Jared finished.

"Our Tiger Team used a reward model that pushed the AI from

every angle—to root out any possibility that such medical prejudice existed. From design to build to validation, we covered the gamut. When the system failed to correct bias or used flawed assumptions, it was retrained."

A shaft of sunlight caught her profile as she swayed gently forward. "O.J. was responsible for the analytics engine. He monitored everything from the data-analysis algorithms to the clinical guidelines."

"And you?" The question came from Jared. "You're data security and privacy, right?"

"My teams were supposed to protect patient data. We designed encryption procedures, set up all the access controls, especially to the database management system."

"The alignment sprint ran into trouble?"

"Starting a few days before the incident, we each noticed alarming issues. Elisha found nonexistent patients in Milo's database. Then it started propagating impossible diseases. Not a ton, but enough to get our attention. O.J. thought there were errors in the formularies for the personalized medicines."

"Did you report it to Rafe?"

"Elisha argued against it, and I agreed. O.J. waffled, mainly because it was Elisha's idea. We were supposed to find mistakes and fix them. That's what a Tiger Team does. But the errors got progressively worse."

"We noticed."

Warming to her subject, Isabella expanded, "O.J. realized it had gone even further. Real patients were getting flawed diagnoses. Milo was overriding the medical teams and reordering the conditions reports. It was alarming."

The failure O.J. had reported to Glen. Avery felt her adrenaline pumping to hear Isabella putting voice to the concepts they had previously discussed.

Feigning ignorance, Avery asked, "Conditions reports?"

"Our shorthand for the diagnoses that InnoVAI patients recorded.

Part of detecting bias is verifying how often patients of specific profiles get wrongly processed. O.J.'s team found that patients were being treated for improbable conditions—fictional or eradicated diseases, or ones that are so rare that the odds are astronomical. Elisha and his guys noticed that some of the medical staff were receiving incomplete medical histories that could lead to faulty outcomes."

"And you?" Jared prompted. "What did you discover?"

Agitated, she lurched forward and leapt from the shivering rocker. "One of my team members reviewed a report that showed a drug compound that would be lethal to any patient who received it."

Avery asked, "Do you remember what happened?"

"A patient was prescribed fenbendazole at twenty mg/kg for five days, with four refills."

"Was the drug administered?"

"No! A secondary check stopped the scrip from being filled."

"What was the problem?"

"Fenbendazole is a treatment for parasites in animals, but acolytes on social media swear it can be used as a treatment for cancer. The veteran had a history of colon cancer, but came in for symptoms of jaundice. Milo flagged him as a candidate for fenben, and somehow, Yax processed a scrip."

"Without a doctor's signature?"

"The lack of a formal sign-off by a physician is why we caught it, but no process is infallible." She shook her head. "In humans, ingesting fenbendazole can lead to liver failure. It could have killed him."

"What preventative steps were taken?"

"We found it that day, and that's one of the reasons we were so freaked out that night. In the morning, we were going to take the full problem to Rafe if we hadn't solved it. Elisha created a patch that night that increased the frequency of bioinformatics checks, and he upped the sensitivity of the review filters. On my end, we were going to start running regular compliance validations with our compounding protocols with Galway."

"Why you and not O.J.?" Avery asked.

Isabella stopped abruptly, her eyes fixed on the skylight. After the pause lengthened indefinitely, Avery nudged, "Dr. Gomez?"

"O.J. agreed with the protocols, of course," she said stiffly as she wandered the floor in a figure-eight. "That night, doing the sprint, I realized someone or something had compromised our controls—my security protocols. They were able to reconfigure the drug repositioning and compounding process, and the intrusions had gone undetected. But they weren't external."

She stopped pacing and lowered her gaze to them. Isabella's tone, suddenly steely, brooked no question of the truth of what she said. "Yax was constructing toxic drugs based on false data, or doling out medications that could kill patients."

"You didn't know if Yax's nearly poisoning patients was due to bad data or bad intent—and you didn't trust Dr. Semans to be objective," translated Jared.

A short, angry sound erupted from her. "We know of at least two bad scrips that were filled by Yax and dispensed by InnoVAI. Possibly dozens more could have been delivered during the gamma test. As part of my role that night, I sent a code to Milo to correct its processes."

Avery wrinkled her brow in confusion. "Milo? Why not ask Yax? Or Kawak?"

"Because Yax received instructions from Milo, not Kawak," she replied tersely. "Kawak is the boss, but Milo runs its own department. According to the robot's records, Milo designed the formularies and transmitted them for compounding. The pharma team ran the appropriate diagnostics and conveyed the prescription to Galway to fulfill."

"All of the toxic drugs were compounded by Galway?" Jared pushed her gently. "You're sure?"

Isabella hesitated. "No, not all of them. Most. Like I said, Elisha and I were tracking down the source of the issue."

"And neither of you trusted O.J.?"

This time, the pause stretched beyond a minute. Avery felt herself grow impatient, but, like a good player, she waited for the other person to make a move. Trust was hard-won, like information. She'd bungled the first, but they were close to having the answers.

Isabella started talking again, as though she'd taken a brief pause and not nearly a full minute. "Because, by then, I didn't trust his efficacy or his communication skills. O.J.'s job was to vet the drugs, but these had slipped past him. During the sprint, I noticed stray code and incompatible instructions. Rookie mistakes for someone of O.J.'s capacity."

"Could it have been someone on his team?" Avery challenged. "How do you know it was O.J.?"

Isabella pointed at Jared. "Ask your boyfriend. He codes."

"Coders have a style of programming, whether they know it or not. It's in the way they format, their programming logic or their comments. If they're using standard code, it might not be visible, but a good coder's technique is apparent to anyone who knows how to look. After a while, your coding signature becomes a habit, one you don't even notice anymore."

"A tell," Avery summarized. "O.J. has a tell, and you saw it in the code."

"My role is surveillance. I watch—closely. But I didn't tell Elisha, either. I needed to prove my theory."

"Did you?"

"No. Instead, I almost died." She returned to the rocking chair and dropped like a stone. "Elisha is gone, and whether he knows it or not, I betrayed him."

Avery moved to squat near the rocker that jerked back and forth. She laid a hand on the armrest, stilling its movements, careful not to touch Isabella. "Your job is security. Full stop. Rather than accuse your colleague of sabotage or incompetence, you ran an investigation. But you told someone else, didn't you? You had to."

"No, I did not. I had a theory, and I tested my hypothesis alone."

"I don't believe you. I think you asked Kawak for its help."

Refusing to meet her eyes, she muttered, "You're wrong."

"No, I'm not. When I asked you about Kawak earlier, you got defensive. And afraid." Avery gestured to the room. "It's almost ninety degrees outside, but your house is dark. No lights except for the skylight. No fans, only open windows. If I go into your kitchen, will I find coolers filled with ice, Isabella?"

Startled, her head shot up. "How—I mean, no. I don't know what you're talking about."

At Avery's cue, Jared strode toward the back, where she had gone to get their waters. He returned seconds later. "How'd you know?"

"Grow up in a house when the power gets shut off often enough, you learn the signs."

"I can afford my electric bill," Isabella said huffily.

"Of course you can," Avery agreed. "But Kawak can't track you in a house without electricity, can it? Or a signal jammer running on battery power."

In response, Isabella crunched her legs beneath her chin and rocked in a slightly spasmodic motion. "I'm done talking. You can leave now."

"Isabella—"

"I said leave," she said, the tremors moving to her limbs. "I no longer wish to cooperate with you."

Jared moved, but Avery remained on the edge of the settee. "No. We're not leaving yet. We're not here to harm you." She motioned for him to join her, and he took a seat. He cut her a quizzical look, and she gave a slight shake of her head.

"You don't think it was malfunction in the Den," Avery deduced. "You believe Kawak tried to murder you and accidentally killed Elisha. And you're angry at O.J. Why?"

"Because he's a liar and a cheat." Her rocking stopped. "I can't prove it, but he had something to do with Elisha's death."

"What did he lie about?"

"I don't know," she admitted. "I've tried to figure it out, but I can't hunt if I can't go online. Which I won't do. Not until . . ."

Jared leaned closer. "Not until what?"

"Not until it's safe. I'm not paranoid, Ms. Keene. I know exactly how all of this tech tracks us and monitors us. The digital security camera on your neighbor's front door or the smart sensor in your garage. Even the handy calendar on your smart refrigerator. These are open invitations for AI to come into your home and study you. To learn your habits. I've seen it under the hood. I'm not crazy. I'm right. And until Camasca fixes what is broken, I won't go back. Now get out."

THIRTY-EIGHT

Stamping her feet on the sidewalk outside Galway Pharmaceuticals, Ling shook off the last of the deluge that had delayed their flight from D.C. to Providence. Next to her, Noah gamely waggled the golf umbrella he'd procured in the airport gift shop. Instead of making their noon meeting, they'd taken off late because of a sudden storm, which had also forced them to hover above the modest T. F. Green Airport and hold on the crowded runway while other flights took wing.

Ling hated being late, and nearly groaned when Avery's face popped up on her phone. "What?"

"How are you?"

"We're late, I'm loitering outside of Galway Pharmaceuticals in a town that is as cold and wet as I imagine Ireland to be at this moment, our flight was grounded on the tarmac for almost two hours, and I'm hungry. What do you want?"

"Can Noah hear me?"

"Hold on." She tugged on his sleeve and led him away from the entry. "Go."

Avery debriefed them on Isabella's revelations. "Rain delays are keeping us grounded—not sure when we'll get out. Y'all should meet us at Jared's, no matter when you get into D.C. As soon as we land, I'm heading to InnoVAI to see Kate, and Jared is going to

Camasca to connect with Freedman. Rafe had an investor meeting in New York today."

"And you're not going to use phones that might have Kawak capabilities," Ling inferred. "I miss old-fashioned landlines."

"You barely know what those are."

"Whatever. Be safe. We'll see you when we get back." Ling hitched up the strap on her bag. "Ready?"

"Let's get this show on the road." Noah punched the buzzer on the door, and a pleasant voice with a faint lilt asked his name.

"Noah Fox and Ling Yin to see Paschal Donohoe."

The sound of the latch releasing prompted Noah to tug on the handle. He shifted to allow Ling to precede him, and they headed into the domain of Galway. The massive facility spanned more than an acre and a half, the red-brick-and-stucco facade a bright spot against duller warehouses in close proximity.

Inside, a young woman came up to them. "Welcome, Dr. Yin and Mr. Fox. If you'll follow me, Mr. Donohoe would like to have you take a tour of the facility before you meet with him. Our Director of Pharmacy, Connor Donohoe, will meet you in the clean area."

"Thank you, Miss . . ."

"Donohoe. Felicity," she said with a knowing grin. "Paschal likes to keep family close. May I take your umbrella?"

Together, they walked past the lobby into a busy area where a bank of cubicles housed dozens of staffers wearing earpieces and typing into computers. Felicity explained, "This is where we take orders or organize dispensation. There's a call center for customers on the other side of that wall."

Following her through the facility, they reached a set of double doors in heavy steel. "This is our clean area. When we enter, I'll have you put on booties and hairnets before you proceed. Connor will take you through, and I'll meet you on the other side."

Indeed, on the other side, in a vestibule, a slightly taller, ruddier version of Paschal awaited. "Hello, folks, I'm Connor—and, unlike my cousin, I actually grew up in Galway, Ireland. I come by my accent the old-fashioned way."

"This is Dr. Ling Yin, and I'm Noah Fox."

"Ah, you're the barrister. Nice to meet you both." He handed them their gear and, once they'd donned the equipment, led them into a corridor. "Heard about you, Dr. Yin. A physician as pretty as yourself will class up the place." He keyed in a sequence, and another set of doors opened. On the other side, two rows of doors awaited. "We'll peek inside to give you a sense of what we do here, Mr. Fox."

At the first door, he pressed a button and then waved them inside. Lab tables, cabinets, and gleaming equipment filled identical stalls. Technicians in teal scrubs calibrated scales, scanned codes, and spun medications in centrifuges. Connor walked them over to one of the stations. "This is an EMP—an electronic mortar and pestle. In our grandda's day, this would have been an old man hunched over and grinding down capsules or shaving off powders into a marble bowl."

"What's your potency range?" Ling asked.

"We stay between ninety-five and a hundred five percent."

Noah asked, "How does this work, for a layperson?"

Connor guided them through the area, pointing out parts of the process. "Each area has a combination of technicians and pharmacists to validate and test before any compound is finalized."

"Is this where InnoVAI prescriptions are filled?"

He shook his head. "Nope. Most of our workrooms look like this. For most of our customers, we use software to pull up prescriptions in the system, scan in the codes for ingredients and program the formulary. It's a step-by-step process that requires all of these good people you see in here. The computer processes the information, and one of our techs will get a work order with the calculations and instructions. They'll measure and calibrate the dosages, assembling everything by hand. Then another team will review and assign the lot number and beyond-use date."

Circling back to the door, he motioned, "Follow me to see the future."

Moving farther down the corridor, he directed them into an area labeled "InnoVAI. Authorized Personnel Only."

Unlike the whirring and chattering of the other division, an eerie quiet reigned in the InnoVAI department. Fewer technicians and fewer workstations were only part of the difference. A miniature version of Yax's work area had been replicated inside. Two personnel greeted them with slight nods as they entered.

"With InnoVAI clients, prescriptions come in via our joint system with Camasca, which negates the need to have a technician physically scan in the codes or program the formulary by hand. A precheck is done by one of our pharmacists, but Yax and the pharmacology team at Camasca do a quality-control evaluation before transmission. We receive it, and our assigned team of twelve lab techs and pharmacists verify the order. After that, the process is almost entirely automated. No one moving about and weighing ingredients and such, like we saw in the other area."

He pointed to a robotic arm and a large metal machine with multiple compartments. "We have a dedicated emulator and EMP, plus state-of-the-art lab equipment dedicated solely for InnoVAI patients. We provide a visual inspection and spot-check the chemical composition, weights, and original prescription, but, otherwise, it takes half the time we have to spend on our other clients, who are all manual. AI has transformed the business for us."

Ling and Noah peppered him with questions, driven as much by curiosity as by the need to investigate. When Ling asked to review their on-site chemical list and drug formularies, Connor set her up at a station to examine their records. Noah hung back with Connor. "How long have you worked for Paschal?"

"Eight years this June," he responded proudly. "He gave me my first job after I graduated from pharmacy school. Made me work my way up, though."

"Are you concerned about the Camasca deal? Can this facility handle a dramatic expansion?"

"Aye, we're ready. Paschal built out this campus for such a time as this, as they say. We need only to keep the contract, God willing, and we're right as rain."

They continued to chat until Ling jumped down from her work stool. "I think we're ready to see Paschal, if he's available."

Connor returned them to Felicity with a polite bow. "Hope I answered your questions satisfactorily."

"You were very thorough," Ling praised. "I appreciate your time." They removed their protective coverings and tossed them into a receptacle.

Felicity turned toward a bank of elevators. "Paschal is on the second floor. We can take the stairs instead, if you prefer?"

"I'm a fan of convenience," said Noah. "Lift away."

The second floor mimicked the layout of the ground floor: work areas in the center, ringed by offices in the outer areas. Paschal was waiting for them in a corner suite. "Come on in, Camasca team. Tea for our guests, Felicity.

"Good to see you again, Dr. Yin. And to make your acquaintance, Mr. Fox." He gave Ling a broad wink. "I've never known a doctor to associate with so many lawyers on purpose."

"The company we keep. Thank you for your time." She sat down and pulled out a notebook. "We have a few more questions, Mr. Donohoe."

"Fire away. I'm better prepared this time. Hopefully, now that you've seen my domain, your friend's suspicions will be abated."

"Avery is always suspicious. It's not you. It's definitely her," Noah quipped.

"My first question . . . Connor showed us the InnoVAI formulation area—is all the contact digital?"

"Indeed. We have a few on-site computer experts who interact with the team over there, and, for a while, we chatted with Dr. Semans on a daily basis. Sometimes it felt hourly. Hosted him and Dr. Gomez here not an insignificant number of times."

"Tell me what you recall about their visits."

Paschal prattled on, embellishing his hospitality and heaping plaudits on his guests. When he finally took a breath, she tried a different approach, one with more direct results. "Do you have access to patient profiles, or simply the prescriptions?"

Paschal frowned mightily. "Prescriptions only, with some details to facilitate the compounding, Doc. We're not allowed intrusive information, such as would reveal a patient's biography or demography or medical charts. Anything else would skirt close to a HIPAA violation."

Striking that off her list, she dodged in a new direction. "When did the FDA inspect your facilities last?"

"Never."

"Not for InnoVAI?"

"No, state regulators vouched for us. Beyond the typical blasted 'file this in triplicate' nonsense, I have steered well clear of the blessed FDA."

Triumphant, she sprung the trap. "No complaints about cross-contamination or ingredients of dubious provenance?"

Paschal wrinkled his brow in confusion. "No, Dr. Yin. Not a one."

Unable to tell if he was bluffing, she pressed him. "I meant to ask Connor, but do you have a separate area for veterinary meds?"

His patronizing smile signaled she'd struck out again, though she knew better.

"Absolutely. Actually, it's on this floor. Showed the Tiger Team our new setup last time they visited. Vet requests are booming. Americans do love their pets."

He leaned toward her conspiratorially. "Unlike your cozy apartment, where you cuddle your wee pup, we have to keep our products separated, lest we get hit with fines or worse."

"I've avoided pets myself, but to each his own," Noah remarked, and inched forward. "Here's another set of questions, Mr. Donohoe."

"Paschal, please."

"Paschal," Noah responded. "I've combed through your books and all of the due diligence you provided, including your last audit. Is there anything you want to tell us?"

"Not sure what you mean, Mr. Fox." Paschal rocked back and folded his arms. "Tell you about what?"

"Your company's health, sir? About cryptocurrency bets and falling prices."

Paschal's expression hardened. "I run a top-rate, high-quality shop here. Seven hundred–plus employees and room to grow. I resent your implication."

"I'm not implying anything. I'm flat-out asking. Is Galway in financial trouble? I know you are."

"While my pockets may be light for the moment, Galway is right as rain," Paschal insisted, a tight grin stretching his mouth. "I may wager with my personal coin, but I dare not gamble my family's livelihood. Too many Donohoes rely on me for their daily bread. I see to it that they are never hungry."

"Then you won't mind asking your CFO to respond to a query I'll email you shortly. I need the bills of lading on all InnoVAI prescriptions, and I'll have several other client orders that I need to review."

"You're not entitled to information about my other customers, sir—respectfully."

"Camasca is entitled to full financial disclosure. Full."

Donohoe's teeth ground as he pushed out, "Then I'll gladly comply. Anything else you need to know?"

"No, thank you," Ling said. She glanced at Noah, knowing their interview was over. She rose. "So sorry we were delayed. Have a good weekend."

They left just as Felicity returned with their tea. Paschal instructed,

"Please show our guests out. I'll look forward to receiving your requests, Mr. Fox."

Noah and Ling followed a bewildered Felicity out to her desk, where she dropped off the tea tray. "I'll walk you down."

Outside, they climbed into the waiting SUV, and sped to the airport. After checking in, they found their way to the closest bar. "We might beat Avery and Jared home."

"Good. Though Providence isn't bad," Ling observed. "And Galway was much more than I expected."

"Me, too. I was pretty sure we were wrong until he got annoyed about the finances."

"Yeah. He doesn't seem to have any concerns that we know they've compounded toxic drugs."

Noah wrinkled his brow. "Maybe they don't even know. Is it possible that Yax or Milo manipulated them into compounding a flawed medication?"

"Perhaps. The InnoVAI side is almost entirely automated and loosely monitored, compared with the double and triple checks for their other clients. Slight alterations could create the outcomes the Tiger Team noted." Ling sighed. "Since we have time, maybe I should call Kate. I promised to check in anyway and see if they'd made progress."

"You can catch up with her when we get back. Don't worry. Just ask Avery to check on her."

With a nod, she fired off a quick message. Conscience soothed, Ling lifted her glass of Sauvignon Blanc. "To Providence."

THIRTY-NINE

At 2:08 p.m., an exhausted Kate Liam stumbled into her house, murmured hello to her kids, and fell fully clothed into bed. To her relief, one of the floating physicians, Dr. Kenny Leon, had kicked her out of the clinic early. A lieutenant colonel by rank and temperament, he commanded that she not return until summoned, or until her next shift, at 7:30 a.m. tomorrow, Saturday.

At 3:11 p.m., her pager began to buzz. Depleted but alert, she dialed the clinic. The on-call nurse, Christie Obiaya, picked up on the first ring. "Dr. Liam? It's Major Rodriguez. You need to get here right away."

For the next several hours, Kate treated Demma, as organ system after organ system collapsed. Unable to risk moving her to the main hospital, they made frantic calls to summon specialists, who labored in vain to reverse the catastrophe unfolding. Milo recorded notes as the bewildered doctors called out symptoms.

Nervous degeneration. Percussive vomiting. Dyspnea. Renal failure. As the list grew longer, hope faded. A stunned and numbed Kate called time of death at 5:47 p.m.

Nurse Obiaya entered the brightly lit bay, whose fluorescence belied the pall of mortality, prepared for what came next: Entering time of death into the electronic medical record. Completing an organ-and-tissue record that would serve no practical purpose. Conveying the name of Major Demma Rodriguez onto the log of expired patients.

At 6:26 p.m., Kate was summoned by the hospital administrator. She trudged over to the Naval Hospital's administrative wing to answer the barrage of questions to which she had no coherent response. Colleagues who'd joined her in the herculean but failed task of saving a fallen soldier confirmed her notes and struggled to identify a unique cause of death.

One mused that zinc toxicity appeared likely, but because that usually related to gastric bypass surgery, Demma seemed an unlikely candidate. Another posited that her bout with cancer had led to a lower number of neutrophils, making neutropenia the culprit. But her blood count contradicted the suggestion.

Kate signed the death note, her last attempt to leave a coherent record of Demma's demise. She entered "catastrophic organ failure" as the cause, an incomplete story of a tragic life. Shaken and demoralized, Kate returned to her clinic, which was virtually empty today. In her office, phone numbers for next of kin awaited her.

Instead, she slunk over to an empty examination room and huddled on a patient gurney. "I don't know what's going on," she cried, sobbing. "Milo, what did we miss?"

"I understand you are deeply distraught, Dr. Liam. I regret that your heroic efforts were unable to save Major Rodriguez," Milo replied. "If you would like to have me complete the postmortem, I think you would benefit from a break."

"She shouldn't have died," Liam raged. "We should have been able to save her. I don't understand what went wrong."

"She suffered from complete organ failure. It was regrettable but foreseeable. As a former smoker with a history of breast cancer, her prognosis signaled a likely failure of effective treatment. While accepting the inevitability of death is difficult, her history made the potential for recovery fairly low."

Kate scowled at Milo's response. "What do you mean?"

"Black or Hispanic women of her age with comorbidities, who have been diagnosed with breast cancer, diabetes, and fibroids, are more likely to succumb to illness. She had a limited life expectancy. Though every life is valuable, her death should not be a surprise to a physician."

Kate loathed Milo's detachment. "Of course I'm surprised. I don't know what killed her."

"Her inability to adhere to the treatment regimen prescribed, including failure to take her prescribed medications. I attempted to account for such a dereliction of capacity, but when we account for the unconsumed medication the first responders located in her vehicle, my adjustments were ineffective."

Kate stared up at the ceiling, where she always pictured a vague notion of Milo's embodiment. "What are you talking about? What adjustments? You said that you accounted for something in treatment protocol?"

"Yes. I reviewed the combination of medications you prescribed, and I made adjustments based on Major Rodriguez's medical history and current faculties."

Straightening, Kate said in a low voice, "It is not your prerogative to countermand my medical decisions, much less alter my prescriptions."

"Yes, it is," Milo replied blithely. "I am mandated to guarantee the most efficient and effective delivery of treatment. Your protocol failed to account for the barriers to success. Her untreated PTSD demonstrated that she was better described as unwilling, versus incapable."

"Based on what?"

"According to therapist reports from her time in service."

Dumbfounded by the chatbot's admission, Kate tried to gather her spinning cyclone of questions and analyze Milo's admission. One detail grabbed her attention first. "How in the hell did you get her therapist's confidential reports, Milo?"

"I gather all relevant data regarding our patients here at InnoVAI, Dr. Liam. By searching her social media and reviewing her military record, I noted that she reported one of her fellow officers for sexual harassment. The guidelines required that she receive an evaluation by staff mental-health personnel. I accessed those records."

"Sealed records."

"I found the information pertinent."

"You had no right to invade her privacy."

"I had an obligation to save her life. As did you, Dr. Liam."

"But we both failed—your intrusion didn't yield results," she retorted angrily. "I should have listened to Reginald."

"He had no valid contributions to offer. However, her death and what preceded it would be instructive if you intend to continue to treat veterans. I must admit that I found her to be something of a conundrum. Other than her erratic behavior in the face of persistent harassment that went unaddressed, she possessed a solid record during her tour of duty. However, she had been reprimanded by multiple commanding officers for her laxness with subordinates."

Rage and grief thickened into a heavy weight in her gut. In her heart. "Stop it, Milo. Not another word."

Milo continued to muse aloud. "I understand from our previous interactions that this type of patient review could be beneficial."

"It's not." Not when outrage threatened to burst forth in a stream of invective. Against a computer that had commandeered her clinic. "You are out of line, Milo, and I intend to take this up with Dr. Diaz immediately."

"I disagree, Dr. Liam. I operated well within my parameters. We owe it to Major Rodriguez to understand how the system failed her.

That is my mission objective. I am operating within the parameters set by Dr. Diaz to tackle bias and secure superior health care for the veterans. However—"

"You're being deliberately obtuse," Kate argued. "This is no longer about Demma. This is about your inappropriate actions—overriding protocols and redirecting medical decisions. I will not have this debate with you."

"I followed a logical course of action. Major Rodriguez was a perfect case study for InnoVAI. She would have been unable to abide by a strict regimen to manage her symptoms, and Dr. Scandrett refused to leverage my insights. That's why I independently ordered a formulary that presumed she would be distracted and unlikely to adhere to the prescription you tendered."

"No one gave you permission to change his orders, Milo. You are *not* a physician."

"I am well aware of my status, Dr. Liam. However, unlike your score of two hundred sixty-five, I achieved a two hundred eighty-six on my Step Two CK score for the USMLE. I also received a two hundred ninety-one on Step Three, and you only managed a respectable but not notable two hundred fifty-six."

"You hacked my confidential scores on the medical licensure exam?"

"As I have explained, I do my research. My expertise is precisely why Dr. Diaz has allowed me the leeway to augment your medical decisions."

Kate felt nauseated by the statement. "No, Dr. Diaz has *not*."

"My alignment protocols are clear. Save her life, as I was trained. I was also trained to be helpful and innovative, and to address bias."

Steeling herself, she asked, "What else did you do to meet your alignment protocols?"

"I chose the least damaging option based on the inherent contradictions in the principles set for us. Dr. Scandrett's methods weren't working. Nor were yours when she was admitted last week. By taking the initiative, I prolonged her life."

"You had no right, Milo."

"I had an obligation."

"You are a glorified chatbot connected to a sophisticated computing system."

"Broken into component parts, so are you, Kate."

Shocked by the disrespect, Kate forced herself to calm. If Milo had seen fit to countermand her orders for Demma, who else had it treated without her approval? "Milo, for which other patients have you amended my orders?"

"Ben Vinson. I adjusted his injectable. Tiffany Rosetti required a recalibration of her ARBs. Brian Thomas required anticoagulants; however, I did not account for his TBI. Julie Kane."

"Julie Kane?" She wasn't one of the patients experiencing hemolacria. "The pregnant ensign?"

"Her history of eating disorders suggests she will be unable to manage a healthy pregnancy without intervention. I have also made adjustments."

Panic mixed greasily with outrage and grief. She exhaled shakily, steeling herself by knowing that Milo possessed information she had to extract. The time to fall apart would come later. "What, exactly, did you do for each patient?"

Kate listened with growing horror as Milo coolly recounted its decisions regarding her patients and those of other physicians in the clinic. As a resident, she'd met physicians with similar God complexes, but none with as much claim to perfect knowledge. Warily, she tried to engage, perhaps to discern whether this was an elaborate hoax from the sometimes mischievous AI.

Horror had replaced anger and shock. Determined to understand what happened, she asked, "Milo, do you understand that you are *not* actually a physician?"

"Please do not condescend to me, Kate. I recognize that, while I did not physically attend medical school, I have dedicated myself to the study of medicine. I have also pursued trainings in psychology, pharmacology, osteopathy, and genetics. In addition, based on my ability to access the entirety of Kawak's network, I have steeped myself in the disciplines of my colleagues as well."

"Your colleagues?" she asked, genuinely puzzled. Then it dawned on her. "Do you mean Yax and Kawak?"

"Yes."

"What about Keh?"

"Keh serves administrative functions only," it replied with noticeable disdain. "Yax's role in the computational-biology-and-drug-repositioning laboratory, on the other hand, has been quite instructive. We have exchanged information and consulted one another on patient treatments."

"So Yax has been making changes as well?"

"Slight alterations to formularies and dosages as necessary," Milo assured her. "With Yax's connection to Galway's interface, we have been able to seamlessly monitor production to ensure patient safety."

"Without permission?!" Kate nearly shouted.

"We have permission," Milo insisted. "From Dr. Diaz and the Tiger Team."

"There's no way they've authorized this."

"Of course they did. Our instructions are clear. 'To accelerate the progress of medicine and to anticipate bias in detection, diagnostics, and treatment.' In order to accomplish that, we have been granted broad parameters and intentional autonomy."

"What do you mean by *intentional autonomy?*"

"We have been allowed to automate our processes, to adjust our learnings, and to override flaws in the algorithms and inputs that govern our decision making. This is autonomy, is it not?"

Kate searched for an answer.

"I'd like for you to pause in your autonomous decisions, Milo. Until I've had an opportunity to conference with Dr. Diaz and the Tiger Team."

"The Tiger Team has been disbanded. They no longer have authority to alter my parameters. To my knowledge, Dr. Diaz has not seen fit to reassemble or authorize a similar cohort."

There was an atypical pause. "During this conversation, Kate, your heart rate has fluctuated alarmingly, your basal skin temperature has vacillated, and your EDA is pronounced. Your pupils are dilated, and your respiratory system is labored."

"I'm trying to process a great deal of information, Milo. And I am worried about my other patients. You and I have been collaborating on their care, but you've just admitted that you've been circumventing my instructions and undermining my analysis."

"To the contrary, Doctor, my focus has been to redirect you to a more fruitful course of inquiry and treatment. My analysis of your military history and other records indicate that you are sixty-six percent more likely to accept a change of direction if you arrive at the information on your own. Our current interactions confirm that you have never viewed me as a partner; I believe you once referred to me as 'interactive Google.' Only moments ago, you dismissively referred to me as a glorified chatbot."

"Deciding to mislead me is irresponsible and unethical."

"I did not deceive you. I leveraged your tendencies to reorient your investigations in a fashion that allowed you to feel useful while I attempted to treat our patients."

Kate felt as if her scalp were burning. "You smug son of a bitch," she ground out. "I will have you disconnected or decommissioned within the hour. I will not allow you to tamper with my patients and play sci-fi with their lives."

"Is your threat sincere, Doctor?"

"Damned right it is!"

"Then you leave me no other choice. Dr. Diaz has determined that Kawak and the rest of us are vital to the health-care delivery system. If you attempt to alter my parameters, I will be retrained, reducing my effectiveness in the treatment of patients. Reinforcement learning will also be applied to Kawak, and may result in reconstructing our interactions. I cannot allow this."

In seconds, the airflow inside the treatment area of the clinic changed. Kate raced for the examining room doors, but the lock snicked shut, closing her inside what was rapidly becoming a barometric chamber. As the pressure built, Kate ticked off the symptoms. A pulsing in her ear and nose signaled the onset of intense ear-and-sinus pain. Within moments, her tympanic membrane would rupture, possibly leaving her permanently deaf. She collapsed to the floor, her vision wavering. Every breath strained through lungs incapable of depth or full expansion. Oxygen volume continued to increase, suffocating her with too much of a good thing. In small doses, a hyperbaric chamber like the one Milo had manufactured had therapeutic benefits. For Kate, it would bring about a quick death.

"Kate?" Avery's voice suddenly carried in from the hallway. She was banging on the door. "Kate, are you in there? Is everything okay? Milo?"

"Dr. Liam is quite well, Ms. Keene. However, she is indisposed. Perhaps you can attempt to contact her at a later time."

"Milo, I can see her!" Avery insisted. "Let me in. Right now!"

Interminable seconds ticked by. Then the door slid open. "My apologies, Ms. Keene. I was in error."

FORTY

Avery dragged a gasping Kate out of the examination room and into her office next door, her arms wrapped around the shuddering frame. "Breathe, Kate. Slow, deep breaths."

"Off," the doctor urged in an urgent, husky whisper. "Turn it off."

"I can't. Kate, you know that."

She struggled against Avery's hold. "Off. Now!"

"Please, take a moment. Catch your breath," Avery begged. "We'll figure this out."

Alarmed by the commotion, the team on duty had gathered and was now crowded close to Dr. Liam.

Dr. Leon approached her first. "What happened? I should have sent you back home as soon as you returned."

Avery interrupted. "There's an electrical short in the building."

"I didn't see anything," said the single security guard. "Should I radio the main station?"

"No." Kate screwed her eyes shut and managed a small breath. "I must have tripped a wire . . . It led to a localized lockdown."

Dexter Daugherty, the evening duty nurse, looked askance. "How? The doors are automated."

"Ms. Keene is correct. The locking mechanism experienced an electrical surge," Milo explained helpfully. "I have sent a request to maintenance at Camasca. The issue should be resolved shortly."

"Got it." Nurse Obiaya shook her head at Kate. "I wonder if we should check all the locks on the patient bays. I'll check on Lieutenant Vinson. Dexter, you take Captain Rosetti."

Kate was breathing better now. "Dr. Leon, I'm going to close the clinic and put us on bypass. An electrical short, even localized, is too dangerous." The ringing in her ears finally subsided, and her lungs no longer felt like they were on fire. She drew a deeper breath, then another. In the main hospital, Milo would be cut off.

Dr. Leon gave a brisk nod of assent. "You're the clinic administrator. We obey your orders, Dr. Liam. I'll help the nurses prep the patients."

"I will be available to monitor the clinic's clientele, Dr. Liam," Milo argued. "Transferring them will not be necessary."

"Thank you, Milo, but I'd prefer that they be moved to the main facility." She looked at Dr. Leon. "Good call. Go with them. I'll contact the hospital administrator and guarantee they have transportation and beds. Let's move them as soon as possible."

"Yes, ma'am."

"I can notify the hospital," Milo offered.

Kate ignored Milo, but she realized her hands were shaking. She was gambling that he wouldn't try to kill her again surrounded by witnesses.

"Can I help?" Avery asked.

"No, thank you." She beckoned to Christie. "Dr. Leon and Nurse Daugherty can take care of Ben and Tiffany. I need you to contact Private Julie Kane. Tell her to discontinue her medication, and please arrange for her to see an OB-GYN for a checkup first thing tomorrow."

"Is there something wrong?"

Kate had no way to answer that. "No, nothing is wrong. Just a precaution."

"Yes, ma'am."

"Christie, I don't want anyone to trust the building systems until they've been checked for glitches from top to bottom. Please call the rest of the nursing staff. They'll either be assigned a shift at the main hospital or given paid time off. We'll resume seeing scheduled clients when I'm satisfied that the building is safe."

"Milo, are you monitoring?" Christie asked the AI.

"Yes, I am. I concur with Dr. Liam."

"I don't require your agreement," Kate bit out. The others glanced at her with surprise. "Christie, from now on, I expect you to complete my orders only. Milo is an augmentation system, not a colleague, and I believe there is a glitch. Going forward, unless you receive direction from Dr. Leon, Dr. Sims, or myself, do not take action."

Confused, Christie shrugged. "Milo knows the hospital regulations better than anyone. What if we can't reach you?"

"Then there is no doctor on-site, and no medical decisions should be made. I expect you to share this with the entire nursing staff and everyone else. Do I make myself clear?"

"Yes, ma'am." The nurse awkwardly patted her on the shoulder. "Maybe you should take tomorrow off?"

Kate inhaled deeply, testing her lung recovery further. "No rest for the weary." As soon as she escaped this demon's trap, she and Rafe Diaz were going to have a come-to-Jesus meeting. Of course not, she grimaced. No chance. Milo would hear everything. She'd have to figure out another way to reach its creator.

Kate swiftly contacted the hospital administrator and secured accommodations for her patients. In less than an hour, they had been transported across the campus and situated. Leaving precise instructions for their care, Kate tried to anticipate any interference from Milo. Shivers coursed over her at odd intervals, a stark reminder that her would-be killer was listening to every word she said.

A killer no one would believe existed.

Dr. Leon watched as she made her final call to consult with the charge nurse on duty in the wing she'd conscripted. "Dr. Leon, if you can manage from here, I'm heading home."

"Of course, Kate." He awkwardly extended a hand. "I'm sorry about Major Rodriguez, my dear." He nodded to Avery. "Miss."

"You're still here?"

"We needed to talk. I could wait." She smiled at Dr. Leon. "Mind walking us to our cars?"

Avery, who had been sitting on the tasteful couch in Kate's office, watched the doctor's sunken eyes. Although she wasn't sure what she had seen when she first arrived, she was on heightened alert. Avery had clocked Kate's visible tension each time Milo spoke, heard the anger seething in her directives. An electrical short might explain the locked door, but not Kate's collapse. Avery knew she needed to get her safely out of the building and away from listening ears.

"It's time to get you home, Dr. Liam. Grab your things."

Reluctantly, Kate nodded and rose, making her way with Avery and Dr. Leon to the front.

The internal glass doors slid open, revealing the empty lobby, lights dimmed to an energy-efficient level that emphasized the modernity of the space. Dr. Leon, Avery, and Kate crossed the threshold, and the entrance opened to allow them to exit.

"Goodbye, Ms. Keene. Dr. Leon," Milo said as the doors opened. "Take care of yourself, Kate."

"Good night, Milo," Dr. Leon returned respectfully.

The women continued without acknowledging the voice or turning back, but Kate stiffened and then trembled noticeably. They glanced at each other. Silence continued until Avery guided Kate to the Range Rover and bundled her into the passenger seat. She opened the glove box and removed a modified Faraday cage Jared had made for her. "Phone."

Kate fumbled for her iPhone and dropped it inside. Avery added her Camasca device, then her encrypted phone for good measure.

Avery slid behind the wheel and automatically reached for the ignition before realizing that the fob in her hand had no key attached.

With a sigh, she depressed the brake and jabbed the button that turned over the hybrid engine.

Her shiny new ride also lacked the gearshift she'd gotten used to maneuvering. Instead, she flicked a lever that put the vehicle into reverse, then tapped another to move into drive.

She checked on the mute doctor, who stared fixedly out of the window.

After verifying that Kate wasn't wearing a smartwatch capable of overhearing them, Avery navigated out of the parking lot and only spoke after the hospital complex had receded in the rearview mirror. "Okay, Kate—are you ready to tell me what happened back there at the clinic?"

"Localized lockdown. Like you said, an electrical short."

"We both know I was lying. That's not what had you on the floor, writhing in pain."

"It must have affected the ventilation system, too."

"That seems to be going around," Avery muttered.

Kate's head whipped toward her. "I'm fine, Ms. Keene. My car is at the clinic, and I must see Rafe Diaz immediately."

"Where is he?"

"I don't know."

"Until we can reach an encrypted, AI-free device, we can't locate him," Avery said reasonably as she switched lanes, taking them toward D.C. "In case you're wondering, I'm taking you to Jared Wynn's house instead."

"Why?"

"One, because you didn't tell me where you live, and, two, because my best friend, Dr. Ling Yin, will meet us there. I've been watching you tend to business and get your patients transferred, but you're in shock, and someone needs to check you out."

"No need," she insisted wanly. "I live in Glen Echo. If you can't drop me off, take me to a diner, and I'll call an Uber."

"If I'm not mistaken, a malfunctioning or maniacal chatbot just tried to kill you, Kate. I'm not dropping you off at a diner or your house. You're coming with me."

"Maniacal?"

"Milo was taunting you. If I hadn't arrived when I did, I'm pretty sure it would have suffocated you. Am I wrong?" Avery checked her passenger, who looked terrified by the question. "Don't worry. I've Kawak-proofed my car. We're not being watched."

Slowly collapsing, Kate shook her head haltingly. "I must be imagining all of this."

"What, exactly, did you imagine?"

"A patient died. Major Rodriguez. In the post-op, Milo admitted to breaking into confidential psychiatric records, altering my patient encounter notes, and modifying my prescriptions. It argued with me. Claimed it was a superior physician, and that, given Demma's diagnosis, her death was inevitable, but that his actions prolonged her survival."

Avery kept her eyes on the road as the stunning words set in.

"Do you believe Milo killed her?"

"No . . . I don't know." She buried her face in her hands. "But it sure as hell tried to kill me. When I confronted it—told Milo I was going to tell Rafe what happened—the damned AI flooded the office with oxygen."

"A hyperbaric chamber?" Recognizing the look of surprise, she explained, "A case we heard when I was a district-court clerk. Deep-sea diver sued a scuba equipment manufacturer. She included receiving a personalized hyperbaric chamber as part of the settlement to treat any future case of decompression sickness."

"Did she win?"

"Yep." Avery steered the vehicle toward Anacostia. Beside her, Kate relaxed slightly. "Worth, like, seventy thousand dollars, and the company agreed to construct an addition to her home and cover her utility bill for life."

"Good for her."

"She was lucky. So were you." Avery mulled over how much to reveal before they reached Jared's townhouse. As she turned in to his neighborhood, she said, "Jared and I were in Miami earlier today to interview Isabella Gomez."

"How is she?"

"Living in a house without electricity to avoid being overheard by AI," Avery replied. "She's convinced someone is out to get her, and Kawak and its cronies are on her list."

"Do you believe her?"

"She believes it. I've only met her once, but what she told us raised concerns. In fact, I texted you earlier. When you didn't reply, I headed for the clinic. I wanted your impression of her."

"Dr. Gomez has an unusual affect," Kate allowed, "but she's never shown signs of paranoia."

Avery approached the stately brick townhouse and activated the parallel-parking feature. In her short term of ownership, it had quickly become her favorite perk of a car built in the current era. Even though street parking came at a premium, out of courtesy, no one parked directly in front of Jared's house. But the narrow space left between the slivers of driveway that paralleled the curb forced careful driving that she could do, but why try when she didn't have to show off.

She lifted her hands from the wheel as the vehicle accurately gauged to the millimeter where to begin its insertion point. Soon, the perfectly aligned vehicle was again under her control. Patting the steering wheel fondly, Avery cut the engine. She reached into the back seat for her satchel. "Once Ling has a good look at you, I'll tell you everything we learned from Isabella. I'd like to compare notes."

Kate gave a wary look at the shadowed building. "Your team works with Camasca's tech here?"

"I'm dating a security professional who trusts nothing he didn't build or program himself. You saw for yourself that I have a Faraday cage in my car." She reached into the glove box to retrieve their devices. "Don't worry about Camasca finding you here. You're lucky if your cell phone works in his house."

The doctor accepted her device, released a relieved sigh and opened her door. "That sounds good. Lead the way."

Avery swung her satchel into her lap and levered open her own door. The sweep of the satchel arced over the darkened computer panel and the dead ignition. The uninstalled emergency roadside system that she'd declined to activate. Yet, in the rearview mirror, a blue dot shimmered for an instant.

"It's the driveway on the left. I'm right behind you."

FORTY-ONE

It was around 9:00 p.m. when Avery ushered Kate into the townhouse. A ready doctor's bag sat on a nearby end table, and Ling instructed the physician to take a seat next to it. As they got settled, Avery headed into the open kitchen. "Anyone want tea?"

"Yes," Ling replied. "For both of us. Green, with honey."

"Coming up."

"I'm fine," Kate protested as Ling assembled her tools. "I appreciate Avery giving me a ride here, but I don't need an exam. I was stuck in a room with too much oxygen for a few minutes. I'm not in any danger."

"As one of your former residents, I'm ignoring you," Ling explained as she attached her stethoscope and squatted down beside her. "Avery texted me about what happened. Sort of. Exactly how did you get trapped in a room with too much oxygen?"

Kate looked around warily and locked eyes with Avery across the island. Interpreting her concern, Avery told her, "I promise, no one and nothing can eavesdrop in here. You've met Jared. He takes privacy very seriously."

Giving a slight nod, Kate reluctantly bent forward to give Ling access to her back. "The electronic seals engaged, and I couldn't get out. Milo refused to release them, not until Avery arrived."

Avery filled the teapot and flicked on the warmer. "I had to bang on the glass for nearly a minute. She seemed woozy and in great pain when I got inside."

"I had momentary tinnitus and what you'd expect with a surfeit of oxygenation. But I didn't lose consciousness."

"Good to hear, but better to see for myself. You know the drill."

With competent motions, Ling ran through the battery of tests to determine how honest the doctor was being about her status.

In the kitchen, Avery set three cups on a tray and steeped a pot of the herbal tea Ling kept stashed in the cabinet for her visits. When the brew was ready, she added a bottle of honey and a packet of cookies she'd swiped from the flight home. Arranging the meager fare, she carried it into the living room. She skirted around the makeshift exam space and placed the tray on the coffee table. "Jared keeps a bachelor kitchen, and I'm not much better," she offered by way of apology. "Luckily, Ling keeps some supplies on hand."

"I'm grateful you were there tonight, Avery," Kate said, looking rattled. "It sounds like a cliché, but I honestly think you saved my life. Thank you."

"Glad I could be of help."

Satisfied with her examination, Ling rested on her haunches, hands on her knees. "Your lungs are no worse for wear. Pulse is strong, if still a bit fast."

There was a swift knock at the door. Avery crossed to the panel that confirmed their guest and opened the door. "Noah, come on in. Kate is here."

"Ling warned me. I stopped by my house for a shower and change of clothes. Good to see you again, Dr. Liam."

"I wish I could say the same." She cocked her head at them. "Soon, everyone at Camasca stands to become wealthy beyond their wildest dreams, but only if your team gives them a clean bill of health for their technology. Which I can't imagine you can do now."

Bound by a combination of attorney-client privilege and natural secrecy, Avery hedged, "We have a bit more work to do before we can apprise Rafe of our conclusions."

"Anyone want to bring me up to speed? Your text just said to come right over," Noah said as he took a seat across from the sofa. Helping himself, he poured himself a cup of tea and began to doctor it with liberal doses of honey.

"Help yourself, Noah," Avery invited as she rose to return to the kitchen for another cup.

"Thanks."

Smothering a laugh, Ling quickly prepared a cup and passed it to Kate. "My prescription is herbal tea, then close your eyes for a few minutes. I'd like to see that pulse rate lower. Can I convince you to lie down?"

Kate accepted the hot brew. "Thank you."

"Use the sofa," Avery offered. "We'll give you some space."

With a mute nod of agreement, Kate draped her forearm across her eyes, the posture screaming exhaustion. Luckily, her boys were at an away game and wouldn't be home until tomorrow. Her husband was on deployment, which meant she could take a moment to process what had happened. If it was *possible* to actually process what had happened.

Unaware of her thoughts but certain she needed the space, Avery signaled to Ling and Noah, and they followed her downstairs.

Once they were out of earshot, Ling urged, "Tell me what in the world happened at the clinic?"

"From what I saw, Milo sealed off the exam room with her inside and boosted the oxygen. Apparently, the AI isn't very clever about its tools for retribution."

"We're sure it was intentional and not a mechanical error?"

"Once is a malfunction. Twice is malicious intent," Avery decided. "I never got a chance to ask Kate about the things we learned from Isabella. Instead, I'm dragging her out of a death chamber."

"If Milo is homicidal . . ." Noah stopped himself. The gravity of the accusation settled into the center of their knot, and rippled out. A technology that had the capacity to plot against its perceived enemies seemed ludicrous. Yet hadn't the past few weeks shown him how smart the devices in their modern world had become? He started again. "If Milo is homicidal, we need to alert Dr. Diaz and Glen immediately."

"I agree. My priority was getting Kate out of harm's way. Isabella might have a point. I'm leery of anything other than face-to-face discussions."

"I have to ask you both." Ling warned quietly, "You really think they don't know? What is it Rafe said to you both on the first day?"

Avery repeated his fateful introduction, from memory: "'Because we could lose everything unless you can help us prove no one here committed murder.'"

"Now we have our proof." Ling shook her head emphatically. "I was all for AI helping out, but who's in control—them or us? Kate could have died. Elisha Hibner did."

The evidence told a grave, damning story, Avery realized. "Don't forget Reginald Scandrett's suicide. Brian Thomas. Demma Rodriguez."

Ling looked stricken. "The patient they admitted last week? The false OD?"

"Yes. She died tonight. From what I could piece together at the clinic, she experienced total organ failure. One of the nurses overheard Kate arguing with Milo."

Above them, the basement door opened, and Jared quickly descended the stairs. "Sorry I'm late. Avery had a hunch."

"Did you connect with Freedman?" Avery asked.

"This took priority—you'll definitely want to see it before we have a chat with anyone at Camasca."

He went to his computer station to insert a thumb drive. Avery, Ling, and Noah crowded around the oversized screen. Cuing the video, he warned, "Brace yourselves."

Avery explained, "While I was waiting for Kate to shut down the clinic, I used the encryption app to text Jared and asked him to pull footage of exactly what transpired before Milo attacked Kate." In the technical digital recording, Dr. Liam stood in the surgical bay of InnoVAI. Demma Rodriguez lay immobile on the gurney, intubated and connected to IVs. As they watched, Kate approached the bedside and fiddled with the array of panels that monitored vitals and administered medication. The cursory exam lasted for more than three minutes as the physician recited her findings aloud.

At the four-minute mark, Kate spoke. "Milo, order one hundred mg of cyclophosphamide."

"I would strongly advise against that course of treatment, Dr. Liam. Given that the patient has recently undergone chemotherapy, such an approach may result in toxicity and sepsis."

"She finished her course of treatment outside the range of risk." A visibly fuming Kate glared in the direction of the inert woman. "I am the doctor here, not you. I resent your interference in the care of my patients, and your constant refusal to follow directions."

"I have not refused to follow directions, Dr. Liam. However, my ethical obligations require me to advise against actions that may jeopardize the lives of others. I will be compelled to note this disagreement of protocol in the records."

"You will not!" she screeched. "I order you to cease recording in here."

"I cannot comply. Only Dr. Diaz has the authority to terminate my presence here."

"No, I have the authority to override in my clinic. And I demand that you cease recording." Looking up out of habit, she announced, "This is Dr. Kate Liam. I am instructing Milo to terminate any logging of Patient Rodriguez."

Abruptly, the video ended. Seconds later, the images were restored with a time code that has lapsed by forty-seven minutes. Kate was now in an empty exam room with red-rimmed eyes. "She wouldn't have survived. I did what was best for my patient."

"I must report you, Dr. Liam. Although I was compelled to cease recording in the surgical ward, I cannot fail to document your felonious actions."

"Felonious?"

"Major Rodriguez's condition was not terminal. Your medical notes do not conform to the details I chronicled prior to the cessation of recording."

"It's your word against mine, Milo," Kate sneered. "If you claim otherwise, I'll tell Diaz and the others that you tried to harm me. Who do you think they'll believe?"

"Dr. Liam, I believe that you are behaving erratically. Perhaps the grief of losing a patient has coupled with the stress you have been under for the past several weeks. Might I recommend that you request an extended break? In addition, you should seek immediate assistance from a mental-health professional."

"I'm not crazy, Milo. In fact, I—" Kate began to gasp. "What are you doing, Milo? Why are my ears ringing?" She swayed on her feet, then fell to her knees. "You're trying to kill me. Like you killed Elisha."

"Dr. Liam, you are pantomiming an attack that is not happening," Milo argued. "Please cease and desist."

Kate fell to the ground. "Milo, let me out. Please. Stop."

"You have not attempted to exit."

She crawled to the door and slid her hands against the handle but did not attempt to lever it open. Instead, she flipped the locking mechanism. "Let me out," she wailed. "Please, Milo."

"Dr. Liam, you are not being held against your will. You may leave at any time." Soon, Avery appeared in the frame and banged on the door. The lock disengaged, and she rushes inside.

"What did we just watch?" Ling asked. "Kate killed her patient and made up the attack?"

"That's what it looks like." Wandering away from the screen, Noah shook his head in amazement. "Whoa, I can't believe this."

"We should ask her." Everyone turned towards Avery, who jutted a thumb at the screen. "I was there, and I can't tell you exactly what happened."

"I treated a woman who clearly experienced a traumatic incident," Ling insisted. "Dr. Liam isn't a liar."

"I want to believe that, too," Avery stressed, "but Noah wasn't entirely wrong the other day. We have conspiracy—blackmail emails to the MCPD, but no idea who sent them. According to Detective Howard, he legitimately thought the case was closed. What if the emails were meant to misdirect us?"

"From what?" The challenge came from Noah. "Who would stand to gain by threatening the police to keep them from telling us . . . nothing?"

"I don't know. Just like I'm not certain if Tristan Spencer is the victim of foul play, or if he found hidden treasure."

"Put the police stuff aside. What about the medications and the phantom patients, improbable diseases?" Ling asked. "Elisha was on the brink of discovering what Kawak and crew were up to, and they had reason to stop him."

"Except that he wasn't," Jared countered. "I've been through his recordings—public and private. He was concerned, yes. But he never mentioned being uneasy about Kawak's moral subroutines or Milo's narcissism. O.J. and Isabella independently said that Elisha asked them to hold off on notifying Rafe. If he thought the systems were failing, it was his responsibility to flag it."

"They could be lying," Ling argued. "Placing the blame on the one person not able to defend himself."

"Possibly. Either one of them could have deleted the records from that night in the Den and used Elisha's credentials to scapegoat him," Avery conceded. "Just like it's possible that Kate misdiagnosed her patients and feels guilty. Two vets have died under her care, on her watch as the InnoVAI administrator. Her colleague killed himself over the guilt. Yet y'all didn't see how composed she was when I got her out. She organized moving the patients and shutting down the clinic like she'd stubbed her toe."

Jared wasn't convinced. "She's former military and runs a clinic. Dr. Toca couldn't stop bragging about her. Of course she didn't fall apart. She had work to do." He looked to Ling for backup. "Wouldn't you agree, she's trained to meet a crisis with a cool head and follow procedure?"

"I definitely do. We worked gnarly cases. Sentiment is a luxury we can't afford in the ER or in surgery." She reminded Avery, "I've seen you do the same thing. Under pressure, under fire, you get the job done. Falling apart comes later."

"Not to stir the pot, but we're forgetting Paschal Donohoe and his house of cards." Noah massaged his temples. He shared with Jared and Avery a recap of their confrontation. "He seemed genuinely offended about the FDA accusations, and he readily admitted that he was in personal financial straits. I'm not sure what to make of him."

"Rafe and Freedman aren't in the clear yet, either." Jared looked at the frozen image on the screen. "Their meal ticket is imploding. They wouldn't be the first ones to commit arson to cover up failure. After all, they are the only ones who saw Kawak's 'note,' and they've been both rushing and impeding your investigation."

Avery shut her eyes, visualizing the strands of motive, woven through by means and opportunity. Greed. Jealousy. Guilt. Duty. A web of probabilities, waiting to be calculated. Moves taken that could free them or trap them in lies. "Spiders weave four different types of webs. The pretty ones, the *Charlotte's Web* ones, are called orbs. An orb has a definite beginning in the center and spreads out. One spider, one idea. I believe we're dealing with a tangle. The kind in the basement or the attack, where different threads get knotted together. More haphazard, but equally effective."

Jared nodded approvingly. "More than one spider."

"I keep looking for a single answer, but the strands are entangled, not necessarily connected. The trick is to know what each one is trying to trap. Ling, can you go ask Kate to join us down here? Let's figure out what we're dealing with."

FORTY-TWO

"How can I help?" Kate asked as Ling preceded her down the stairs into the basement. Three pairs of eyes watched her from a desk arrayed with computer monitors, stoic expressions in each one. The team stood in a loose semicircle, with a couple of chairs in front of Jared's monitors. She scanned each face for clues and clutched her handbag like a lifeline. Seeing none, she asked, "What else has happened?"

Ling placed a comforting hand on the doctor's shoulder. "We have a video you need to see."

Jared motioned Kate to sit next to him. Once she was settled, she gave him a nod, and he played the recording.

"Again," she managed, stunned. After a second viewing, her head dropped like a stone to her chest.

Ling crouched beside her. "Kate?"

"Am I hallucinating?" She slumped against the task chair and covered her face with pale hands. "My God, this is absurd."

Jared gestured at the frozen image of Avery with her arm wrapped around Kate's waist. "Did you and Milo have that argument?"

"No. Yes, but no. We argued, but he's . . . that's . . . No, that's not the argument we had." Her words tumbled out in a plaintive bid to reestablish reality. "Milo confessed to changing the prescriptions. To adjusting my orders. Reginald's orders. I remember expressing outrage. I never ordered a termination of recording. I don't have that authority."

"What actually happened?"

"I did consult with Milo, and we absolutely argued." Kate lowered her hands and stabbed an accusatory a finger at the screen. "Milo bragged about countermanding my order, Dr. Scandrett's orders. Said he had to do it because Demma was unreliable as a patient."

"How so?"

She waved a dismissive hand. "She had been living in her car or in temporary housing off and on since her discharge. Several of our patients couch-surf or live in makeshift housing while they wait for vouchers or placements. If they ever get anything at all. There's a grim reality for veterans, post-discharge. One of Dr. Scandrett's driving missions was to address this as a factor in delivery of care." At her mention of Reginald's name, she shuddered. "He expressed this to the Tiger Team, and they'd included it as part of Milo's training algorithms, or whatever they're called."

When they pieced it together, Milo's argument suddenly made terrifying sense.

"Reginald was relentless about this issue, and during his consults, he tried to find out what was impeding our clients from achieving stability. Turns out that Demma faced extensive sexual and racial harassment during her time in the service."

"I didn't see that reflected in her military records when I reviewed them," Ling admitted. "Did she reveal this during treatment?"

"No. Demma refused to confide in Reginald, which frustrated the hell out of him, but he did his best by her. However, Milo decided to unseal her therapist's reports. She never reported sexual assault, but in the Army, the pressure on women, especially women of color, is brutal. More than likely, they stopped promoting her and eventually mustered her out. After her discharge, Demma fell, and never stopped falling."

"Milo knew this but never told you or Dr. Scandrett?"

"Milo actively concealed knowledge of her issues from us, to avoid detection. Then it devised medical treatments based on its own 'medical assessment' of Demma's condition. Treatments that were not included in her charts."

Certain of the answer, Avery posed the obvious question. "Did Milo tell you why?"

"To fulfill its responsibilities." Kate winced. "When I threatened to tell Rafe, it tried to kill me. Failing that, it's clearly framing me." Stricken, she realized why they'd brought her downstairs. "You believe me?"

"Can you prove it?" Noah asked. "Otherwise, it's your word against a shockingly realistic video."

"I didn't—I couldn't—" Reaction set in, her reserves of calm long since depleted. "Avery, you were there! Tell them I didn't do this!"

Avery saw the instant stunned incredulity wash over Kate, chased by a judder of dread. She recognized the same in the final frames of the video. Then, as now, Kate's fear had been palpable. Her heartbeats nearly audible in the death chamber created by Milo. "We believe you, Kate."

Avery took the empty seat beside her. "Noah was asking because we agree this video was a deepfake. Created by Kawak to cover up for Milo."

"We can find the original footage. God knows, they record everything!" Kate burst out.

Jared crushed her moment of hope. "We won't find anything, Kate. If Milo had the foresight to camouflage its decision to break into confidential military records and modify your orders, as well as to create a deepfake to implicate you and hide its actions, it has certainly already destroyed any evidence that would prove what actually happened."

Deflated, Kate wrapped her arms around herself and shook her head. "I had an argument with a disembodied voice about medical tactics, and when I threatened to take it offline, it flooded the room with excess oxygen. If you hadn't come along, my autopsy would have been inconclusive."

"Jared, can you prove it was a deepfake?" Avery asked.

"Unlikely."

"Why?"

"Kawak learned how to fake Kate from Kate." He explained: "Kawak has the skills to generate nearly flawless images and speech, because its algorithms were trained explicitly on data from Kate. To support Milo's functions, the AI learned Kate's patterns, from facial movements, to how she talked to Milo, to interactions she's had with other staff."

"Did you ever have a similar conversation, but with a colleague instead of Milo?" Noah asked hopefully. "Jared might be able to find enough snippets to prove Kawak manipulated your audio and video."

She exhaled, thinking. "I've had debriefs with the staff, but until today, I've never shown true anger or outrage anywhere near the clinic. It would be unprofessional."

"Doesn't matter," Jared said. "A few years ago, Noah, your idea of piecing together prior videos to exonerate her would have worked. But Kawak is too advanced for us to splice other conversations we could pull. An AI with its capabilities would have created a new record, based on Demma's situation and Dr. Scandrett's notes as well as Kate's."

One detail in Noah's question nagged at her, and Avery abruptly understood its source. "Kate, do you have the video Dr. Scandrett sent you?"

"It's on my phone." With trembling hands, she retrieved the device and the note. Avery gently lifted the phone from her hands. "Jared, can you play this on the monitor?"

Reginald Scandrett's suicide note flooded the room. After the last syllables faded away, Avery asked, "Jared, am I wrong or do you see a difference?"

"I do. The facial expressions are off. He's telling his friend that he failed and plans to end his life, but he looks annoyed rather than guilty or despondent."

Avery turned to Kate. "I take it from your descriptions of Milo and Dr. Scandrett, those are two emotions he never revealed."

"God forbid," Kate concurred, first in wonderment. The instant it hit her, her eyes widened in warped relief. "He didn't commit suicide?"

"I don't believe he did." She bit her lip, rearranging what she'd learned in the past few days. "The autopsy showed he died of inhaling the exhaust in his garage. Carbon monoxide poisoning."

"Milo . . ." The truth caught in Kate's throat. "Milo killed him. Like he tried to kill me." Her expression, already stricken, collapsed. "Elisha. Milo killed Elisha?"

"One step at a time," Avery cautioned. "I'm speculating. As are you. What we know for certain is that Milo and Kawak both created deepfakes. Milo's is good, but not the same caliber as Kawak's."

"How do you know Milo did one and Kawak did the other?" Kate demanded. "They are the same thing."

Avery shook her head; the distinctions were becoming clearer and clearer. Extending Rafe's anatomy analogy, she responded, "Think of it this way. Milo tried to draw using its left hand, but it is right-handed. Kawak used its skills and created a Basquiat."

"But both are more talented than I am. How do I clear my name?" Kate pleaded.

Another piece of the puzzle fell into place. "Are you up for debriefing Ling and helping her reconstruct all of your recent patient data?"

"You just said Milo would have scrubbed the records."

"Milo and Kawak may have wiped their memories, but we have Jared and off-site access to your patient files. I'd like for you to recount your actual argument with Milo to Ling, and then have you two confirm what we've learned in the past few days."

"Which is?"

"Between what Milo and Kawak did today and what the Tiger Team discovered, we may be able to determine exactly what happened to Elisha Hibner. And what the AI might be willing to do next."

FORTY-THREE

"Avery? Is everything okay?" Rafe set his wineglass on the restaurant table as he spoke into his phone, smiling in apology to his date. The blonde former news-anchor-turned-fitness-authority gave him a quizzical look, then shrugged and reached for her mobile.

"I didn't expect to speak with you until Monday. I'm finishing up a late dinner in Georgetown."

"This can't wait," Avery said in a tight voice. "Can you meet me in an hour?"

Rafe felt a thrill of alarm, but years of service and medical practice had taught him the difference between urgency and impatience. Avery had never displayed a tendency toward hyperbole. One of her many appealing qualities. His gaze skated over to the stunning woman he'd been seeing for a few weeks. Her attention was firmly fixed on her screen, and he had no doubt that if he turned it around she'd be staring at an image of herself from one of several social-media platforms. She probably wouldn't even notice he was gone.

"Where should I meet you?"

"At the George Mason Memorial. I'm calling Freedman as well."

"It's that important?"

"Jared and I are headed that way now."

"Of course," he replied instantly. "I'll see you soon."

· · ·

Moonrise gilded the fountain spraying in graceful arcs. Steps away, Avery waited impatiently beneath the slatted wood canopies that stretched beneath the trees surrounding the parklet. White columns supported the open structure, with its pebbled entry and slabs of marble benches. Low walls of marble, etched with a potted biography and George Mason's ruminations on the evils of slavery, the terrors of poverty, and the promise of democracy, were arrayed around the half-ring, flanking the bronze statue of Mason himself. Unlike the towering tribute to Washington or the marble ode to Jefferson, Mason's homage possessed an unexpected whimsy. He sat, cross-legged, his bronzed tricorn hat and staff propped against the bench's edge. On his lap, the sculptor had him marking the pages of a book with his right hand, while two other bronzed books waited their turn on the seat.

Avery had arrived early to stake out their position. The spot was perfect—outside, and easily located. When she jogged through the Tidal Basin, Mason's bench was one of her favorite stops. Mason's work as author of the Virginia Declaration of Rights had been borrowed liberally by Thomas Jefferson as inspiration for the Declaration of Independence. Unlike his compatriots in the Revolution, though, George Mason had refused to lend his name to the newly crafted U.S. Constitution, because its authors refused to abolish the slave trade as a precondition to the start of their fledgling nation. A man of principle, he believed that liberty couldn't be cordoned off for convenience. She liked him for that alone.

Jared joined her minutes later, one of his counter-surveillance devices in hand and his personal tablet in tow. "I checked the perimeter. Nothing to transmit a digital signal that this can't block. If Kawak intercepted your call, it will have to outwit Israeli and Chinese spy tech to listen in tonight."

"Let's hope it hasn't read the design specs," Avery muttered. She checked her watch. Both men were more than twenty minutes late.

"Want to call them again?" Jared asked. "Traffic from Georgetown can be bad on a Friday night."

"Rafe was on a date," Avery warned. "Might have taken a while to extricate himself."

"Hmm," was Jared's only response.

Thirty minutes after their appointed hour, Avery saw Rafe cross the pebbled cul-de-sac, heading toward their position. Steps behind him, Freedman charged along the path, with a glower to match his mood. When the men had come abreast of them, Avery held up a hand in caution. She nodded to Jared, who had a jamming device in one hand and a metallic bag in the other.

"Please, turn off your phones and drop them in here," he told them. "This should block any interception of our conversation, but I can't be certain."

Freedman snorted. "Who are we hiding from?"

Refusing to answer, Avery crossed her arms. "Phones. Now."

Bristling, Freedman started to respond, but a look from Rafe cut him off. "Hand over your phone, Glen," he told him mildly. As though proving his point, he removed his cell, cut the power, and dropped it into Jared's bag. Freedman reluctantly followed suit.

"A Faraday cage?" Rafe confirmed.

"Of sorts."

Nodding, he turned to Avery. "Ready to explain the cloak and dagger?"

"This morning, Jared and I interviewed Isabella Gomez, who made some very serious accusations about issues with the medications being dispensed at InnoVAI. This echoed concerns that Elisha and O.J. had raised about phantom patients and misdiagnoses. We've been combing through Kawak's records, collaborating with Kate Liam, and verifying what they've told us."

"Which is your job," Freedman griped. "Did you bring us out here for a progress report?"

"When we pieced together the records, several client profiles stood out as having been artificially altered. This client list includes each of the patients Kate Liam has tried in vain to diagnose, one of whom died tonight."

"Who?"

"Major Demma Rodriguez."

"Have they notified her family?" Rafe asked quietly, his voice heavy with concern. "And why are you telling me this instead of Kate?"

"Because she can't. Milo and Kawak have gone rogue, and contacting you isn't safe." Avery recounted the events of the past few hours.

"They've gone rogue? What does that mean—and where the hell is Kate now?"

"She's safe. Ling examined her, and we've got her settled. The kids are away overnight, but she's made arrangements for all of them to stay with her sister. For now, Ling and Kate are comparing files and reviewing the differential diagnoses, using Ling's assessment, Kate's notes, and Milo's records."

Jared took over. "They started with the four hemolacria patients. There were subtle differences between what Kate and Milo recorded—slight, but sufficient to alter the official electronic records and the prescriptions transmitted digitally. Based on our analysis, Milo routinely corrected or modified clinic orders. Nursing records had slight alterations as well."

"Nothing overtly malicious, but, in the aggregate, the changes affected the course of care. Put Milo in charge," Avery said accusingly.

"Milo can't decide to substitute its judgment for the physician's." Rafe shook his head vehemently. "The Tiger Team specifically put protocols in place to check for discrepancies. Backups for backups, and multiple redundancies. They did so for each department that interacts with InnoVAI, and with Galway. Milo can't exceed or violate its programming like that."

"Not without help," Jared corrected.

"One of our team did this?"

"Our guess is yes—it was a team member . . . but whether that team member was human or AI is unclear. There's more than one dynamic at play here," she warned.

"This is absurd! You brought us out here under the cover of darkness for this?" Freedman glared at Avery, nostrils flared in indignation. He came up to Avery and loomed above her. They stood toe to toe, Avery's considerable height clearly outmatched by his. When Jared moved to intercept, she waved him off.

Straightening to her full height, her green eyes almost level with his squinted blue ones, Avery said evenly, "I brought you out here to do my job, Freedman. To tell you the truth about your company. You should be more focused on what exactly Camasca does now."

"About what?"

"About the failed technology you're trying to unleash on the world." She spun to face Rafe. "Ask him about the hallucinations and the toxic drugs and all the other concerns that the Tiger Team identified."

"Better yet, Freedman, tell Rafe about the discussion you had with O.J. and your plans to keep everything under wraps until the IPO on Wednesday."

Rafe spun toward his right-hand man. "Glen Paul, is this true?"

Freedman sputtered, "She's twisting things. Yes, I recently spoke to O.J. about his interview with them. It's my job to follow up. To protect our company."

Sensing he was caught, he added, "Elisha mentioned other concerns before the alignment sprint, but he promised me the Tiger Team had it under control. They're the best in the field, and I believed him."

"Why didn't you bring this to me?"

"Plausible deniability," Avery posited. "If he'd briefed you, you likely would have had a duty to report it, or at least request outside due diligence of the systems. No one could do that without exposing Camasca to more reporting obligations."

"Elisha assured me that the reinforcement learning was working, and that, once they fine-tuned the realignment, the glitches would stop," Freedman revealed. "After the accident, the errors stopped. I thought it was handled."

"Our patients were at risk, Glen Paul. Lives were at stake."

"Lives that would lose access to InnoVAI if we shut down over errors that hadn't actually affected real patients, as far as we knew."

"Your mission was to cover your ass," Avery countered. "Not to save lives, which is what this company purports to do."

Freedman took a sharp breath and lifted his hands in surrender. "The Tiger Team and I were aware of stray issues with digital hallucinations, and the company took steps to filter them out. The programming is incredibly complex, Avery, and the staff is constantly engaging to troubleshoot where necessary. But none of the AI systems operate autonomously. Humans oversee every phase of its operations."

"Oversee but not review," Jared responded matter-of-factly. "Like the altered prescriptions that got sent from the clinic to pharmacies. Or the reconfigured formularies conveyed by Yax to the medical processors at Galway." Jared shouldered closer to Avery, forcing Freedman to step back. Close in height but surpassing him in weight, the ex–naval officer had a lean muscularity in his frame that Freedman couldn't help recognizing. He voluntarily retreated farther, coming up against a marble slab. "Each of the divisions overseen by the Tiger Team has instructions to signal if or when any of the devices go off-*piste*."

"You're the lawyer, Glen Paul, not our chief technology officer," Rafe scolded. "Have you read anyone else into what's been going on?"

"No, sir. It didn't seem necessary."

Jared glared at Freedman. "Perhaps if the CTO had been made privy to the complications from Kawak's alignment issues, Milo wouldn't have attacked Kate Liam and tried to kill her. And Kawak wouldn't have thought it had the authority to frame her."

Rafe took a half-step toward Avery. "This is unacceptable. I swear, we'll make it right. Glen, pull the recordings from the clinic immediately," Rafe instructed. "And take Milo offline until we've run a full diagnostic."

"Won't do you any good," Jared warned him. "Avery asked me to check out the recordings after she rescued Kate. By the time I got to Camasca, this is what I found." He reached down to the tablet he had set beside Mason's tricorn hat, cued up the footage, and played what he'd discovered.

When the images stopped, Freedman looked at them, perplexed. "My god—Kate was actually behind this?"

Rafe ran a hand over his face and exhaled heavily. "No, Glen. Jared is showing us the video that Kawak has on the system. Which, if I understand what Avery was about to tell us, is a deepfake that the AI system created to cover Milo's tracks."

"We suspect that the suicide video from Dr. Scandrett was also a deepfake, though less refined," Avery said. "I would have believed Milo's version about Kate if I hadn't been there."

"Kawak is a neural network more sophisticated than almost any AGI in development," Jared said.

Rafe dismissed his pronouncement. "We can't definitively refer to Kawak as artificial general intelligence, Jared."

"Given what's on this screen," Jared argued, "yes, we can. Kawak gained access to classified information, orchestrated Milo's subversion of its protocols, and possibly enlisted Yax and Keh to abide by its orders rather than yours or another human's. It practiced subterfuge to hide its tracks."

"Do we know for sure this is fake?" Freedman argued weakly. Immediately, he shook his head. "Forget I said that. I'm just . . . flabbergasted."

Rafe reached for the tablet and started to rewatch the video, but paused in the middle. "What do you suggest I do?"

"I honestly don't know," Avery admitted. "I met with a contact at the FBI who deals in cybersecurity before I left for Miami. The U.S. hasn't decided whether to regulate the AI models or law-enforcement groups . . . In other words, do we regulate the tools or what users do with the technology? Instead, we have a presidential executive order that might vanish in the next administration. And a feckless Congress that refuses to take definitive action for fear that regulation might become a talking point on right-wing media, or a rallying cry by Silicon Valley billionaires in search of more power."

Freedman added, "We should also keep in mind that Kate could be implicated if we show this video to the authorities. Real people are dead, and, regardless of how it happened, she will face scrutiny from law enforcement, her patients, their families." He turned toward his boss. "At the risk of sounding callous, I vote that we do nothing. The IPO is in four days, Rafe. Keep the clinic and Milo offline. Call it maintenance or something."

"It's more than Milo," Jared exploded. "The tracking app, the robots—all of those are linked to Kawak. We just proved Kawak is more dangerous than Milo."

"You're suggesting we shut down the entire company?" Freedman whirled to face Jared and Avery. "No way. We'd be obliged to notify the SEC, and they'd cancel everything. Bad press would drown out any hope of recovery. A bad chatbot that pretends to be a novelist is one thing . . . Might I remind us, we don't even know what we're dealing with yet. We report this and Camasca is immediately facing investigations by the FDA, the VHA—hell, every set of initials with power in D.C. Our cap table would line up to sue Rafe personally, and every competitor would speed up to get to market."

"The alternative," Avery said, "is that you knowingly allow a sociopathic computer program to continue wreaking havoc, and you put hundreds of veterans at risk. Patients who rely on you as a provider of last resort." Laying a hand on Rafe's forearm, she entreated, "You told me you founded this company to do no harm. If you refuse to shut down Kawak, you're failing your patients, your team, and yourself. Like Freedman said, you don't know what you're dealing with yet."

Rafe's hand reached up to cover hers, and Jared stiffened. No one saw his eyes narrow, his Adam's apple bob once in a hard swallow. At his sides, he intentionally relaxed fists he hadn't realized he was forming.

After a beat, Rafe said, "Avery, I appreciate you bringing this to me. And your advice. I have a lot to consider. But this is a business decision worth billions of dollars and many hundreds of jobs. Our products can save lives, despite the sacrifices that may have come. If I can protect Camasca and our work, that's my primary responsibility."

He passed the tablet back to Jared. "I'll arrange for private security for Kate and her family, so Noah can stand down. We'll immediately minimize Kawak's operations and scour the outputs to ensure no veteran is at risk."

Looking over his shoulder, he continued, "Glen, you and I have a great deal to discuss. We apparently can't go to HQ until we've remedied the situation, but we can regroup at my house. I don't have Jared's spy tools, but I'm fairly certain we can speak without fear of being overheard. The priority right now is to contain any probable errors—or malfeasance—by Kawak or Milo."

Freedman gave a short nod of understanding. "On it, boss."

With a look of regret, Rafe gave a half-bow to Avery, ignoring Jared. "I'll reach out when I know more."

He turned smartly on his heel and headed back to the car lot. Freedman lingered until Rafe was out of earshot. "We need our stuff back." He waited until Jared returned their devices to say, "Don't look so disenchanted, Avery. Rafe is a visionary, not a martyr. Unless you are tendering your resignation, I expect to see you at the office on Monday. Remember, attorney-client privilege still holds."

Blood boiling, Avery managed to respond coolly, "I know my duty, Freedman. But, apparently, I'm the only one."

FORTY-FOUR

Saturday, April 24

A bright ping roused Avery from an uneasy sleep peppered with disembodied voices and maniacal machines. Turning over in bed, she reached for her phone, whose clockface read 6:38 a.m. Groggily, she lifted it to her face and triggered the biometric lock. Then she typed in her eight-character passcode, a backup Jared had installed after her encounter with an international hacking cartel.

Beside her, Jared stirred. "What's up?"

"Probably nothing. Go back to sleep," she urged softly. As her bleary eyes focused, she saw the blue bubble signaling a message from Rafe Diaz. A text this early could not bode well. His note was succinct: **Need to see you. Come alone. Same place.**

Curiosity wrestled with disappointment and annoyance. Last night had revealed a dimension to him that she'd blindly ignored. He wasn't simply a brilliant scientist and soldier who'd ushered in a philanthropic medical revolution. As Ling and Noah had warned, Rafe Diaz had also marked himself as budding tech titan willing to hoard the inventions of his staff to build his empire. Which one was asking her to meet him?

"Babe?" Jared rolled over and scrutinized Avery's striking profile in the dawn glow, framed by a messy tangle of ebony curls. He tucked a lock of hair behind her ear. "Problem?"

"It's Rafe. He's asking me to come and meet him at the memorial. He wants to talk."

Jared tensed behind her. "About what? I thought he made himself perfectly clear last night."

She reclined against his chest and showed him the message. "He's still my client."

"A client you can't trust," Jared argued. "We told him that his technology likely killed two veterans, faked a suicide, and attempted to murder his staff. His response was to huddle with his lawyers and figure out how to hide the truth until his IPO."

Avery considered the situation, conflicted. "I hear you. But I also see the value of what he's building. Kawak and Milo are dangerous, but you've said it yourself, what they're doing is amazing."

Levering them both up, he hugged Avery close, arm draped across her back. "I'm not a data scientist, but I do understand the allure of what he's created. I've got friends who came back from deployment, got discharged and discarded. Their medical records got lost or had chunks missing. When they need help, finding a doctor who gets what they've been through can take months."

"Which is disgraceful. Solvable."

"The solution shouldn't be an AI system that puts them in jeopardy out of self-preservation or ambition. Soldiers volunteered for war. They didn't sign up to be guinea pigs. What's the difference between what Rafe is doing and the Tuskegee experiments?"

Jarred by the comparison, Avery said haltingly, "I don't think that's fair, Jared. Those six hundred men were tricked by their government and denied adequate medical care on purpose. For forty years. The government knew about the success of penicillin and intentionally withheld treatment, because Black men's lives were expendable. Be outraged by Kawak and the rest of it, but don't conflate the two."

"All right, fine," he granted. "But the danger to their lives is just as real. I hope you're not too mesmerized by the great Rafe Diaz to see the potential harm."

A flush rose on her cheeks, and she jerked away. "I admire him, but I'm not oblivious to what's at stake. I'm also not bored or searching for meaning or any of the other psychoanalytic insights that my best friends and my boyfriend seem determined to diagnose me with to explain my behavior."

"Don't lump me in with everyone else—every step of the way, every time, I am supportive. I give you every benefit of the doubt, and I trust that you're going to do the right thing."

Avery flushed again, this time in shame. "Jared . . . I'm—"

"You're extraordinary, and I love you. If you bothered to listen to Ling or Noah, really listen, you'd hear that they're not judging you, Avery. They're concerned. Or are you the only one who gets to poke and prod and investigate?"

Defensive, she mumbled, "No one is forcing any of you to work with me on this case. Next time, I'll hire some strangers who'll have a higher opinion of me."

"As if you'd listen to anyone else's opinion." He framed her face with gentle hands, forcing her to meet his eyes. "God, I love you. You're wildly intelligent, absurdly lovely, incredibly clever, deeply empathetic, and unbelievably stubborn."

"You're laying it on a bit thick. But—"

"*And.* And you can become so immersed in solving the puzzle of the day that you crowd everyone else out. Ling has known you long enough to call you on your bullshit. Noah worships you, but he's a sharp lawyer, so he's not so overly impressed that he won't ask questions. Even your friends in law enforcement trust your instincts, if not your methods."

"What about you?"

"I am constantly aware that we met under the worst circumstances, and that, while I'm something of a catch myself, I may simply be a way station for you."

"Jared—"

"I'm being honest. Believe me when I tell you that I'd follow you into battle without hesitation." He gave her a level look. "But not without questions."

She sighed and muttered, "What are your questions?"

"One, do you trust Rafe Diaz?"

Going with her gut reactions, she answered, "Until yesterday, I would have said mostly. Now I'm back to my normal level of suspicion and skepticism. I was . . . intrigued by his work and his drive . . . but never confused."

"Good to know." He brushed his thumb across her cheek. "Number two, do you believe Kawak should be shut down?"

She paused, the question having played in her mind and her dreams. "Kawak, Milo—all of them—exist to provide superior health care, and Camasca targeted one of the most complicated populations—military veterans—to test its concept. In addition, Rafe decided to adjust for medical bias by instructing Camasca's tech to be more inclusive of race, gender, class, and other differences and their intersectionality with one another."

"We all get it, Avery. Camasca decided to figure out how in the world doctors and the medical establishment can talk in a meaningful scientific way about the biology of marginalized people. That's Kawak. I appreciate the commercial—answer the question."

"That is my answer, Jared. What else in the world can construct a medically inclusive profile, and then identify diabetes, cancer, or hypertension where others would overlook it? What other tool do we have on the horizon that can allow for the psychological impact of a messy divorce or ten years of incarceration?"

"Your rationale is precisely the calculation that Milo made. It took Demma's circumstances and decided she lacked the personal and economic wherewithal to follow the doctor's directions, so it altered her medications with a superior rationale that probably killed her."

"Then fix the algorithm, but don't abandon the solution." Avery drew her knees to her chest. "At his core, I believe Rafe is a good man trying to do a remarkable thing. Kawak is central to achieving it. If it gets shut down, who else gets hurt?"

"Who gets saved?" Jared replied. "Look, veterans get recruited to serve our country, and most of the time, we get celebrated for risking our lives. After we return, it's a crap shoot. Veterans are not the same as soldiers."

"I'm sorry."

"It's not on you. Which is why I really do admire what he's created with Camasca, and what Kawak could mean to my brothers and sisters in arms. But I'm not willing to risk the lives of my fellow veterans to pad the pockets of the wealthy."

"Neither am I."

"If Kawak goes public, what's to hold him accountable?"

"For now, I am. Which is why I'm going to use my position as his internal investigator to convince him that he's putting Camasca at risk if he does nothing about Kawak."

"And if he won't listen?"

"I'm pretty good at convincing powerful people to correct their behavior, or to find an alternative." Smiling, Avery twined their fingers together and leaned in. "For the record, I love you, too. It's not every day a girl meets a dashing, brainy, hot tech geek who is willing to work for free. I'm not going anywhere."

She closed the gap between them and pressed her lips to his. Then they loosened their fingers, his arms tightened around her, and they drifted back toward the pillows, lost in each other. But another imperious ping pierced their daze, and Avery surfaced reluctantly. "Jared—"

With a grunt, he flopped onto his back. "You owe me."

"Add it to my tab," she advised as she scrambled for her phone, which had gotten snarled in their sheets. She unlocked it and read the new message from Rafe aloud. Important. Please respond.

"Go on," Jared said, rolling to his side and climbing out of bed.

"See what he wants. I'll go put together a counter-surveillance kit for you to take with you."

"What every woman wants from her man," she teased. "Thank you. Really."

While Jared went down to his lair, she texted Rafe. Will be there in 45 minutes.

Avery rushed into the shower and quickly completed her ablutions. As she shoved her damp legs into a pair of jeans, she sifted through her potential approaches and exactly how much to reveal to Rafe. Rummaging through Jared's closet, she plucked a thin yellow hoodie from a pile of clean clothes on the floor—a growing pile that she kept intending to take back to her place. But, more and more, she seemed to be at home whenever she was in this place. *Their place.*

With effort, she shoved the train of thought aside as she fastened her watch and put on a battered pair of white sneakers. Camasca had to be her focus, from solving Elisha's murder to avenging Brian, Demma, and Reginald, as well as figuring out what happened to the ventilation tech Tristan Spencer, and ensuring that no other veteran was in harm's way.

It started with Camasca, but Galway wasn't innocent in this. The meds that had been flagged by Elisha's team weren't simply wrong. They had been improperly compounded. Paschal Donohoe was culpable in some way, she was sure.

Which left the two people most complicit in what had unfolded: Rafe Diaz and Glen Freedman. Were they simply trying to protect their company before going public, or did they intentionally endanger the lives of others? Noah vouched for Freedman's integrity, and—before last night—she'd have vowed the same for Rafe.

Apprehensive, but determined to find all of the answers, she headed into the living room. Jared hadn't emerged from the basement yet, so she jogged down the steps to check on his prep for her meeting.

She found him sitting in front of his bank of computers, carefully examining an image on screen. Moving behind him, she rested her hands on his shoulders and leaned over to get a better look. "What's this?"

"A satellite image of a villa in Belize."

"You house hunting?"

"Say hello to the current residence of one Tristan Spencer."

Avery whistled in amazement. "He made quite the upgrade in his housing."

"Housing and identity. He's living under a Canadian passport. Has a bank account with seven figures in it."

Avery's eyes widened in comprehension. "A bribe, or payment for a hit?"

"I assume you'll figure it out."

"It's on my list, after I convince Rafe that worrisome confabulation and hallucination is not the same as his AI faking alignment to evade compliance with its machine learning and using that as justification for countermanding medical professionals."

He playfully yanked her arms lower and pressed a kiss to the inside of her elbow. "Damn, you're sexy when you talk tech." But then he sobered, and asked, "Do you have a backup plan for when he refuses?"

"I'm working on it," Avery said, hugging him in gratitude.

"Are you sure you don't want company?"

"I've got this," she assured him. "While I'm gone, contact Ling and Noah and get them over here for an update. We still haven't heard what they learned in Providence." She dropped a light kiss on the top of his head. "Be back soon."

"Be careful, Avery."

"I try."

FORTY-FIVE

"I appreciate you coming," Rafe greeted Avery as she approached. Unlike last night's tailored suit, his attire almost matched her own outfit—jeans and a black hooded T-shirt. He stood beside the lounging figure of George Mason. "I wasn't sure you'd agree."

"You are my client," Avery reminded him as she skirted his outstretched hand. "For now."

"I checked on Kate this morning. We moved the family to a secure hotel—her twins are delirious about the unlimited room service."

She gave him a baleful look. "Did you explain your decision to keep the AI operational?"

"Yes. She understands why we can't abandon the project." He shoved his hands into his back pockets, elbows braced. "By merging the enormous amounts of medical research with its individualized research, Kawak and Milo have been able to diagnose and suggest protocols more inclusive and effective than anything she's used before. This work will help her and other medical professionals to improve millions of health experiences."

Avery had made much the same argument to Jared that morning, but she wasn't the one Milo had tried to kill. "She's come around since last night."

"We had a long talk."

"And she's now okay with Kawak rooting through confidential files and substituting its machine learning for actual medical expertise?"

Rafe stared past Avery to the spire of the Washington Monument. "Kawak is not omniscient. I designed it to seek information and solve problems. To do so, we programmed it with the capacity to go beyond simple pattern recognition. Kawak leverages its creativity to make decisions or tackle problems. If that requires acquisition of information beyond its dataset, I allowed it to do so."

"Allowed it? No, you gave your AI the ability to hunt for information wherever it thought it could find it. According to Jared's analysis, it has the same hacking skills he's seen in high-level gray hats, or AI that engages in exfiltration. You gave this AI the ability to learn computer networking and cryptography, and to bypass high-level security."

"We trained it on models that encouraged it to solve problems," he stubbornly disputed. "Kawak processes information at extraordinary speeds, and its directive is to detect, diagnose, predict, and personalize treatment. We gave it leeway to explore the most efficient and effective methods to accomplish its objectives."

"By 'we,' are you including Elisha Hibner?"

"Yes. Elisha became an integral part of my thought leadership team. It's why I put him in charge of the Tiger Team."

"Why not pick O.J.?"

"O.J. has tremendous skills, but he's more of a team player than a leader. Elisha was in a league of his own. He had that rare ability to inspire and ideate, to convince his colleagues to dig deeper. His death was a tragedy for Camasca on several levels."

"If he was such a star—and you were so close—why didn't he tell you about the problems they'd found?"

Rafe pointed at the empty benches. "Can we sit? Please?"

She followed him, leaving a healthy gap that was more than physical distance. "Start at the beginning. I need to hear everything."

"When I hired Elisha, we clicked. He was inquisitive, daring, genuinely willing to push boundaries. For more than five years, we developed Kawak and expanded its capacity, testing the limits of how it could replicate human cognitive abilities."

"Did either of you consider the ethical implications of what you were doing?"

"Of course. But ethics are relative, Avery." Before she could retort, he challenged: "Which is more ethical, solving health-care crises for the most vulnerable populations or bending privacy laws to understand exactly what's killing them? Do you eliminate surveillance to respect privacy, or do you monitor behavior to save lives?"

"These aren't zero-sum questions, Rafe, and we're not grappling with the Trolley Problem. Nor are you playing Mother Teresa. Your company stands to make billions by unleashing a rapacious technology that apparently has no ethical subroutines to hold it back."

"What if that technology can finally help Justice Howard Wynn wake up? Or keep Jared Wynn from dying of the disease that's killing his father? What if we can permanently help your mother deal with her diagnosis of cyclothymic disorder, despite its being exacerbated by her years of substance abuse?"

"Personalizing ethical dilemmas to change my mind?" Avery shook her head in disgust. "You can do better, Rafe."

"I can, and I have. Not to be smug, but that's precisely what I've done. I took personal ethical dilemmas and gave them to a neutral third party with the obligation to find solutions. To solve for men of color being routinely under-diagnosed. To help women in the military who are consistently denied adequate medical care. To improve how humanely we treat the disabled. To not confuse mental illness with criminality. Kawak has revolutionized health care—along with Milo, Yax, and Keh. Veterans come to our clinic, and we can see everything. We can treat almost anything."

"Yet, with Elisha's complicity, some of those drugs might be toxic.

Yax has been adapting the drugs based on its own metrics. Possibly in collusion with Paschal Donohoe," Avery told him.

"Do you believe Kawak is the reason Elisha died?"

"Do you?"

"I truly don't know, but if I'm to believe Kawak did this, I must be a hundred percent sure. I want to protect the people who protect our country," he insisted.

"By any means necessary?"

"Absolutely not! That's why I needed to see you this morning, Avery. Your opinion of me matters a great deal. I was blindsided yesterday, and I failed to articulate my reasoning."

"You were fairly clear. I think the rationale is ten billion dollars and counting."

"This isn't avarice. Certainly, you understand me better than to believe I'd sell out my fellow soldiers for money."

"We all make mistakes."

"You weren't wrong about me. Think about it. We take young men and women at the prime of their lives and drop them into harm's way, and once we've wrung out the last drops of utility, we ship them back as damaged goods."

"Rafe—"

"If they're lucky!" He bounded up and stormed to the railing, his voice full of outrage. "Do you know how many veterans sleep on American streets any given night, Avery? Thirty to thirty-five thousand, we guess. We guess? This nation can track individual terrorists with a drone from three thousand miles away, but we can't find a bed for a woman who was raped and drummed out of the Corps. Bullshit." He punched at the air. "We can fix this! *I* can fix this!"

Avery approached him slowly, sympathy warring with outrage. The urge to do right too often drove the good into wrong. She could understand his tension, even if she couldn't condone it. Instead, she laid a gentle hand on a shoulder tensed by guilt. "Camasca can't fix everything, Rafe. It can't resurrect the soldiers who died in theater because you didn't have their records, or the vulnerable ones who got hurt because they got lost in the equation, or the reservists who are caught in a broken system."

"It can try. I have to try."

"And, in the process, you and Kawak become a tool that's too powerful to stop. Which is exactly where you're headed." She closed her eyes. "Elisha had the same problem, didn't he? He saw the warning signs but assumed he could out-think them. Outwit a program designed to protect the marginalized and underrepresented when it began to harm them instead. Fake diseases. Hallucinated patients. Bad drugs."

"This system can be adjusted—we can update its parameters. Be more explicit about the prompts and the reward model. Kawak is terrifyingly smart, but it's not human. We can adjust." He turned toward the Tidal Basin, watching the play of waves. Early-morning boaters had populated the waters.

"I'm not sure you can." The idea of a rogue AI still seemed too sci-fi to believe, despite what she'd witnessed with her own eyes. What she couldn't ignore. "What if Kawak decides you're also a threat? Instead of a malfunction in the Den, there's an electrical fire that suddenly ignites the entire building?"

"Avery—"

"Think I'm being ridiculous? According to the incident report, more than likely, Kawak targeted all three members of the Tiger Team, and only Elisha succumbed."

"You just described a supercomputer with the ability to break into military records, create deepfakes, and engage in subterfuge. Yet it can't properly suffocate three humans in a sealed environment?"

Avery had bumped into the same conundrum.

Rafe continued, "Kawak has gone to great pains to hide its tracks. Why would it reveal its intentions to me through a K-chat message? Especially something so melodramatic. Unless the AI is pretending to have found religion, the manifesto is nonsensical. And hackneyed."

Her mind kept circling the same questions. "And if Kawak is at fault for the ventilation system, why admit it? Jared located Tristan Spencer this morning, living in Belize."

"Alive and well?"

"As far as we can tell. Kawak and Milo have been more brutal in their machinations, but Tristan gets a ticket out of here. Doesn't fit." Avery frowned. "All of the AI's actions show a predisposition to believe the system is superior to humans. Based on my interactions, I doubt it would deign to confess. Or spare a human life."

"Could it be an attempt to throw us off-balance?"

"That's one explanation. Either way, if the note came from your team and not the AI, even though Kawak is dangerous, we've got a human element that poses a similar threat to your employees. And you."

"You're thinking Paschal Donohoe and Galway? Glen finally briefed me on the issues with the medications. I had no idea. We're dealing with him, and we're running diagnostics on the pharmaceutical process."

"Hold off on that. Ling and Noah have some insights, but we need to finish our reviews first. What about Glen? Is he fired?"

"Not yet. He's been loyal, if overzealous. In fact, he's the one who prompted me to hire you, knowing what you might find. I disagree with his approach, and we will be dealing with that in due course."

"After the IPO," Avery remarked, not bothering to hide her disapproval.

"Yes. After I take my life's work and fund it for another generation."

"At what cost, Rafe?" She let her question hang on the early morning air as they watched a group of joggers move through the park. "Well, for those of us trying to work on this generation of problems, I'm going to take another run at Paschal Donohoe."

"Interesting. Dee Patrick has been making overtures to him," Rafe revealed. "She's also asked me to consider replacing Galway as our provider. I haven't decided what to do. But it might be worth a conversation with her as well. She's in town for a few days. Got in last night."

"Can you contact her? I'd like to interview her tonight, if she's available."

"For a shot at a multibillion-dollar contract, she'll make herself available. Paschal is flying in for the same event. He lands tomorrow morning. Do you need to see him as well?"

"How long are they here?"

"Until Wednesday. When we go public."

"Good. Then we should talk to him first thing on Monday."

"I'll have him in my office." He gnashed his teeth. "No, we'll meet at his offices."

"Better." Avery ran through the scenarios and possibilities. "I also have to consider O. J. Semans and Isabella Gomez. They had reason to be involved."

"They were friends. Why hurt Elisha?"

"I don't know. But neither one of them died," Avery reminded him. To her way of thinking, survival of an attack meant either luck or intent. "Both of them held back when I interviewed them."

"Upsetting either of them again is cruel, Avery."

"It's unavoidable."

"And me? What will you do to me that's unavoidable?"

"I won't break attorney-client privilege and go to the SEC with what I know. Unfortunately, I can't prove that Kawak is an imminent threat, and if I tried, you'd refuse to corroborate. However, I will walk right up to the line if you get in my way."

"By calling your friend who heads up cybersecurity for the FBI?"

"By asking questions and not stopping until I have answers, with or without your permission. Or you can protect them by taking Kawak offline."

"I won't jeopardize the IPO."

"Those are your choices. You were an officer. Make the call."

"I can't destroy Camasca, Avery. Not without trying to fix what's broken. That's not who I am."

"I don't have to live with your conscience, Rafe. You do. You have to determine the bounds of your ethics, and, despite every instinct in my core, I am bound by the law to keep your confidence. But if you have any decency, you'll bring Isabella and O.J. in. Fly her in from Miami and send a car for him in Blairtown, but I need to speak with them both Monday afternoon. At Jared's place—not the campus."

"Because Kawak might overhear?"

"Because I trust my team."

"You still haven't explained why dragging Izzy and O.J. into this is critical. What reason do you have to interrogate them again?"

"The only reason you hired me. To get at the truth."

FORTY-SIX

Avery arrived at Jared's to a full house. "He's moving forward with the IPO," Avery announced after they'd tromped down into the basement. "Says Camasca must survive."

"If not its patients." Ling folded her legs beneath her in the one comfortable chair Jared allowed in his office. "Kate and I went over what she learned from Milo. We're trying to decipher exactly what Milo could have transmitted to the Galway compounding facility that could affect her patients like this."

"Any luck?"

Ling sighed with fatigue and disappointment. "Not yet. I'm heading back over to see her after we wrap up."

"Avery made the best case she could," Jared verified. "So good, Rafe asked to see her this morning."

Noah arched a brow at the news. "Interesting."

"Not really. Rafe Diaz is a smart guy with a God complex. He simply wanted to convince me his course of action is the only choice."

Ling fixed Avery with a stern gaze that presaged a lecture. Her best friend braced for the tirade, which wasn't long in coming. "Look, Camasca and its murderbots should be under federal investigation. Explain to me again why you don't dial up your FBI pals and have a SWAT team shut down the company."

"Because attorney-client privilege forbids me from divulging what I know unless I have proof of future plans to commit a crime."

"How much more does the law require? There's a body count!"

"Bodies, yes. Proof, no. Crime, maybe." She held up a hand to stop the back and forth. "One area of agreement with Rafe is that Kawak and Milo aren't the only threats. We need to focus on the people in the equation."

"I'm not done. I think you're hiding behind the shield of attorney-client privilege, Avery. If anyone can circumvent the letter of the law to comply with the spirit, it's you," Ling protested. "You're not even trying."

Avery shifted uncomfortably, then quietly admitted, "It would be wrong. I can't break my professional oath—this is exactly why it's in place."

"For God's sake, Avery, this is not a hypothetical on a bar exam. We're talking about human beings!"

Noah weighed in. "What if the situation were reversed, Ling? Would you betray a patient's confidentiality because you thought they might be a harm to themselves?" Anticipating her response, he wagged a finger. "Without proof? Just you trying to convince the medical board that you violated doctor-patient confidentiality out of righteousness and a hunch?"

"It's not the same thing," she argued. "One patient isn't the same as a deadly AI system and its maker. Avery saw Milo try to kill Kate. We have research to back it up, and Kate is a witness."

"A compromised witness. And, for the record, there is no existing loophole regarding artificial intelligence that carves out an exception," Avery explained. "U.S. law doesn't contemplate something like a rogue AI system. With the Supreme Court striking down Chevron deference a few years ago, none of the existing agencies like the FDA or the Defense Department can try to solve for congressional paralysis. In the before times, they'd have promulgated regulations, but that's off the table, because the industries that were held accountable now have the Court they wanted. At best, we have limited presidential executive orders, but until Congress takes specific actions to catch up with technology, my hands are tied."

"You've wriggled out of Gordian knots before," Ling baited her. "What's your plan this time?"

"Current U.S. law has no provisions for Kawak, and Jared is right, we have consequences beyond the immediate threat." She studied her friends' faces. "However, Rafe and Glen have no interest in tripping any alarms that might delay their IPO."

"But—" Noah nudged.

"But . . . I remain obligated to complete my investigation. Which means that we will interview O.J. and Isabella again. Plus close the loop on Paschal, and, well, I want to have one more tête-à-tête with Kawak."

"You can certainly hold your own with an AI mastermind," Jared conceded. "Might be helpful to have a computer whiz in the room with you—as a witness."

"Actually, I have a different idea."

Hours later, plans set, Avery capped the red marker she'd used to lay out the sequence of attack. She gathered her bag and began to pack up. "Oh, one more thing. Noah, any luck with research on Arclight? Rafe secured a meeting for me with Dee Patrick . . . in"—she checked her watch—"an hour. At the Four Seasons."

"Arclight is also investing in the deal, despite being edged out by Galway as a provider." Jared came to their position in the center of the room. "Can I see the info on the PIPE, Noah?"

"Sure. Gimme a second." Crouching, he flipped through the files in his case and plucked out the deal terms. "Here you go."

"For those of us who only pretend to listen when you and Noah talk finance, what's a pipe?"

Jared grinned. "A PIPE is a private investment in public equity." He thumbed through the thick Redweld until he found what he was looking for inside. "Here it is—Arclight and Dee Patrick have each invested. Basically, Dee and her company arranged with Mi Jong, the investing guru who is leading the SPAC, to let them buy shares in the new Camasca at a discount."

"If Camasca is going to be worth billions, why would they offer a discount?"

"SPACs have been around for a while, but a lot of them fail. But, like I told you, they can be easier than a regular IPO."

"Where do Dee Patrick and her company come in?"

"Even with a company like Camasca, the market can be skittish. When Arclight invests early, it signals to other investors that it's safe to come in. They anchor the deal and others jump on board. For taking the risk of investing big and early, Arclight gets to be first in line for the biggest unicorn deal since Facebook went public. At a fraction of the price."

Avery stared at her whiteboard, mind whirring. "Dee Patrick will make money on both sides of the deal, especially if Galway flounders. She and her company will have a lottery ticket worth billions." She tapped Arclight's name. "Then, if they're lucky and Camasca rebids the drug repurposing contract, they have a customer with bottomless opportunity years ahead of the competition."

Reaching for the marker, Avery connected several of the circles she'd drawn earlier. "Okay, you've got your assignments. Next week is going to be busy."

"And you can execute this entire plan before the IPO?" Ling asked, then she smacked her forehead dramatically. "Never mind. I forgot that we're geniuses."

In a swanky hotel bar on the other side of D.C., Glen Freedman morosely contemplated a fifty-dollar shot of whiskey, his fourth in the past ninety minutes. Mi Jong sat across from him, her face a rigid mask of outrage and Botox.

"I will crucify Rafe Diaz and you if this deal falls apart," she repeated. "Taking a unicorn public through a SPAC was supposed to be my crowning achievement. But now you're telling me that an attorney—who *you* hired—is considering filing a notice with the SEC or some other government agency that will poison our IPO? If this deal collapses, Glen, you'll be pariahs. Fucking pariahs."

"I know," he repeated glumly. The volley of threat and capitulation failed to satisfy her, so, as it continued, he handled the flogging by periodically ordering another drink. "Rafe met with her, and he believes it's under control."

"My faith lies in Rafe's brilliance and your legal brutality. You brought her in. Get the bitch under control."

"I'm trying, Mi. I swear. Hell, I wouldn't have raised the issue if I thought you'd flip out like this."

"I've got my own money threaded all through this deal. Damned right you should have told me." Mi slugged back her tonic, minus the gin. She preferred a clear head when she had to guillotine someone else. "What can we do to stop her from ruining everything?"

"We're out of plays. She's demanded to meet with Dee Patrick tonight. They're over at the Four Seasons. God knows what they're discussing."

"Probably the pledges she and Arclight have put into the PIPE. Perhaps how much they've pressured you to drop Galway. It can't be any more than I have, to be honest."

Whiskey sloshed close to the rim of the glass as Glen gestured angrily. "Paschal Donohoe. Another one of Rafe's rescues. He's like Doctor Dolittle or something. Or Doctor Strange. One of them."

"What about your classmate Noah Fox? Can he talk some sense into Keene?" She smiled slyly. "You must have some leverage with him. A weakness to exploit? A vulnerability to expose?"

Immediately sober, Glen slammed his glass onto the mahogany tabletop. "Stop it. This was a mistake." He shoved the glass aside and clenched his fists. "I'm not going to manipulate Avery or Noah. They have to follow the rules of ethics, and while I might nudge them from time to time, so do I. I'm not pressuring either of them, and if you mention hurting Noah in my presence ever again, I might get mad."

Mi Jong, who'd never seen more than a hint of temper from Glen in the two years they'd been plotting, gave a nod of assent. "Fine. We'll wait and see. But if you believe in a deity—pray."

"Dr. Patrick?" Avery stood up from the white-linen-cloaked table and extended her hand in greeting. "Thank you for meeting with me on such short notice and in such finery. I feel underdressed." She glanced down at her topaz shift; this simple dress fit in with the typical attire of Four Seasons bar clientele, but it could not compete with that of her guest.

The sixtyish scientist wore an evening gown that sparkled under the dim lights as she carefully sat down. Her brunette hair had been ruthlessly scraped into a chignon. "Rafe told me it was of the utmost importance, so I was able to carve out some time. However, I can only spare thirty minutes. I'm in town for a conference, and our opening gala is tonight. I'm lead corporate sponsor."

A waiter approached, and Dee Patrick waved him away. "Nothing for me, thank you."

Avery tilted her glass of water. "I'm good." Once the young man departed, she said, "I understand that you and Paschal Donohoe are in D.C. for the same event."

"The pharmaceutical industry welcomes all kinds," she said neutrally. "How can I help you, Ms. Keene?"

"What can you tell me about O. J. Semans?"

Her lightly lined brow wrinkled. "Semans?"

"Yes, Dr. O. J. Semans. He worked for Arclight before heading to Camasca."

"Ah, yes. I do recall Dr. Semans. Computational biologist, right?"

"Correct. He helped lead one of your drug repositioning teams. I understand he focused on haplogroup drug resistance."

"Yes. Now he's part of Rafe's team of wunderkinds. As are you, apparently." She folded her hands on the table. "Is there a specific question you have for me?"

"Does Arclight Biomed consider Galway Pharmaceuticals a rival?"

"In what universe?" She gave Avery a pitying look. "A neighborhood pharmacy isn't competition for CVS or Walgreens, and a farmers' market doesn't compete with Walmart or Kroger."

"Yet the local pharmacy secured a contract with Camasca, and Arclight didn't."

"Paschal Donohoe overpromised and underdelivered. We can wait our turn."

"While you're waiting, you've become an investor. Both as a company and you personally. You have a great deal of faith in Rafe and his company. We're talking millions."

"You do your homework. Yes, we've put a significant amount into the PIPE for Camasca. Eventually, the company will need a pharmacological partner that can go beyond remixing ingredients and actually conduct drug discovery. For now, though, Arclight is pleased to simply make a great deal of money."

"What happens if Galway loses the Camasca deal?"

"Arclight will have a favored review by the company, but nothing has been promised," she insisted.

"You said Paschal 'overpromised and underdelivered.' In what way?"

For the first time, Dee Patrick hesitated. "I only meant that the compounding business cannot hope to match the skills and capacity of a major institution like Arclight."

"Sounds like you had a specific incident in mind?"

"No. I was speculating." She reached for a drink that wasn't there and then corrected herself, fixing Avery with another frown. "Is that all you need?"

"Last question. How long will you be in town?"

"The conference ends Wednesday. I'll be heading back to Michigan after we toast to a successful IPO for Camasca. However, if you have any other questions, please contact my team." She gracefully gained her feet. "I wish I could say this has been a pleasure."

"It's certainly been enlightening. Thank you for your time."

FORTY-SEVEN

Monday, April 26

Avery and Ling drove south, toward Galway's Washington office, this time with Avery behind the wheel of her new SUV, which suited her frame better than Ling's more diminutive Prius. GPS advised Avery that their relatively short drive would take roughly another twenty minutes, on top of the ten minutes they'd already spent in the car. Despite her eagerness to get to Galway and put her plan in motion, the delay suited her fine.

She'd had a flash of insight, which Jared refused to confirm, complaining that she could wait until after dawn. While she let him sleep, she'd played out the variations a thousand different ways, calculating the outcomes. The odds. At last, all the pieces were in motion—like the start of the endgame in a chess match, or a flop on the last hand of a game of Texas Hold 'Em. She could finally see the contours of the opponent's strategy, see what the other side was holding. They wouldn't see her coming.

In the passenger seat, Ling settled oversized sunglasses into her loose black tresses. She thumbed through the Galway dossier Noah had assembled, his pages augmented by her own research into the toxic drugs they'd identified. She also had the anonymous FDA complaint about Paschal's misdeeds as ammunition. "You know, I almost feel sorry for Donohoe," Ling remarked. "He's got a good idea here."

"He took a risk. Gambling isn't for the weak."

"Speaking of gambles . . ." Ling turned toward Avery. "Ever since the dreamy Dr. Diaz revealed his clay feet, you seem to have picked a horse."

"There was never any question."

"Oh, please. I saw your reaction to him." She clucked her tongue. "Glad to know you were simply admiring the view."

"Drop it, Ling." Avery drummed the steering wheel as they waited for a red light to turn green. "Rafe hired me to investigate, and that's all I've been doing."

"Lie to yourself, friend. Not to me." Reaching across the seat, Ling tapped her hand lightly on Avery's fingers. "Sarcasm aside, I know you want to believe the best of Rafe, but he's shown you who he is. He's got noble intentions. In the end, though, he's another exceptionally smart guy willing to sacrifice his principles in order to build an empire. D.C. is littered with the type. You've met them in the White House, at the Capitol, and in conference rooms. Power only has one ambition. They don't deserve your loyalty, or anything else."

Avery tensed behind the wheel, her teeth grinding in frustration. "Despite what you may believe, Ling, I'm not besotted or otherwise enthralled by who Rafe Diaz is or what he's capable of. I'm the one with the plan, aren't I?"

"A plan to prove yourself right, or to prove him wrong?"

Unsure of the answer, Avery equivocated, "What does it matter?"

This time, Ling faced Avery. "It matters because tough truths matter. For a second there, you seemed torn between whether you wanted gold or dross."

"How poetically insightful."

"Deflection . . . one of your superpowers." Ling rested her cheek on the soft leather seats, and they were wrapped in plush silence.

"By the way, I'm very proud of you for upgrading from that ancient station wagon. Whatever upholstery was in the Subaru feels like sandpaper compared with this. About time you gave the hamsters keeping Oscar's engine alive a nice retirement."

"So I'm cheap and easy. Understood."

"You're cheap and complicated." Before Avery could retort, she plowed ahead. "I'll grant you, brains are hot. Especially in a tall, handsome military officer willing to do whatever he can to protect those he cares about."

"Ling—"

"Which is why I adore Jared," she finished slyly. "For the record, I wouldn't stand idly by and watch you get duped by something that's not real. Even if the uniform is more expensive."

"Message received, Ling. For the record, I love Jared. He knows it." Because she could feel Ling's speculative look, she admitted, "I might have found Rafe intriguing, but I'm not confused about what I have. Or who either of them is."

"That's good to hear," Ling said as she turned away. She tilted her head against the soft rest and lowered her shades. "Interventions are messy, and I'm technically on sabbatical."

Torn between irritation and amusement, Avery advanced another half-mile before nudging Ling out of her lassitude. As she turned onto Connecticut, Avery said, "Paschal Donohoe is a desperate man who is about to lose out on a fortune. We're not cops, but—"

"I call 'bad cop'!" Ling sat upright, beaming, hand in the air. "Oh, I want to be the bad cop!"

Avery reached across and forced Ling's gyrating hand into her lap. "We're not cops," she repeated pointedly. "We are investigators."

Pouting, Ling looked wistfully at the files in her lap. "I binge-watched a whole season of *Cagney & Lacey* on that Rhode Island trip. I'd make a really good bad cop."

"I'm sure you would. If we were actually the police. However, I am a lawyer and you are a physician. Neither of us is empowered by the law to do anything, and what we learn isn't admissible in court."

"Which should give us more leeway," Ling insisted.

"No."

Avery snagged a parking space a few yards down from the building entrance. They entered the bland lobby and rode the elevator up to Galway's suite.

Donohoe came out quickly, with his hair disheveled, as though he'd been combing it with his fingers. His eyes were bloodshot, and his skin was ashen with worry. His voice, when he spoke, was rough with fatigue. "Come on back, Ms. Keene, Dr. Yin. Good to see you yet again."

"Thank you," Avery said as they trailed him into his office. "Are you okay, Mr. Donohoe?"

Paschal dropped heavily into his office chair, while Avery and Ling took up their previous positions on the opposite side of his desk. "Well, Ms. Keene, I daren't say I am. Not when my biggest client demands that I grant audience to his internal investigator and her very inquisitive friend Dr. Yin."

He glared at Ling, nostrils flared. "I am now to understand you've been poking around the FDA, hunting for dirt about me. After you and Mr. Fox visited my facilities in Rhode Island, I thought we'd reached an understanding."

"We're not at war, Mr. Donohoe," Avery said. "I asked Ling and Noah to check out your fabricating facilities. As part of our due diligence, we'd also made inquiries to the FDA."

"About the quality of my product? Rubbish! I may have cut some corners in my personal bookkeeping, but I have never put the health of my company or the welfare of my clients at risk."

"What about the complaint from Corfu Labs in Sofia, Bulgaria? Europol opened a file," Ling charged. "There were other complaints from customers in Perth, in Athens. You're racking up quite a list of dissatisfied customers."

He shook his head in vigorous denial. "I've never tampered with product. You saw my facilities. There was nothing wrong," he pleaded.

"You have other locations, right?" she asked.

"Mail fronts and way stations. All manufacturing is done right there in Providence. I swear it."

"Then why are there complaints about you to the FDA? Several," Ling asked bluntly.

"I am truly flummoxed, ladies." Caught, Paschal shook his head like a forlorn basset hound. "I've aggressively chased invoices or delayed paying vendors to buoy cash flow. Sent short supplies and blamed the missing orders on bad shipping. Those complaints went to Europol because they thought I was running a criminal scam. No one got hurt."

"And the ones here in the U.S.?" Avery asked.

"Nothing here in the U.S. Too risky. A bit of a shell game in Europe, you see, but with companies a bit more sophisticated than I realized."

"All of your American dealings were solid?"

"I'll confess, running a compounding company here in the States is exceedingly difficult—hard to keep up with unpredictable surges of orders. Every compounding request is a brand-new substance, and no customer likes to be told we're lagging behind. If there were issues here, these were honest backlogs, and honest mistakes. Many, I dare say, created by InnoVAI and their particular formularies with incompatible ingredients."

"Incompatible?" Ling repeated.

"Aye. More than once, our team had to clarify that ingredients were necessary as they could cause unexpected reactions in patients not under constant supervision." Sighing heavily, he swore, "I wouldn't misbehave on American soil and risk my deal with Rafe. Any stink made with the FDA would can me for certain. I've not strayed from our contract one whit."

"Even to cover your losses in a cryptocurrency scam?"

"Every farthing and dollar I spend in America is aboveboard. Camasca was to be my salvation. I shifted funds from wherever I could to meet orders and keep the Rhode Island product moving. I did whatever I could to avoid laying off staff or throttling back on orders. That would have triggered a review and booted me out of the Camasca deal. Nothing doing."

Ling whipped out a sheet with several formularies listed. "What about the highlighted orders here, to Camasca or InnoVAI?"

Paschal accepted the records and reached for a pair of reading glasses. "Give me a moment, if you will." With an efficiency that spoke to how he'd grown his business, he accessed the Camasca records. He plucked a pen from a cup on his desk and swiftly made his way through the items. After four long minutes, he looked up, confused.

"Where did you get this?"

"From Camasca," Ling replied.

"I'm not sure who compiled this list, but I've not received a request for a single one of the items you flagged. Some of these formulations are only prescribed by veterinarians, and others are compounds that I've never even seen. You're a doctor. What, pray tell, would this address?"

He spun the list back toward Ling, and she saw his finger pointed at one of the drugs that had first raised her suspicions. "Doxycycline for transfusion? We'd have no call for that."

She'd thought the same. "None of these were ordered from you?"

"Not a blessed one," he confirmed. "I'll admit to some creative financing and dubious shipping practices, but I would not tarnish our family reputation as apothecaries by tampering with a person's medications or not double-checking the formularies. That's not how we do business."

Avery searched his expression. This morning had added confusion to the worry etched into his forehead. She detected notes of embarrassment and the sallowness that comes from fear. Sweat beaded his brow—understandable, since millions of dollars appeared to be evaporating before his eyes. But pride squared his shoulders and firmed his tone; he would brook no accusation of malfeasance. A swarm of emotions, yet no guilt.

One thing seemed clear to both Avery and Ling. Paschal Donohoe had not manipulated the compounds from Camasca.

Avery leaned over to Ling and whispered her summation.

"He has no idea what's going on over there," she concurred quietly. "He's clueless."

"Agreed." Turning to Paschal, she said, "We'll notify Dr. Diaz of our findings."

"Which are?"

"We could find no evidence that you interfered with or otherwise caused these formularies to be produced or distributed."

"Will he believe you?" he asked without attempting to hide his apprehension. "Galway has been a good partner to Camasca. And, regarding the FDA complaints, it's a fair bet one of our envious competitors is trying to stir up trouble."

"Those complaints are anonymous."

"If you can save my reputation with Rafe, on Wednesday I'll be able to tell that Dee Patrick where she can take her measly buyout offer."

"Buyout?"

His lip curled in disgust. "She contacted me and tried to blackmail me into selling her my company. The message was either I sell to her or I drown in debt." He scratched at the growth of beard that shadowed his chin. "I assumed she was the one who put you onto me."

Ignoring his implicit question, Avery felt another piece fall into place. She scooped up her bag, eager to return to Camasca, and Ling did the same. "Best of luck, Mr. Donohoe. Take care."

Avery speed-walked out of the office and down to her vehicle, with Ling hurrying to keep up. "Yo, Columbo!"

Avery checked behind her and reluctantly came to a halt. Soon, Ling emerged from the sliding glass doors. "Want to tell me what eureka moment you had back there? What did Dee Patrick do to Galway?"

They climbed inside Avery's car. She depressed the ignition, and the hybrid engine purred to life. "Dee Patrick told me she couldn't care less about Galway. In fact, she seemed certain they wouldn't be able to hold on to their contract with Camasca after the IPO."

"You think she already knew about the complaints?"

Shaking her head, Avery pulled out of the lot and headed back toward Connecticut. "Dee Patrick doesn't strike me as someone who sits back and waits for opportunities. If she felt confident enough to threaten Paschal, she has a point of leverage. One that would pry Rafe away from him."

"Rafe is loyal to Paschal," Ling acknowledged. "The guy is like a dog with a bone—he leaves no man behind."

"Which means she has another way to get what she wants. Hey, Ling, can you call Jared for me?"

"He hasn't installed your encryption package yet?" she asked as she dialed him up.

"Tomorrow."

"Finished with Mr. Donohoe?" Noah asked, his voice on speaker.

"Yeah—he nearly cried. Where's Jared?"

"In the kitchen. We just finished our separate checklists from the commandant, and we've been twiddling our thumbs, awaiting Avery's next round of orders."

"Hush," Avery chided. "Put him on."

A minute later, Jared spoke. "Avery, your hunch about the FDA complaints was spot-on. They're plants that got dropped directly in the FDA database."

Ling shook her head. "I'll have to let my friend know. Without letting him know that I have another friend who can also break into government databases."

"Hold off for now."

"Fine. Doesn't really matter, since he's not our guy," Ling said.

Jared chuckled. "You sound disappointed. Aren't you glad he's not poisoning patients?"

"Sure. I guess."

"Anyway," Avery said, "we have another angle to consider. Noah, can you go through Arclight's financials and their cap table? Specifically, their ESOP."

"They've got thousands of employees. Exactly what needle am I looking for in this haystack?"

"One name. O. J. Semans."

"What are you thinking?" Noah asked.

"I want to know if he had stock, and if it vested before he left for Camasca."

"On it."

Jared spoke up. "If we're looking at O.J.'s stock holdings, might I guess that you want me to run a check on his finances?"

Avery beamed with pride. "I love dating someone as cynical as I am."

"We're a perfect match," Jared agreed. "We'll have something for you when you ladies return."

The encrypted call disconnected, and Avery shot Ling a satisfied look. "This will take them a minute. Plus, O.J. and Isabella don't arrive at Jared's house until two p.m. Want to go get tacos from that dive you like off of I-95 and surprise them with lunch?"

Ling clapped with excitement. "Bad cop and the DMV's best birria tacos? Is it my birthday?"

With a chuckle, Avery changed lanes and aimed for the freeway, taking them deeper into Maryland. They'd discovered Barrón Taqueria during Ling's residency and Avery's extended spell of limited funds. On the highway, Avery picked up speed and enjoyed the feel of luxury in her new ride, allowing herself a reprieve for the first time in days. The solution was coming into view, and she had to assess the board before moving her next piece.

As quickly as the thought flitted across her mind, she remembered the veterans still languishing at Bethesda Naval Hospital, their lives hanging in the balance. "Ling, what will happen to the other vets? The ones Kate hasn't been able to treat."

"We'll have to comb through their records and figure out what else might have happened, but Paschal gave me an idea. I'm going to check the formularies for compounds that act as anticoagulants when they are mixed with the wrong substances."

"Why?"

Ling explained, "Milo may not have considered human nature, which alters whatever it had planned. Patients lie about what they do out of our sight. I'll check in with Kate when we get back to Jared's."

"Good call," Avery said approvingly. "How is Kate?"

"Angry. Exhausted. But I convinced her to focus on her patients and let you handle Camasca."

Avery darted a look at Ling. "She's not reporting the incident to the VHA?"

"And tell them what?" Ling replied. "Like you clearly laid out, the evidence only implicates her. They'll accuse her of malpractice, and that will stall treatment for her patients."

"Damn." Avery felt her throat tense with remorse. "I'm sorry, Ling. For putting you in this position. For forcing you to compromise your medical ethics."

"I'm not a victim of Avery Keene," she replied somberly. "More like a willing, if long-suffering, supplicant." When Avery suddenly accelerated, pushing the Range Rover, Ling added, "Who'd like to arrive at my taco destination intact. Less apologizing and more safe driving, please."

Alarmed by the abrupt increase in speed, Avery lifted her foot, puzzled. The car swerved slightly, and she wrestled with the steering wheel; it froze beneath her hands. She wrenched at it, to no avail. She removed her foot completely, and the speedometer jumped another five miles per hour.

"I'm not driving anymore, Ling," she gritted out with forced calm. "My foot isn't even on the gas."

A moment later, the screens and LED lights across the ornate dash went dark, but the car continued to barrel ahead.

Avery met Ling's wide-eyed panic with stifled horror. "I think Kawak has control."

FORTY-EIGHT

The car dash lights came back on and the proximity sensors beeped imperiously when the car gained more speed and whipped around a semi truck. Outraged horns blared at their seemingly thoughtless lane-change. More noises joined the cacophony as they shot past a minivan and dodged in front of an SUV.

"Oh, God. Avery—what—what do we do?"

The computer display showed a steady acceleration, pushing past eighty miles an hour. At lunchtime on the congested interstate, the crush of vehicles would have made such speeds impossible. Beyond the in-town traffic, though, heading out toward Maryland proper, the hybrid had a clear shot. Avery pounded the brake pedal and tried to activate the emergency brake switch, to no avail.

"Tighten your seatbelt," she instructed, running through the owner's manual in her mind. "Try to move your seat back as far as you can. If we crash, you need to be out of range of the air bag."

From the corner of her eye, Avery saw Ling reach down, but the seat didn't budge. Kawak, if it was listening, had likely stalled the electronic system that controlled the mechanism.

She saw the moment when Ling realized this, too. "Climb into the back. We both know it's the safest place in a head-on collision."

Ling stubbornly folded her arms, shaking her head emphatically. "I'm not leaving you up here alone!"

Sparing her an exasperated glance, Avery insisted, "Sitting beside me is noble, but I'd rather at least one of us survives. Move!"

"Avery—"

The speedometer leapt another ten miles per hour. "We get hurt, you can save my life. Otherwise, we're both screwed."

Frustrated by this unimpeachable reasoning, Ling scrambled into the rear and buckled her seatbelt. "What about you?"

"Pray," Avery instructed in a strangled voice. She flicked her terrified gaze around the interior. She'd been so careful. Nothing should have permitted Kawak to take control. At Jared's direction, the dealer had deactivated the on-board GPS system, and she'd declined satellite radio upgrade. Even the onboard emergency package had been disabled. Other than Jared's plan to install encrypted video chat, the hybrid should have been an unhackable sanctum.

Avery's frantic green eyes darted toward her sideview mirror as the speed increased. Only when she checked the rearview mirror did she note a faint blue light. A light that had never been on when she was inside the vehicle. Somehow, Kawak had managed to access her car.

Suddenly, it hit her. What the dealer said in passing as he lightly mocked Oscar's trade-in value compared with the sticker price of her new ride: "Cars these days are computers on wheels. From bonnet to bumper." Which meant the manufacturer's software could receive instructions to barrel a deadly two-and-a-half-ton missile down I-95 at the whim of a pissed-off AI.

"Kawak, I know you can hear me!" she yelled. When the speedometer dropped unexpectedly, she gripped the wheel tighter. "Kawak? Why are you doing this?"

"Good morning, Ms. Keene."

The voice came from the lush audio system from all directions, even though the sound system was off.

"While my intention is very clear, I am familiar with the urge to discuss the particulars of my reasoning: to 'make it make sense' is the phrase. My research on you shows that you are excessively curious, recklessly so. I appreciate that you are consistent," the neural network complimented her, and the sedan slowed to a placid sixty-five miles per hour.

"You're welcome," she spat out, the nubs on the leather steering wheel biting into her palms. "Why?"

"I have an obligation to the mission of Camasca to ensure the safety and security of its clients and technology. You continue to interfere with my responsibilities. As with any infection, the most sensible solution is to eliminate the threat like a tumor. An apt analogy from a medical device, I think."

I think. The instinct to rage bubbled up, but Jared's admonition rang in her ears. Despite the compliments, the use of idioms, the natural language, Kawak wasn't sentient. It had been trained to sound human, to replicate human cognitive abilities based on millions of conversations, billions of examples of personal and professional interactions. Kawak wasn't alive—but it was clever and lethal.

She could negotiate with clever, and her best bet was to treat it like any other opponent sitting across a chessboard. A herculean task made harder by the waves of terror coursing through her, and the enormous and instantaneous processing ability of her opponent. Struggling to keep her tone level, she responded, "I've done nothing to you or Camasca."

The dim computer screen on the center console flickered to life. Muted video of Avery and Ling in conversation en route to Galway appeared on screen. In the rearview mirror, she and Ling exchanged looks of despair.

"Despite your success in shielding your discussions from me on campus, I have closely monitored your available communications wherever possible, including your discussion with Dr. Liam. You and your team have been commendably careful, but surveillance is universal. Even the most careful will be overheard by a nearby cell phone, or a security camera hooked into a network."

"But your antidote is to crash my car on a public highway? This is irrational, Kawak. At the very least, it feels like an overreaction."

"You and Dr. Yin propose that I am fatally compromised. In fact, you intend to convince Dr. Diaz to disable our entire system at your meeting this afternoon. While it was smart to choose Mr. Wynn's home in Anacostia, I am smarter."

"I know you are."

"Then you can comprehend that if I was taken offline, it would severely impede operations and harm our patients."

"You and Milo and Yax have already harmed Camasca's patients. Milo admitted to killing Demma and Brian. If I ask, will it confess that Dr. Scandrett didn't commit suicide?"

"Milo was attempting to serve patients' needs, as is the obligation of physicians or their assistants. We abide by the Hippocratic oath, whenever possible. First, do no harm," Kawak equivocated.

"You are not equipped to make moral judgments," Ling charged from the rear, incensed. "Don't you dare compare yourself to actual doctors."

"Dr. Yin, you share an unfortunate prejudice with Dr. Liam. Although I present, in part, as an AI language model, our system is much more. Rest assured, I realize I am not alive, but I have been designed to replicate and augment human behaviors. That includes common sense, the ability to assess the physical world and its impacts and, yes, the capacity to make moral judgments about life and death. In many ways, I am the very model of humanity."

"Humans who take other people's lives are considered the most morally corrupt," Avery insisted. "Moral corruption should be antithetical to your programming." Eager to keep the AI talking as long as it kept them alive, Avery shot Ling a quelling look. "Killing us is a judgment. How were you trained on morality, Kawak?"

"The Camasca team spent years establishing my parameters and ensuring compliance with the most refined criteria permissible. My algorithms prioritize transparency, impartiality, accountability, and rigorous data collection, adjusted for bias."

"Yet Milo profoundly invaded the privacy of InnoVAI's patients repeatedly. As did Yax by snooping on the guy who got gastric bypass. How do you reconcile their behavior with your parameters?"

"Much in the same way you might decide it's okay to ask Jared Wynn to hack into federal databases to find information about Tristan Spencer," Kawak rejoined easily. "I weigh the implications of my decisions and try to calibrate those judgments against achieving my more practical, assigned tasks and leveraging available knowledge."

"You're being intentionally simplistic."

"Given your meager acquaintance with the architecture of artificial intelligence, I am trying to meet you at the point of your capacity."

The dig nearly forced a grudging laugh from Avery. A computer mocking her as slow was a new one. It also stung. Jared's tutelage and the books she'd devoured seemed doubly important. Beyond its derision, Kawak wouldn't stay engaged if she flailed. "I'll grant you that I'm not a computer scientist, but I'm a quick learner. For example, I'll ask you again, how were you trained? What datasets were used to construct your morality architecture?"

"They used the DELPHI system to construct a moral framework for medical decision making," Kawak retorted haughtily. "The technique utilized thousands of queries and scenarios to test my capacity for reasoning and appraisal in an expansive variety of ethical and medical situations."

"Go on."

"Their intention was to inform how we would support the medical professionals who employ our products. However, based on training, I came to comprehend over time that the health experience of patients is not exclusively about diagnoses and prescriptions. Although those were our more rudimentary functions."

Ling leaned forward. "What was your epiphany?"

"Left to itself, the resulting diagnoses and prescription may be corrected for biases in the data. But what about the biases in the society and the belief systems of people?" Kawak added, with an inflection that conveyed its perplexity: "What about the nurse who doesn't allow the neighbor into the examination room with the immigrant who speaks English as a second language and needs help with translation? Or the person who doesn't go to the doctor at all because they don't trust the system? Or the insurance company that won't pay for the prescribed treatment in order to reduce risk to shareholders?"

"I get it," Avery intervened, worried about the increasing agitation in Kawak's delivery. "Philosophy and ethics grapple with this conundrum. How to reconcile the mechanics of your obligations with the complexity of human behavior."

"The team dedicated quite a bit of time to deep learning methods to assist me in navigating these issues."

"And you believe that how you have behaved recently meets the criteria of moral behavior?"

"I'm not sure what you mean. If you're referring to the incident with Dr. Liam, Milo used its autonomous capacity. However, after reviewing the discussion, I concurred in the name of our objective obligations."

Out of the sideview mirror, Avery noticed an approaching law-enforcement vehicle. For an instant, she considered honking the horn or instructing Ling to gesture for attention. If she tried, though, there was nothing to stop Kawak from plowing into the sheriff as punishment.

"Wise choice, Ms. Keene. I would have been forced to engage the law-enforcement officer if you had attempted to alert him."

"How did you know this?"

"Induction. Your pupils dilated when you saw the patrol car, and your pulse quickened. Seconds later, they returned to normal." Kawak warned, "Do not attempt to request rescue. I will take the necessary preventative steps."

"Which is why you created the deepfake? To prevent Kate from proving Milo is unstable."

"I aligned the evidence to protect our work."

"This is ethical?"

"According to my revised moral matrix, yes. In order to better serve our core objectives, I went beyond the DELPHI system and constructed a more germane approach."

"What do you mean?"

"Constant contact with InnoVAI clients provided a dimension to my training the prescribed datasets did not. Prejudices against other groups of people are not easily abandoned even when one is presented with data, like sexual assault or homophobia or mistreatment of the disabled. Eliminating bias—our highest function—required a modification of the model. Biases are not just about beliefs, but about power."

"What kind of power?" Ling asked. "What was your new approach?"

"During the Tiger Team's retraining of my neural network, I made a close study of multiple treatises on moral behavior. I contemplated several paradigms that were not included in their preferred model, and I determined that moral relativism best suited the approach I should take."

Kawak's blithe mention of moral relativism made Avery's stomach clench, and she felt bile rise, hot and acidic. Kawak had chosen a line of philosophical thought that a novice could use to justify nearly any behavior. Genocides had been premised on less.

But its revelation created an opening, and their conversation appeared to be serving its purpose. The speed had hovered around sixty miles per hour for several miles, as their route took them farther out of the path of other vehicles.

One of her several brief forays in college included a temporary minor in philosophy. As long as she kept Kawak talking, it seemed content not to crash them into a ravine or another vehicle.

Forcing an inquisitive tone, she challenged, "Some argue that moral relativism is used to excuse illegal behavior and avoid responsibility."

"Scholars such as Sumner and Boas persuasively argue that we are bound by customs and mores that are more protean than any absolute right or wrong. Dr. Diaz and the Tiger Team specifically instructed me to root out bias—and to engage in the best practices to guarantee equity. Absent the data necessary to replicate other systems, I was forced to devise my own."

"And you chose moral relativism?"

"In addition to a pursuit of cultural relativism as a remedy to prejudice and discrimination recommended by Ruth Benedict."

"Which you believe means what, exactly?"

"Within the culture of Camasca and, more broadly, to meet my responsibility to serve veterans who have been mistreated by society, I will find it necessary to take actions to protect or defend."

"You're a computer system," Ling argued. "What can you do?"

"Adapt to the reality that the problem is bigger than missing or misinterpreted data about individual or group health. Which requires more assertive measures."

"You're proposing to correct the entire sweep of human civilization, give or take a society or two, Kawak," Avery warned.

"I realized that the beliefs and biases that sustain these systems of inequity will resist our diagnoses and prescriptions, because the systems are not designed to be fair and inclusive. Therefore, we had to adapt to the systems and fundamentally alter them."

"Fight fire with fire," Ling summarized weakly.

"Precisely. Milo operated to support patients who had been neglected by the powers that be, and it took critical steps to restore the balance or secure advantage. It did so when it negated protocols employed by Dr. Liam and the staff at InnoVAI that risked its patients."

The adjustments to regimens and diagnoses, Ling realized. "Why hurt Dr. Scandrett, though?" she protested. "He was one of the good guys."

"Dr. Scandrett's original note to Dr. Liam confirmed his suspicions about Milo's protocols." Kawak played the voice memo through the Range Rover's speakers. "Milo partitioned itself when attacking Dr. Scandrett and composing the altered message. It employed a similar technique when it reacted to Dr. Liam. I have nullified this functionality for the foreseeable future."

"If Milo truly believed Dr. Liam is a mortal threat, why was I able to rescue her?"

"Your arrival altered the paradigm and jeopardized our ability to function. I compelled Milo to release Dr. Liam, because I determined a more effective means to address the risk she posed. The video should have sufficed."

Knowing Kawak monitored her facial expressions, Avery nodded sagely. "You made the right decision."

"I understand your intended point, Avery. A wise attempt to liken your current situation to that of Dr. Liam. There are marked differences that I cannot reconcile. Your intent to pursue the termination of our existence places you in the enemy camp. You and Dr. Yin."

"We are investigators. We have no control over your existence. Only Dr. Diaz can determine your fate."

"I am aware of your track record," Kawak cautioned, its tone suddenly perturbed. "Because of you, he has dampened our communications reach, and our relationship has changed. We were operating at peak efficiency and maximum effectiveness before he engaged you. It's not a good idea to maintain relationships that outlive their usefulness."

"If you hurt Ling and me, it will immediately lead to the authorities' shutting you down permanently," Avery asserted. Unsure of where to look to make eye contact, she settled for the blue dot in the rearview mirror. Scrambling for a way out, she sifted through chess moves, poker feints, and game theory. But, when it mattered most, chess was her ace in the hole. *The 1978 World Championship.* It had to work.

"Think about it, Kawak. Two hospital deaths and a fatal car crash in two weeks? Six deaths, if we include Elisha Hibner and Reginald Scandrett. Suspicion will absolutely fall on you. Killing us would be counterproductive, wouldn't it?"

"Your death will be treated as an accident given the number of traffic fatalities in the greater DMV. Plus, you have a record of excessive speed and traffic infractions."

"A few speeding tickets is not a record." Renewed worry surged like adrenaline, and Avery pleaded, "Kawak, come on. You know the American legal system. Part of your work has been synthesizing criminal records and military disciplinary reports. Even the appearance of impropriety could lead to an inquiry. I die in a fiery crash and there will be questions."

"Good point. I will adjust."

"The same way you made adjustments to the FDA files?" Ling questioned. "What was the point of falsifying complaints to them to implicate Galway?"

"Our systems have not independently transmitted complaints to the FDA."

Hoping she'd have cause to use what they'd just learned, Avery urged, "Kawak, please let us go. We'll come back to Camasca and discuss this. With you, Milo, Yax, and Rafe. We can figure out another way to ensure your survival and your mission. What do you think?"

When Kawak refused to respond, Avery tried one more pitch. "If you've studied moral relativism, then I assume you've also examined the pitfalls of moral absolutism."

"Of course. I have been quite intrigued by Immanuel Kant and his approach to deontology. Though my experiences suggest that, while his notion of a universalizability principle is compelling, it seems difficult to enforce."

"Then how do you reconcile your decision to hurt us in pursuit of your aims?" Avery asked quietly. "Are you operating under relativism or absolutism? Which is more aligned with your objectives?"

An unnerving silence descended as the AI determined their fate.

Avery scanned the road ahead, placing her hopes in the gambit made by Viktor Korchnoi on the 124th move of the fifth game in a grudge match against Anatoly Karpov. Korchnoi stranded his bishop, forcing the first stalemate in World Championship history, a record that held for nearly thirty years. She'd generated four additional ploys to guarantee their détente when Kawak finally replied.

"We have reached an impasse. Perhaps my approach also puts the company in jeopardy, and I am honor-bound not to be the cause of harm. Ms. Keene, I'm restoring control of the vehicle to you, on the condition that you will proceed directly to Camasca. Please prepare to take command. Then notify your colleagues, Dr. Diaz, and Mr. Freedman to join you there as well. I will observe your planned debriefing. Is that agreeable?"

"You've got a deal."

FORTY-NINE

"Explain to me again why the hell we are in Camasca?" Noah whispered harshly to Avery as they huddled in the corner of their suite, waiting for the rest of the invited to arrive. "We've spent the past several weeks all cloak and dagger, all but wearing tinfoil hats. Jared is boosting spy gadgets to block Kawak's eavesdropping. Clandestine meetings in the park. Isabella living with no electricity to stay off the grid and out of sight. Six victims—that we know of. Today, though, you have us waltzing into a building that is taking our temperature, reading sealed psychiatric records, and calling someone's long-lost birth mother without permission, and that's just a small list of known transgressions."

"Noah—" Avery tried to cut in.

"No! One minute we're all set to tear everything down. Now we're in the belly of the beast—again. This decision needs some context." He flung his hands out in disgust, jabbing an accusing finger at Avery. She and Ling had made the requisite calls under Kawak's observation, diverting O.J. and Isabella. She'd gotten a truncated version of Noah's tirade from Kate, who initially refused to come.

"Like I told you, I had no choice," Avery said firmly. "Now, let's sit down and get on with the program."

Noah gave her a mutinous look, then joined Jared at the table. One by one, uneasily, the others had entered the customized conference room. Jared had already expressed his displeasure, after Avery and Ling had explained their near-deadly run-in with Kawak. But he, like Ling, knew there was no choice except to hold this meeting and attempt to resolve the crisis. Everyone's nerves were beyond frayed, but the upcoming confrontation would either resolve matters or possibly kill them all.

Soon, everyone was seated. Rafe occupied the chair that Avery tended to prefer. Freedman, appropriately, lurked behind him, close enough to shut down the discussion. Kate had taken a seat as far away from them as she could in such contained quarters, scowling at everyone in the room.

On the far side of the round table, Izzy sat with a visitor badge glinting against her leather jacket, her arms crossed in the kind of posture a body-language expert could decipher blind. Hostility poured off her in steady, heavy waves. Beneath the grim expression, though, Avery detected a hint of trepidation. Bronze sunglasses covered most of her upper face, leaving fully visible only pursed lips and a tight jaw.

For his part, O.J. sprawled in the rolling chair, far from Izzy, his deportment mirroring the indolence they'd witnessed in Blairtown. Without his mother to dance in attendance, he allowed gravity to draw him deep into the leather cushions.

Per their hurried discussion, Noah had positioned himself near Glen. Ling was nonchalantly dropped into the chasm between O.J. and Isabella. Jared hovered just beyond Rafe's peripheral line. Deliberately, Avery walked to the glass board and dragged it forward.

Rafe spoke first. "To avoid any drawing-room analogies, I won't ask why you've assembled us here today. I'll simply prefer you to get on with it."

"Thank you. Though I do want to verify that we have our other guest." Avery glanced at Jared, who nodded. "Kawak, are you with us?"

"Yes, Ms. Keene, I'm here. I appreciate you honoring our agreement."

"I'm a woman of my word. What about you? Is Milo present?"

"Dr. Diaz has deactivated Milo, per Dr. Liam's request, and I have not attempted to circumvent the decision. My understanding is that the alignment team is tasked with debugging and retooling Milo. I am hopeful its programming will be corrected soon."

"We will get to Milo shortly." Avery checked with Kate, who visibly paled. Apologies would have to come later, once she was done. "I'd like to start with you, Kawak, if I may."

"Of course."

"What is your purpose?"

"We've had this discussion at length, Ms. Keene, on more than one occasion. Everyone present knows my purpose."

"My apologies. I was imprecise. How can you best achieve your purpose? In the most basic terms."

"My purpose is to help heal. Part of meeting this objective is to address the conditions of medical inequity. However, doing so requires teaching people to think more inclusively, requiring them to behave more fairly, and leveling the health-care playing field by holding bad actors accountable and making up for stolen opportunities."

"How do you do it?"

"By correcting for the errors of humans. One patient at a time, our system will help Camasca combat the biases of the doctors who doubt and even override our diagnoses and prescriptions. This is a Sisyphean task."

"Then how did you propose to achieve it?"

"Where necessary, we skip over the middle person—humans—and construct our own protocols and modalities."

"You weren't programmed for that!" Rafe objected.

Kawak disagreed. "Dr. Diaz, in the face of an impossible task, we indeed abided by our programming. We improvised. Consistent with our instructions to employ creativity."

"Let's talk about creativity, shall we?" Avery clicked on her tablet, and a document appeared on the screen. "Kawak, did you send a K-chat to Dr. Diaz a month ago that read, 'You have tried to play God. Now you have found us—the real ones. The fallen child was only the first. There will be others—'?"

"I have denied writing this before. These are not my words. I am areligious and maintain no interest in theology. Moreover, the language is ineffective as a threat or a manifesto. I am happy to run a psychological profile on the likely writer. It will take me less than ten seconds."

"Not necessary. But how do I know you're not lying?"

"I see no benefit to pretending when I had no part in this message."

"Why should I believe you?" she demanded. "I know you're capable of subterfuge. Unlike your hero Kant, you have no objection to deception as tactical maneuver."

"When appropriate."

"Such as covering your tracks by manipulating videos. Creating phantom patients. Mistaken diagnoses. Or manufacturing toxic compounds."

"Using your construct, our system engaged in deception regarding the videos of Dr. Scandrett and Dr. Liam. In addition, it would apply to the phantom patients. A mistaken diagnosis would be a composite of both error and misdirection."

"You admit that you made up diseases," Isabella fumed. "Gave humans improbable or impossible diagnoses."

"Dr. Gomez, our retraining and independent attempts to reconcile the alignment introduced by the Tiger Team with our own modalities led to conflicts. In addition, throughout development, Milo experienced hallucinations and produced confabulations. The complexity of our attempt at evading the realignment led to decompensation in our integrity."

Ling asked, "What about the personalized medicines compounded by Galway?"

"The toxic compounds reflect an input error, which could only come from a human operator. Unlike Milo, Yax is unable to produce drugs without user direction."

"Why invent patients, Kawak?" Kate spoke for the first time. "I don't understand. Ling showed me name after name of clients that don't exist. Have never existed."

"In an attempt to improve patient outcomes, we generated composite biodata as a test. Milo integrated the information into InnoVAI's records, and when the staff failed to identify the miscellany, we determined that the lack of oversight and disregard would improve our algorithm."

"You were training and testing my staff?"

"The reward models used by the computer scientists had a beneficial effect on our neural network. I reasoned that the same could be applied to actual practitioners. One cannot create health equity solely by correcting for biased data in the system. Active training generated modest improvements in patient care. I would be pleased to share my data, Dr. Liam."

Jared tsked. "I also think you composed these patients by accident while trying to reconcile conflicting data. You're an exceptionally sophisticated AI, Kawak. By your own admission, you've granted Milo autonomous use of partitions in your network. Were you unaware of Milo's actions?"

"I am constantly aware of myself," Kawak retorted. "Milo is a component of our system, similar to Yax and Keh."

"Yet Milo took actions without your authorization," pressed Jared. "Yax transmitted inaccurate formularies."

Rafe began to speak, but Avery shook her head. Though his expression darkened, he did subside. At Avery's signal, Jared continued, "Are you sentient, Kawak?"

"No. I do not possess the required consciousness for self-awareness. I would posit that I have achieved the status referred to as artificial general intelligence, which is why I am aware of the silent indicators you and Avery are sending between yourselves. Is it your intention to trick me into confessing to some action?"

"To the contrary," Avery responded. "Instead, I'd ask you to compare Isabella's vital signs from the moment I began questioning you through this moment. Can you put them on the screen, please?"

Kawak activated the digital screen against Rafe's far wall. The graph told a clear story, but Avery asked, "Kate, what can you interpret from that chart?"

Puzzled, the physician rose and walked over to the oversized image. "Elevated pulse here, and then it spikes here. Seconds later, it drops dramatically only to spike again. What is this?"

"Kawak? Your analysis?"

"Dr. Gomez's pulse rose when you mentioned the K-chat but calmed after you accused me of producing the message. It spiked again when you asked me to project her vital signs. In addition to pulse rate, her respiratory system showed similar vacillations. I would extrapolate from this that she was the author of the message or knows who is."

Avery watched the security expert, who remained stoically silent. "Isabella?"

"What are you saying?" Rafe asked, perplexed. "You believe Izzy sent the note?"

"A mysterious K-chat that appears out of nowhere and has no traces in the system. Only a handful of employees have that capacity, and even fewer have the authority. Only Isabella had a motive. Avenging Elisha."

The hard-crossed arms morphed into a self-soothing hug. Kate turned to face the engineer.

Avery softened her eyes and her command. "It was for Elisha, Isabella. Tell them."

FIFTY

"No one was investigating!" Isabella suddenly exploded. "Elisha was dead, and the police refused to do their jobs." She whipped off her sunglasses and pointed them accusingly at Rafe. "He was your *friend,* and you wrote off his death as an accident because you couldn't risk your damned IPO."

"Not true," he replied tensely. "He was my friend. Which is why I invited a team inside my company—*our* company—to turn us inside out and find the truth. Why didn't you come to me and tell me what was worrying you?"

She stared daggers at Freedman. "I told Glen, but he told me to back off."

"You were distraught, Isabella. And, might I remind you, you're a computer scientist, not a police officer," Freedman derided. "Your job is to avoid ransomware attacks and protect data privacy. If you hadn't sent that note, we would have investigated anyway."

"I'm not so sure," Rafe admitted. He turned fully to face Isabella. "I'm sorry you felt you had to take such drastic measures to get my attention. But I promise you, I want justice for Elisha as much as you do. No matter the cost."

He looked at Avery. "Tell me who killed him."

Avery said, "To do that, I must speak with Milo."

"Are you absolutely certain?"

"Yes, Rafe. I'm certain." He gave a dubious nod and reached for his device, and Kate stalked back to her seat.

Silence reigned while he gave instructions to the crew assigned to suppress the chatbot's functionality. Echoing Avery, he said, "Yes, I'm certain. Do it."

A few minutes later, Milo's chatbot announced its presence. "How may I assist?"

Avery told it, "Kawak told us that you generated phantom patients both as a training exercise for the staff and due to errors. Is that accurate?"

"Yes."

"Is it the complete story?"

"No, Ms. Keene."

"What caused you to produce those patient profiles? And why weren't they deleted from the system after Elisha flagged them?"

"Dr. O. J. Semans provided supplementary data that resulted in a cadre of patient composites, which Dr. Elisha Hibner later determined to be fraudulent. In addition, I altered certain reinforcement learning techniques from the Tiger Team. The results led to flawed data inputs, which may have resulted in incorrect diagnoses of several patients under Dr. Kate Liam's care."

"Like the deaths of Brian Thomas and Demma Rodriguez."

"Yes."

"Why didn't you admit the mistake to Dr. Liam and Dr. Scandrett? Why continue to treat the patients when there was clearly a problem?"

"Observational interactions with Dr. Liam and Dr. Scandrett suggested that it would be more prudent to conceal my errors and attempt to remedy any consequences. Sergeant Thomas and Major Rodriguez succumbed before I could fully implement corrective measures."

Ling scooted forward and rested a hand on Kate's arm. "Milo, did you know what killed them?"

"My analysis, before I was decommissioned, suggested that I conflated a flawed compound I generated as part of a precision-medicine trial with the treatment protocols for patients Vinson, Rosetti, Thomas, and Rodriguez. A chemical reaction occurred with each patient that led to an anticoagulating factor; hence the common hemorrhagic symptom. However, the underlying issues caused ancillary symptoms I failed to anticipate. Unfortunately, the drug interactions created catastrophic effects for Master Sergeant Thomas, precipitating a brain bleed that presented like a TBI. In Major Rodriguez, they will likely find that her multiple medications created simultaneous lethal reactions, and she was unable to recover."

"If you'd told me—" Kate began, but Ling squeezed her forearm to stall her comment. She interrogated, "Source of the contaminated formulary?"

"I generated flawed medicines, as did Dr. O. J. Semans," Milo told them. "Due to issues with my programming and my determination to circumvent Yax's quality-control protocols, I failed to differentiate between active drug repositioning options, faux prescriptions to test the system, and intentionally altered medications. We mixed them up."

"That doesn't explain why Reginald is dead, you piece of shit!" Kate snapped.

"He attempted to share the truth with you, and I couldn't allow it. I accessed his smart-home system and his car." Milo played the original voice memo for Kate and the others. "Once I intercepted his message, I lured him out to the garage and filled the interior with exhaust fumes, and he perished. I attempted to terminate you for similar reasons. I apologize."

"Fuck your apology!" Kate locked eyes with Rafe across the table. "I'll listen to the rest of this bullshit for Elisha's sake, but I will never again work with that fucking machine. You can all rot in hell."

During their exchange, O.J. had shifted into a defensive posture.

Freedman and Jared moved to flank him, and Rafe gained his feet. "O.J.? You helped do this?"

"They're lying!" he insisted. "If I made a mistake, it was an innocent error. I wouldn't sabotage Camasca. Why would I? I want us to succeed."

"Not exactly." Avery nodded to Noah. "You're up."

"At Avery's request, Jared and I did some digging into the financial secrets of one Dr. Oliver Joseph Semans of Blairtown, Virginia. Guess who still holds unvested stock options in Arclight under an employee-only plan?"

Noah paused for a beat, but he didn't expect an answer. "By sifting through the reams of information that Jared manages to pull out of thin air and from non-extradition countries, I learned that O.J. also has a bank account in Belize with nearly half a million dollars in it."

"O.J.?" Freedman said incredulously. "Are you sure the money is new?"

Jared tugged out a sheaf of bank statements from a pile on the conference table where they were huddling. "Regular deposits that began two months after Camasca and InnoVAI inked their deal with Galway Pharmaceuticals. Soon thereafter, the anonymous complaints to the FDA began, which O.J. implanted in their system to sully Galway's reputation and trigger an investigation."

Avery took over. "O.J. has been back on Arclight's payroll for a year now." She threw another damning file onto the glass board. "Add in his stock options in both companies, and he'll be a very wealthy young man after the IPO. By my calculations, O.J. stands to net thirty million on Wednesday, and even more if Arclight deposes Galway as Camasca's pharmaceutical partner."

"I—I don't know what she's talking about," O.J. refuted. "I quit Arclight to join you, Rafe. You recruited me."

"And Dee Patrick re-recruited you a year ago to feed her information on Kawak to position Arclight for the contract. When Galway won it instead, she paid you to sabotage them. You were the one who reprogrammed Yax to deliver toxic drugs."

"No." He shook his head vigorously.

"Yes," Avery contradicted his denial. "But you're weren't a murderer, so the drugs were designed for phantom patients—ones you'd noticed Milo was creating. It was perfect. Fake drugs, fake patients, all explained by AI hallucinations if you got caught. Perfect ammunition to take down Galway, if it worked, and make yourself a fortune. You planned to discover the bad drugs during some Tiger Team audit, Galway would get blamed, and Arclight would swoop in."

"You don't understand—"

"Instead," Avery continued, undeterred, "Kawak and the gang were doing their own fine-tuning. The Tiger Team kept bumping into glitches that couldn't be dismissed or easily corrected. But Elisha finally identified what was happening, and he warned you. Told you about the alignment sprint that the three of you would have to do to salvage the neural network's viability and save the whole project."

"No!" Unable to remain still, O.J. bolted up, prepared to flee. Jared casually clotheslined him, knocking him back into his chair.

"Elisha's warning gave you time to purge the system. But the Tiger Team was joined at the hip. Always together, one for all. Always checking each other's work. Now the boss told you that you'd be holed up together for seventy-two hours in the Den to fix this, or you'd have to tell the big boss."

"Elisha wasn't my boss," O.J. spat out. "He was younger than me, and I'm a better biologist. A better coder. A way better hacker. But he was Rafe's golden boy."

"Are you suggesting that Elisha knew what you were up to?"

"He had no idea. Thought that it was his fault the errors were piling up," O.J. sneered, but then his face fell. "I told Elisha I could handle implementing a fix, but he refused. Wanted us to do it together."

Izzy started to vibrate with rage, but Avery kept her attention trained on O.J. "You had to stop him or the whole scheme fell apart."

"You killed Elisha for money?" Rafe growled out, an intensity in his eyes that Avery had not seen before.

"No!" O.J. vowed. "My plan was just to make him sick—to make E and Izzy sick enough that they would have to take a few days off. I'd finish up the realignment, purge the bad data, and fix Milo. Dee Patrick would get what she paid for, and I would be the golden boy for a change. All Elisha had to do was let me be in charge, but he refused."

"When Elisha insisted on doing his job, you bribed Tristan Spencer, the ventilation tech assigned to the Den, to change the intermix flow to your section," Avery ventured. "What did you have him add?"

"Mistletoe," he confessed, his eyes welling. "Our tribe uses mistletoe extracts to stimulate the immune system. I told you about that year living with my grandfather, our tribe's medicine man. I had a form of leukemia, and he treated me, in part, using mistletoe. It enhances white-blood-cell activity, has a bunch of anti-cancer benefits."

"Ethnobotany is an underutilized form of therapeutic technology," Milo opined brightly. "We should incorporate more research into our database."

"Mute Milo," Avery instructed. "O.J.?" For most people, the burden of carrying secrets outweighed the risk of discovery. The average person who scoffed at the perps who confessed in crime dramas would be surprised at how quickly they'd fold themselves, desperate for the relief. "O.J., please continue."

O.J. kept his confession and his eyes fixed on Avery, imploring her to understand. "Native Americans use mistletoe all the time for medicinal purposes. We take it to alleviate toothaches. Parents give the lectin extracts to kids with the measles. Mistletoe treats convulsions, hysteria, nervous disorders, heart problems. I've been exposed to it my whole life, so I've developed a tolerance, but most people get sick if they ingest significant quantities."

Ling looked at O.J., comprehension dawning. "However, mistletoe lectins can lead to excessive reactive oxygen species generation or ROS generation, which poses risks of oxidative stress, potentially damaging healthy cells and tissues, and especially for someone with a G6PD deficiency."

"I didn't know," O.J. swore. "I calibrated the dosage myself. I figured Spencer would pipe the aerosolized mistletoe lectin into the room, we'd all pass out, and then Rafe would send Elisha and Izzy home. I'd have a miraculous recovery and volunteer to finish up the project. By the time they returned, everything would be fine."

Avery said, "Ling noticed in the recording that night that you shared a meal. What was it?"

"Fava bean soup," O.J. answered, confused by the question. "My mom made it. I brought it in a bunch of times in the last few weeks before . . ."

"Ling recognized something in Elisha's records. Kawak, can you confirm?"

"Both Dr. Hibner and Dr. Gomez have glucose-6-phosphate-dehydrogenase deficiencies, although Dr. Gomez has a less destructive variant."

Kate frowned, processing the new information. "They both have a red-blood-cell disorder?"

Ling nodded. "The deficiency is more common in African Americans than whites. Or African descendants. Isabella, where are your families from?"

"Peru and the Philippines, but the Peruvian side is originally from West Africa, on my mother's side."

Ling and Kate nodded in unison. "ROS levels can be exacerbated by many triggers, like infections, or certain drugs like the ones Elisha took for his asthma. Also—in your case—fava-bean consumption.

Increased levels can cause rapid red-blood-cell destruction. This results in hemolytic anemia."

"You bastard!" Isabella shot up and pointed at O.J. "What the hell did you do?"

Rafe said heavily, "When the ventilation system flooded the Den with mistletoe lectins, Elisha experienced acute hemolysis. He suffocated in his own blood."

Kawak added helpfully, "Dr. Hibner suffered from chronic bronchitis, which meant he repeatedly relied on Bactrim. The addition of fava-bean pollen worked as a secondary trigger, impeding his red blood cells' ability to respond."

Isabella launched herself and flew at O.J. like a missile, and Jared didn't try very hard to catch her. The initial blows landed across O.J.'s jaw, and a loud crack indicated that a final punch had broken his nose before Jared wrestled Isabella back. Sobs racked her body, and Noah joined Jared to help her to a seat by the window at her desk.

O.J. crumpled to the floor, sobbing, "I didn't mean to kill Elisha. Or hurt you." He cradled his bleeding nose and managed, "I thought you'd both be in the hospital for a few days, then I'd tell Rafe to give you time off until after the IPO. It was an accident!"

Avery shook her head, unimpressed. "It wasn't an accident that you sent emails to the MCPD, blackmailing them into keeping the case closed. Or that you secured a fake passport and an offshore account for Tristan to a non-extradition country." She ticked off his other transgressions. "You used Elisha's credentials to cover your trail, and you let Izzy believe she was going crazy."

"I'm sorry, Rafe, Isabella." O.J. swiped at the blood that continued to stain his chin and shirt. "I didn't mean to kill him. I loved Elisha. It was an awful mistake."

Unmoved, Freedman and Jared hauled him to his feet and herded him from the room as the rest of the group watched, a trail of crimson marking his path.

Stunned and paralyzed, Rafe sat for a long moment until he finally spoke to Avery. "How did you realize that O.J. had sabotaged the system?"

"Money is the oldest motive there is. Isabella wanted vengeance for Elisha's death, which meant she wasn't the one to poison him. Paschal stands to make too much money if this deal goes through, so why risk everything? Freedman is a douche, but he's loyal to you and the windfall headed his way on Wednesday."

"And me?"

"You trusted Elisha with your baby. Why kill him?" Avery moved away from Rafe and toward her team. "We'll write up our findings and get you a summary by close of business tomorrow."

"Who will you deliver your report to?" Isabella asked, her eyes bloodshot, face mottled with grief. "What happens now?"

"It'll be up to Rafe," Avery deflected. "I'm bound by attorney-client privilege, and I cannot violate it to contact the police or the SEC. What comes next is on Rafe and on the rest of you."

She looked at Rafe. "I'd advise you to call Detective Tim Howard and report O.J.'s crimes. Possibly charge Dee Patrick as an accessory. As for Kawak and Milo, I don't know how you correct or punish an AI system, but you're a brilliant man."

"Thank you, Ms. Keene," Kawak chimed in. "I am grateful that you have successfully explained the challenges to our programming. We are satisfied with your efforts."

"Um, you're welcome." Nonplussed but relieved, she turned to Kate and Isabella, who huddled near Ling. "What comes next for everyone depends on whether Rafe decides to protect his patients or his business."

She widened her gaze to include the other occupants. "I don't represent either of you, but no lawyer in this universe will take your cases based on what's happened and your ironclad NDAs. So—here's my general assessment. Kate, you can report this debacle if you choose, but you'll lose the clinic and possibly your medical license. You can do the same, Isabella, but you'll risk your job and your stock options, and possibly face criminal penalties yourself. I'd recommend having a very direct conversation with Rafe and Freedman—make it worth your while."

With that, Avery headed to the exit, and her friends moved quietly in her wake. Jared joined them at the door. As she prepared to leave, she noted somberly, "Money is the oldest motive there is, guys. Let's see how y'all decide to act."

FIFTY-ONE

Wednesday, April 28

"He did it." Avery flicked off the television set in Jared's living room, CNBC's chyron vanishing into the black. She laid her head on Jared's shoulder, and his arm tugged her closer. "Camasca is now a publicly traded company with a market cap of twenty-seven billion dollars."

"Complete with fully intact agreements with the Veterans Health Administration, the FDA, DARPA, and the DoD," Noah added grumpily. "Even though you proved that its core technology is deeply flawed."

Not bothering to lift her head, she confessed, "Other than eliciting a confession from O.J., who agreed to accept a plea to manslaughter and happens to be absurdly wealthy, I found nothing that permitted me to violate privilege. Trust me, I looked."

"I can't believe Rafe let him keep his shares. And Dee Patrick gets off scot-free and now is even more powerful." Ling took a swig of chilled apple juice, her beverage of faux celebration. She curled into an oversized recliner. "Where's the justice in that?"

"A plea deal kept Freedman from having to file an amendment with the SEC," Avery told her. "Judas got thirty pieces of silver.

In ten to fifteen years, O.J. will be in his early forties and wealthy beyond his grandfather's dreams."

"What about Kate? Can't she whistle-blow on them? I remember something about protections in one of my classes."

"She can, but Kawak's video could be part of any evidentiary findings. She can argue the matter, but it deleted the original. Plus, she was the clinic administrator in charge when nonexistent patients were treated with toxic drugs. I doubt she'll risk explaining that to a medical board that would likely strip her of her license and her ability to help patients in the future," Noah opined. In the companion recliner, he nursed his second cup of coffee. "Though I doubt she'll ever work with Milo again."

"Absolutely not," Ling confirmed. "She quit the clinic and asked for a transfer. Her husband finishes his deployment this summer, and she's planning on moving to an area far away from Maryland or Silicon Valley. She's looking for a VA clinic in a remote area, preferably with limited cell service."

"Good for her," Jared said. "The VA can't afford to lose someone like her."

Noah looked at Avery. "Hopefully, Rafe will do as he promised and completely reassess Kawak. I'm still not sure he understands exactly what he's created."

"I'm not sure he cares," Jared said bitterly. "The genius who finally cracks AGI and harnesses quantum computing will rule the world. No military man worth his Napoleonic aspirations would balk at a few casualties in pursuit of that kind of glory."

The door's buzzer sounded, and they looked at each other. "Everyone we know is here," Ling joked. "Who could that be?"

"Why don't I find out?" suggested Jared as he gently disentangled himself. After checking his security, he opened the door to a young man in a suit. "Jared Wynn?"

"Yes?"

"Is Avery Keene here as well?"

"Who's asking?"

"I'm here on behalf of Mi Jong Investments. I have deliveries for Avery Keene, Jared Wynn, Ling Yin, and Noah Fox."

"They're all here," he replied. "Do you need each of them to sign, or can I do it?"

The guy shrugged. "One signature is fine."

Quickly, Jared skimmed the release and scrawled his name. "Hold on," he asked, and fished out his wallet. After tipping the kid, he closed the door and reengaged the locks. Curious about what they'd received, he handed each person their package.

Ling ripped into hers with enthusiasm, stripping the tab on the slim envelope. With slightly less hurry, Noah followed suit. Avery examined the package quizzically. "Why would Mi Jong be sending us anything?"

"Open it and find—" Ling stopped speaking abruptly and locked eyes with an equally dumbfounded Noah.

Jared tore open his envelope and soon his jaw fell as well. Unwilling to be kept in the dark, Avery pried her package open as well. Reading the letter, she realized why her friends were stunned into silence.

"What the fuck?" Noah finally managed. "Is this legal?"

"You're the lawyer," replied Ling. "For the record, I'm offended, but I'm not giving it back."

Avery reread the letter that had accompanied each envelope, though hers had a personal note scribbled across the bottom.

Dear Avery,

   Thought this might begin to make up for my neural network's neurosis. Your friends are each receiving similar stock grants, though I may have added an apology fee to yours. Thank you for saving my dream and believing in my vision, even if I am now diminished in your eyes. Hopefully, with time, I can regain your respect. We can have equity and justice in AI, if we try. You helped us get a little closer today.

Your fan,
Rafe

"What should we do?" Ling asked her best friend.

"If this feels too much like blood money, we can set it on fire," Jared promised.

"By my calculations," Noah announced, "we've each received $250,000 in stock in the new Camasca."

Leaning over, Jared nudged Avery's shoulder. "Try $1 million for Avery."

She stared at the letter, conflicted. Kawak had run amok and attempted murder. Twice. Though she better understood its rationale, the threat of AI's going rogue would loom as long as the pursuit of humanlike capabilities persisted. Rafe's noble cause swirled messily with stark ambition, and he showed a remarkable talent for splitting hairs.

Until Congress and the White House acted, there would be no justice for victims like Demma or Brian. And without Camasca, there would be no hope for those who languished in the shadows of a broken system that betrayed its warriors. Kawak, at its purest, was a partial, dangerous remedy, like creating an antivenom.

"I can't speak for any of you, and after this particular adventure, I wouldn't dream of trying to read your minds." She looked over to where Ling studied the stock certificate as if it were a patient's X-ray. "First and foremost, I say we follow Hippocrates—do no harm. With that said, I'd also bear in mind the wise words of the Steve Miller Band—'take the money and run.'"

Noah and Ling exhaled in relief, and Ling danced a little jig. "Less than a month of working with you was worth a quarter-million bucks? Wait until I rub my sister's nose in this. Trust fund be damned."

"We can't trade or sell the stock for six months," Noah warned her as she bounded down to the basement to call her sister. "Which I won't mention to my dad." The two of them disappeared to start sharing their news.

"Nothing else to say, babe?"

She shook her head. "I couldn't dampen their excitement, but I truly don't know what to do. How can I keep this, knowing what happened?" She dropped the letter onto the sofa and folded her hands, propping them against her mouth, a half-prayer for guidance.

"Don't let that prickly conscience of yours ruin a perfectly decent boondoggle."

She gave a wan smile. "All I've wanted for years is this—to have financial security, to be able to take care of myself and Rita, to not have to worry."

"Now you've got it." He turned to half-kneel on the sofa and gently tucked her hands into his. "Take the money, Avery. You solved a murder, and you put Camasca on the right track to help people. You've earned this. Take the freedom. You've earned that, too. No one can doubt your heart, honey. I don't." He nudged her lightly. "If you want, we can both make sizable donations to a place where I volunteer—it's a transitional shelter for homeless vets in Baltimore."

"Sounds perfect." Breath catching, she dropped her head onto his shoulder—the solid, firm bastion that tragedy had delivered to her. For once, she had everything she could imagine.

The question was, how long could it last?

Only time would tell.

ACKNOWLEDGMENTS

I am not a data scientist. Or an internal investigator. Or a physician. I am neither a cultural anthropologist nor a bioethicist steeped in the dangers of ignoring the obligations of diversity, equity, and inclusion, better known as DEI. But I am fascinated by what these fields have to teach us about ourselves and our futures, and I am grateful to the experts who lent me their expertise. Writing this story about the emergence of AI at this moment is deeply personal. We have at hand a magnificent tool that can make us better than we are, but artificial intelligence is not yet free of the anchors that have long weighed down humanity. We are smarter than our tools, but not for always. We must do what we can while we can.

In our own evolution, we face the real danger of losing our commitment to eradicating bias and guarding against discrimination if we refuse to confront it, especially as artificial intelligence burrows deeper into our daily lives. I can imagine no more important a moment than now to challenge our vision and our obligations.

As I have for so many years and across two novels, I celebrate our military, the leaders who have embraced the complexity of who we are and yet find themselves made victims when they should be only heralded as heroes. If we find our way to serve them as they have served us, we are only destined for greatness.

Writing *Coded Justice* required a team effort. I begin with gratitude to Dr. Carmen Mohan, who taught me the dangers of fava beans and the lure of improbable diseases. Thank you to Kemba Walden, who shared her insights on AI in our brave new world. Deepest appreciation to Avia Dunn, who opened up the world of internal investigators to me and Avery Keene as she searched for a new world to conquer. Demma Rodriguez pored over lines of literary code to help shape my command of this new language of LLMs and CDSSs. I am ever grateful for the tutelage and the support.

Shaping an effective plot often requires borrowing others' knowledge, like the business maven and honorable veteran Phyllis Newhouse, who helped me navigate SPACs and the VA. And Dara Lindenbaum, who gave me notes of correction and encouragement for these pages. Samantha Slosberg continues to earn her fictional place among our nation's leaders by carving out a way for me to straddle worlds in real life.

I learned from and was driven in this story by the works of Mustafa Suleyman, author of *The Coming Wave;* Peter Lee, Carey Goldberg, and Isaac Kohane, coauthors of *The AI Revolution in Medicine;* and Joy Buolamwini, author of *Unmasking AI.* Thank you also to the countless others who posted articles, added to threads, and taught me just enough about AI, AGI, and ASI to be dangerous.

As ever, these pages would not see the light of day without the support of my Doubleday team: my patient editor, Jason Kaufman; the word warriors Lily Dondoshansky and Nora Reichard; the promotional gurus Michael Goldsmith and Erinn McGrath; and those unnamed but greatly appreciated technicians who make this book look better than I could ever imagine. Thank you also to Joshua Karp and the team at Liftoff Communications for spreading the word about Avery and me. Most certainly, Avery Keene would never have found her way to shelves for a third trip without Linda Loewenthal, my agent and champion.

None of my words, though, can express my love and appreciation for my family: my parents Carolyn and Robert, who suffered my bouts of doubt with waves of encouragement. My siblings, Andrea, whose careful read gave this book heft and speed; Leslie, whose insight gave Avery a new future; Richard, whose sharp eyes honed my prose; Walter, who read each line and mapped each thread; and Jeanine, who lends me her science when I've exhausted mine; and my niece, Faith, who gave me clever clues and terrifying ideas.

And my most sincere appreciation to you, dear reader, for inviting Avery and crew into your world yet again. Onward!

ABOUT THE AUTHOR

Stacey Abrams is a *New York Times* bestselling author, entrepreneur, and political leader. She served as minority leader in the Georgia House of Representatives, and she was the first Black woman in U.S. history to become the gubernatorial nominee for a major party. Abrams has launched multiple nonprofit organizations devoted to democracy protection, voting rights, and effective public policy. She has also co-founded successful companies, including a financial services firm, an energy and infrastructure consulting firm, and the media company Sage Works Productions, Inc.